HIDDEN RUNAWAY

A DCI Jones novel

KERRY J DONOVAN

Copyright © 2021 by Kerry J Donovan
Published by Fuse Books 2021
ISBN: 9798751723682

All rights reserved.
No part of this book may be reproduced in any form or by any electronic or mechanical means, including information storage and retrieval systems, without written permission from the author, except for the use of brief quotations in a book review.

The right of Kerry J Donovan to be identified as the Author of this work has been asserted in accordance with the Copyright, Designs, and Patents Act, 1988.

All characters in this work are fictitious. Any resemblance to actual persons, living or dead, is purely coincidental.

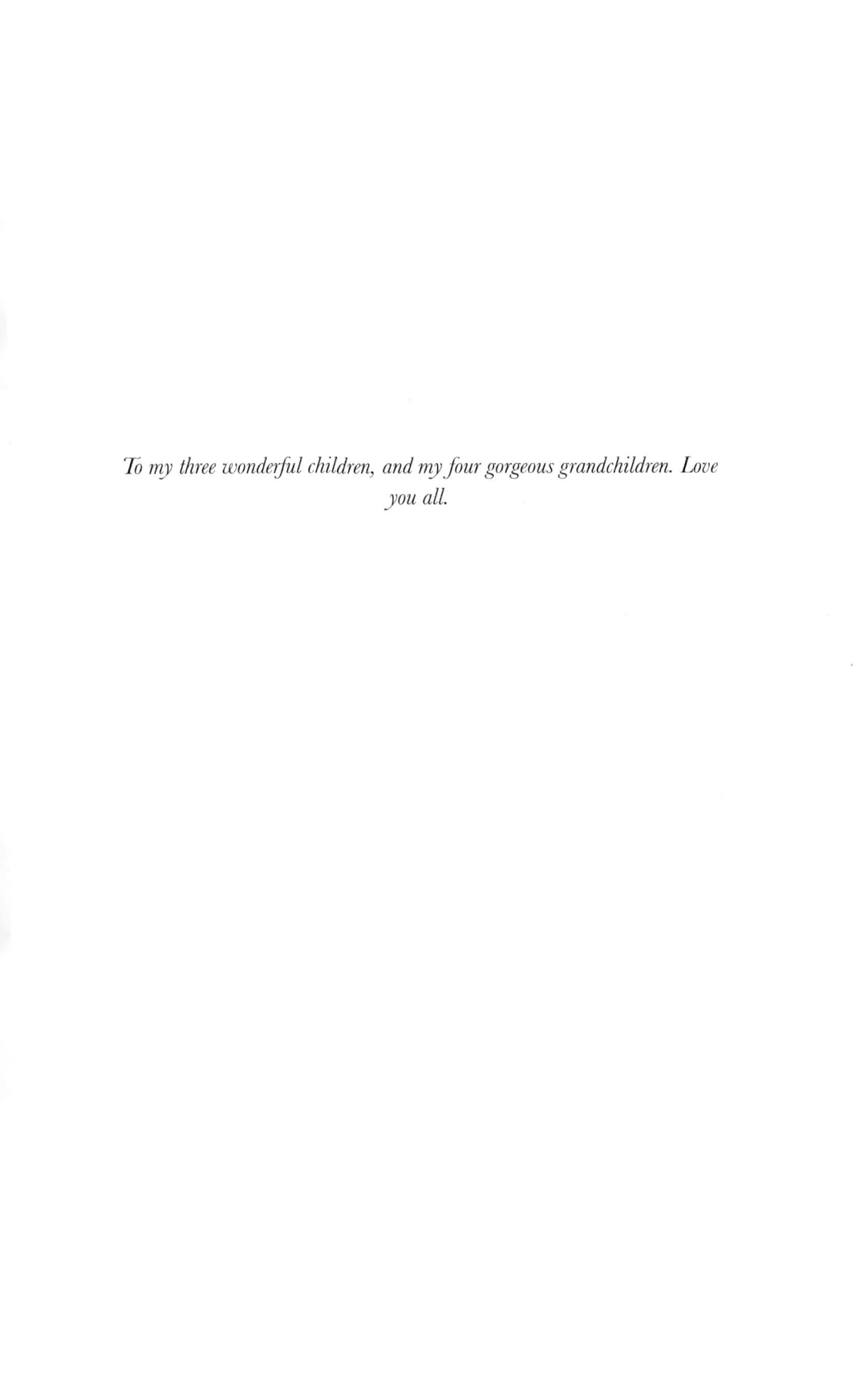

To my three wonderful children, and my four gorgeous grandchildren. Love you all.

Part 1

*"Gone. Our baby's gone.
Find her, Chief Inspector.
Please find her."*

Chapter One

YOUNG LOVE – *Ellis Flynn*
Early afternoon, Birmingham

HARSH LIGHT FROM an early summer sun bounced off the pavement and dirty shop fronts. Ellis Flynn leaned against the railings outside Joe's Piercing Salon with a hand raised to shield his eyes and scanned the street for his latest target, the delectable Hollie Jardine. She had long, strawberry-blonde hair, blue eyes, and the innocent, open smile of a new teenager. She fitted the requirements to perfection.

The time on his Tag Heuer knock-off showed her as fifteen minutes late.

Daft mare.

He kept the pleasant smile—the one he practised regularly in the bathroom mirror—pasted in position.

Five long weeks he'd spent cultivating this one. Long, long weeks. It hadn't been difficult, though. He'd been charming and attentive, drawing her to where she accepted the belly button piercing. It was yet another way to bind her to him. A couple more trinkets and she'd be ready, hooked. She'd be his to do with as he wished.

When he'd suggested a belly piercing would look wonderful on her softly rounded stomach, Hollie, the one Ellis thought of as "Hottie", had hesitated at first.

"All the women are wearing them these days," he told her.

"I can't have a piercing," she whispered, but he could tell by the glint in her eyes the idea really excited her. "Dad would have a fit."

"When's your father gonna see your stomach?" he asked as they strolled hand-in-hand in the park on the other side of town, well away from her home and her schoolfriends. "You walk round the house half naked, do you?"

She blushed, eyes wide, hand covering her mouth. "No, of course not. I'd never be allowed to show my tummy like that … not in my house. Dad's too … old. Too stuffy."

"Well, that's okay then. It'll be our little secret. Meet me after school tomorrow, and I'll buy you a silver bar. Deal?"

The daft bitch hesitated for a moment, but then she smiled. "Yes. It's a deal."

"Don't be late. You know how I hate being kept waiting."

Sixteen minutes late. Sixteen fucking minutes. She'd fucking pay. Slowly, but she would pay.

In the distance, a head full of wavy blonde hair bobbed into sight.

There she was. Finally.

'Bout fucking time.

Hottie tottered around the corner twenty-five metres away, on black four-inch heels, looking awkward—a new-born lamb taking its first steps toward the slaughterhouse. Ellis smiled at the thought, then turned on the charm.

She wore the top he'd bought her a week earlier, yellow to match her hair, and short enough to expose a belly with enough puppy fat to raise their client's blood pressure. Another of his presents showed through the semi-transparent top, the silk bra—34C—barely holding the girl's assets in place.

He widened the smile and strode towards her, soon drawing

Part 1

close enough to catch sight of the make-up—mascara, grey eye shadow, blusher, and plum-coloured lipstick. Subtle it wasn't. Why didn't she learn how to do it properly? If he had more time, he'd point her to a decent "how-to' video on YouTube, but he didn't have more time. More to the point, neither did Hottie.

She drew the attention of a beggar camped in the doorway of a derelict off-licence. The tramp mumbled something as she passed and tried looking up her way-too-short skirt. She skittered sideways and rushed towards Ellis—towards her man, her protector.

Her protector.

Yeah, right.

One of her heels caught in a broken paving slab. She stumbled. Ellis raced forward, caught her, and pulled her close. Her breasts mashed against his chest, nipples pushing through the silk bra and the cotton top. She looked up and smiled through the travesty of makeup applied with plenty of gusto but very little skill.

"Hi, babe," he said. "You look fantastic." He smoothed the wavy blonde hair. "Did that bloke say something to upset you?"

He pointed at the bag of rags in the doorway.

Hottie nodded, sniffed, and buried her face in his chest. Ellis hoped she didn't fuck up his expensive shirt with that god-awful paint job. He placed an index finger under her chin and raised her head with the gentlest pressure.

"It was horrible, Eddie," she sniffled, dabbing her eyes with his offered handkerchief. "Said he'd … he'd give me a fiver for a … *blow job*." She mouthed the last two words.

"Did he now?"

Ellis 'Eddie' Flynn, gritted his teeth, dropped the smile, and affected an expression of quiet concern.

"That's terrible, but we mustn't blame him. Probably the drink talking. I'm sure he's a good man under all that grime. Let's forget about him. Right … you sure you're okay?"

"I'm fine now I'm with you, babe." She smiled and grabbed his upper arm.

Ellis bunched his bicep. Girls loved ripped muscles, and he worked the weights hard to keep in good shape. He took the handkerchief back and dabbed her eyes some more, removing another three coats of lacquer.

"Ready for your present, angel?"

"Are you sure they'll do it? I … I mean don't you have to be over sixteen for a piercing?"

"What? Are you kidding? Nobody's going to ask your age. You look eighteen if you're a day."

Hottie lifted her chin higher and beamed. "Do I really?" Her eyes widened, tears drying. "You're not just saying that?"

"Hollie, babe," he whispered, and kissed her smooth forehead—the only place clear enough of the war paint to touch. "Trust me. I'd never lie to you. Now, c'mon, or you'll miss your appointment. I've already chosen the perfect little silver barbell. You're gonna absolutely love it."

Ellis took her hand and escorted her into the shop.

The piercer and tattooist, Joe, a fifty-something biker and former "associate" of Ellis's late and unlamented father, winked at him before turning to the girl. "Hello, Ms Jardine. Please take a seat. This won't take but a minute. Lift your blouse a little please … and lower the skirt … yep, that's perfect. Now, I'm going to clean the area with an alcohol wipe, it might feel a little cold at first."

Hottie gave Ellis a nervous smile and gripped the arms of the chair. She looked like a child at the dentist's, preparing for a filling. He nodded encouragement and stepped forward to hold her hand.

EVENING, Hollie's House.

Hollie peeled back the dressing protecting the livid puncture wound at her navel—her adult badge of honour. Five days, and it still hadn't healed properly. She didn't expect it to take so long, but she could put up with the irritation. It was no worse than the curse. She'd put up with anything for her gorgeous Eddie. Wonderful man. So big, strong, and handsome—and that six-pack made her go weak at the knees. Caring too, the way he looked after her and never asked for anything in return. And as for those smouldering eyes which had the power to stop her heart … wow!

She's been so lucky to find him.

The clothes he bought were revealing and grown-up—just like the ones in the magazines she hid at the bottom of her closet. They were lovely, soft against her skin, too. So much nicer than the cheap cotton rubbish Mum made her wear.

Hollie remembered the fight she had with Mum the day they went to buy her first set of adult underwear. The old-maid things Mum wanted to buy for her were baggy and hideous. Hollie just had to make a stand. Living with such ancient parents was such a cross. They didn't understand what it was like growing up in the twenty-first century.

"I can't change for games wearing those, Mum. I don't go to a convent school," she whispered, to keep the discussion out of the ears of the snooty shop assistant. "The girls will call me, 'Sister Hollie'. I won't be able to concentrate during lessons. And you know how hard I work to keep my grades up."

She picked up a modest matching set in pink lace.

"But, those are too … old for you, baby girl."

"Oh, please, Mum. You wouldn't want the girls to bully me, would you?"

Mum had wrinkled her nose and held the garments up to the light between finger and thumb as though she'd catch something from them

"You don't want to look like Amy, do you?" she'd said. "She's become a little tart with her make-up, short skirts, and the hideous smoking. Yes, your father and I have seen her light up the moment she's out of sight of her house. That girl's a bad influence on you, baby."

"Amy's my best friend, Mum. Please don't talk about her like that."

"And I don't like the way her older brother looks at you, either. Like you're a piece of meat. Evil, that one. All boys that age are the same."

"Was Dad the same?" she asked, all innocent-like.

That stopped Mum dead.

"You father is a good man, darling."

"I know, Mum. Can I have them? Please? *Please?*"

Eventually, her mother relented and, after the first time, the rest was easy. Over the following few months, Hollie had managed to build a nice little wardrobe of underwear and short skirts. Dad didn't approve, but he never argued with Mum, not ever. He was a such good man. Ha!

Typical Dad. Anything for the quiet life.

Not long after that, she met her Eddie, with his long hair, and his muscles, and his car. He treated her with respect, and as though she was a woman. Walking home from school one day, there he was. So different from all those boys in school who stared at her, and tried to brush against her in the halls. Even the Deputy Head, kept looking at her with the same expression Mum warned her about. Grey eyes, they were. Looked right into her, but mainly at her boobs. He made her feel naked and exposed. The evil man suggested things, too. But only when no one else could hear. Animal things.

Hideous creature.

She couldn't say anything though—no one would believe her. After all, he was the Deputy Head. Above reproach. Untouchable.

"Hollie, dear. Breakfast is ready," Mum called from the kitchen. "Hurry, or you'll be late for school."

School, school, bloody school.

What's the point in school when she'd already found her man? When she already knew her future?

Mum and Dad had nagged her for as long as she could remember.

"Work hard, baby. Keep your grades high."

"Yes, Mum."

"We've never had a doctor in the family, Hollie love. Now wouldn't that be a fine thing?"

"Yes, Dad. I'll work hard. I'll make you proud."

"That's my girl."

Part 1

But she wasn't "Daddy's little girl" anymore. She was Eddie's *woman.*

Hollie closed the bedroom door behind her, and padded down the stairs, schoolbag slung over her shoulder.

"Coming, Mum."

AFTERNOON, *Birmingham City Centre.*

A light shower drove a giggling Ellis and the Hottie into the cover of a glitzy shopping arcade. Her eyes shone as she stared through the window of a cut-price jeweller's. The childish idiot cooed at the shiny baubles. Ellis, patience itself, indulged her every whim.

"See those?" He pointed to a tray of silver bracelets on the bottom shelf. "Choose one and it's yours."

"Oh no, I couldn't—they're far too expensive," she said, eyes big as hubcaps—and just about as intelligent.

"Hollie. You'll upset me if you refuse."

"They're all so beautiful. I can't choose."

The cool of the arcade made the Hottie's breath fog the glass.

"See that one? The one with the teardrops?" Ellis pointed at a mid-priced bracelet, silver with glass beads inserted between the links. "Matches the colour of your eyes. What d'you reckon?"

"It's gorgeous, but the price …"

"Not a problem. You're worth it, babe."

Ellis bent forward and tapped a finger to his cheek. When she moved in for the kiss, he turned his head and their lips met. Hottie giggled and pressed hard—too hard. He darted out an exploratory tongue and met little resistance. She responded and their spit mingled.

Sloppy and fucking horrible.

He broke the embrace.

"Oh my gosh, I … I'm so sorry, Hollie," he whispered. "Don't know what came over me. I've never been that pushy. It's … just that you're so … sweet."

Hottie's face creased into a pout.

"Please don't be upset. That was lovely. I don't mind, really I don't. In fact"—she lowered her eyes to his chest—"we could go to the next level. If you like."

Gotcha.

"Are you sure? You're so young."

Hottie's chin dimpled, and her eyes watered.

"The other day you told me I looked like a woman."

"Well, yes … but you're only thirteen."

"No. I'm *fourteen*," she shouted, loud enough for a passing elderly couple to hear. The miserable wrinklies shook their heads at him before scurrying deeper into the mall.

Fuck's sake Ellis. Way to keep a low profile, dumbass.

"Kidding, babe. I know exactly how old you are. I'm counting the days 'til your sixteenth birthday, when we can be together, forever."

He dragged out the winning smile once more. Used the bloody thing so often, his cheeks were starting to tire.

Hottie sniffled.

"Why do we have to wait so long? I'm ready now."

Double gotcha.

"No, it wouldn't be right. I couldn't do anything so rash. We can wait. Now c'mon. Let's go get that bracelet."

For the rest of the afternoon, Hottie kept playing with the shiny trinket. Couldn't stop thanking him. Ninety fucking quid it cost, but the shop offered a cash-back arrangement. They held hands again and Hollie skipped.

The stupid kid was actually skipping for fuck's sake! Fuck's sake, how naïve.

"Look," she said, and yanked on his hand. "A photo booth. Can we, please?"

Shit. Not a good idea.

"Sorry, Angel. I'm all out of change and we don't have the time."

"Oh please, I'll pay." She fumbled in her handbag and yanked out a little pink purse. "Please, it won't take long."

Part 1

"So long as I get to keep the film so I'll have something to look at when we're not together."

"Oh, Eddie. You're so sweet."

"I know."

Yeah, right. You're mine, little girl. All mine.

———

LATE AFTERNOON, *Edgbaston*.

Arthur always made Ellis nervous, deliciously nervous. Older and much wiser than him, Arthur expected obedience and reverence. In return, he gave Ellis a sense of belonging and hope—and safety. And of course, love. Ellis would do anything for Arthur, anything he asked.

He messed the gear change and crunched when dropping into second as he pulled the old camper van to a halt at a T-junction. The big old diesel idled at high revs.

"Why the disguise?" Ellis asked.

"Why not? And the name's Jennings this trip, right?"

"Jennings?"

"Right. Don't forget."

"I won't, but the blond wig and those green contacts. Boy, they're so weird. The real Jennings must be one ugly mother."

"He was."

"Was? He's dead now?"

"Yes. Kept askin' too many questions."

"Sorry, Art… er, Jennings." Ellis swallowed hard, and pointed out the window on his side. "There she is. Told you she wouldn't let me down. For once, the stupid bitch is on time, too."

In the front passenger seat, "Jennings" scrunched lower and followed the line of Ellis's finger.

Hottie, still wearing her school uniform, walked along the path and came to a halt at the empty bus stop. A small white suitcase, gripped tight in both hands, rested against her thighs.

"Damn it, boy. You didn't tell me we're picking her up outside a fucking school. This old camper's too bloody conspicuous."

"Please don't be angry with me," Ellis said, rushing his words. "I had to. She thinks we're going on holiday. Could hardly make her walk too far, could I."

The older man rested a hand on Ellis' thigh, and his skin tingled under the loving touch.

"Easy, pet, I'm not mad. I could never be mad at you for long. You should have given her the money for a cab, but we're here now, and the ferry's waiting. Let's go. Mustn't keep the wee tart standing there."

The traffic cleared. Ellis engaged first gear and made a right. Hollie started waving the moment the van completed the turn.

"Don't forget, she calls me Eddie."

"Eddie? That's a bit Freudian."

"Huh?" Ellis frowned as he pulled the vehicle to a stop alongside their prey. "Oh, see what you mean. You think it's about my dad, right?"

"Never mind, lad. Just get on with it. Time's wasting."

Ellis unbuckled his seatbelt, scrambled into the back, and slid open the side door. "Hi, darling. Toss me the case and c'mon inside."

Hottie took half a step forward but hesitated when she caught sight of "Jennings".

"Who's he?"

Ellis saw doubt in her eyes for the first time since he'd raised the subject of their trip. She hugged the case to her chest and turned her head toward the school entrance.

"Don't worry, babe," Ellis said, using his soothing voice. It usually worked. "He's a friend of mine. Needs a lift to the station is all. It's only a couple of miles out of our way. Won't take long. We'll drop him off, and have the van to ourselves."

He offered his hand but she refused it.

"I … I don't know. Maybe we should wait … like you said?" She made a half turn.

"Grab her," Jennings barked.

Ellis obeyed.

Chapter Two

THURSDAY EVENING – Edgbaston, Birmingham
Time since abduction: *six hours*

DETECTIVE CHIEF INSPECTOR David Jones parked his venerable Rover 400 saloon behind one of two patrol cars and paused long enough to remove his dark glasses, secure them in their case, and drop the case into the glovebox. He eased out of car and leaned against the door, which closed with a meaty and satisfying clunk.

He rubbed the bridge of his nose, but it did nothing to ease the tension headache brought on by the drive through heavy evening traffic.

Another missing kid?

All he needed.

Stop it, Jones.

If it was bad for him, what must it be like for the parents?

Of course, this might not be an abduction. It might be a runaway. Abductions were the worst, of course, but runaways were just as bad for the distraught parents.

During his decades-long career, Jones had worked so many

missing child cases he'd lost count, but he still hated the emotions they generated. Most of all, he hated the initial interview with the parents and the raw motions they exposed.

No doubt about it, Jones couldn't hack the emotional stuff—the tears, the anguish, the self-recrimination. Give him a riot, a bank job, or a blood-spattered corpse and a gory crime scene any day of the week. Those, he could handle, but yet another missing teenager?

Poor kid. Poor parents.

Parents could never come to terms with what happened. They'd say and do anything to deny the truth.

"Our girl's good as gold, Chief Inspector. She's our perfect little angel."

"She's never been any trouble. Someone must have taken her."

"Oh no, Chief Inspector, she's far too young to have a boyfriend. We'd never allow it."

He'd heard it all before.

Ordinarily, he'd leave this particular interview to Phil Cryer, his trusted Sergeant—a parent himself—but Phil wasn't available. Phil might never be available again, not in an official capacity. Not since the accident.

Everyone else in his unit was either too junior, or too damned useless and lazy to do a good job. Besides, Jones needed to see the family home for himself. He needed to gauge the parents' reactions and search the missing girl's bedroom. Delve deep into their lives.

Hideous.

But all part of the job.

The next couple of hours would be difficult enough for him, but nothing compared with the ongoing torture faced by the parents.

Jones tasted the cool evening air and took a moment to take in the scene. Delaying the meeting as long as possible.

Net curtains twitched. Concerned neighbours peeked from doorways, or huddled together in groups along the pavement for mutual comfort. They knew the reason for the police presence. Those who were parents themselves would sympathise with the Jardines, and they'd keep their own children closer for the next few

Part 1

days. After that, life would return to normal for them, but not for Mr and Mrs Jardine.

Never for the Jardines.

The street had money. Not much, but enough to pay the bills with a little left over for renovations and other improvements. Manicured front gardens, clipped hedges, carefully weeded flower borders, and freshly painted doors and windows showed evidence of care and pride in their homes. These were neither the wealthy, leafy suburbs of the rich and powerful, nor a forest of high-rise tower blocks riddled with crime where evil people could buy or sell a life for the price of their next fix. This was an average, lower middle-class, comfortable street—no more, no less.

Jones left the sanctuary of his Rover, closed on the Jardine house, and paused at the garden gate unwilling to make the next move. He needed time to focus.

He knew exactly what Siân would have said to his delaying tactics.

"Pull your finger out, Davey," she'd have said. "There's a girl out there who needs your help. Man up and find her. It's what you do, isn't it?"

Siân, the only person he'd ever allow call him Davey. Hell, how he'd missed her guidance and her support over the years. Her love. More than thirty years, and a day still never passed when he didn't think of her, or their son.

Well? What you waiting for, Davey? Get on with it, man.

The Jardines' bay-fronted 1930s semi-detached house blended in well with its neighbours. A plum-coloured front door stood ajar in mocking welcome. Irrespective of the outcome of the investigation —good or bad—their house would never feel secure and welcoming again, not to the Jardines.

Kids.

Why would anyone want them? Decades of heartache then they leave, if they survived at all. So many things could happen to a child on the road to adulthood. Some, like his and Siân's baby, Paul, only lived a short while—a whole lifetime in thirteen minutes.

Damn it, man. Get a bloody grip.

The gate opened on well-oiled, silent hinges. Ten paces short of the Jardines' front door, his mobile buzzed. A wonderful reprieve, however fleeting.

"Jones speaking."

"Control here, sir."

He recognised the clipped, efficient tone of the evening shift's Comms Officer.

"What do you have for me, Alan?"

"We found some interesting CCTV pictures, sir. A campervan circled the park behind Hollie Jardine's school this afternoon. Twice. First time at, er … fifteen-thirty-one, and again twelve minutes later. The second time, it stopped for fourteen seconds, and then drove off at speed, heading south … towards the motorway. The camera was a long way off and the pictures aren't particularly clear. The techies are trying their best, but they don't hold out much hope of extracting a licence number for the camper."

"Any sign of the girl?"

"Possibly. There was someone on the pavement before the van stopped, and they'd gone when the van left. We assume it was the girl and she got into the van."

"Voluntarily?"

Jones hoped the girl had gone somewhere with a friend without telling her parents, but an image forced its way into his head—the imagined image of a blonde girl battling an abductor, arms flailing, scratching, screaming.

"The camper blocked the action. It's impossible to tell, sir."

"You've released details of the camper?" Jones rubbed his eyelids. The tension-headache moved from the back of his head to stab behind his left eye. Much worse and he'd have to resort to a painkiller.

Nah, not a chance.

He hadn't taken any medication in years.

"The bulletin's gone out and we're treating this as a Priority One Alert. Every patrol car in the county is on the lookout. I've allocated my best team in traffic surveillance to go through the CCTV recordings along all the projected routes."

Part 1

"You said the camper headed south?"

"Way ahead of you, sir. I've notified the motorway traffic boys and they're on full alert. Not expecting much though. The driver's had a six-hour head start. That camper could be anywhere in the country by now. Might even still be in town, sir."

"Yes, I know." Jones sighed. "Good work so far. I'm at the family home. Call me the second you have anything more."

He rang off, searched the phone's directory, hit the number, and waited for Pelham to pick up. A chill easterly wind ruffled his hair. He dragged the straggly tufts into place behind his ear, and then scratched his chin. The electric razor stored for emergency use in the Rover's cubbyhole would have a workout later—when he found the time.

If he found the time.

Detective Sergeant Charlie Pelham, the Serious Crime Unit's entry for Useless-Article-of-the-Year, and its interim second-in-command in Phil Cryer's absence answered on the eighth ring.

"Hello, boss." Pelham yawned.

"Evening, Charlie. Keeping you up are we?" Jones hated the idea of Pelham running anything more important than a bath, but he needed to put up with things the way they were—at least for the moment.

Pelham cleared his throat—a horrible, wet cough that made Jones cringe.

"Sorry, boss. It's already been a long day."

"Status report please, Charlie," Jones said, not wanting to listen to any more of his griping.

"So far we've contacted the girl's form teacher and ten of her classmates. We're having trouble getting hold of the others. Their mobiles are either engaged or go straight to voicemail."

"Anything interesting?"

Pelham sniffed.

"A couple of the girls fought with Hollie Jardine in the last couple of weeks. They said she'd become a little uppity recently. According to her so-called schoolmates, Hollie Jardine's become, and I quote, 'a bit of a tart'. Whacha reckon? Possible runaway?"

"Hell, Charlie, 'tart'? She's a child, for God's sake."

"Weren't my description, boss. I'm just reporting what they told us."

"Perhaps not, but she's fourteen. Go easy on repeating it with such obvious relish."

"Hang on, boss. I weren't doing nothing of the sort. Leastways, I didn't mean to. So, a runaway, you reckon?"

Jones took a breath. He hadn't meant to snap, but Pelham's attitude always seemed to irritate and, given the situation, it wasn't easy to rein in his feelings.

"DS Pelham," he said, hoping the formality would reinstated the proper tone, "we will treat this as an abduction until we know different. Have you made arrangements to search her school locker yet?"

"The headmaster's unavailable so we can't get his permission. The Deputy Head's gone AWOL, too. You'd have thought they didn't care that one of their kids had disappeared."

"Charlie, sort out an emergency warrant. Break into the damn school if you have to. What've you been doing for the past two hours?"

"Ruddy hell, boss, that's a bit harsh. Phone's been ringing off the hook. We've already been fielding phone calls from the press, and there's only me and Wash."

"For God's sake. Tell the switchboard to route the press calls through to the media officer. That's her job, isn't it?" Jones paused.

It wasn't like him to shout at his team, even Pelham, and it wouldn't help anyone for him to lose his cool.

"Sorry, Charlie. I'm on a short fuse today. Draft in some uniforms to help with the grunt work. Tell the Duty Officer, I sanctioned it. Get Ryan to contact the other schoolmates while you sort out the locker. And have one of the uniforms check the Missing Person's database for similar cases. Use Ben Adeoye if he's on shift. Remember that girl in Nottingham, Amanda Barton? She went missing on her way home from the shops? She was a blonde, too. And there was that young lass from Derby the other month."

"You think there's a gang of paedos targeting a specific type?" Pelham said, his level of interest picking up at last. "I wondered why

Part 1

you was so quick off the mark on this case, boss. Hollie Jardine's only been missing ten minutes."

"Just get on with it, Charlie. And let me know the second you find anything of value."

"Will do, boss."

Jones broke the connection. He took another deep breath and stepped through the threshold into a narrow hallway.

Magnolia paint on the walls, two panelled doors on the right, and a carpeted stairway on the left. The first door, like the front, stood wide open. It led into a lounge-dining room with beige carpet, mid-value furniture, a dark leather lounge suite, and a modest old-school television. Nothing too flashy or expensive. As expected from the outside, here was a well-maintained, well-ordered and comfortable middle-income home.

A man and woman he took to be Mr and Mrs Jardine sat close to each other on a tired and well-worn couch.

The Family Liaison Officer, a slim policewoman Jones had met a few times before but couldn't name, sat beside the distraught woman. She'd offer as much support as she could which, given the circumstances, would be precious little.

Detective Constable Alexandra Olganski, the Serious Crime Unit's only female officer, sat in a chair opposite the Jardines. She stood as Jones entered, introduced the parents to him, and handed him a photograph of their missing child.

"Taken three weeks ago, boss," Alex said.

As Jones studied the photo, his blood chilled.

Christ on a bike.

No way he'd able to keep this case at arm's length even if he wanted to. The missing girl had flowing blonde hair, sapphire eyes, dimpled cheeks, clear skin, and a pale complexion—a child with the open, innocent girl-next-door look.

Oh, God.

Phil Cryer's daughter, Jamie, would be the dead spit of Hollie Jardine in four or five years.

He cleared a chalk-dry throat and asked the questions he already knew would give no real answers.

"Has Hollie ever been late home before?"

Mr Jardine answered, his voice timid and faltering. "Not like this. She always tells us where she is and never stays out unless … unless she has permission. Our Hollie's a good girl."

Of course she is. They all are.

Jardine had the look and demeanour of a town clerk, dark suit, shirt, and tie still tight to the collar, metal-rimmed spectacles, balding with a Donald Trump comb-over. His lower lip trembled, but he wouldn't let the tears fall. Like Jones, he belonged to the "real men don't cry" generation.

No. We don't cry. Not in public.

Mrs Jardine, a small woman in her late forties or early fifties—rather mature for a woman with a teenage daughter—kept her focus on the tissue crumpled in her hand. She dabbed at puffy, bloodshot eyes and clung to her husband's arm as though frightened he would disappear, too.

Jones studied Hollie's photo again. He'd seen similar images a hundred times before. Here was a fourteen-year-old girl on the cusp of adulthood. A little make-up, a few pieces of jewellery, and an evening dress would allow her to pass as a twenty-something woman.

He needed to dig deep but knew his questions would add to the parents' pain. It would hurt them, sure, but he couldn't let sympathy for the parents interfere with finding their daughter.

"How has Hollie been lately? Any abnormal changes in personality? Fights, tantrums, boyfriend trouble?"

Mrs Jardine found her voice, though it was weak.

"Hollie's good as gold. Always has been. Studying hard for her exams made her a little more temperamental than usual, but nothing out of the ordinary for our baby."

A teenager without tantrums? Really?

She shot a furtive glance at her husband, who didn't appear to notice.

The warning mechanism in Jones' head, honed by nearly four decades as a police officer, thirty-three of them a detective, tingled. The mother was hiding something.

Part 1

"How did she get to and from school?"

Mr Jardine extricated his arm from his wife's death grip and stood.

"If it's dry she walks with her friend, Amy. It's only a mile or so if you cut through the park and take the footbridge over the dual carriageway. On rainy days, either Emma drives them, or Hollie takes the bus."

"On a sunny day like today, would she have walked home?"

The father nodded.

"When she failed to arrive, I drove her normal route three times, but there was no sign. After that, I phoned all the hospitals in case … but there's nothing. That's when I called the police."

He crossed to the window overlooking a well-tended rear garden, his back stooped in defeat and fear. Mrs Jardine remained on the couch and stared at the carpet. For all the good it would do, the FLO rested a hand on the distraught mother's forearm.

"And the friend she walks with, Amy. Have you spoken to her?"

"Amy's been off sick since Monday. Says she hasn't seen Hollie for days." Mrs Jardine's timid voice barely carried across the six-foot gap separating her from Jones.

"Can I have Amy's full name and address? DC Olganski can go and have a word."

Jones jotted the information into his notebook, stood, and signalled for Alex to join him in the hallway. He closed the door behind them.

"Did you get a description of the clothes she left home in? Jewellery she wore?"

"Yes, boss. School uniform, no jewellery. I've circulated the full description."

"Good, thanks. Call me when you've spoken to this Amy girl. Push her hard. We need to know what Hollie's been up to recently. According to her schoolmates, she might have had a boyfriend. I'll be here for a little while."

Alex pointed to Hollie's photo and frowned. "*Fan också*. She looks like Jamie Cryer, doesn't she?"

"Really? Hadn't noticed."

She offered a disbelieving smile and hurried from the house.

Jones returned to the lounge. Mrs Jardine hadn't moved from the couch. Jardine remained at the window, head lowered and eyes closed.

Jones cleared his throat and the father jumped.

"I'd like to take a look at Hollie's room now, if I may, Mrs Jardine."

She stiffened and looked at him directly for the first time.

"Why?"

There it was, the defensiveness he expected.

"The more I know about Hollie," he said evenly, "the better chance I have of finding her."

"Steady, Emma, old girl." Mr Jardine turned to face the room and spoke quietly, his voice firm. "If it helps find our girl you can search the whole damned house, Chief Inspector."

They might well have to do that, but first things first.

"This way," Jardine said, pushing himself away from the window.

Jones followed the desperate father up the stairs to a room overlooking the back garden—Hollie's inner sanctum. It offered few surprises. A poster of the latest boy-band flavour-of-the-month and a still from a vampire movie with a pale, emaciated-looking leading man adorned the faded pink walls. A dressing table buckled under the weight of cosmetics, mirrors, and inexpensive jewellery—silver and plastic, much of it pink. A queen-sized bed, complete with a dozen stuffed toys, occupied the wall adjacent to a wide picture window, pink curtains.

Jardine crossed to the bed and picked up a one-eared, no-eyed teddy bear. He stared at it as though it would tell him where they could find his daughter. Jones' breath caught. He'd given Jamie Cryer a bear exactly like it for her first birthday. Even after eight years, the thing held pride of place on the little girl's toy-shelf. He'd given Paul Cryer—the latest addition to his sergeant's family—a stuffed giraffe, and the toddler cuddled it to sleep every night.

Along the left-hand wall, a floor-to-ceiling wardrobe opened to reveal an assortment of clothes, school uniforms, skirts, blouses, tops, and the occasional dress. None was frivolous, or what he would consider inappropriate, but gaps in the rail and empty hangers told an interesting tale. A few of the skirts seemed closer to "micro" than "mini", but fashions change and Jones didn't have much of a clue what passed muster for respectable fourteen-year-old girls these days. He knew what disreputable fourteen-year-olds wore—his work showed him that often enough. He'd need to consult with Alex, or maybe Manda Cryer.

"How tall is Hollie?"

"As tall as you, Chief Inspector. She outgrew Emma and me last year."

The skirts were definitely "micro" then.

"Are any of her things missing?" he asked.

Jardine's lower lip trembled again, and his eyes glistened. A response Jones expected, given the empty spaces in the wardrobe.

"We checked before calling you. A suitcase and some clothes … they're gone." He hesitated before adding in a whisper, "She's taken her passport, too."

Of course she did. Damn it.

He'd been certain from the moment he opened the wardrobe.

"Why didn't you tell us this before, Mr Jardine?" He kept his voice level and controlled, not wanting to spook the poor man.

The desperate father lowered his head.

"We didn't think you'd try as hard to find her."

Jones remained silent until Jardine looked up, his eyes imploring.

"Sir," he said, "Hollie's a minor. No matter what, we'll try our very best to find her. Please believe me on this."

Jardine broke eye contact, stared down at the stuffed toy again, and nodded. Jones knew how it felt to lose a child, and he understood Jardine's pain all too well.

"Hollie's our miracle baby," Jardine said, almost to himself.

"Excuse me, sir?"

"We'd been trying for years without luck. Just about given up hope. And then … IVF. Emma fell pregnant in her thirty-eighth year. I was nearly forty-five. Most people think we're too old to have a teenage daughter. Sometimes, we're actually mistaken for her grandparents. Old fuddy-duddies. We probably smothered her."

His voice broke and he looked up again.

Jones spoke quietly. "You've tried her mobile?"

"No response."

"We'll put a trace on it. As soon as she makes a call, we'll know where she is."

Jones tried to bury the thought that Hollie couldn't answer the phone because she was already dead, but it kept burrowing its way to the surface and haunting him.

"Does Hollie have her own computer?"

Jardine took a deep breath. "No, she uses the family PC downstairs in the office."

Unfortunate. They probably wouldn't find anything useful on it.

"If you don't mind, I'll have one of our IT techs take a look at it. She may have been talking online to someone she shouldn't."

"Oh no, I've put full parental controls on the internet usage."

"Really?" Jones said, unable to mask his doubt.

"Before you consider me too naïve, Inspector," Jardine said, confidence clear in his tone, "I'm a software engineer, and I know all about computers. We didn't allow Hollie to use social media. But please feel free. If it helps, take the bloody thing away."

"Thank you, sir. We will."

Jones hated the next step, but couldn't avoid it. He didn't want Hollie's father to see him rifling through his daughter's private life.

"If you don't mind, sir." He pointed to the door. "I won't be long, and I promise not make a mess."

Jones never made a mess. It was one of his things, a matter of personal pride.

Mr Jardine hesitated, stole another look around the room, and turned away. He took the ragged bear with him.

Once alone, Jones dragged open the top drawer of the dressing table, already knowing what he'd find. Underwear: silk, sheer, neatly folded, bras with a cup size revealing the shape of a woman, not a child. Spaces showed that some of the items were missing.

The other drawers held nothing of particular interest.

Part 1

When searching the rest of the room, his gaze alighted on a large bowl of potpourri on the windowsill. He shuffled the dry leaves, but found no hidden baggies. The textbooks on the single shelf over the bed gave up nothing, no hidden papers, no jottings in the margins, no secreted photos.

The wardrobe proved more informative. In a battered shoebox, he found the thing he hoped for, an old-fashioned, pen and paper diary with a feeble lock. He didn't have to worry about operating systems, passwords, or something equally difficult—like finding the "on" switch.

He flipped to the most recent entry, dated the previous day:

"WE KISSED! Finally. Oh God, it was lovely. Tongues too. I think E's going to ask me today, and I'm going to say yes. Says he can't wait to see me naked at last. He's so hot. I want him to touch me, play with my …."

Jones thumbed backwards through the entries. Numerous references to *"E"* stretched back more than a month. The timeline matched the information given by her school friends. She met *"E"*, who was an older man, judging by the references to his having a car. She kept his identity secret, and her personality changed almost immediately. A classic sign of grooming, or was it too early to tell?

Jones dropped one of Hollie's hair brushes into an evidence bag in case they needed it later for identification, and hurried back down to the front room.

"Mrs Jardine." She turned towards him and his heart stalled at the torment in her puffy, reddened eyes. He'd seen the same look of desperation and fear so many times before.

"Has Hollie ever mentioned a boy with the initial, '*E*'?"

Her eyes flicked towards her husband, and her chin quivered.

"No, we told you. Hollie's a good girl … doesn't have a boyfriend. She's too young and concentrates on her schoolwork. She doesn't waste her time on … boys."

A flickering shadow of recognition passed behind Frank Jardine's eyes.

"Mr Jardine, might I have a word, please? In private."

Mrs Jardine blew her nose and turned away as Jones escorted the father back into the hall. He closed the door behind them and showed Mr Jardine the bag with the brush and the diary.

"I'll need to take these with me. Is that okay?"

Mr Jardine nodded.

"I've read the most recent entries. There's a chance Hollie may have run away with this 'E' person. What do you think?"

The father turned his head away.

"I've never met him. Whenever I asked Hollie, she'd tell me to mind my own business. What could I do?"

Ground her? Or don't parents do that sort of thing anymore?

Mr Jardine fixed Jones with tear-filled, pale brown eyes, and grabbed his arm. "Please find our little girl. She's everything to us. All we have."

The hidden steel behind Frank Jardine's meek exterior showed as the fierce grip on Jones' forearm increased. He felt the man's desperation and couldn't ignore his own empathy for a distraught father.

Somehow, Hollie's photo appeared in his hand. He stared down at it, and Jamie Cryer's smiling face stared back at him.

Siân's voice in his head said, *"Don't do it, Davey. Don't you dare."*

He normally followed her sage advice to the letter, but not this time.

"I'll find her, Mr Jardine. I promise."

Chapter Three

THURSDAY EVENING – Investigations
Time since abduction: nine hours, thirty minutes

JONES YELLED down the phone at the technician.

"What about ongoing police work? Isn't there a, what-do-you-call it, a backup system?"

"I'm terribly sorry, Chief Inspector," the techie said, without sounding the least bit apologetic, "but we've been the target of a series of security attacks over the past few weeks. We need to close the system to initiate a full upgrade or we'll be wide open to hackers."

Nope, the woman didn't sound at all sorry. In fact, her voice held a note of boredom.

"In fact, you're the fourth senior police officer I've talked to this evening. Every force in the country has had more than adequate warning. You should all have failsafe duplicate systems in place. It's part of the national standards." She paused. "And by the way, we chose this time because only seventeen percent of PNC searches are run overnight." Another pause. "I can give you ten more minutes before we pull the plug but that's all. If it's any help, the system should be back online by eight o'clock tomorrow morning."

"What's the point in having a Police National Computer system we can't access? A young girl's life is at stake here."

"Again, I am sorry, sir, but—"

Jones slammed the phone into its cradle and punched the desk with the side of his fist. A sharp pain jarred through his wrist and stung his fingers. He shook the hand.

Wonderful Jones, that'll help. That'll help a lot.

As the tingling in his fingertips diminished, he turned to face the room.

Alex Olganski sat at the computer station, her head bowed, eyes focused on the monitor. Ryan 'Wash' Washington, a hook-nosed, stoop-shouldered Detective Constable, and the fleshy DS Charlie Pelham, sat hunched over telephone handsets. Each spoke quietly. Papers and yellow telephone notes littered the desks. Jones wanted to jump across the room and tidy them into neat piles, but that would only help him, not the case. Ryan and Pelham worked hard, but the information they had gathered over the previous couple of hours was background colour and contained nothing to help locate Hollie Jardine.

Pelham's attempt at searching her school locker ended when the deputy head stated the school didn't have any. The children were "encouraged to travel light" and, "with the advance of new technology, heavy textbooks are no longer strictly necessary".

For his part, Ryan had accessed the school's IT system, but found nothing in Hollie's file relevant to her disappearance. Jones despaired at the loss of real honest-to-goodness paper.

"Who's responsible for overseeing the backup PNC system?" Jones asked the group.

Pelham lowered his head and frowned as he studied an incident report. Ryan answered for him.

"Superintendent Peyton refused to release the funds to expand the local network, boss. Said it wasn't worth it for the amount of time we'd need the resource. Phil tried to talk to him about it when

Part 1

you were in High Court on the Skelman trial, but the Super shot him down in flames."

"You mean there's nothing backed up locally?"

Pelham coughed and shuffled in his seat.

Ryan lowered his gaze. "We have some out of date files on the local servers, but the system's a pig. Nobody's spent any money on it for years. Our in-house system is out of the Ark, keeps crashing. Bloody thing's just about useless."

Jones couldn't believe it. No one could ever accuse him of being an advocate of high-tech, but even he could see the value of uninterrupted access to data files.

Superintendent Douglas Peyton was a bean counter of the worst kind. If Hollie Jardine died because of Peyton's penny-pinching, Jones would cheerfully castrate the useless bastard.

Jones tried to relax his aching jaw muscles and turned to the only working computer in the office. "You've got ten, no … eight minutes, Alex. How's it coming?"

She rattled the keyboard.

"I need to know what search parameters to use. I've entered adult males in this region. What age range? Centre of operation? Modus operandi?"

Jones tugged at his earlobe. All he knew for certain was that Hollie called her boyfriend "*E*". He didn't even know whether it referred to a surname or a given name. Hell, it might even be a pet name.

"Pull out every male with a history of molesting or grooming underage girls. He was old enough to drive, right? So he's at least seventeen. Upper age? Oh, I don't know, fifty-five? He was probably IC1, judging by what Hollie's school friends said. Get me every name you can and we'll go through it later."

He checked the time—seven minutes left.

Alex bowed her head and concentrated on the screen showing the soon-to-be-locked blue search template.

Come on, Alex. It's all down to you now, lass.

She spat out something in Swedish—probably a curse—glanced at Jones, and shook her head in apology. He stood over her and tried to read the digital forms. Her fingers fluttered over the keys, but her eyes remained glued to the screen. Jones wondered when she'd learned to touch-type so well. He also wondered why it mattered.

Alex stopped typing and looked up. Smudged mascara, where she rubbed her tired eyes, drew Jones' attention.

"Boss, please?"

Jones raised an open hand.

"Sorry."

He turned to leave the room, but paused long enough to straighten some of the papers on Ryan's desk. He couldn't help himself.

Jones could think of nothing better to do than pace the corridor outside the SCU briefing room and monitor the time, which rushed past with the speed of Usain Bolt on one of the days he broke the world record. He considered entering his office to organise the papers the admin officer would likely have thrown in a mess on his desk, but couldn't stomach the thought of doing something so mundane.

No matter how many times he told the man to put new files in the in-tray and not on his blotter, he refused to listen. Jones began to wonder whether someone on the team egged the man on, just to annoy him. Well it bloody worked. Jones hated mess in his personal space, and anywhere else come to that.

He wiped a coating of dust from a windowsill in the hall with his handkerchief and shook the cloth out before folding it into a neat square and replacing it in his inside jacket pocket. He wondered, not for the first time, what the cleaners did to earn their minimum wage.

Jones called the control room again. None of the local patrol cars had reported any success. Officers had stopped and searched one campervan fitting the description, but cleared the owners—an elderly Welsh couple—to go. Apart from that, they had nothing.

Jones ended the call and popped his head around the SCU office door. Alex still attacked the keyboard with controlled fury. Neither Pelham nor Ryan had moved from their posts.

Jones' spirits sank. Alex needed to come up with a list of suspects before the deadline. If not, they'd be stymied until morning

Part 1

and Hollie's chances were … He refused to complete the thought and paced the hall for five more interminable minutes.

"Boss, I have it!"

Jones burst into the room to find Alex smiling in triumph.

"Excellent." He touched her shoulder. "Now, print off four copies."

The laser printer hummed, and Jones signalled for Ryan to distribute the output. This time, he didn't wait for the pages to cool.

"There are fifteen men who fit the profile,' Alex announced. "That is, fifteen with a particular interest in teenage children."

With a magnetised strip, Jones stuck his copy to the wall-sized whiteboard and finger-walked through the names. Searching first for anyone he recognised before skipping to the first 'E' he found.

Method, Jones. Miss nothing. Go through each name in turn.

He scratched off two men. One had died of natural causes a couple of weeks earlier, and the other was currently tucked away downstairs in the holding cells, charged with exposing himself near a school playground.

"Doesn't anybody update the PNC? I thought the whole point of a computerised system was to have *accurate and complete* records? Anybody else have anything?" Jones found himself shouting, despite struggling for control.

Pelham pulled at his lower lip before pointing to his list. "You can remove Ewan Priestly. The guy's too pug ugly. No way's he gonna turn the head of a young girl."

Damn, that's one 'E' gone.

"And bin Ivan Zylic, too," Pelham continued. "The Home Office returned him to Serbia. I sat in on his extradition case last month."

"Ryan?"

"Sorry, boss. Don't recognise any of the others."

"Alex?"

"A member of the public attacked the paedophile, Glen Evans yesterday. He's still recovering in hospital, I think." Alex picked up the desk phone. "I'll check." The handset disappeared under her long blonde hair.

Jones didn't miss the initial letter of Evans' name. His heart sank a little more as they struck a second "*E*" from the dwindling list. He turned to Pelham and Ryan.

"Take three names each. Go find them. Report in the minute you clear anyone. Alex and I will take the remaining four. I want every one of these sick buggers interviewed, checked, and crossed off. I don't care how many uniforms you allocate to help with the search. Off you go."

Pelham's shoulders sagged. "What's the point of running around after her? The kid's a runaway. It's obvious. She packed her bags and took her passport, didn't she? This is a waste of bloody time."

Jones turned on Pelham and stepped close.

"What did you say?"

The stink of sweat mixed with stale tobacco forced Jones to breathe through his mouth. He backed away half a pace.

"What the hell's wrong with you, man? What would you do if your Greg disappeared like this? Do I have to remind that you Hollie Jardine is a child? She should be home with her parents. I want her found. Understand?"

"Yes, boss. Sorry," Pelham mumbled. He raised a placatory hand and rushed to follow Ryan through the door.

Jones didn't believe the apology. Pelham's laziness had worsened in recent months, and he constantly stretched Jones' patience beyond its limits. He wanted to kick the lazy bugger off the team, but the crafty old sod had protection from on high in the emaciated, buck-toothed shape of Superintendent Duggie Peyton. As a result, Jones needed to tread carefully.

Alex finished her call and crossed Evan's name off the main list.

"Broken arm and concussion. Definitely, he is not our man."

Jones checked his Seiko.

"Hollie's been missing over ten hours. We're running out of time, if the poor child isn't already dead."

"Our four suspects." Alex pointed to each name in turn. "Aaron Smollett, Jackson Perry, Nigel Simms, and Edward Flynn. Who do you want to look at first?"

Part 1

"Edward Flynn. Edward Flynn. Where do I know that name from?"

The final 'E'. Was he clutching?

Alex shrugged and read from the brief bio.

"I'm sorry, but the name is unfamiliar to me. Born in 1960. He has more than fifty years."

"Would a man in his fifties really turn the head of a teenage girl?"

"Excuse me?"

"Her diary." Jones handed her the pink journal. "The entries read like a young girl with a crush on a slightly older boy, not a middle aged man. But she does use the initial 'E'."

Jones spun on his heel and headed for the door.

"I've had an idea. Send patrol cars to pick up Perry, Simms, and Smollett," he called over his shoulder. "After that, follow me to the archives. We have some old-fashioned police work to do."

THE ARCHIVES, across the road from the smart new police headquarters, had missed the latest round of renovations.

The under-utilised, dusty vault hadn't changed much in the eleven months since Jones last searched through the paper records, but the smell of damp and decay had worsened by a country mile. Cobwebs hung like shrouds, dust clung to every flat surface, and flecks drifted in the still air as large as confetti in a wedding photo. Jones sneezed twice and pulled on a pair of disposable gloves. He shuddered at the grime and the airborne germs, and wished he had a dust mask handy.

According to the Sex Offender's Registry, Edward Flynn's most recent court appearances dated back to 1999. It took Jones half an hour to find the case file. Something scrabbling in the back of his mind told him they were getting close to an answer. The familiar burst of adrenaline accompanying a potential break in the case made his heart rate jump. This was the buzz he lived for—the parmesan grated over his pizza.

Alex arrived as he dropped the thick manila folder on the reception desk. The file hit the surface with a clap and stirred up a thick cloud of dust. He sneezed again and regretted being so aggressive with the folder. He waited for the dust to settle before flipping open the front cover. The excitement melted away the instant he read the first page.

"Oh, for God's sake!"

"Boss?" Alex's eyebrows knitted together.

"Look." Jones pointed to the big red letters stamped diagonally across the top page: *DECEASED*. "So much for my bright idea."

He stepped back to let Alex take a closer look and allowed his shoulders to slump. Now they had nothing but the other names on the SO list.

Alex read the entry aloud.

"Edward Flynn died in prison. Isle of Wight, nearly five years ago. He served twelve of a twenty-five-year sentence for the grooming, kidnap, rape, and murder of a twelve-year-old girl. An inmate stabbed him to death in the prison chapel two days before his release for what was described as good behaviour. It would appear the other inmates were not too happy about Mr Flynn being released so early."

"So it would seem." Jones rubbed his face with his hands. "Flynn's MO matches Hollie Jardine's abduction. Hell, I thought we were on to something. I don't suppose he has a brother, does he?"

Alex flipped a page and continued reading.

Jones closed his eyes, and tried hard to think of something they'd missed, another line of enquiry. He came up with nothing. All they could do was hope one of the other men on the list became a hot candidate, or someone spotted the campervan. But the holiday season had already started, and the mass exodus of campers making the trip to the ports on the south coast made the odds of finding a specific vehicle bloody long. They still hadn't turned up a registration number.

"Boss, I have something." Alex raised her head from the file, her eyes shone. She pointed to an entry in the file under *Next-of-Kin*. "Edward Flynn had a son, Ellis."

Part 1

Jones slapped a palm on the desk and read the information over Alex's shoulder. "Ellis Edward Flynn, more '*E*'s. Is there anything in the file on this boy, Ellis?"

"There's a reference number here. It means he has a case file."

Jones rummaged behind the serving counter for the index list. "Call out that number for me."

"2-3-6-8-9-8-6."

It took him a couple of frustrating minutes to find the number in the index and the file's designated shelving area. They hurried to the correct section of the archive, only to find an unholy mess of misfiled case folders. Hundreds of them, all stacked in haphazard fashion on sagging metal shelving units that were clearly unsuitable for the task. Jones nearly screamed in frustration.

"This is what happens when we rely too heavily on IT and outsource the hard copy filing to the lowest bidder. Nobody's sorted these files in months. Damn it. Heads are going to roll for this bloody mess."

Alex took in the mess and nodded.

"If we take the files and place them on the floor in regular stacks, we can perform a binary split. It will be much faster, *ja?*"

Jones ground his teeth.

"What the hell's a binary split? Yet another piece of technology I have to learn?"

Red spots coloured Alex's high cheekbones. She lowered her head and picked up the first file.

"Sorry, boss. It's a mathematical process."

Jones coughed and followed her lead. He clamped down hard on his frustrations and studied Alex's methodical approach. When she finally came up with the file, it had only taken fifteen minutes. It would probably have taken a damned sight longer without her system. Alex tossed the file onto the table in front of him. A self-satisfied grin split her face.

"So that's a binary split, eh?" He nodded. "Thanks, Alex. Sorry for being so short with you back there."

"It is okay. I also want to find Hollie Jardine."

Jones pointed to the notes. Ellis' folder was considerably thinner than that of his father.

"Do you mind reading the file? Your eyes are sharper than mine."

He paced behind her while she scanned the papers.

"There's not much here, boss. He's never been in trouble as an adult, but there is a sealed juvenile record." She checked the time on her mobile. "Unfortunately, we won't be able to access that specific file for at least six hours."

"Does it give a current address?"

She pointed to a box on the top page. "Tile Hill. You know the place?"

Jones nodded and allowed himself a grin. Perhaps his fears of a motorway trip for the campervan had been premature.

"It's a small town a few miles southeast of us. There was nothing on the SO register about Ellis Flynn so he may be an innocent. On the other hand, he might have taken Hollie to his home."

The information fitted, it felt right, and his internal mechanism agreed. Jones made the decision.

"Call Ryan and Charlie. Get them to meet us at Tile Hill. I'll organise a couple of uniforms for added backup."

Alex rushed from the room but Jones paused a moment and eyed the desk. Although he would have put any other officer on a charge for doing the same thing, Jones picked up both of the Flynn folders and took them along with him.

What the useless filing clerk doesn't know ....

Chapter Four

THURSDAY EVENING – *Tile Hill*
Time since abduction: eleven hours, forty-five minutes

JONES, Pelham, Alex, and Ryan, together with two uniformed constables, pitched up at Ellis Flynn's 1930s, Art Deco house in two police cars and Jones' Rover. Jones ordered a silent approach and they turned off the flashing lights and the sirens half a mile from the house.

Half past three in the morning. Hollie had been missing nearly twelve hours. The odds against her survival lengthened with each passing minute, and everyone in the team understood as much.

The first ominous thing Jones noticed was the *For Sale* sign in the postage-stamp of a front garden.

As the most senior officer on duty, Jones didn't need a warrant under the exigent circumstances rule, and they smashed their way through the flimsy front door. Ellis Flynn wasn't home, as Jones knew in his heart he wouldn't be.

"Ryan, make sure you call the Estate Agent first thing in the morning. See whether they have a contact number for Flynn.

Although I'll be willing to bet he's referred everything through a solicitor."

Ryan jotted a note on his computer tablet.

"Charlie, go talk to the neighbours. See whether anyone knows where Flynn's gone. Actually, canvass the whole damned street and take the uniforms with you."

Pelham sighed, shook his head, and wandered off. Jones scowled at his back and turned to Ryan, the SCU's resident petrol head.

"Take the garage. See if you can find out whether Flynn owned a campervan."

Jones sent Alex to search upstairs, while he took the ground floor.

The house, although tired and in need of modernisation, had been thoroughly cleaned. If the *For Sale* sign didn't make it clear enough, the bare bones furniture covered in dust sheets confirmed Ellis Flynn's intention to leave the house he'd lived in since his birth. Jones found no registration documents, no official papers, passports, birth certificates, or school qualifications. Neither did he find any deeds to other buildings or utility bills for any property other than the one they were ransacking.

In short, he found nothing to tell them where Flynn might have taken Hollie. Nor did they find anything concrete to link Flynn with the girl. Although it made no logical sense, somehow Jones *knew* Ellis Flynn was their man. He felt it in his bones. There was a smell to the place. An aura of decay. A sense of evil.

Alex returned to the front room and shook her head.

"I found nothing upstairs. No clothes in the wardrobes. The linen and bedclothes are also gone. There's nothing in the bathroom, either. Ellis Flynn has gone on a runner."

"Same down here. Nothing personal left in the place, only that photo over there." He pointed to a simple glass-fronted picture frame on the mantelpiece above the fire.

The picture showed a thirty-something woman dressed in clothes from the 1980s—the decade taste ignored. Flynn's mother he presumed. The woman in the frame didn't figure in Ellis Flynn's

Part 1

current life or he'd have had a more up-to-date picture, and he wouldn't have left this one behind.

Why did he leave it here?

He took a second look, and crossed the room in four quick strides. "Do you see this?"

Alex stepped beside him and studied the picture.

The woman in the frame wore her wavy blonde hair long and loose. She had blue eyes, and a toothy, dimpled smile.

"*Jävla helvete!*" Alex said. "She's so much like Hollie Jardine!"

Before either of them had time to speak, Ryan burst through the door, breathing heavily.

"Found something, boss," he said and smiled as he held up two evidence bags. "There's an incinerator in the garden, still warm. But Flynn clearly doesn't know diddly about setting fires. He let it go out. Look."

Ryan handed over the first of his treasure trove—the lower third of a photo booth film strip. A scorched edge showed the fire damage, but the bottom picture remained relatively intact. It showed Hollie Jardine and a handsome man in his early twenties. Hollie smiled and gazed longingly up into the man's face. Ellis Flynn—it had to be him—wore his thick dark hair long. He bore a passing similarity to a young film actor, but Jones couldn't put a name to the celebrity.

In the picture, Ellis Flynn stared into the camera lens, looking directly at Jones through cold, lifeless eyes. It was almost as though he knew Jones was trespassing on his domain.

A cold shiver rushed up from Jones' shiny black shoes. Ryan's voice broke through his thoughts.

"…garage is definitely large enough to hold a campervan, boss. There are discarded oil and air filter boxes in the bin, along with used diesel glow plugs. It looks like he might have prepared the camper for a long drive. But that's not all." With a smile and the flourish of a stage magician pulling a card out of his sleeve, he held up a second evidence bag. It contained a sheet of paper covered in oily fingerprints. "I found this on the floor under the workbench. It's a till receipt for a new shower pump to fit a caravan … or a campervan."

Jones clenched his fist. "Okay, that's confirmation enough for me. Any sign of a registration document?"

Ryan shook his head.

"Sorry, boss. I'd check the online driver's listings for a registration number, but the PNC's a bust and the DVLA won't be open until eight o'clock tomorrow morning."

Bloody computers—bloody DVLA.

Jones' mobile buzzed and he answered before checking the caller id.

"Chief Inspector Jones?" Mr Jardine's pleading voice hit him like a blow to the gut.

Jones regretted giving out his personal number, then immediately reprimanded himself for being so callous.

"Mr Jardine, I'm sorry, but there's no news ye—"

"We've just had a reporter knock on our door."

Already?

"Really?"

"He was from the local paper. A man called Wilson. Said he was in close liaison with the police and asked me to comment on research showing most abductees are killed within the first six hours!"

'Old' Luke Wilson. Wait 'til I get my hands around his pencil neck.

"Mr Jardine, we have no reason to think the worst." Jones tried to sound calm and comforting but knew it wasn't working. "You mustn't give up hope. In fact, we're looking into a lead. Tell me, has Hollie ever mentioned an Ellis Flynn?"

"Oh God! Is that the man who took her?" Jardine's voice cracked.

"We're not certain, but do you recognise the name?"

"Ellis Flynn? No, Hollie never mentioned him, but I never knew the name of any of her friends. I can't ask Emma, either. The doctor gave her a strong sedative and she's asleep. She's taken this so badly."

Jones let Jardine ramble on for a few moments, offered him

some useless platitudes, and rang off as Pelham strolled in with a smirk on his flaccid, stubble-blurred face.

"Looks like I were right after all, boss."

"About?"

"Hollie Jardine's gone and run off wi' this Ellis-bloody-Flynn character."

"What makes you say that?"

"Spoke to the neighbour. The old biddy weren't too happy to be woke in the middle of the night, but she were pretty helpful in the end."

"In what way?"

"Turns out that Hollie Jardine's been visiting Ellis Flynn a couple of afternoons a week." Pelham consulted his notepad. "Mrs Tomlinson—that's her next door—said she were shocked on account of the girl looking so young. She even arrived in her school uniform one day."

"Did she give you a description of the camper?" Jones asked, trying to ignore Pelham's look of smug satisfaction.

"Yes, boss. And I quote, *'It's a big, white monstrosity. Takes up two car parking spaces and blocks out all my light'*. Mrs Tomlinson's in her eighties, boss. Wouldn't know the difference between a campervan and a dumper truck."

"She's certain it was Hollie?"

Pelham sucked his teeth and twisted his thin lips into a wry grin. "Yep. She recognised the photo. Nobody's abducted the silly little fool. She ran away with Flynn. This is a bloody waste of time. We could be tucked up in our nice warm pits fast asleep instead of chasing around town after a bloody idiot runaway."

Jones stepped closer and braved the stench of sweaty armpits and stale cigarettes.

"By all means go home to your bed, Sergeant Pelham," Jones said, quietly. "But if you do, you can empty your desk and resign yourself to writing parking tickets for the rest of your useless career."

Pelham's jaw dropped.

Jones locked angry eyes with his sergeant and counted off the points on his fingers.

"A fourteen-year-old girl is swept off her feet. She packs a bag, and takes her passport. An adult male who's been grooming her for weeks fuels up his camper and whisks her away to who-the-hell-knows-where. Now, I don't care that she apparently went willingly, and I don't care about your bloody warm bed. If Flynn touches one hair on her head, it makes him a paedophile, and I'm going to have the bugger strung up by his scrotum. Do you understand me, Sergeant Pelham?"

"Er, sorry, boss. Just kidding," Pelham offered. His cheeks flushed, and he averted his eyes from Jones' steely glare.

"This isn't a joking matter, Sergeant. Even if Hollie did go voluntarily, she's still a minor and we need to find her."

Pelham swallowed hard.

"Yes, boss. What do you want me to do?"

"Go back to the station and phone all the ports in the country. Flynn's taken a campervan, so I doubt he plans to use an airport. Check whether he's booked on an overnight ferry to the continent. Check the Channel Tunnel too, and don't forget all the sailings to Ireland. With a name like Flynn, he might have relatives over there. And if you find a booking, remember to get a vehicle description and registration."

Pelham hesitated.

"Well, get a move on, man!" Jones shouted. "Alex, Ryan, you go help him. Go melt some telephone wires."

"What are you going to do, boss?" Alex asked from the doorway. The other two clearly didn't have the nerve.

"Me?" Jones said, adding a grim smile. "I'm going to wake my favourite memory man."

Chapter Five

FRIDAY MORNING – *Pre-dawn*
Time since abduction: thirteen hours, thirty minutes

JONES' Rover screamed through quiet country lanes, his foot jammed hard on the throttle pedal. The blue flashing lights cast an eerie glow on the hedgerows as he flashed by at twenty miles per hour above the maximum speed limit. The car lurched on soft springs each time he hit a dip in the road, but his right foot remained flat to the floor mat.

He hated using the phone while driving, but he'd never learned to operate the hands-free Bluetooth thing the techies had issued, and time was a luxury. Nor could he work the voice recognition thing either. On a straight stretch of road he risked a glance down and hit the call button.

It took a while for his call to be answered with a sleepy, "'Ullo?"
"Philip, ah great. I'm afraid I need your help."
A muffled voice replied.
"Huh? That you, boss?"
"Did I wake you?"

A loud yawn and a groan was followed by, "Christ's sakes, David, it's four-thirty in the morning. Of course you bloody woke me!"

"Sorry." Jones took a breath. "Sorry about breaking into your sick leave, but I'm in a bind. I would have called our international hacking guru, Corky Whatshisname, but he wouldn't be able to help this time."

"What?"

"Corky, the hacker. Sean Freeman's buddy."

"Boss, you're confusing me."

"Sorry, Phil. A girl's disappeared."

"Okay, right. The teenager, Hollie Jardine. It's all over the news. But what can I do? I know nothing about it."

Before answering, Jones snapped a double gear change to negotiate a T-junction and dropped back into top.

"You spent a couple of years working with Joe Davies in the Juvenile Crime Unit, didn't you?"

"Yeah. My last assignment before joining the SCU." Cryer stifled another yawn and kept his voice low. "So?"

"I need access to your memory banks."

"Hell, boss. Can't this wait? Paulie's teething. We haven't had a full night's sleep for weeks."

"I doubt Hollie Jardine's getting much sleep either," Jones snapped, unfairly.

The glow of the city's streetlights grew in the distance.

Not far now.

"Ouch, I deserved that, I suppose. Can't you get someone to help you run a database search?"

"Love to, but the bloody system's down for a wash and scrub, or whatever it's called. I wouldn't ask, Phil, but the girl's been gone over twelve hours. And you know what that means."

Phil sighed. "Right, boss. I'm awake now. What do you need?"

"I'm guessing when you were at the JCU, you spent the quiet times reading old case files. Like you do now?"

Again, Phil sighed. "Right, I understand. Where are you at the moment?"

"Fifteen minutes out. Put the kettle on and wake up that wonderful memory of yours. I'll need all you can tell me about the child molester and murderer, Edward Flynn. And, more importantly, his son, Ellis."

A baby cried in the background.

"Oh great, we've woken Paulie." Phil grunted. "I'll leave the back door unlatched. Keep the noise down when you get here, yeah?"

Chapter Six

FRIDAY MORNING – Mrs Memory
Time since abduction: thirteen hours, thirty minutes

MANDA CRYER ROLLED onto her back.

"Was that David?"

"Who else is gonna call at this time of the morning? He's on the missing girl case—Hollie Jardine. Thinks I can help him. Sorry, I should have disconnected the bloody phone."

Phil pulled back the covers and grunted as he sat and eased his injured leg over the edge of the bed.

Manda rolled over and scrunched her eyes against the searing light from Phil's bedside lamp.

"Philip Cryer, don't you dare talk like that. There's a young girl missing and you'll do what you can to help. You know you will."

She grimaced with him as he struggled out of bed, grabbed the walking stick, and shuffled towards the *en suite*. He still dragged his left leg badly. It hurt her so much to see her man in so much pain.

"David thinks I might know something."

She sat, and rubbed her eyes.

Part 1

"I'll go and settle the little monster before he wakes Jamie."

"It'd take a neutron bomb to wake that little madam."

As Paulie's cry grew more strident, Manda bounced out of bed and pulled on her dressing gown.

"I feel sorry for David sometimes."

Phil popped his head around the bathroom door. He held a toothbrush in the air. Toothpaste foam dribbled down his chin.

"Why?"

"He doesn't have many friends outside of work."

She picked up a screwdriver from her bedside cabinet, poked it into the large hole in the bedroom door, and used it as a handle. The door, stripped of its paint and ironmongery, had been awaiting its primer coat for weeks, as was just about every other wooden fixture in the house. Phil had promised to get to it when his leg recovered.

"It'll be great when it's finished," had become something of a family motto.

Manda returned with Paulie in her arms. She handed the lad to Phil who hugged the boy close.

"Hello my little man," he cooed. "Did the nasty telephone wake you up, then?"

Paulie grumbled for a few seconds, snuggled into the crook of his daddy's arm, and fell back to sleep in a flash.

Manda smiled at the picture of the two most important men in her life.

"I suppose David's on his way?"

"Yeah. I'll go fill the kettle. He'll want his tea and I'll need a gallon of coffee to wake me up and keep me alive. You stay here and have a lie-in." He sniffed the air close to his son. "Better change him first, though."

"I'll sort him out and be down in a little while. I'm glad David's coming over. At least I can send him away with a nice cooked breakfast. The poor man looks more and more emaciated every time I see him. Needs a good woman to take care of him."

Phil stared at her with exaggerated patience and made a slow shake of the head.

"Don't get ideas about setting him up with any more of your friends. Remember what happened last time?"

Manda sniffed. "Ailsa Carpenter would have been perfect. David never gave her a chance."

Phil placed the sleeping infant on the bed, propped between two pillows. "I almost fell off my chair when she offered to share her dessert with him. Thought the bloke would have a fit."

He chuckled.

"Yes, well next time I set him up with one of my girlfriends, I'll brief her a little better. David might have a thing about dirt and dust, but he's a lovely man, and I hate seeing him lonely. Never fear, I'll find someone for him one day."

Phil paused at the door. He leaned on his cane and made an awkward turn to face her.

"The boss has already had a go at me about your matchmaking efforts. Doubt he'll allow a next time."

Manda smiled and kissed Paulie's forehead. "I understand your lab has a vacancy for a Scenes of Crime Team Leader after poor Mr Prendergast's … meltdown."

"That's right. And?"

She smiled and let Phil see it.

"As it happens, Robyn's looking to move out of London."

Phil shot her his special look.

All those years ago, the nineteen-year-old Amanda Durbridge knew Phil Cryer as a friend of a friend for months before he used the look on her. Manda's lumbering, handsome bear of a husband could still give her goose bumps with that one searing glance. And still the lovely man had no idea.

"Robyn?" he said, giving her a wide-eyed nod. "Didn't know she wanted to leave London. You could have something there, love. At least they'd talk the same language. She's almost as fastidious as the old man. Worth thinking about," he called over his shoulder, and then laughed.

"Why the giggle?"

"I just pictured the two of them trying to work out the best way to brew the perfect cuppa and, worse still, which side of the bed to sleep on."

Phil disappeared through the doorway and thumped down the stairs. The tip of his walking stick clicked on the bare wooden treads.

Manda smiled to herself and started planning how to engineer a meeting between David Jones and her best friend in the world, Dr Robyn Spence, PhD.

Robyn, a senior forensic scientist for the Metropolitan Police would do very nicely indeed. Manda wondered why she hadn't thought of her as a match for David sooner.

She pulled a fresh terry-cloth nappy from a drawer under the bed-the horrible and environmentally unfriendly disposables would not do for her little angel.

Chapter Seven

FRIDAY MORNING – Pre-dawn
Time since abduction: thirteen hours, thirty minutes

THE PREDAWN SKY promised another warm summer's day.

Jones rolled the midnight blue Rover to a sedate stop in front of the Cryers' small, detached house. He closed the car door with a clump and pressed the button on his key-fob. The fizz-click of the central locking system echoed through the quiet residential street and startled the neighbour's cat. It darted through a hole in the Cryers' dilapidated fence and scuttled out of sight in the primped herbaceous border.

The gentle morning breeze rustled the leaves in the nearby trees. On any other day Jones would have paused to soak up the sights and sounds of daybreak, but this wasn't the time, or the place. This far into the city, no dawn chorus welcomed the day, and only the gentle grumble-rumble of incessant traffic on the nearby trunk roads ate into the silence. Spaghetti Junction, with its tangle of motorways, dual carriageways, and slip roads lay a mere four miles due east. The Cryers' street would never qualify as anybody's peaceful haven.

Jaded after the night's frustrating searches, Jones stretched his aching neck. The cervical bones clicked in protest. A yawn, deep and long, reconfirmed his exhaustion. Sleep would be great, but he'd made Hollie's father that ridiculous promise, and rest wouldn't help him keep it. Besides, it' wasn't as if anything awaited him at home but an empty bed, and another long and near-sleepless night of talk radio.

He pushed through the tatty garden gate, and followed the raked gravel path to the side of the house. He avoided the trip-hazard toys and arrived at the lopsided fence panel that acted as the Cryers' security gate to the back door. The off-square hinges and poorly fitted lock stood in mute testament to Phil's DIY ineptitude. Jones cringed. He'd offered to help refit the blessed thing but Phil couldn't see anything wrong with it, and Jones had to let the matter drop. Not his place to force the issue.

He tapped gently on the back door, and let himself into the new, professionally-fitted kitchen. Black granite surfaces topped fauxwood carcasses. They looked nice, but Jones wondered how long they'd last under the heavy workload of a growing family.

Phil stood beside his black-on-red cooker and spoke quietly. "Come in, boss, tea's brewing."

Phil's mussed blond hair, early morning stubble, and bleary eyes showed a man rudely awoken. Jones probably looked as bad—he certainly felt it. He still hadn't found time to use his emergency electric razor.

"Love a cup. Sorry for the intrusion, Phil. I really do hate disturbing you, but … well, you know." Jones kept his voice low.

"Yes, boss. I know."

Phil retrieved Jones' designated, double-sized cup and saucer from its special place in the wall unit, and filled it with the pale brown nectar.

Jones took a sip.

"Lovely. Really need this after the night I've had."

"Come through to the lounge."

Phil hobbled into the open-plan lounge-dining room and dropped with an airy thud into his leather chair. He waved Jones to sit.

"I'll stand, otherwise I might drop off. I'm shattered. How's the knee?"

Phil waggled an open outstretched hand. "Getting stronger every day." He twisted in his chair and avoided meeting Jones' eye. "I'll be fit for work soon though, as long as I don't have to chase any more villains over rotting rooftops."

"I told you not to follow Collins, but you wouldn't flaming well listen."

Phil raised both hands to forestall the inevitable lecture. "We've been through it a million times, boss. Hot pursuit. Learned my lesson though. Never again."

Jones still hadn't forgiven himself for failing to prevent the accident. Why the hell had they been scrambling over rooftops chasing a killer? Utter madness! The image of the rusty metal spike sticking through Phil's thigh would give Jones nightmares forever.

At least Phil hadn't lost the leg. He could walk again, thanks to a ten-hour operation and long long months of painful physiotherapy, but only time would tell whether he'd ever be signed fit for work.

As it happened, Jones had cashed-in all his favours, and more, with the Deputy Chief Constable to keep Phil's place on the Unit open. He owed his young friend that much. The rest came down to the physio, the FMO, and Phil's willingness to suffer through the torture of rehab.

Jones took another sip of tea.

"Okay," he said, "now tell me all you know about Edward and Ellis Flynn."

Phil took a breath and closed his eyes. Once again, Jones marvelled at his protégé's facility for full recall.

"Edward Roy Flynn, born … April 18th, 1964. Tile Hill. Home birth. Not so unusual in those distant days." Phil opened his eyes. "I have the whole record available" — he tapped his temple — "but he's dead now, so I reckon you're more interested in his boy, Ellis, right?"

"You could say that, unless you think Edward has risen from the grave." Jones instantly regretted his sarcasm and raised a hand in apology. "Sorry Phil, fatigue's darkening my mood. Carry on, please."

"Ellis Flynn. Born 12th, November … 1993, in Birmingham Hospital for Women, Edgbaston. Five weeks premature. The result of a beating his mother received from his ever-loving and paedophile father. Turns out that Edward Flynn kept his wife chained in the cellar after she tried to run off when the boy was three or four. Daddy Flynn was one sick arsehole." Phil paused and squeezed his eyelids together. "Um … oh yes, right," he continued. "Young Ellis spent much of his childhood in and out of one institution or another: hospitals, care homes, and, finally a youth detention centre."

"1993? So, Ellis Flynn's in his late twenties? Looks younger in his photo." Jones tugged his earlobe. "What about the detention centre? Does that explain his young offender record?"

Phil nodded.

"Ellis was caught fiddling with his neighbour's five-year-old daughter. He was thirteen at the time. The girl's father beat him half to death."

Jones' skin prickled and the blood pounded in his head. Even if Hollie accompanied Flynn voluntarily, the man's record confirmed the danger she faced.

Phil leaned back into his chair and continued. "Young Ellis spent five years locked away at, er … the Derbyshire Detention Centre … a former Grammar School, funded by the Ministry of Justice. The Headmaster-stroke-Governor throughout Ellis' stay was a chap by the name of Dr Buckeridge, a qualified and well-respected educational psychologist. The place closed a year after they released young Ellis. The bloke's been out a little under ten years." He opened his eyes and shot Jones a knowing glance. "You know what sort of an education he'd have received from the inmates in a place like that, right?"

"Yes. They're training schools for hardening criminals. Didn't have much of a start in life, did he?"

Phil's expression darkened as he stared at the white-plastered ceiling above his head, where the nine-year-old Jamie lay asleep.

"Bollocks to that. Don't waste your sympathy on Ellis-bloody-Flynn, boss. There's no excuse for kiddie fiddling. Bastard got what he deserved."

Jones could understand Phil's feelings, and once again wondered how he could sleep at night for worrying about his babies, given the job he did, and the things he saw. That sort of anxiety would send Jones to an early grave. He was much better off alone.

Yep, that's right, Jones. Keep telling yourself that.

"Anyway," Phil continued, "last I read, nothing's been added to the file since his release. So he might have been keeping his nose clean."

"Or he's flying below the radar. The original molestation is a real worry, though. He might be following Daddy's lead."

Jones collapsed into a chair and rubbed his face in his hands. He raised leaden eyelids and stared at his subordinate.

"Anything in either file to suggest where Ellis might have taken her?"

Phil closed his eyes again.

"They banged up Edward Flynn for one murder, but the police attributed three other disappearances to him. The CPS dropped the other cases after the murder conviction for lack of evidence. Let me see …" Phil rubbed his forehead. "Edward Flynn raped and strangled Alicia Keen. Twelve-years-old, poor darling. Dumped her body in woods outside Great Malvern. He owned a holiday cottage in the Cotswolds."

Jones shook his head and sighed heavily.

"That information was in Edward's case file. I sent the locals to check it out overnight, but the place has been abandoned for years. No signs of any recent activity."

Again, Phil nodded.

"That cottage was subject to a Confiscation Order. The courts decided Edward Flynn exhibited, and I quote, 'a criminal lifestyle' and couldn't prove how he earned the money for a second home.

Part 1

Under the Proceeds of Crime Act 2002, they sold the cottage to pay victims' compensation. That was back in 2010."

"Anything else?"

"Sorry." Phil opened his hands as a sign of defeat.

"Hell." Jones stood again and crossed to the patio doors. The rising sun caught the dew. It sparkled like ice on the lawn.

"Just a minute, I'll get the files from the Rover. It might prompt something. Forgot to bring the damn things in with me. Getting old."

Jones returned after a few moments and handed the buff-coloured folders across.

"Hell, boss. These aren't copies. You stole the actual files from the archives." Phil tutted and shook his head.

"Borrowed. Didn't want you to see them, but thought they might help. Does it spark anything?"

"Give me a chance, boss. I'm not a clairvoyant. Mind if I open the file first?"

"Sorry." Jones frowned and looked away. "The case is getting to me."

While Phil speed-read the file, Jones drew open the patio doors and stepped into the small, well-tended garden. The multi-coloured flower borders demonstrated another of Manda's talents. As well as having a gift in the kitchen, she owned a set of very green fingers.

He waited as long as he could before returning to the lounge.

"Anything?"

Phil turned a page and revealed a photograph showing a single story farm building with off-white walls and a tiled roof. Phil clicked his fingers and leaned forward.

"Fuck, what happened there? Should have known this. Tired I guess. I have remembered something else. This photo appears in Ellis Flynn's case file, too."

"Yes, I thought it was the place in the Cotswolds. Go on," Jones said, latching onto Phil's excitement.

"During the confiscation case, the court found another holiday home, but they couldn't continue with the claim because of its location."

"Really?"

"Yes. The second house is in Brittany."

France!

A smile widened Phil's round, unshaved face.

"The court deemed the location issues too complicated and let the house ownership stand. You'll never guess who inherited after Edward's death."

"Little boy, Ellis?"

"Bingo."

"Bloody hell. The bugger's taken Hollie to France!" Jones reached into his pocket and dragged out his mobile. "Excuse me, Phil. I need to call the office."

Pelham answered after the first ring.

"Serious Crime Unit. Oh, it's you, boss." He sounded alive for once. "I was about to call you. We found him!"

"What? Where is he? How's Hollie?" Jones heart hammered.

"Sorry, I mean we found his trail. He boarded the twenty-one-fifteen ferry to Calais. He's been in France since a little before midnight last night. Alex is on the line with the French police. They'll have to take it from here."

Jones' warning mechanism flared.

"Damn it Charlie, stop her!"

"Come again?"

"The gendarmes are a bunch of bloody cowboys! If they find Flynn, they're likely to go in shooting. They don't take kindly to British criminals running loose over there. Hell, they might even call in the CRS, and those boys take no prisoners."

"The CRS? Yeah, I've read about them. Vicious buggers. Rumour has it they think the French Foreign Legion little more than a girl's prep school."

Jones' mind flashed back in horror to his earlier dealings with the *Compagnies Républicaines de Sécurité*, the French version of the SAS, but with even more attitude. He blanched at the memory of the botched operation. The three fugitives he chased to Paris all died at the hands of the CRS, as did an innocent bystander. That was back in 1996, but the reputation of the CRS hadn't mellowed over time.

Part 1

An idea hit. It would be risky, but ….

"Before you put Alex on the line, did Ben Adeoye find anything on MisPer database?"

"Yeah, like you suspected, there's bunch of similar girls gone missing all over the Midlands region. All over the country come to that, but nobody's made a link to a single operation."

"When the system's back up and running, add Ellis Flynn to the search string. See if it shows up anything. In particular, filter it down to girls matching Hollie's description."

"It's top of my to-do list," Pelham replied with a loud yawn. "I'm not a complete moron," he added in a stage whisper.

Once again, Jones wondered why he put up with the lazy lump, but after a few seconds' pause, punctuated by Pelham's mumbled curses, Alex spoke.

"Yes, boss?"

"How far have you reached with the French authorities?"

"I'm waiting for someone to return my call. Is everything okay?"

"No, not in the slightest."

"Excuse me?"

"Sorry, thinking aloud. Can you leave the office? I don't want Charlie or Ryan to overhear this conversation."

"Why not?"

"Humour me." Jones waited and counted away the seconds of silence.

Phil frowned and raised an eyebrow. Jones held up a hand to stay his question.

"Boss," Alex said, voice echoing. "I'm in the lavatory, you can speak freely now."

"I'm going to France. Phil's given me a lead on a property Flynn owns over there. I want to scope the place out before involving the locals."

"What about Superintendent Peyton? Does he approve?"

Not bloody likely. The useless lump would pass it over to the French if only to save on the airfare.

"Don't worry about the Super. I'll run it by him later."

"But you can't go alone, boss. It is risky. I should go also."

"Absolutely not. I'm out on a limb here. If anything goes wrong I can't have you anywhere near the fallout."

She paused before asking, "What would you like me to do?"

"When the French call, give them a potted version of the case. No details. Then go home. That way they can't chase you up again."

"I don't like this, boss. I really don't."

"Neither do I," Jones said, and disconnected.

"Did I hear you right, David?" Phil asked, leaning forward.

Jones raised an eyebrow at Phil's rare use of his given name.

"Don't you bloody start, Philip. I'm going. Won't let the damned French bugger things up again."

The kitchen door flew open. Manda Cryer stood in the doorway, arms akimbo.

"David Jones, what on earth do you think you're doing using that gutter language in my home?"

She dropped her arms along with the false scowl, swapping it for a wide smile as she rushed across the room. She stood on tiptoes to plant a wet kiss on his cheek. Jones accepted the smacker without reaching for the handkerchief, but he did think about it.

"Oh look at you." Manda grabbed him by the upper arms and leaned back as though appraising him for a new suit. "When did you last have a decent meal and a proper sleep? You look terrible, and I don't think I've ever seen you with stubble."

"Morning, Manda. You look absolutely wonderful."

She tutted and raked the fringe of auburn hair back from her forehead.

"You old charmer. I've only just woken up. I'm a real mess."

"Never in a millions years. How are the little ones?"

She wagged a finger at him.

"Jamie's dead to the world, and I've only just got Paulie down again. So, in answer to your next question, no you can't see them at the moment."

Jones nodded and threw her what he hoped was a shamefaced frown.

"Sorry to call so early, but I needed Phil's help."

"Yes, I know. Don't worry about it. Phil's glad to do anything he can." She spun towards Phil and the scowl returned. "Aren't you, darling?"

"Yes, dear. Right, dear. Anything you say, dear." Phil threw his hands in the air. "And what's more I might have broken the case. What d'you reckon, boss?"

Jones threw him a thin smile.

"You know what? I think so too, but only if you can remember the address of Ellis Flynn's holiday home."

Phil beamed, pulled a lever on the side of his burgundy-coloured leather chair, and stretched out as it opened into a full-length recliner. He cupped his hands behind his head and purred as he snuggled back into the soft leather.

"You know me, boss. Never forget a thing."

Chapter Eight

THURSDAY EVENING – Ellis Flynn
Time since abduction: thirteen hours, forty minutes

ELLIS SHIELDED his eyes as a blood red sun dipped behind the swaying masts of small boats anchored in the harbour. The stuttering movements of the spars had increased over the past half hour with the growing wind and rising swell. The pleasure yachts yearned for freedom, and tugged at their anchors, but escape wouldn't come.

Escape never came.

"Crossing's gonna be rough tonight," he said, almost to himself.

Ellis glanced at Arthur—no, Jennings, in the passenger seat. His mentor stared back, his expression calm, reassuring. Even at the worst of times, the man could always make Ellis feel safe.

"You've chosen well, lad. She'll do nicely," he whispered.

"I knew you'd like her in the flesh. Photos don't do her justice, do they? Just what you ordered, right? Naïve, big blue eyes, big boobs?"

"Yes, Ellis. You're right, son. The clients went ape over the pictures. They can't wait to see more of her. Placed loads of advanced orders."

Jennings gave him a thin smile and Ellis breathed deeply in relief.

"Did I do well?"

"You did well, my boy. She's the best yet. Perfect skin. Glowing. She'll look great under the lights."

Ellis beamed and stole another look in the rear-view mirror.

"Didn't take me long to reel 'er in. I'm getting better at is. Won her over with a smile and a pair of silver earrings. Look, she's still wearing the bloody things."

He hiked a thumb towards the back of the camper.

Jennings frowned and shook his head.

"Yeah, but as I said, it was a damn stupid thing, picking her up outside the school. Asking for trouble. This bloody bus is so bloody recognisable, and now I'm sitting inside the bloody thing. You should have said before collecting me. We need to be more careful, son."

Ellis swallowed hard. He hated when Arthur looked at him that way—sadness mixed with disappointment. Made Ellis think of his Dad. The evil bugger.

"Sorry, Arth—"

Arthur cut a hand through the air. "Jennings, remember! And it's too late for apologies. We're here now and we've got orders to fill."

"I can't help it … she got scared. That disguise of yours terrified her. No wonder she tried to back out."

Jennings studied the back of the camper.

"Stupid little cow. Won't be long before she knows all about fear."

"She won't be missed for another hour or two, so the filth won't have been alerted yet. Are we … cool?"

Ellis held his breath.

He tried not to sound so fucking feeble, but he hated letting the man down. It made him feel inadequate. He tried to stop the tears forming and his chin wobbling.

Jennings reached across and brushed Ellis' cheek with his fingertips. The touch of a parent comforting his errant child.

Ellis' skin tingled under his touch, and he sniffed back the tears. Jennings knew exactly what to do and when. He loved the older man like a father, and a million times better than the arsehole who'd married his mother and sired him.

Ellis wiped his eyes and turned in his seat to study the girl. She lay on her side in the foetal position at the bottom of the storage chest that formed the campervan's bench seating. He'd removed the seat cushions so she'd have enough air for the journey from Birmingham. Didn't want the little tart dying of suffocation before they reached journey's end, now did they? That would not do.

Not after the last time.

"Should I check on her?"

"Nah. Leave her for a while," Jennings leaned against the headrest and closed his eyes.

Ellis wished he could be as confident and relaxed as his mentor, but the gut-wrenching nerves still attacked him. He stared in the mirror again.

Hottie existed solely for pleasure for as long as it lasted. A couple of days. A week? It didn't matter. Plenty more bodies like hers could be bought for shiny baubles and fancy meals.

The cow twitched in her sleep and the covers slipped to expose a long smooth thigh and large round buttock. Pale white skin showed where her blouse pulled out from the waistband of the black skintight micro skirt. The tiny silver bar, with a ball at each end, pierced the girl's belly button. The skin around the piercing showed red, not quite healed, but close to it.

She twitched again.

"Poor cow's having a nightmare," he said.

"She'd better get used to it." Jennings snorted and licked his lips. "Won't be long now Ellis, my boy. Take it easy. Have patience."

Ellis smirked.

"She practically begged me to take her. Then changed her mind. Stupid bitch."

"She'll be begging again later on."

Part 1

Jennings smiled the thin smile of his and the new green eyes seemed to glow in the dim light. Ellis trembled. The excitement of anticipation was almost as good at the act itself.

This one, Hottie, was the youngest and prettiest yet.

She would struggle, scream, and plead, but it wouldn't do her any good. She'd go the way of all the others before her. Ellis felt no remorse—he'd much rather dish out the punishment than be on the receiving end. His cock stiffened at the thought of the games to come. He smiled and Jennings nodded, staring at Ellis's crotch.

"You like this one, don't you. Turns you on."

"Yes, Arth—, er, Jennings. She does. So Goddamned hot. Can't wait to show her what a real man's for. Can't wait to show her off to the world, either."

"Aye, son. But we both need patience. Won't be long now."

One more step to freedom. The cottage beckoned. Hottie would entertain both of them—and the viewers—for a little while. Then they'd move on to someone else found in a different region. Could life ever get any better?

The car in front inched forward in the queue. Ellis slipped the campervan into first gear and closed the gap. Another five vehicles separated them from passport control. After that, they faced a forty-minute wait to board, an hour's sail to Calais, and a nine-hour drive to the cottage. The drive through the night would be a complete fucking ball-ache, but he could take it. Patience was a virtue after all, and the delay would only heighten the anticipation.

The delights of the cold, dark cellar and the bright, white place waited. Each room, fitted with anchoring points, chains, and leather straps, would fill with Hottie's screams and, eventually, her blood. Rooms of darkness and light, both equally nasty, and neither offering any comfort.

Ellis smiled, and his skin prickled with anticipation.

The queue nudged along again and he maintained his place. The ticket kiosk grew larger in the windscreen. Guards would be able to see inside the campervan soon.

Jennings jerked a thumb towards the back.

"Better check her now. But be quick about it."

They had travelled this route with their special contraband before. Nobody had ever stopped them on the outbound journey, only on their way back *into* the UK, but there could always be a first time.

Ellis yanked hard on the parking brake, and it ripple-clicked on its ratchet. He sidestepped between the front seats to access the compact living compartment, and leaned in to open her eyelid—pupil wide, non-responsive. To make sure, and because he really wanted to, Ellis smacked Hottie's exposed arse-cheek, hard. The slap echoed in the confines of the van, but the girl didn't move.

A big red palm print formed on her pale buttock.

Yep, still out cold.

They'd given her plenty enough anaesthetic.

The orthopaedic neck brace he fitted to keep her airway open worked. Hottie still breathed. Unlike the stupid bitch a few weeks ago.

"She's fine. Still dead to the world. Be out for a while yet, I reckon."

Ellis lowered the plywood panel hinged to the side of the box to hide their prize from prying eyes. He covered it with jeans, t-shirts, and a couple of jumpers, replaced the seat cushion, and patted it into place.

Perfect.

A concentrated search would find her, and he would not be able to relax fully until they were aboard the ferry, in safety, but that had always been part of the excitement, part of the glorious rush.

Ellis made his careful way back to the driver's seat.

"This is where I get off, son," Jennings said. "You gonna to be okay without me holding your hand?"

Ellis smiled.

"I'll be fine. No need to worry about me … honest."

"But you're one of my boys, and I always worry about my boys. It's what I'm all about. You know that."

Ellis beamed.

He was cared for, protected, and it made everything worthwhile.

Jennings reached a hand to the footwell and grabbed his small overnight bag. The man never went anywhere without the bloody thing. Ellis often wondered about its contents but could never gather up the courage to ask.

After a nodded goodbye, Jennings pushed open the passenger door, and eased himself to the ground, stifling a grunt. Leaning on his walking stick, he crabbed sideways between two lanes of queuing vehicles.

Ellis never asked about the injury, and his surrogate father never explained, but the limp had worsened since they met all those years ago. He watched his saviour shuffle the forty metres along a walkway marked with crosshatched yellow paintwork, and push through a door showing a sign, *Foot Passengers Only*.

"Catch you later, Arthur," Ellis mumbled and swallowed.

Alone again, he was vulnerable. Scary-wired.

The cars in front cleared and he rolled the camper to a stop alongside the passport control kiosk. A middle-aged sourpuss with glasses and a hairy mole on her chubby chin took his papers. She compared the passport photo with his face and shone it under a lamp.

Ellis gave her the benefit of his most winning smile and she thawed, as they always did. He always affected the poor cows that way—the benefit of having a pretty-boy face. Mum told him he'd be a heart breaker one day. How right she was, but it wasn't only hearts he broke.

Ha!

The tubby woman with the most boring job in the world craned her neck to stare at the back of the cabin. Ellis held his breath but kept the smile fixed in place until she returned the passport. He forced himself not to snatch it from her stubby little hand.

"The wind's getting up, sir. I hope the crossing isn't too rough."

"Thank you," he replied. "But I'm an excellent sailor. I'll be fine. Have a lovely evening."

Courtesy paid dividends, Mum used to say—before Dad beat her to a pulp for the final time. But it was her fault. It was always her fault. She shouldn't have answered Dad back. Should have been more reverent. More loving. It might have saved her life.

Ellis tried to picture his mother before the bad days, but all he saw were bruises and broken teeth. Dad thumped her and she deserved it. Mum should never have tried to run away. That's why Dad resorted to the chains. Ellis hated the chains, and remembered how they chafed his wrists and ankles. Chains still had a place in his life but, these days, in a completely different way.

Oh yes. Completely different.

He gunned the big diesel engine and inched towards the security gate, to the most dangerous part of the crossing. If they stopped him now or if Hottie revived and started kicking ….

Three cars in front passed without stopping. The more vehicles they allowed through unsearched, the lower his chances of earning a free pass.

A black-faced security guard in a black uniform looked in his direction.

Shit, no!

The guard pulled over the car in front—a big blue Volvo—and waved Ellis through.

He nearly wet himself with glee.

"Jesus. So fucking close," he muttered.

He waved his thanks to the security man and slid the big camper around the Volvo. He couldn't stop grinning as he followed the filter lanes to the back of the pre-boarding queue.

Yes!

Twenty minutes later, the freight trucks finished boarding and Ellis' line cleared. He made the ferry's parking deck without trouble, engaged the hand brake, and barked out a low whoop of joy.

The other passengers rushed to claim their prime seats, but Ellis didn't need to hurry. There'd be at least thirty minutes before the remaining cars boarded and the crew secured the bulkhead doors. He had ample time to deliver another dose.

Once again, Ellis side-stepped into the back and drew the privacy curtains. He closed his eyes and raised the seat cover, heart beating loud. Was she still alive? They'd lost one like this before when she suffocated on the way to the ferry. If it happened again, Jennings would go ape-shit and they'd have to start all over, but from

Part 1

a different location. Birmingham was closed to them now. Forever closed.

He opened his eyes and relaxed when the rise and fall of the magnificent swollen tits told him all was well. The livid slap mark remained, complete with newly formed raised welts.

Jesus, what a turn on. Made him so fucking horny.

"Evening, my lovely."

Ellis pinched her bruised buttock. She stirred. Excellent, she'd see him prepare the medicine.

He took a small black leather case about the size of a mobile phone from an overhead compartment.

Hottie's eyelids opened a slit and closed again. Ellis slapped her thigh, not quite as hard as before, he daren't risk making too much noise. Hottie's chin dipped as much as the neck-collar would allow. Her lids flickered and opened, eyes struggling to find focus before she turned her head and recognised his face. Her breathing behind the gag deepened and she tried to scream, but managed little more than a muffled squeak.

"Shush. If you hadn't changed your mind about our little trip, you could have ridden up front in the nice comfortable passenger seat with my friend and me. You only have yourself to blame, my precious little girl."

Ellis made his crazy Gollum voice.

Hottie froze, eyes wide. A small blue vein on her temple bulged. Fresh urine mixed with the stale and the smell flooded the compartment, stinging the back of Flynn's throat.

"Oh dear," he said in his normal voice. "You've wet yourself. You naughty little girl. That will earn you a very special punishment when we reach our new home."

Ellis raised his hand slowly. Her eyes followed it all the way up, and all the way down as it landed hard, on top of the palm print. Tears flowed from behind lids squeezed tight.

Hottie whimpered.

"It's lucky I lined the compartment with plastic so the piss won't leak out and give me away. But it does mean you'll have to lie in your own waste for the next twelve hours, unless I mop it up with this."

He lifted a kitchen roll to her eye-line.

"Shall I do that for you? I'd hate you to develop a rash. That wouldn't do. Not at all. You have to be perfect, to begin with."

She closed her eyes, and he slapped her again.

"Open your eyes, little girl. I ain't asking the same question twice."

Hottie's eyes flickered open and her brows steepled in supplication. She looked from Ellis, to the paper roll and back again. Again, she whimpered, and his hard-on threatened to burst a seam on his jeans.

He already started gaining control of the girl's mind as well as her body. His excitement mounted.

"Raise your hips."

Hottie's eyelids squeezed shut and her pelvis tilted as much as the restraints would allow. As soon as the paper touched the crack between her buttocks, she dropped her hips back to the mattress and turned away.

"Okay, if that's the way you want to play it. Stay wet, I don't care."

He leaned deep into the box, licked a salty tear from her cheek, and bit her earlobe.

A high pitched, but quiet whimper erupted through her nostrils, forcing out a bubble of snot. Her hips rose again.

"That's better. Behave yourself and we'll get along. You love my attention, don't you? But you know what happens when you're naughty, right?" He reached between her legs and pinched the inside of her thigh, five centimetres away from her crotch. Tears flowed again. She screamed, shook her head, pushed her feet against the end panel, and tried to pull away from his pincer grip. Her head cracked against the inside of the box and bent back. Neither panel deflected as much as a millimetre. Hottie relaxed her knees and squeezed them together, and continued to squeal through the gag.

"This box is strong so you aren't going to break it. Relax." He pinched again, harder this time. "Get it?" he snapped, and maintained the pressure.

She moaned again and jerked her head in the nearest approximation of a nod possible while wearing the neck brace. He released his fingers.

"Now we understand each other, turn on your back. Watch what I'm doing and be quiet."

She struggled to turn against the bonds. A button popped on the white cotton blouse and exposed more of the cleavage formed by the large breasts and a silken push-up bra. It was the cleavage and the size of her young, fresh tits that first drew Ellis' attention when he drove past her school on the hunt.

Well, if she showed them, she must want them looked at. Right? And if she wanted them noticed she was fair game. Gagging for it. He smiled at the pun.

A tiny freckle on her left tit showed above the line of the bra. He wanted to nibble it, but Arthur needed to see everything he did to her if he was to savour each humiliation. Arthur wouldn't touch the girl himself, not until the end. He enjoyed watching and directing the operations. Ellis loved doing the touching, and being told what to do. Theirs was a symbiotic partnership made in heaven.

Well, if not actually in heaven ….

Once on her back, Hottie's eyes focused on the black case as he undid its zip. He removed the syringe, already full of a pale yellow liquid. Hottie's eyes widened again. She shook her head violently, and struggled against the gaffer-tape bindings.

Ellis fixed her with a dead stare. She quivered and stopped moving.

"That's better." He tapped the syringe tube. "This is a mild sedative. Don't worry. We've worked out the dosage very carefully. You're not in any danger."

Not yet.

The girl raked her head from side to side. He smiled and licked his lips. A dribble of saliva dripped to mix with the sweat on her forehead. Jennings wouldn't want that, so Ellis cleaned it with a surgical wipe taken from the case.

Hottie shivered as he uncapped the needle and flicked the tip. An air bubble dislodged from inside the glass tube and rose to the top. He squeezed the plunger a fraction and the bubble escaped through the hole in the needle.

"This will keep you calm during the crossing." He stuck the point into a raised vein in the crook of her elbow and depressed the plunger, slow and steady, as Jennings had first shown him all those years ago.

Hottie whimpered again. Her whole body trembled.

"Stay still while I make you more comfortable."

He checked the time. Five minutes left. He needed something to tide him over for the journey. He took the tip of his right index finger and caressed Hottie's cheek, lowered it to her chin, and moved it down to the swell of her breasts.

Hottie shivered again and snivelled but her movements slowed. Not long now.

Ellis hadn't touched her before. They'd never been intimate. He was saving the moment until they reached the chamber. Thus far in their short relationship, he'd been the perfect attentive gentleman, but that was going to change.

He undid the remaining two buttons and parted the blouse. The white bra popped into view. He thought about removing it, but kept the big reveal for later, for the comfort and privacy of their new home, and to let Arthur's camera capture the action.

Moving his hand lower, his fingers traced the gentle ripples of her abdomen, which trembled under his touch. She groaned again and stared, imploring as he reached the site of the piercing. The red swelling around the hole still looked raw.

"Must have a word with Joe about sterilising his equipment better."

Hottie's eyes closed.

Chapter Nine

FRIDAY MORNING – I love you, Uncle David
Time since abduction: fourteen hours, thirty minutes

JONES TRIED to do justice to Manda's breakfast offering—bacon, poached eggs, black pudding, baked beans, grilled tomatoes, and two slices of toast and marmalade—but nervous tension played havoc with his stomach acid. He did little more than pick around the edges of the plate, although he did manage to sink two large cups of tea.

"Thanks, love. Delicious." He dabbed his lips with a napkin, folded it into a triangle, and placed it on the side-plate. He lined the hypotenuse with the table's edge, centred the knife and fork on the breakfast plate, and pushed up from the chair.

"David," Manda chided, "you barely touched it."

"Sorry, but …" He patted his stomach and screwed up his face. "Sensitive, you know."

Manda nodded.

"Now," he said, "let's see if Phil managed to book my flight."

"Why are you going alone? It's dangerous." Manda stared across the kitchen at him. Dark creases wrinkled her brow.

Yes. But it's better than letting the trigger-happy CRS crash through doors like Hollywood action clowns.

He thought about Hollie's picture; the blue eyes, blonde hair, and then about the child asleep not four feet above his head. He found it more and more difficult to separate the two girls in his mind. Jamie looked like Hollie, and Hollie became Jamie. He'd never forgive himself if the gendarmes took over and Hollie caught a bullet in the crossfire. He couldn't tell Manda about the two girls' physical similarities. Why burden her with that exquisite nugget of pain?

"I'm only going to take a look before contacting the locals. It's safer that way. Believe me."

He gave her a peck on the cheek and turned to head towards Phil's office.

"David." Manda caught his arm. She bit her lower lip and locked worried brown eyes on his. "Is Hollie, well … is she … still alive? She's been missing so long."

Jones squeezed her hand. What could he say? Without going into too many details, he, Phil, and Manda had often discussed cases around the dinner table. Manda made a great sounding board and knew the missing case statistics better than most civilians.

He straightened. "I'm not giving up hope yet, love."

"Be careful." She tweaked his tie and patted down a ruffled collar.

He found the action comforting, somehow maternal—not that he remembered ever having a mother.

"There's someone I want you to meet when you get back, so don't mark that ruggedly handsome face of yours."

"Honestly Manda, you and your matchmaking." He tried to scowl, but couldn't do it justice. "How many times have I told you that ship has sailed? I'm too old and too set in my ways."

"Nonsense, it's never too late. You'll make someone a wonderful husb—"

"Okay, okay." He raised his hands in surrender and backed

towards the door. "Have it your way. Can't wait to meet the next one. Who have you got in store this time? Another humus-eating, food-sharing poet?"

He could never be angry with someone who tried hard to make his life better. Manda wouldn't ever believe that his ticks and compulsions were set firm. She couldn't believe he'd ever tried to change. Didn't know that he'd even considered therapy once, but his ingrained habits were as much a part of him as were his hands or his eyes.

Without his attention to detail, he wouldn't be half as good a detective, and without the job, he had nothing but a half-built wreck of a house slap bang in the middle of nowhere.

"No, David. You and Robyn have such a lot in common. You'll get on well. I promise."

And one day a squadron of porkers will request landing permission at Heathrow.

"Robyn? Right. I'll look forward to meeting her."

"Uncle David!"

Jones spun to see Jamie, dressed in a pink onesie, standing at the top of the stairs.

"Ready?" she yelled.

"Okay," he said, pretending to be put out. "If you must."

He held out his arms. She bounded down the stairs and leapt off the fourth step from the bottom. He caught her mid-flight, as they'd practised so many times, and hugged her tight. She wrapped her arms around his neck. Jones buried his head in her hair and squeezed. She was warm and smelled of shampoo.

"Jamie. Why aren't you in bed?" Manda scolded.

The lass pulled her head away and made her serious face, with a deep frown and a pout the image of Manda's.

Jones' heart lurched.

The little girl studied him for a second before speaking.

"When can Daddy go back to work, Uncle David? Mummy says he's getting under her feet and making the place untidy."

Jones chuckled.

"Well now, Poppet, we have to wait until Daddy's leg is all better, don't we?" Jones squeezed again.

"Uncle David, you're hugging too tight."

"Sorry, love, but you should be in bed. It's too early for little girls to be awake. Shall I tuck you back in?" He sneaked an enquiring look at Manda who nodded her approval and added an exasperated smile.

"Yes please, David. She'll be too tired for school without another two hours."

"Oh, Mu-um. Please can I stay with the grown-ups? There's so much noise going on I'll never get to sleep again."

Manda crossed her arms and gave that, "Oh no you don't, my lady" look.

Jones climbed the stairs, all the time rubbing Jamie's back. The little girl's head slumped to his shoulder and her eyes drooped. Once in her room, he kissed her forehead, laid her in bed, and tucked the duvet under her chin.

"Sleep tight, little one."

"I love you, Uncle David," she mumbled, half asleep.

"Love you too, Poppet."

He took a final look at her sleeping form, locking away the memory, before closing the door softly and descending the stairs.

The doorbell chimed as he reached the hallway.

"I'll get it," he called, and opened the door to Alex. A shoulder bag dangled at her side. "What are you doing here? Trouble with the French?"

Manda popped her head through the kitchen door and beckoned Alex into the house. "Great, you're here at last."

Jones scratched his head. "What going on here?"

Alex fixed Jones with a steady, cool stare.

"You're not going to France alone."

"But I have to."

Manda turned on him. "David, this is the best way. Alex speaks French. And what happens if, er … when you find Hollie. Wouldn't it be better if she sees a friendly female face?"

"You're in on this too?"

Part 1

Manda and Alex had backed him into a corner, but he did see the logic and relented.

"Okay, Alex, but if things go wrong you'll have to tell the authorities I ordered you to accompany me. Understand?"

Alex nodded and looked away.

"Yes, boss."

Jones didn't believe her for a second, but knew from the determined set of Alex's jaw he couldn't change her mind.

Phil turned and smiled when Jones and Alex entered the cluttered room that posed as his office. Poorly fitted shelves sagged under the weight of books, lever files and other assorted reference material, including past papers for the Inspectors' exams.

"Alex. Glad you made it," Phil winked at her and blanked Jones' angry frown. "You're both booked on today's flight to Brest Airport, Finistère. Departs Birmingham International at 07:30, and lands 09:00 local time. Return flight departs tomorrow at 09:00 our time, 10:00 local. We got lucky. The service runs alternate days except weekends."

He paused long enough to check the clock on his computer screen.

"You'll need to leave within half an hour. And I reserved you a hire car, a Range Rover Defender. I've checked Sattrack—"

"What now?"

"Satellite imagery, boss." Phil grinned. "Here, I'll show you."

He spun the swivel chair to face the large computer monitor and hit a few keys. Jones tried to follow his actions but Phil might as well have been playing a Space Invaders arcade machine. Before long, an image of the Earth appeared on the screen. Phil scrolled the dial on his computer mouse and the picture zoomed in to show France, Brittany, and then a country landscape.

A patchwork of green and yellow fields surrounded a small wooded area. A stream meandered through the trees and passed beside a small group of buildings.

"Is one of those Flynn's cottage?"

"Think so, boss. It's the only habitation for a few hundred metres. An old farm about a kilometre from the nearest road. See that track?" Phil pointed to a ribbon of white running from a two-lane tarmac road straight through the fields. The lane turned sharp north, disappeared into the woods, and ended in the clearing occupied by the buildings.

"Yes."

"Looks rough, that's why I thought the Defender might come in handy, especially if it rains. That lane's the only way in or out of the place except on foot."

"Isolated," Alex added. "And we'll be arriving in wide daylight."

"Broad daylight," Phil corrected, adding a wink.

"Thank you, Philip." Alex said. "Broad daylight. It may be difficult to approach the farm unseen."

"We'll have to take care," Jones said, needing to regain control. "The track twists and turns at the end before entering the woods. There might be enough cover to hide us at least part of the way. What's that grey line near the buildings?"

Phil shrugged.

"Not sure. Could be a wall surrounding the woods."

"Let's hope it's tall."

"You're certain we shouldn't notify the locals?" Phil's worried expression matched the one used by Manda.

"Absolutely certain. I saw the French approach to hostage negotiation back in '96. Don't want to go down that route again. At least not until we've checked the place out. I'll tell Charlie to hold off notifying them until we know what's happening. Alex and I'll cross into France as civilians." Jones stretched his aching back. "In any event, speaking to the French authorities face-to-face is bound to be better than going through official channels." He turned to Alex. "What about your passport?"

"Julie is delivering it to the airport. And you?"

"Always keep an emergency grab-bag in the car. Change of clothes, first aid kit, passport. Used to be a Boy Scout, and I'm always prepared."

He checked his watch again. Time to go. He nodded to Phil on his way out and wondered whether he wasn't making the worst mistake of his professional life.

Chapter Ten

FRIDAY MORNING – *Ellis Flynn*
Time since abduction: fifteen hours, five minutes

ELLIS DROVE the big camper due west for over five hours. The horizon brightened behind them and the clear sky promised a wonderful sunny day. He hummed the first few bars of *Oh what a beautiful morning*, but kept the volume low. He didn't want to wake Jennings who had leaned the back of his seat as far as it would go and lay open-mouthed, snoring gently beside him. Relaxed and peaceful.

During one stop to check on the Hottie, Flynn had thrown a blanket over Jennings. The smile and a "thank you" he'd received for his trouble made Flynn's heart soar and shortened the journey by hours.

He stopped the camper every hour or so, but the Hottie slept the sleep of the innocent, tucked away in her little box. Could the day get any better?

Hours passed and the drone of the camper and the endless

straight roads made him drowsy. He needed to stop soon or risk falling asleep. Crashing the camper would be more than a disaster.

At eight-fifteen, Ellis yawned and rubbed tired eyes. He needed a final stop to rest and check the package again.

A grumbling stomach told him a spot of breakfast wouldn't go amiss either. He dropped the indicator stalk and cut right onto the slip road to *L'Aire de Lamballe*—a municipal picnic area adjoining the picturesque coastal high road. In France, he never took the *Autoroute*, since the automated ticketing system would leave a trail a blindfolded man could follow.

The morning sun at his back, orange and friendly, gladdened his heart. The empty rest stop welcomed him in to its open arms.

He drove to a quiet spot as far from the rest-room facilities as possible and parked in the shade of a stand of conifer trees. His heart rate spiked as the moaning, thumping, and muffled squealing from the living area grew louder. Here came the start of the new adventure.

"Excellent," he murmured.

Jennings stretched, lowered the blanket, and rubbed sleep from his eyes. Lord knew how he coped with the contact lenses, they must have caused agony.

"Sort her out, son. She'll do herself a mischief, and that's our job."

Ellis drew the confidentiality curtains behind him and turned to face the noise.

The seat cushions bounced under the force of Hottie's intensifying blows. The gagged screams rose in volume. She'd tire soon enough, but he didn't want her hurt. There was plenty of time for that.

Ellis knew what it was like to wake up bound, gagged, and in the dark. It had happened to him many times when Dad punished him for wetting the bed, or answering back, or simply for being alive.

Hottie would be grateful to him for letting her see daylight. He'd endured the same feelings towards Dad way back then.

Let the mind-games continue.

Ellis pulled the seat cushion, clothes, and the panel away. Hottie squeezed her eyes shut against the bright morning light and froze. He dipped his head into the trunk, and stopped an inch from her face. The fear in her eyes made his heart sing, but the smell of urine had ripened overnight, and he wrinkled his nose.

"Keep your fucking noise down, bitch," he whispered, knowing the lack of volume would be more terrifying than a screamed threat. "Can't hardly hear myself think."

Her eyes narrowed and the tiny pupils shot out hate.

Wonderful, there's some fight left in her.

Ellis stroked Hottie's hair. She pulled away but the bonds and the neck brace restricted her movements, and she couldn't get far.

"Quiet, little one. Calm." His hand moved towards her chest. Hottie squealed and twisted, but he pushed her shoulder against the base of the box, her potential coffin. He pinched her earlobe with his free hand. "Don't misbehave, or it'll be much worse for you."

The girl screamed through her nose and bucked under his hands, but he kept the pressure until she stopped moving. Tears ran down her cheeks and puddled in her ears.

"That's better. Stop struggling and I'll stop hurting. Deal?"

Hottie didn't answer. He slapped her face gently—no bruises wanted at this stage.

"I asked you a question," he hissed. "Do we have a deal?"

Her head jerked in a restricted nod.

Ellis released his grip and paused for a moment to view his prize again in all her part-naked glory. He leaned closer and whispered in her ear. "Do you need the bathroom, my sweet?"

She frowned, apparently confused by his change of approach.

"I won't ask again," he said a little louder.

She blinked tears away and nodded.

Ellis took a switchblade from his pocket and waved it under her wide eyes. She followed the blade the same way she'd followed his hand aboard the ferry.

His heart raced at the fear he saw and smelled. This was too, too good.

"I'm going to cut you free now so you can use the toilet. You can have a shower too, but only if you promise to be quiet. Can you do that?"

Another nod.

"Now, don't move a muscle until I tell you, okay?"

Hottie let out a low whimper. Ellis grinned and cut the tape holding the gag in place. The girl yelped as he ripped the sticky tape from her lips. A small split on her upper lip oozed blood. He removed the neck brace.

Two more cuts released the tape at her hands and feet, but she didn't move.

"Good girl. You'll be stiff from lying in the box all night, so take your time, and then go clean yourself." He gave her the gift of his most captivating smile. Such a lucky little Hottie.

"I want you nice and fresh for when we reach our new home. And don't try opening the window in the shower-room. It's sealed and the thick Perspex won't break."

Ellis offered his hand, but Hottie didn't take it, so he snaked it into the box and yanked her out by the wrists. Such a well-built creature, he needed both hands to drag her upright and prop her against the side of the van.

"Why are you doing this to me?" she pleaded, her voice a coarse whisper.

He slapped her hard across the face.

"I didn't say you could talk, bitch! Now get in the shower. You stink. And hurry, we don't have all fuckin' morning."

She turned and dived into the shower. He enjoyed the view. He'd be the first man to fuck her—and the last. She wouldn't enjoy the experience, but both he and Jennings most definitely would.

Jennings would stare. He never fucked any of them and left that part to Ellis, which was fine by him. Jennings did nothing but direct the action and do the cutting, or as he preferred to call it, the editing. Ellis chuckled at the inside joke and prepared breakfast.

From behind a gap in the curtains, Jennings grinned and nodded his glorious approval.

Chapter Eleven

FRIDAY MORNING – *Airborne*
Time since abduction: eighteen hours

ALTHOUGH A MONUMENTAL STRUGGLE, David Jones resisted the urge to pull on a pair of latex gloves and don a crime scene facemask against the fug—he didn't want to draw too much attention to himself. Budget airline seating made him shudder. As far as he was concerned, in the hygiene stakes, they were only one step up from public buses. The dirt and grime was overwhelming, and the body odour suffusing the recirculated air, overpowered his senses.

On the seventy-five minute flight, he suffered the usual audio bombardment of adverts for food, drink, perfumes, lottery tickets, and jewellery. At one stage, he wondered what bright spark in the Irish airline's sales team believed that travellers on cut-price flights would want to buy costume jewellery.

He spent much of the flight trying to make sure the snot-ridden, bouncing toddler in the adjoining seat didn't wipe his nose on the sleeve of Jones' jacket. He managed a scant few minute's nap between announcements for the next must-have travel essential. What the hell was a *pouch bag*, and who on earth needed one?

Jones prepared himself for the descent into Brest Airport by closing his eyes and trying to imagine himself in a tidy, calm place—his kitchen. It sparkled. White and spotless. Everything had its place. Nobody else's clutter messed with the lines. No grubby children to cause him distress.

That's it, Jones. Keep calm.

In the seat to his right, Alex, a regular air traveller, slept through the whole trip with head back and mouth gently open. A thin trail of saliva formed at the side of her mouth. Jones' eyes were drawn to the frothy white bubbles and it took all his will power not to wipe the dribble away with a tissue. At least it was better than looking at the snot-faced brat on his left.

Once again, he debated the logic of bringing her.

A few years from retirement, Jones didn't fear the professional fall-out, but the same didn't apply to Alex. She'd accompanied him out of a sense of loyalty. If things went horribly wrong, her career would be in the toilet. Yet there she was at his side, risking everything to help him find a missing girl who might already be dead.

Don't go there, Jones. Think positive.

No doubt about it, he needed her language skills and Hollie would need her kinship, assuming they found the girl alive. But Jones couldn't help worrying that he'd jeopardised the career of a valuable officer on little more than a hunch, and a deep-seated mistrust of a foreign police force. He didn't have to imagine Siân's reaction to his inherent distrust of rural and foreign police forces. In so many words, she'd called him arrogant. They'd had a very similar conversation the morning he'd arrived in South Wales for his summer secondment.

9th June, the day they met. A Monday. The date had been branded into his memory. She'd collected him from Carmarthen railway station and driven him to the regional police headquarters to meet his temporary boss, Inspector Gareth Hughes. Jones had taken one look at the under-resourced, pokey country police station

Part 1

—a badly converted vicarage—and hadn't been able to keep the disappointment from his bearded face.

Constable Siân Savage had seen right through his pretentions from the word go.

"Davey Jones," she'd said, eyes shining in the light of the noonday sun, "get your nose out of the air, boy. We can't all work in the big city. Despite our lack of funding and manpower, countryside forces have their uses, and their compensations." She grinned at him during the scolding.

Her bright smile did it for the young Constable David Jones. He'd fallen for her hook, line, and police radio. They'd spent the summer together, working hard, playing harder. Happy, tragic days. Days he wouldn't have missed for worlds. Despite the harrowing ending.

A glance out the cabin window showed a rugged granite coastline that turned into lush green meadows and dark woodland, seamed with tarmac roads. It looked beautiful, but he hadn't come to soak up the vistas.

Finistère, the knobbly bit on the western tip of Brittany.

He'd never visited this part of France and didn't know what to expect. The last time he dealt with French authorities he got by with a few phrases of the language and the locals' ability to speak English, but that had been in cosmopolitan Paris. He doubted the same held true in the rural backwaters of Finistère. As well as French, they spoke Breton, here. A cousin to the Welsh language, apparently.

He studied Hollie's photo for the hundredth time and tried not to see Jamie Cryer.

Hold on, lass. If you're here, I'm coming.

A smooth-voiced pilot announced their imminent landing, and Alex stretched awake. She licked the side of her mouth, took a tissue from her handbag, and dabbed her chin.

"Sorry, boss. That can't have been very attractive."

"No idea what you mean." Jones stared through the window and acted the innocent.

She smiled knowingly.

"I believe you."

After a steep, ear-popping descent and a shuffle over the concrete apron to the terminal building, they arrived at the head of the customs queue. Alex lugged a small overnight bag. Jones carried nothing but a camera case containing four items of police equipment and a pair of binoculars. The items had caused a huge fuss at Birmingham International Airport's security gate. In the end, he'd shown his warrant card to three security officials of increasing rank before they allowed him to board without checking the items as cargo. He feared the French border guards might be worse.

"*Bonjour monsieur, passeports s'il vous plaît.*"

The pretty, uniformed official's smile surpassed by miles the po-faced greetings delivered by his fellow-countrymen at BIA. He flashed the thin blue travel document and expected the third degree, but the woman took no more than a glance at it and waved him through.

No bells, no whistles, no fuss.

Jones followed Alex to the car-rental kiosk, decorated in an eye-watering lemon yellow, and handed her the rental agreement Phil had printed for them some three-and-a-half hours earlier. The speed and efficiency of international travel in the Information Age never ceased to astonish him. Once again, he vowed to sign up for IT classes, when he found a quiet week between cases.

Dream on, Jones.

Alex did the talking, and after a few minutes of efficient paperwork, the salesman pointed them towards the car park. Their gleaming Range Rover Defender stood in the centre of the lot—black, powerful, imposing.

As they approached the car, the centralised locking system clunked and the door-locks disengaged at the same time as a loud two-toned electronic bleep. Jones opened the right-hand door, and climbed into the cab before realising the steering wheel was on the other side.

Damn it. Bloody idiot.

Lickety-split, Alex jumped in the driver's seat.

"Good idea, boss. I'm used to driving on the proper side of the

Part 1

road." She kept a straight face. "And you can rest. You look really tired."

Jones hesitated but gave it one last try.

"Listen Alex, I'm still worried about your being here. It's not a good idea. Why don't I drop you off near a police station, er, *gendarmerie*? Give me a couple of hour's head start before raising the alarm. It'll take the locals a while to organise a raid. Meanwhile, I'll check Flynn's cottage alone.

"When the gendarmes arrive I'll be able to give them the lay of the land, and you'll be protected from any fall-out."

Alex turned to him, and she shook her head firmly.

"Boss," she said, "you need a second pair of eyes, and I can take care of myself. Now we should let that be an end to the discussion, *ja?*"

She set her jaw again and Jones gave up. She'd earned his respect long ago and changing her mind would take more time than they had to spare.

"Yes, Constable Olganski," he sighed. "Please carry on. But don't blame me when we're handed our discharge papers."

She relaxed and broke out a considered smile.

"No, boss. I won't."

Alex powered up the GPS and programmed their destination, the tiny hamlet of Carhoët Grande, Finistère. While the device calculated the route, Alex pressed the big red ignition button in the centre of the dashboard.

Given that the Defender's console resembled the cockpit of an aeroplane, with full-bore flashing LED lights and digital display screens, Jones half expected the motor to sound like a jet engine on take-off. Instead, the big diesel purred into quiet life with nothing but the slightest vibration transmitted through to the leather seats. A far cry from the beat-up farm vehicles he remembered from childhood. Hell, the powerful diesel ran more smoothly than his beloved Rover's petrol engine.

The brash American voice on the GPS announced an ETA of 11:33, some nineteen hours after the abduction. Would they be in time to do something other than identify a corpse?

Damn it, Jones. There you go again.

Alex pushed the lever into drive and they pulled away from the airport. Jones leaned back into the soft seats, absorbing the aroma of new leather and Alex's subtle eau-de-cologne.

Six kilometres from the airport, the GPS pointed them east to the N165 dual carriageway, towards the coastal town of *Quimper*.

An early-morning sun shone low through the windscreen. Jones lowered the visor and closed his eyes but the smiling face of a blonde fourteen-year-old girl played on the cinema screen behind his lids.

Bloody hell.

"Won't this bloody truck go any faster?"

Alex floored the throttle and the needle crept beyond the one-hundred-and-fifty kilometres per hour mark.

Jones closed his eyes again and tried not to dwell on the indignities that Hollie Jardine might be suffering. If Ellis Flynn had taken on the mantle of his sick father, she'd be undergoing all manner of mental and physical hell about now. Jones hoped and prayed he was wrong.

Perhaps the young girl was basking in the sun in a flower-strewn cottage garden in the middle of Brittany. Perhaps Ellis Flynn didn't harbour any feelings of malice.

Yeah, and perhaps tonight's moon will be a beautiful shade of sapphire.

Chapter Twelve

FRIDAY MIDDAY – Ellis Flynn
Time since abduction: nineteen hours

ELLIS GLANCED in the rear view mirror again, as he had done for much of the previous hour-and-a-half. Hottie had taken too long to shower, so he'd handcuffed her to the cooker unit, wrapped in a towel and dripping wet. She held the towel tight, but every time he turned the wheel, she shot out a steadying hand, and the towel slipped, giving him a delightful peep show. At one stage he stamped on the brake pedal without warning, to see her land spread-eagled on the floor, legs splayed, big round arse exposed, complete with the livid purple palm-print.

Jennings enjoyed the game, too, and spent most of the journey facing the back, baring his teeth in a devilish smile and taking photos with his mobile phone. He kept his face hidden behind the head restraint. Only his see-all eyes showed beneath the ridiculous long blond wig.

Ellis spotted his turn, dropped down the gears, and inched along the rutted lane, downhill all the way. The big camper slewed and bobbed like a dingy in a force nine gale until he pulled it to a halt in front of a gate that looked ready to fall apart under its own weight.

"Here we are, darling. Home at last, and in plenty of time for lunch."

Ellis didn't think he could wait much longer to sample the delights of their latest houseguest, but priorities first. The cottage needed warming and airing after a month's disuse. He had a fire to light and tools to sharpen—weeks of damp would have dulled their honed edges.

They had plenty of time to party. He'd leave Hottie to simmer on the metaphorical hob first, before carving into the meat. The house would be full of cobwebs, spiders, dead flies, and mice—the perfect atmosphere for their new plaything. And, to top it all, he couldn't wait to see what she made of the cellar. The shock alone had made some of their guests collapse in dread.

Fucking ace.

Ellis jumped out, opened the gate, and returned to the cab. He took care to manoeuvre the big camper into the Dutch barn, which stood on the far side of the cottage, and hid the camper from all but the resident wildlife. He took great care to avoid the weak spot in the floor. It wouldn't do to damage any of the equipment.

Jennings watched the performance from his seat and gave him an appreciative smile.

"Nicely done, my boy," he whispered. "Can't be easy to reverse-park this monster." Jennings patted his knee. Electric sparks passed through Ellis and his heart thumped hard. Wouldn't be long now. He'd be getting his jollies soon enough.

God knew where he'd be without Jennings' tutelage. Locked away with the rest of the prison scum probably. Ellis owed the older man so much, he'd do anything for him.

"I'll go power up the generator and check the recording equipment," he said. "You okay with the tart?"

Ellis grinned and spoke up for Hottie's benefit. "Yes, Mr. Jennings. I'm perfectly okay here. Me and the tart are going to be fine."

A cooling breeze rustled the branches and leaves around them.

Part 1

Birds called and the stream out back babbled happily over the pebbles.

"There's no place like home, eh?" Jennings asked. He climbed awkwardly from the cab, hobbled around the side of the barn, and headed towards the house.

Ellis opened the camper's side door and stared in appreciation at their trophy.

"Okay, my lovely," he whispered. "Time to get you settled."

Hollie Jardine screamed.

Chapter Thirteen

FRIDAY MIDDAY – Midday
Time since abduction: nineteen hours, fifteen minutes

THE MEDIEVAL VILLAGE of Carhoët Grande clung to the sides of a steep wooded valley. Oaks, chestnuts, willows, and conifers clustered together in an uninterrupted wilderness, coddling the hamlet like a baby blanket.

A row of stone cottages, a grocery, a restaurant, and the ubiquitous *Bar Tabac* rolled past Jones' window. A pair of old men sat at a table in the sun. Each nursed cigarettes and a pre-lunch glass of *Pastis* and water, a hideous aniseed drink Jones had tasted once and couldn't abide. The world carried on as normal while, quite possibly, a young girl fought for her life not three miles distant.

Somehow, life goes on.

It was one anomaly Jones could never come to terms with, despite the passing years.

The spire on the town's granite church pierced the sky, the clock on its eastern face showing eleven-twenty-three. He checked the digital clock on the dashboard and his Seiko—all the times

Part 1

matched. Idly, he wondered how many church clocks in England would be accurate more than twice a day.

The village ended abruptly and the road continued into quiet countryside. Beautiful and tranquil here, but what lay ahead?

The voice of the GPS announced, "*In two-point-five kilometres, turn right.*"

"You can switch off that damnable American now. It's the next turning."

Alex pressed a button on the dashboard and eased back on the throttle.

They needed to pause. Needed to breathe, to plan. Rushing in half-cocked would be something worthy of the CSR. So far, he'd done little more than react since linking Hollie to Ellis Flynn. Now, he needed to behave like a professional. Not easy when every time he thought about Hollie Jardine and Ellis Flynn, his heart almost stopped.

Jones took a breath, wiped his face with the hankie, and folded the cotton into a neat square before returning it to his pocket.

"Is the aircon working in here?"

Damp patches under his arms spread to meet the one soaking his back. He should have bought water at the airport. Talk about a lack of preparation.

Two-and-a-half kilometres beyond Carhoët Grande, they made a right and hit a rutted, single lane farm track.

"Take it easy here, Alex. Try not to raise too much dust."

"I can see cover down there."

Alex pointed to the expanse of trees and brush to the left of the track about half a mile below, and slowed the Defender to near walking pace.

Jones' heart thumped. He wiped moist hands with his hankie, and focused on a young oak that punched through the verge close to the lane. The rough black trunk grew straight and true, its branches spreading wide, reaching to the clear blue sky. At any other time, Jones would see the sapling as beautiful—a bright, strong hope for the future. Today, it reminded him of the hanging trees in the black-and-white cowboy films he'd absorbed as a boy in the orphanage.

As a child, he only had the westerns and his books to keep him company, but Hollie had parents who loved her. Jones wanted, no, he needed to reunite them.

They bounced along the potholed lane for eight hundred metres before the track jagged left and entered a heavily wooded world of mottled light and cooling shade. After three hundred metres, the undergrowth thinned enough to show where the track ended at a ramshackle, three bar gate.

"Stop here."

Alex reversed the Defender into an opening in the bushes that pressed in on the track.

Jones released his seatbelt and extricated the equipment that so excited the BIA security guards from the camera case.

"These might come in handy." He handed Alex a pair of handcuffs.

The other articles found secure resting places in the front pockets of his sleeveless fishing jacket. He hung the binoculars around his neck, closed his eyes, and took another breath.

"Alex."

She locked blue eyes on his and lifted her chin.

"Boss?"

"Whatever happens I want to thank you for being here. I appreciate it." He cleared his throat.

"*Det gör inget*. It is nothing." She smiled. "I wouldn't not miss this for anything. I joined the police for the travel and the excitement."

"Right, let's get going. Comms ready?"

Jones fitted a small plastic device in his ear and Alex followed his example. He clicked his hand-unit twice and the corresponding double burst of static in his earpiece—the earwig—told him his unit functioned properly. Alex tapped her ear and nodded.

They exited the car, keeping the heavy undergrowth between them and the cottage.

At the edge of the treeline, Jones signalled a halt and raised the binoculars. He cupped his hands around the lenses to eliminate the possibility of glare from the sun reflecting off the glass.

The gate, now less than a hundred metres away, spanned an

opening in the two-metre high granite wall. Piles of stones lay at irregular intervals along the base of the wall, forming gaps like missing teeth. Jones' tongue searched out the space left where he'd lost a molar a year earlier.

At some stage, he needed to have the bridgework done.

"Excellent," he said, pointing to a break in the stonework some fifty metres east of the gate. "If we scale the wall at that gap, we'll be out of sight of the buildings and close to the woods. Ready?"

Alex nodded. Her eyes shone and she produced one of her confident smiles. Jones had seen her in action before and knew she wouldn't let him down—he hoped he'd be as effective.

He checked the bushes behind them and confirmed no one could see the big Defender from the cottage. Nobody on the lane would see it until passing directly alongside.

Good enough for now.

They took it in turns to sprint at the crouch across the grassy space between the edge of the bushes and the wall. Once under its protection, they hurried to the break where the wall stood less than two feet high.

Jones paused for a second to recover his breath. "Wait here until I reach the woods. I'll signal you when it's safe."

He scaled the stonework with ease, and crawled to the safety of a large oak. A buzzard screeched in the treetops. A large animal—possibly a deer—crashed through the woods a few metres away. Jones couldn't see it in the stippled light.

His heart thumped and he struggled to stay calm. When did he last do any serious fieldwork? Early 1970s? Was it that long ago? A lifetime. His short spell in the army returned to him in a rush. Days and nights spent crawling through marshland with a rifle in his sweaty grasp, and dirt on his hands. The filth.

For God's sake man, get a grip. Concentrate.

The air, warmed by the early summer sun, smelled of acrid dandelions and sweet rape flowers. A stream burbled somewhere beyond the cottage, but otherwise the only sounds came from the wildlife, and a distant tractor.

Jones focused the lenses on the cottage, searching for signs of life. Despite the morning heat, he shivered at the images running through his head.

The cottage, forty metres away, slouched low to the valley floor. The top metre of the granite walls and the black slate roof showed above overgrown grass and garden shrubbery gone wild. A thin trail of lazy smoke rose from the chimney and climbed towards the sky. His heartbeat peaked again.

Someone's home. We were right!

Tall trees towered over the rundown farmstead and cast shadows against the sun's brilliant glare. They might seem ominous to Hollie, if she was still alive to see them, but they offered decent cover for Jones' clandestine approach.

Cover, of sorts.

He raised the comms unit and whispered, "Okay, Alex. Nobody in sight. Over you come. Over."

He kept the binoculars to his eyes while Alex crawled across the field and came to a crouch beside him. He looked up to the cloudless, deep blue sky. He'd prefer to wait for dark, but at this time of year that meant a ten-hour delay.

Too bloody long.

"Make your way around to the back and come out by the barn," he whispered, pointing to a spot behind the cottage. "Any noise you make should be masked by the stream. I'll hide behind that birch, and wait 'til you're in position." He pointed to a tree with a light trunk and dark leaves.

"Why not come with me and we can both approach from behind the cottage?"

"No, that won't work. Someone has to keep an eye on the front in case Flynn decides to take Hollie somewhere else. More to the point, you'll be better at crawling through the woods than me."

Alex nodded and placed a hand on his forearm.

"Good luck, sir."

You too, lass.

She crept towards the dark undergrowth, and barely made a sound. Her dark brown trousers and jacket blended into the woods as well as any camouflage kit he'd ever seen. As she disappeared,

Jones chided himself for having any reservations about bringing her along.

He took a second to clear his head before crawling for thirty metres inside the edge of the tree line. He knelt at the base of a hydrangea bush next to the birch tree. Its dense foliage and wide blue flowers offered a perfect hunter's hide.

A meadow, twenty-five metres across, lay between him and the cottage.

He waited.

A zephyr rustled leaves in the upper branches and caused ripples in the shadows below. Nothing else moved near the farm.

Jones raked the house with the binoculars again. A pair of untrimmed rosebushes, dotted with faded pink flowers, clung to the wall beneath two windows. He could see nothing behind the dark rippled glass. The rose bushes offered potential hiding places, but the sun bathed the south-facing wall in its bright light—not best suited for a covert approach.

A storm porch jutted one metre out from the front wall, its brick-built walls solid—windowless. A closed front door, sun-bleached, red faded to pink, offered the only access. As a place to lie in wait, the porch couldn't have been designed any better.

Time passed with the flowing speed of cold molasses over a glacier in winter.

C'mon Alex.

The welcome sound of static clicked in his earpiece.

"*In position, boss,*" Alex whispered, breathing heavily. "*And there's a white campervan inside the barn. We found them! What should I do now? Over.*"

Jones considered asking her to look inside the camper, but couldn't risk setting off the vehicle's alarm. The thought gave him an idea, which he filed away for later.

"Can you make it to the rear of the house, unseen? Over."

"*Yes, easily. There are no windows on the north face of the cottage. There are plenty of shadows here, also. Over.*"

"Okay, stay where you are for the minute. I'm going to break cover. Don't move until I call. Jones, out."

The overgrown garden between him and the cottage's gable wall left him exposed and vulnerable, but a direct approach was his only option. He couldn't spare the time to follow Alex's trail.

Jones skirted as far to the right as he could, and drew level with the gable wall. Here, he'd be invisible from the cottage unless Flynn decided to step outside, or poke his head through one of the windows.

Crickets chirruped in the fields around him. The stream, the breeze disturbing the foliage, and the flutter of low-flying sparrows offered a background wall of sound to mask his approach.

On all fours, Jones spider-crawled down the hill towards the building. Insects scattered in his path.

The tall damp grass soaked through his khaki trousers. Every ten metres or so he paused, held his breath and listened. Silence, save for the comforting and intermittent sounds of nature.

He edged to the left and aimed for a quiet corner where the gable wall dived back towards the barn. A water butt, fed by a down-pipe from a sagging gutter, offered a half-decent hiding place. Firewood stacked against the wall beside the barrel would give even more cover.

The sun scorched his exposed neck. Sweat formed on his scalp and trickled down to form a drip on the end of his nose. He wiped the droplet away with the back of his sweaty hand.

A flat concrete yard, mottled with dark green lichen, separated the edge of the overgrown garden from the cottage. The next part was even more risky, but with no alternative, Jones jumped to his feet and darted across the gap, grateful for the rubber-soled silence of his hiking boots.

He raced past the woodpile, juddered to a back-jarring stop against the rough wall, and dropped into a crouch behind the barrel. His heart raced fit to explode.

A film of slime and dead insects covered the surface of the water in the rain barrel. The damp smell of rotting firewood attacked his sinuses. Jones pinched his nostrils together to stifle a sneeze.

He held down the PTT button and whispered into the mic.

Part 1

"In position, Alex. Make your way to the rear of the house. Tell me when you find a window. Jones, out."

The double click of static told him Alex had received and understood his message.

Jones stood and rounded the water butt, scraping his back against the wall. He shuffled sideways to the corner of the house.

A mosquito's shrill whine stopped. A sting on his cheek told him where the damned thing landed. He resisted the urge to slap, and brushed it away in silence.

Move, move now!

The window cut into the front wall about two metres from where he stood. He edged around the corner of the house and pressed flat against the wall, face first. He kissed the hot stonework and prayed Flynn didn't take that moment to open the window and air the cottage.

Jones edged sideways and peered into the window recess.

Damn it.

Bright sunshine bounced off the rippled glass forming a mirror reflection of the garden.

He couldn't see inside!

Chapter Fourteen

FRIDAY MIDDAY – Ellis Flynn
Time since abduction: Twenty hours, seven minutes

ELLIS SWUNG his arm in a slow arc. Pale yellow torchlight skipped over damp walls blackened by decades of grime.

"Take a good look around, my pretty." He allowed the light to rest on the anchoring points let into the stonework. The beam moved left, alighting on the leather straps and whips hanging from hooks on the oak beams overhead.

Black stains on the straps reminded him of earlier guests, now departed. They never stayed long here. He and Arthur, sorry, Jennings, tended to use the cellar as a taster, tenderising their guests for the next place. The clean place. The well-lit place. The place where the movie magic happened.

Windowless and airless, the cellar's single access came from the wooden ladder propped against the wall below a small trapdoor.

"This will be your new bedroom, if you don't behave. Get used to it."

Hottie stared at him through swollen, tear-stained eyes and

shook her head. She pleaded in silence. Her hands reached out in supplication.

"You can speak, if you wish, but don't scream. I'm the only one who can hear you and I won't be happy."

"Please don't l-leave me down here. I'll be good, I p-promise," she whispered and raised a hand to brush back a strand of matted blonde hair.

The chain, one end manacled to her wrist, and the other gripped in Ellis' hand, rattled on the concrete floor.

"You'll stay here until you've learned how to behave properly."

Hottie moaned. Her glistening, dirt smeared face crumpled.

"P-Please! It's so c-cold down here." She shuddered and shied away from a rustling sound in the far corner. Mice had joined the party, or rats.

"I-I'll be good, I will."

She tried a smile, but it looked more like a grimace.

Ellis grinned, the morning's briefest of warm-up sessions had done nothing but stiffen his desires. It also ensured Jennings had set the sound levels for the recordings right. Wouldn't want to spoil the upcoming show with poor sound quality.

"You cried the whole way through our little game earlier. Pitiful, it was. What fucking use could you be upstairs? Hey?" He lunged towards her and she cowered away. "See? You're scared of me. You can't come up and stay with decent folk until you can demonstrate you're worthy of the comforts we provide."

Hottie stepped close and threw her arms around his neck. "Please," she begged. "I-I'll learn to be a good girl. I-I promise."

Ellis prised her scratching fingers apart and pushed her away. Hottie sank to her knees and cried in silence.

He smiled. He'd won and he knew it. This subjugation hadn't taken as long as it did with some of the others. It went to show that if you took them young enough, they were putty. That's what Arthur had taught him from the very beginning.

"Promise?" he asked, softening his tone.

Hottie looked up at him, her eyes pleading.

"Yes, yes, I promise. Please sir, don't l-leave me down here."

She never looked more beguiling. Battered and bruised, and sexy as all fuck. Ellis couldn't have been happier. He wanted to take her there and then, but Arthur wouldn't have liked that. The cameras weren't set up yet. He sneered to keep up the pressure.

"How do I know I can trust you?"

Hottie scrambled to her feet, her chin trembled.

"W-What do you want me to do, s-sir?"

"That's better. Treat me with respect and we'll get along fine. You're learning your place in the world."

"Yes, sir." She reached a trembling hand towards Ellis' groin and rested it against his pulsating cock. She looked up into his eyes. "Is that okay, s-sir."

"It'll do for now."

She lowered her eyes and reached for his zip. He pulled away.

"Not down here, you can come upstairs. Move back while I climb the ladder."

Ellis could never do it in the dark. He needed the light and the warmth, and, more recently, an audience.

Hottie took an obedient step back, head lowered. He clambered up the ladder and climbed into the lounge, ducking to avoid the encroaching staircase.

"Please don't leave me here," she wailed from the dark.

He yanked the chain.

"Okay, up you come but take care. One slip or complaint and I'll leave you down there. Right?"

"Yes, sir," she whimpered.

She sounded ever so grateful. Ellis beamed and anticipated the delights in store for the next few hours and—if she played really nice—days.

Chapter Fifteen

FRIDAY MIDDAY – *Midday*
Time since abduction: twenty hours, seven minutes

JONES SCUTTLED BACK to the relative safety of the gable wall.

"Alex," he whispered, "I can't see inside the house. The sun's too strong. What's it like your side? Over."

He wiped the sweat from his forehead with his shirtsleeve. He tried to calm his breathing but it kept catching in his throat.

"*I've found a window at the side. Wait one moment. Over.*"

Jones tapped his earpiece.

"Alex? Are you there? What is it? Over."

"*Ellis Flynn. I can see Ellis Flynn! Over.*"

"And Hollie? Over." Jones held his breath and prayed.

Please be there!

The thunderous silence stretched to infinity.

"*There's no sign of her. Over.*"

Damn!

"What's Flynn doing? Over."

Another pause and more crushing silence.

"Climbing out a square hole in the floor. Over."

"A cellar? Over."

"Yes. It might be where he's keeping Hollie. Over."

"I hope so." Jones' spirits lifted. "What's he doing now? Over."

"Can't look. He's too close to my window. Over."

"Hold on. Don't do anything. Jones, out."

He dropped to his hands and knees and crawled past the rosebush under the first window. He rounded the storm porch and the front door, passed under the second window, and stood with his face millimetres from the stonework, shrouded in shadow.

He inched across until the corner of his right eye cleared the window's reveal. The warm stonework smelled of dry moss and grazed the tip of his nose. He took one lightning fast look and pulled his head away.

Open-plan room. Bare walls, stone. Dark beams on the ceiling. Fire in the hearth, at the far right of the room. Two old sofas in front, soaking up the heat of the flames. To the left, an open-tread staircase. Between the window and the staircase stood a big oak dining table and chairs.

He risked another peek.

Flynn stood near the staircase, his back to Jones, peering into the cellar. The bastard clutched a chain and a lit torch in one hand. The other held a knife with a wicked-looking six-inch blade, serrated along its top edge. A drop-point hunting knife.

The chain led down into the cellar.

Jones risked everything to stay at the window. If Flynn turned, his element of surprise would be lost but he needed to be certain. Flynn yanked on the chain. A moment later, someone emerged.

Hollie!

Relief flooded through Jones, but the damage—both psychological and physical—had aged the girl ten years. The sight chilled his blood.

A dark bruise coloured Hollie's swollen left cheek. A split in her upper lip looked raw and painful. Long blonde hair, lifeless and greasy, hung around her neck and shoulders, as pale and wispy as a shroud.

Part 1

Jones gritted his teeth and grasped the stone window edge with both hands. He wanted to move, attack, but the safety mechanism in his head demanded caution. He hadn't come all this way to screw things up now.

While Flynn remained within striking distance of the girl, Jones could do nothing. Without a firearm, or sniper support, he needed to separate Flynn from his captive.

As Hollie climbed out, Jones stayed in the window, framed and exposed.

When she spotted him in the window, she did nothing more than raise her arm in front of her face. Hollie, God love her, still had some presence, some steel behind the apparent defeat.

Jones flashed his warrant card and a light behind Hollie's eyes sparkled bright.

Flynn punched her in the chest. Hollie recoiled and stumbled to the floor.

Bastard. You'll pay for that.

Hollie looked up and Jones mouthed the words, "I'll be back", praying she understood. He pulled away from the window, leaned against the wall, and took a breath.

What now?

The campervan!

"Alex?" he whispered, and heard the double click of static. "Don't ask any questions. Run to the camper right now. Smash the windscreen. If nothing happens, lean on the horn and make it sound like a car alarm. Keep going until I tell you to stop. Have you got that? Over."

Two more clicks of static filled his ear.

How long did he have?

Jones crawled under the window once again. A thorn from the rosebush tore at his cheek. He ignored the pain and stood with his back to the storm porch wall, close to the front edge, and waited.

One elephant …

Two elephants …

He reached thirteen elephants before a piercing, cacophonous wailing shattered the silence. Startled birds flew from the canopy of trees and rippled into the pale blue.

How would Flynn react? He surely couldn't ignore the din.

Jones shuffled forwards and risked another cautious glance through the other side of the window.

He watched Flynn loop the chain through one of the staircase steps and snap a padlock through the links. He touched Hollie's cheek. She pulled away.

Not long now, Hollie.

Jones wiped sweaty palms on the front of his jacket and retrieved the two black cylinders from his pockets, one for each hand. He stood, leaned against the porch wall, and waited. He tried slowing his breath. Here was his one chance to end this clean.

His fists shook. How long had it been since he last tackled a criminal hand-to-hand? Did he still have the strength and speed?

Timing and surprise were essential.

The cottage door burst open. Footsteps crunched on gravel.

Jones lunged forward, raised both arms, and pressed a button on the black device in his left hand.

Pepper spray shot into Flynn's face, hot and painful.

The kidnapper howled in agony, hands reaching up to clutch at stinging eyes, an action that served to drive the caustic chemical deeper. Flynn squealed again and retched. He bent double.

Jones pressed a release on the second object, and the telescopic truncheon sprung to its full, one-metre length. He swung the shiny metal bar through the air and it whistled down in a vicious arc, connecting with the notch between shoulder and neck of Flynn's head.

Blood exploded from the wound, and warmed Jones' hand. He followed up the blow with a kick to Flynn's groin and felt as much as heard a satisfying crunch as a part of the kidnapper's pelvis shattered.

Flynn collapsed and fell face-first into the concrete path with a sickening, bone-snapping crump.

Jones could not have cared less.

With his breath rattling hard in his chest, Jones raised the baton

Part 1

again. It took all his self-control not to snap the bar down on the back of the bastard's head again, this time with even more force.

He counted to three, and lowered the weapon. He hadn't come so close to losing control since Siân and Paul ….

Hollie Jardine screamed.

"Hit him again! Hit him again!" She tugged at her chains. "Help, me! Please, help me."

She pointed to a small bunch of keys lying on the kitchen table.

"Don't worry, Hollie, I have him," Jones yelled above the din still erupting from the camper. "Won't be long."

With his knee in the small of Flynn's powerful but flaccid back, Jones dropped the pepper spray into his pocket and raised the comms unit. Surprisingly, his hand trembled.

"Alex," he shouted. "Cut the noise and come give me a hand. Jones, out."

The alarm ceased its incessant wailing, but the after-echo rang loud in Jones' ears. Peace returned slowly.

Alex sprinted around the side of the house and skidded to a halt. She took one look at the prone Flynn, and broke out the biggest, brightest smile Jones had seen in a long while.

"Nice one, boss."

"Go take care of Hollie, but pass me the cuffs first. I don't think this sick fuck is getting up any time soon, but I want to make sure."

Alex's jaw dropped.

"Boss," she said.

"What?"

"You never swear."

"Sorry," Jones mumbled. "Won't happen again."

Adrenaline coursed through his system, his stomach churned. He sucked air through his mouth and waited for the nausea to subside and his hands to steady. He dragged Flynn's limp arms behind his back and fixed the bracelets in place. They closed around his wrists with a satisfying ratchet click. He over-tightened the cuffs.

Try getting out of them, you sick bugger.

He patted Flynn down and took a switchblade from the back

pocket of his jeans. He searched, but couldn't find the serrated knife.

Jones thought about putting the creep in the recovery position, but couldn't really be bothered. He didn't want to touch the sick animal any more than absolutely necessary. He brushed dust from the knees of his trousers and entered the cottage. Without thinking, he rushed to the kitchen and ran cold water over his hands and face. He searched, without success, for a bar of soap, and refused to dry his face on the foul-smelling dishcloth hanging from a hook on the wall. He wiped his filthy, blood-splattered hands on his handkerchief and turned to face the room.

"Boss?"

"Yes?"

Alex, with Hollie on one of the sofas, pointed to the sink.

"Crime scene."

Jones nodded and stuffed the stained handkerchief back into his pocket.

Alex used the keys to release the shaking Hollie, took a throw cover from one of the sofas, and draped it over the traumatised girl's shoulders.

Jones closed the gap between them, smiled, and adopted his most avuncular tone—the one he used when speaking to Jamie and Paul Cryer.

"Good afternoon, Hollie. So nice to meet you at last. My name's David, David Jones, not Davey though. Never Davey," he smiled wider and shrugged.

"Don't have a locker at the bottom of the sea, either."

He knew it was pitiful, but hoped it offered a little comfort.

"We're from Holton Police station in Birmingham. This is Alex, but I suppose she's already introduced herself?"

Alex nodded and placed an arm around the girl's shoulders.

"Yes, yes. Of course she has. Your mother and father asked us to come and get you. I take it you'd like to go home?"

He smiled again.

Hollie raised her head. Her whole body trembled and she tugged a lock of hair away from her face.

Part 1

"Yes … oh, God. Y-Yes please," she said between racking sobs.

Hollie cradled her stomach and bent double. Tears flowed down her battered cheeks.

"He can't hurt you anymore," Alex said quietly.

Hollie buried her face in Alex's chest. Her shoulders heaved.

"Alex," Jones whispered in her ear. "I'm going to secure Flynn and take a look around."

Alex nodded. "See her arm?" She pointed to three needle marks in the crook of Hollie's elbow and added quietly, "Drugged. We should take her to a doctor. She also needs an assault kit, yes?"

Alex whispered the words "assault kit" but Hollie pulled herself upright.

"No, no. He didn't. He … " she gulped. "He was going to, but … no. The green-eyed … monster wouldn't let him."

Her chin dimpled and she sniffled through the tears.

"It's okay, Hollie," Alex hushed. "You're safe now. We promise."

An egg-sized lump formed in Jones' throat.

A low groan from the doorway brought a scream from Hollie. She tore herself from Alex's arms and scrambled to the far side of the couch and then her mouth gaped wide in silence.

"Steady, Hollie." Jones raised a hand to calm her, but she flinched away from it. "He's never going to harm anyone again, I promise. Stay here by the fire and I'll sort him out."

Alex reached out an arm, but Hollie waved her hand away, too. Her terrified gaze fixed on the open doorway, staring at the legs framed in the rectangle of sunlight.

Flynn's left foot twitched and Hollie screamed again.

"Turn away, Hollie. I'm going to bring him in here and give him a taste of his own medicine." He meant the chain, but wasn't sure either Hollie or Alex understood his intentions.

He crossed to the doorway, bent low, and took a firm grip on each of the man's ankles. He dragged the pervert over the rough flagstone floor to the corner diagonally opposite from the couch where he would be part-hidden by the table. Flynn's face bounced and scraped along the way. One of his teeth snapped but Jones didn't give a flying fart what happened to the man's previously unmarked, movie-star face.

Jones wrapped the chain twice around Flynn's ankles and snapped the padlock closed. Dark blood matted the hair at the back of Flynn's head.

Such a shame.

"There you are, Hollie. He's going nowhere."

Jones let out a breath and turned towards the fireplace in time to hear a howl of rage. Hollie flew towards him with Flynn's hunting knife gripped in both hands.

The knife arced through the air. Stainless steel glinted in the sunlight beaming through the open door.

"No!" Jones yelled.

The six-inch blade plunged between Flynn's shoulder blades. Flynn didn't move.

Alex sat frozen, open-mouthed.

Hollie screamed and raised the knife again.

Jones sidestepped the blade and dived behind the frenzied girl. When the knife reached the top of its arc he reached out, grasped her wrists, and twisted.

Hollie screeched and struggled and kicked, but released the weapon, which tumbled to the floor. The blood-soaked blade landed point first and snapped clean off at the bolster. The metal bounced across the flagstones and came to rest against Flynn's face.

Hell! No, no, no.

Hollie collapsed to the floor and curled into a ball, wailing and mumbling something incomprehensible about, "the other one."

Alex leapt from the sofa, scooped Hollie up, and walked her back to the tattered couch by the fire.

She turned to Jones, tears in her eyes.

"Boss," she managed, "I'm so sorry. I looked away for only a second."

Jones shook his head, dropped to the flagstones, and sat, cross-legged beside Flynn, forearms resting on his thighs. Bubbles of blood formed in the corner of Flynn's mouth.

What the bloody hell do I do now?

Chapter Sixteen

FRIDAY MIDDAY – *The Cellar*
Time since abduction: twenty-one hours

JONES SAT and watched Flynn's life end in a puddle of blood and a final, weak sigh. Hollie's knife thrust must have severed an artery.

Good bloody riddance.

He shed no tears for Flynn, but what about Hollie and the long-term effects of killing her tormentor? He'd witnessed the results of PTSD many times during his career and didn't wish to see Hollie suffer any further.

On the couch, Alex spoke in soothing tones as Hollie rocked, and cried and mumbled. Jones heard the words "eyes" and "green" a couple of times, but the context didn't make sense.

A green-eyed monster?

Jealousy.

Had Flynn displayed jealousy over Hollie's childhood being better than the one he'd barely survived? Was that how Flynn's mind worked?

Heaven help us.

No point trying to guess what went on in the mind of a paedophile.

Jones struggled to his feet—not an easy proposition with legs made of jelly—and surveyed the scene.

Flies had already arrived, attracted by the scent of warm blood. The broken knife blade on the floor next to Flynn's head dripped the red stuff. Its handle—feet away—held Hollie's fingerprints.

What a bloody mess.

"Alex?" he whispered.

She turned to face him, still holding tight to Hollie.

"Stay here. I'm going to make a phone call."

Pausing long enough to cover the body with a rug from the second couch, Jones stepped outside. The warm sun, at odds with the cool dankness of the cottage, mocked him with its welcoming brilliance. Birds still chirruped and the stream out back still gurgled merrily. The rippling water caught the strong sunlight, flashed, and twinkled through the trees.

Life returned to normal.

Jones shook his head to clear the cobwebs, and hit the power button on his mobile. He cursed as the signal bar registered zero. He scanned the horizon. Would he have better luck at the top of the hill? He considered taking the Defender part-way up the hill, but that would leave Alex and Hollie alone.

Jones didn't have a clue what to do next. He had a dead body, a crime scene, and a victim guilty of a serious crime, possibly manslaughter. No jury in the UK would convict her, but this was France. What would they make of Hollie's actions over here?

Jones stared at the empty sky. Thoughts tumbled through his congested mind.

Circumstantial evidence suggested Hollie had left the UK voluntarily. An aggressive prosecutor might argue her bruising was the result of rough, consensual sex, despite her youth. An English runaway killing her lover in a fit of apparent jealousy might offend the French psyche. At the very least, he and Alex needed to take photos to document the poor girl's injuries.

Jones didn't know the age of consent in France. It might not be

Part 1

the same as in England. Nor did he know whether he was rambling in shock, or being reasonable. He saw dead bodies all the time, but had rarely witnessed a killing first hand. Hell, he'd actually played an integral part in this one.

The only thing for certain was that he knew as much about the French legal system as he did about knitting.

Did the French have an equivalent of the UK's diminished responsibility clause? Was temporary insanity a legitimate defence in France? The questions kept forming. Could he risk Hollie's freedom to the vagaries of a foreign country's judicial system?

On the other hand, would Hollie benefit from receiving a free pass on the killing? No. Ultimately, she had to face the consequences of her actions, but not here, and not now. She needed to be home and under the care of her parents and her family doctor, at least for the time being.

Jones bent and absent-mindedly yanked out one of the dandelions sprouting through cracks in the courtyard. He studied its white gossamer seedpods and blew them into the air. He'd be there years if he wanted to clear the place of weeds.

He looked at the dandelion stalk and thought of Flynn's body lying under the cover. At least he'd removed two eyesores from the farm. A beginning, of sorts.

Phil Cryer would probably be able to tell him all about the French legal system, but Phil wasn't here and Jones couldn't contact him. He brushed dirt from the knees of his ruined trousers, and inspected the dirt ingrained into his palms and under his fingernails. He shuddered. Would he ever get his hands clean again?

For God's sake, Jones, not important. Not now.

Jones puffed out his cheeks and re-entered the cottage.

"Alex," he spoke softly. "Can I have a word?"

He beckoned her from the open doorway. Hollie lay on the couch, eyes closed. Perhaps asleep after the trauma? Alex wrapped the cover around the girl. She walked towards Jones but kept her eyes on Hollie.

Jones scratched at his stubble and shuddered at the thought of the grime transferred from his hands to his chin.

"Does your mobile have a camera?"

Alex nodded. "I've already taken photos of Hollie and … Flynn." She nodded to the corner.

"Well done. I'd like to get Hollie to a doctor, but I'm not sure I want her to stay in France."

He told her of his reservations regarding French Law. She frowned in concentration while he spoke and looked as though she wanted to interrupt but held off until Jones finished. She nodded.

"What do you propose?"

Hollie stirred, sat up, and threw back the covers. She trembled when her eyes found Flynn's covered body, and seemed to have great difficulty tearing her gaze away to find Jones and Alex. A puzzled frown creased her forehead.

"Where's the other one?" she asked, her voice still weak, but stronger than before.

Jones and Alex looked at each other and then stared at her.

"What did you say?" Jones closed the gap to the girl.

Hollie's chin quivered. She drew the blanket up to her neck.

"The s-second man. The one in charge. He … stayed in the background, w-watched while Eddie hit me. Encouraged it. Egged him on." Her eyes filled again. "And he hit me with his stick."

She lowered the cloth a little and pointed to a thin but angry bruise on her upper arm.

Jones knelt in front of her and slowly reached out a hand, but Hollie shied away. He allowed the hand to fall.

"Do you know who he is? Have you seen him before?"

Hollie shook her head and blinked. Fresh tears fell. She cast her eyes downward.

"He didn't s-say much. Mainly watched."

"Flynn didn't call him by name?"

"Dunno."

Jones had to tread carefully, but needed to press on in case the girl shut down again.

"What did he look like?"

"Green eyes. Walked with a limp. Fat face. Long white hair." Hollie shuddered and lowered her head.

Part 1

"A limp, you say? What leg? How bad?"

Steady Jones, she's in shock. Don't push too hard.

"I don't know," Hollie cried. "H-He spent most of his time sitting ... watching, playing with his ... thing. That smile ... oh God. The evil smile."

"When did you last see him?"

Hollie gripped the cover and drew it under her chin.

"He said they needed groceries ... before Eddie took me down to the cellar. Oh God, the cellar ..." She moaned, and her eyes clouded at a memory.

Fat Face went shopping? One thing at a time, Jones.

Jones hated to ask about the cellar but couldn't avoid it.

"What's down there, Hollie?"

Her face crumpled and she buried her head in the cloth.

Alex cut in. "Boss, that's enough."

Jones stood and took a pace back. "When she's ready, get a better description. And keep your ears open. In case 'Fat Face' comes back from his shopping trip."

Alex nodded.

He hurried across the room and bolted the front door.

"I'll have a quick look around for something useful."

Jones scoured the room and couldn't believe his luck when he found a shotgun in a cabinet behind the staircase. He called Alex across.

"How is she?"

"Resting." Alex nodded at the weapon. "Finding a gun was lucky."

"That's what I thought, but I'm guessing, in the country shotguns are ten-a-penny. And anyway, no self-respecting abductor would be without one."

"Not funny, boss."

"Sorry. You're the firearms expert. Take over here."

He backed away.

Alex freed the gun from its retaining bar and examined its condition.

"Old, but as far as I can tell, operational." She found boxes of cartridges at the bottom of the cupboard and loaded both barrels. She took a few more from the box and dropped them into a pocked in her gilet.

Jones kept his distance from the weapon and pointed to the front door.

"Keep a lookout while I see what's in the cellar. I need to know what spooked Hollie so badly. It might determine what we do next. Won't be long."

"What about preserving the scene?"

He straightened and scowled.

"Damn it, Sergeant. I know what I'm doing." The moment the words passed his lips, he felt guilty as all hell and raised a hand in apology. "Sorry, Alex. That was unforgiveable."

She nodded and took a guard position at the window, alternating her gaze between Hollie, who was curled up in the foetal position under the tatty cover, and the view outside.

Jones turned towards the staircase. He balked at the idea of descending into the inky black hole, but he couldn't deny his professional curiosity. It took a couple of frustrating minutes to find Flynn's rubber coated flashlight, which had rolled under the dining table. Thankfully, the thing still worked.

Years of experience took over. He pulled on a pair of latex gloves and plastic shoe covers—he always carried some with him—and reversed into the dark.

What he found chilled him to the core.

The cold, damp, tomb-like cellar with dripping walls, a concrete floor, and oak beams, smelled like a long-blocked sewer.

Cobwebs shone translucent and silver in the torchlight's focused glare.

Jones swung the beam. Each illuminated item jabbed another hole through his heart. He breathed through his mouth to reduce the smell and deaden his gag reflex.

Chains.

A rough wooden table the size of a mortuary slab with anchoring points at each corner. Gleaming stainless steel tools, each with a recently honed edge were lined on a tray, side-by-side, like

Part 1

implements in an operating theatre. They were the only pristine things in the room.

Jesus, it's a horror movie.

Worst of all, against the wall behind the steps, stood a large grey chest-freezer.

Jones had to look.

Covering his mouth with a clean handkerchief, he sucked in a lungful of foetid air and held his breath. Despite all his years investigating violent crime he'd never been able to get used to the sickly sweet stench of rotting human meat. He'd been here before in many a murder scene, but this time it was different. With Hollie involved, it was more … personal. More immediate.

Jones reached for the chrome-plated handle. It was cold. He tugged.

The lid hissed as the vacuum seal broke.

Empty, but the brown stains, the smell, and the globules of liquefied fat, told him enough. Long blonde hairs, human hairs, stuck to the metal hinges.

Jones gagged and slammed the lid shut.

The discovery changed everything. Hollie was definitely not the first female brought to this … abattoir.

No way on earth would Jones even think of leaving the crime scene unattended. The freezer had contained at least one body, probably more, and recently. They needed to be found. The poor girls, whoever they were, deserved a proper burial. Their families needed whatever little closure a proper funeral could offer.

But the living came first. Hollie Jardine needed his protection.

Jones couldn't leave the cellar quickly enough. He raced up the ladder, dropped the trapdoor, and slid the cast iron bolt into place. He tried to hide his shock.

"Boss? Are you okay? You're very pale."

Jones studied Hollie.

She sat up against the corner of the couch, arms wrapped around bent legs, head resting on knees, eyes closed.

If Jones had missed the connection between Flynn and Hollie, she would have ended up like the other victims in the cellar. He took huge comfort from the fact that his actions had proved justified, but what the hell should he do now?

Jones stepped around Flynn's covered body. A circle of dark blood stained the fibres of the cloth over the dead man's head—the photo negative of a halo. Whispering, he told Alex what he'd found in the cellar.

"We need to get Hollie out of here."

"What about the accomplice?"

Jones sighed. "When you were in the camper, did you see Hollie's suitcase?"

Alex nodded again. "Yes, and in all the excitement I forgot to tell you I found these also." She released her hold on the shotgun barrel and reached into the inside pocket of her gilet. Her hand came out with four passports. "One belongs to Hollie. The three others are from whoever was in the freezer perhaps?"

"The sick buggers kept the passports as trophies. But we have Hollie's, which makes my decision easier. You're taking her back to England."

"What?"

Jones raised his hand. "Hear me out. When you reach the airport, phone the gendarmes before boarding the plane. I'll stay here guarding the scene until they arrive. They'll need answers. But I don't want Hollie questioned until she's been treated at home and I've learned more about the French legal system."

Alex paused. Her cool blue eyes clouded and her lips formed a straight, thin line. "I don't like it, boss. We shouldn't leave a crime scene, and what about the second man, Fat Face?" She hooked a thumb towards the window. "He might be up on the hill, waiting for us."

"I'll ride shotgun until you reach the road and then backtrack with the weapon. You race to the airport as fast as the Defender can take you. Get Hollie home. I'll do the rest."

Alex's expression changed. Her jaw set to its "decision made" default.

"Right, boss. I'll go and collect the suitcase from the camper. You want the weapon?"

Part 1

Jones raised his hands and took a step back.

"No, no. Take it with you. We'll be fine here for the moment." He took the collapsed truncheon from his jacket and gave her a reassuring grin. "I'll be okay with this."

He pressed the release button in the handle and the shiny telescopic bar slid open and locked with a quiet click. Attached to the bulbous tip were a semi-congealed gobbet of blood and a few strands of Flynn's dark hair. He wiped it on the cloth covering the body.

———

ALEX RETURNED with a small white suitcase and passed the shotgun to Jones who leaned it in the corner.

Alex touched Hollie's forearm. The girl jumped.

"I will help you dress, yes?"

They disappeared into a small bathroom near the kitchen.

Jones was washed out, exhausted. Every muscle ached. He rotated his shoulders and arched his back. Fatigue had reduced his ability to concentrate. He slapped his cheeks and rubbed his face but it didn't help for long.

The dream of a long soak in a hot bath and a pint of beer drove its way into his head and grew with insidious clarity. What would he pay to lie in a nice clean bed on crisp cotton sheets? When did he last have a decent night's sleep? Days ago.

Days. God, he was exhausted.

A sparkle of light jabbed into his peripheral vision.

Another glimmer flashed on the hill. The sun reflecting on moving glass?

A windscreen?

A third flare. Each glint flashed lower down the hill than the last. A vehicle, for definite, driving at speed down the track. Jones' heart rate spiked, the fatigue gone in an instant.

"Alex!" he called. "We have visitors."

The bathroom door flew open. Hollie, dressed in blue jeans and a demure cotton blouse followed Alex to the couch. She looked better after her wash and brush up. The bruise around her eye was less obvious.

Makeup?

Alex dragged one of the couches into the far corner of the room to form a protective, triangular cell. She pointed for Hollie to crouch down.

"Stay until I return," Alex soothed. "We won't let any harm come to you."

Jones returned his attention to the activity outside. Another flash, and then another. Alex picked up the shotgun and joined him at the window. Her breath rippled the fine hairs on his neck.

They had seconds, no more. Alex and he swapped places.

Jones gripped the truncheon tight. Not that it would be much use in a firefight.

From her little corner den, Hollie whimpered.

Chapter Seventeen

FRIDAY MIDDAY - ARTHUR "JENNINGS"
Time since abduction: twenty hours, forty-eight minutes

AT THE HEAD of the dusty, rutted farm track overlooking Flynn's cottage, "Jennings" peered through a small pair of binoculars. He focussed the lenses on the skinny, grey-haired old man standing in the courtyard and fumed.

Five minutes earlier, the bastard had clubbed his creature, Ellis, over the head with a shiny metal rod and followed it up with a cowardly kick to the groin. The boy, his boy, dropped like a felled tree. His face hit the concrete and bounced.

My poor, wee boy.

How long had it taken to mould Ellis into the man he became? Years, bloody years. All wasted.

Fuck it.

Angry, frustrated tears fogged his vision. He blinked them away.

Too far away to shout a warning, Jennings could do nothing but sit behind the wheel of the beat-up old Citroën, and watch it unfold.

He saw everything. The angry tears rolled down his face. They dried in the cooling breeze blowing through the car's open windows, and he rubbed away the dry salt tracks.

Who the fuck was the old bastard? A gendarme? How in God's name had he found them so quickly?

Jennings stared at the grocery bag resting on the passenger seat. If only he'd headed straight back to the farm, maybe he could have helped. Nah. He was not much more than a cripple, a watcher not a doer. More likely, the French piggies would have nabbed him too. A lucky break.

But why only one gendarme? Where were the others? Lying in wait? Watching him even now?

The middle-aged gendarme came out into the open again. He stood in the doorway and raised something to his ear—a mobile phone.

You'll be lucky all the way out here, Piggie.

He wouldn't find a signal this far out of town.

The gendarme lowered the phone and stepped back into the dark. A few seconds later, he returned with a tall blonde woman who had wide hips and a massive rack.

So, the old boy did have help. Where are all the other gendarmes?

Jennings scanned the valley with his binoculars. No vehicles in sight, but that didn't mean much. The woods might hide dozens of police and he'd never know.

Jennings couldn't think. The loss of his main boy, Ellis, clouded his mind and stabbed at his heart. Ellis, the heir to Jennings' business empire, was down and hurt. An image of his protégé, smiling at him from the driver's seat of that fucking camper van, flooded his mind with loss and anger. He let out a low groan.

French or not, protected or not, the grey-haired fucker would pay. Jennings would bring down a reign of terror on the bastards who interfered with his business.

Slowly, Jennings' mind cleared.

His glorious retribution could wait. He lowered the binoculars, reached across to the passenger seat, and reached for his ever-

Part 1

present shoulder bag. It contained his emergency kit: spare cash, meds, a change of underwear, and his electronic ears. Just like a good Boy Scout, Jennings always travelled prepared for the worst.

Careful not to strain his lower back, he tugged the bag closer, leaned over ,and unzipped its front pocket. He extracted a black device twice the size of a mobile phone, stuck a plastic jack in his ear, and hit the power button. He dialled in the frequency for the bug planted under the dining table in the cottage. The signal had a range of five miles, more than enough to allow him plenty of breathing space.

Jennings paused for a moment and gave up a silent prayer for his poor, lost soldier.

"Someone's gonna pay, lad. Mark my words."

He turned the ignition key, the Citroën coughed into ragged life, and the exhaust growled and popped.

He glared down at the cottage.

"Whoever you are, you old bastard, you're gonna pay! Nobody fucks wi' me and mine."

He threw the old rust bucket into gear and chugged away.

Chapter Eighteen

FRIDAY AFTERNOON – Safety in numbers
Time since Ellis Flynn's stabbing: twenty minutes

FLASHING blue lights pulsed through the bushes, weak against the bright sunlight.

"Gendarmes?" Jones whispered.

"It looks that way, boss."

Thank God, I think. But how?

Two police SUVs, Renaults, similar in size to the Defender, bounced into view through clouds of billowing yellow dust. Obscured by the trees until reaching the sparse undergrowth of the lower slope, the lights in all their wonderful blue glory, exploded into view. A short burst of police sirens shattered the recently attained silence and reprised the camper's alarm.

The lead Renault, protected by black metal bull-bars, drove straight through the flimsy gate, barely reducing speed. The rotten spars offered little resistance and exploded in a barrage of flying splinters. The truck slid to a sideways halt in a storm of dust, and shot a hail of gravel at the cottage.

Part 1

Behind it, the second Renault arrived in close order and pulled to a stop alongside the first. They formed a 'V' in front of the cottage, blocking any potential escape via the track.

Four gendarmes jumped from the far side of each SUV. Helmeted, and dressed in black, quasi-military uniforms, they took up defensive positions behind the vehicles. Eight red laser sights trained on the front of the house, four on each window.

Jones never thought he'd be happy to see gendarmes. He relaxed and nearly whooped for joy, but then remembered why he hadn't called them in the first place.

"Alex, for God's sake, lower the shotgun." He pulled her away from the window. "Go back there with Hollie and keep low until I've introduced myself. Er, … What's the French for 'don't shoot'?"

Alex arched an eyebrow and dipped her chin at the same time.

"Boss, don't be ridiculous. This is precisely why I am here, isn't it?"

It had been a while since anyone had scolded him. He thought about it for a moment, but realised the logic and with reluctance agreed.

"Remember, if they ask, you're here under my orders. Right?"

Alex shook her head.

"I'm not going to lie."

She lowered the rifle to the floor, pulled out her warrant card, and shouted through the closed door.

"*Ne tirez pas! Ne tirez pas! Nous sommes des policiers! Nous sommes des policiers!*"

Hollie stood and Jones raised his hand.

"Wait there, lass, this won't take long."

I hope.

Alex unlocked the front door and stepped into the courtyard with both arms raised high making sure the new arrivals could see her ID card. She kept repeating that she was a police officer.

Jones stepped into the light and raised his arms, but stayed near the doorway, keeping himself between their weapons and Hollie.

The clear, authoritative voice of a man bellowed an order. The laser sights wavered and lowered to the concrete but remained switched on. The same man asked a question. Alex responded. She pointed at Jones and gave his name and rank.

An officer behind the second vehicle stood upright. He barked another command and the lasers vanished. The other gendarmes stood, lowered their automatic rifles, and removed their helmets, which must have been stifling in the midday heat.

The Officer-in-Charge placed his helmet on the bonnet of the Renault. He reached into the cab to retrieve the peaked flat cap of a gendarme—a *kepi*—and marched towards Alex. He beckoned her to meet him half way.

Over six feet tall, slim build, close-cropped dark hair, and a pencil-thin moustache. The man reminded Jones of the Claude Rains character in *Casablanca*, but taller, and much slimmer. He exuded an air of quiet authority and wore his holster on the left side.

Jones lowered his hands and tried to follow the interrogation, but his schoolboy French wasn't up to task. Instead, he had to rely on his interpretation of their body language and, given his frazzled nerves, any conclusions he made were probably unreliable.

As the seconds dragged by, Jones' frustrations grew. He was little more than a spare wheel. He hadn't felt so redundant at a crime scene for decades. Not since his rookie years back in Wales, and even then, he could understand the language, and he had Siân as translator and back-up.

Alex said something and the OIC yelled another order. The gendarmes snapped to attention and replaced their helmets. They formed three pairs and peeled away, presumably to search the grounds. The remaining gendarme hurried to the opening in the wall and took up a guard position with his back to them, facing the track.

Something touched Jones' arm. He jumped, spun around, and raised his fists in defence in time to see Hollie jerk away and cover her face with both hands.

"Don't hit me!" she squealed.

Jones' heart turned into a lump of molten lead.

Part 1

"Oh God, Hollie! I'm so sorry," he breathed. "You scared me half to death, lass. Are you okay?"

Hollie peered at him through the gaps between her fingers.

"Am I in trouble?"

She sounded so young and frightened, Jones wanted to reach out to her, but held back.

"Not if I have anything to do with it. Alex is talking to them."

"Why are the soldiers here?"

"They're gendarmes, police officers like me. Don't let the uniforms fool you. They're the good guys."

I hope.

"That tall man sent his officers to search for the other … bastard, the one with the green eyes. He's now asking Alex about Eddie."

"Eddie?"

She pointed a shaky finger at the fly-speckled cloth covering Ellis Flynn.

"His real name's Ellis. You understand French?" Jones asked.

She nodded.

"A … a little," she said, and lowered her hands. "Spanish and German too. I-I want to be an interpreter."

She still looked pale, but sounded a little more controlled.

"Good girl. What are they saying now?"

"The officer asked Alex how Eddie … Ellis, died."

"What's she saying?"

"She said he needs to talk to you. He's now asking about me."

Hollie's lower lip trembled. She moved towards Jones and grabbed hold of his arm in much the same way as her mother had held on to her father the evening before.

Hell, was that only yesterday?

Hollie trembled and her heart fluttered against his arm. She pressed her forehead into his shoulder.

"Everything's going to be all right, lass. I'll protect you, but you must do something for me."

Jones disengaged her arms gently. The cut on Hollie's lip had reopened. A thin trickle of blood seeped down her chin. Her youth and vulnerability hit him hard.

"When the officer comes over, say nothing. Absolutely nothing." He reached a hand to her chin and lifted her head gently. He held her head up until they made eye contact. "Listen carefully, Hollie, this is very important. If he asks you anything, pretend you don't understand French. I'll handle this, okay? Don't say a single word."

She nodded.

"Boss?" Alex called and signalled for him to approach.

Jones whispered in Hollie's ear. "Come with me, but remember." He made a zip-the-lip sign.

Hollie gave him a thin smile and then grimaced and touched a forefinger to the cut. The smile was the first time Jones had seen any expression on the girl's face other than terror and shock. It gave him hope for her future.

They joined Alex in the sunshine. Hollie hugged Jones' arm again.

Alex straightened.

"Boss, this is Colonel Jean-Luc Coué of the Finistère Gendarmerie." She turned to the Frenchman. "*Colonel Coué, permettez-moi de vous présenter l'inspecteur-chef, David Jones de la police des Ouest Midlands.*"

Jones coughed. "*Bonjour, Colonel Coué,*" he said. "*Je suis* ... er ... *regret.*" He tried his best to think of something in French but the side of his brain responsible for language had packed its bags and taken a holiday. He opened his hands and shrugged. "I'm sorry, Colonel but as you see my French is non-existent." He turned to Alex. "Could you translate that for me?"

Alex took a breath but Colonel Coué raised his hand and smiled. "That will not be necessary, Chief Inspector. I have a little English. But before we continue with the formalities I understand the young girl, 'Ollie, is in need of medical attention, *n'est-ce pas*? May we offer some assistance?"

He spoke gently, his refined French accent easy on the ear.

Jones couldn't think of anything to say but, "Yes, please."

Coué spoke into his personal radio and a couple of seconds later

Part 1

the female gendarme arrived at a jog from the direction of the barn. She opened the tailgate of the first SVU, and reappeared with a field medical kit. The acting-paramedic and a highly maternal Alex escorted Hollie into the cottage.

Coué signalled for Jones to follow him and they stepped across the threshold of the cottage and stood just inside the door. The Frenchman took his first sight of the crime scene. Jones studied him closely.

Rather than approach the body as many inexperienced officers might have done, Coué stood where he was, and scanned the room with a slow, sweeping gaze. He pursed his lips and smoothed his pencil-thin moustache with the thumb and index finger of his left hand.

"Chief Inspector, please uncover the body and place the blanket to one side."

Jones understood the Frenchman's reasoning. Jones had already touched the cover and the body and could not contaminate the crime scene further than he already had. Coué, on the other hand, needed to maintain his distance. Thus far, the man's professionalism had impressed Jones immensely. He returned to stand next to the colonel.

After a few moments, Coué spoke again.

"If you will bear with me for a little longer, I will return."

Once outside again, Coué withdrew a satellite phone from a leather pouch attached to his utility belt. He raised its chunky aerial and paced the courtyard, speaking in clipped sentences.

Jones understood about one word in twenty.

Coué repeated Flynn's name a few times and said the French words for "accomplice", "registration", and "vehicle". Jones wished Alex had the ability to be in two places at once and translate for him, but Hollie's needs trumped his.

Minutes later, Coué's men returned from their extensive searches and huddled near the SUVs awaiting further instruction. Jones didn't need language skills to know they'd found nothing of interest. Three of the men lit cigarettes and stood off to one side.

They all spoke in low tones and cast surreptitious glances in Jones' direction while their boss continued his call.

After breaking the connection, Coué stared at the sky. A few seconds later, he indicated Jones should precede him into the cottage and they stood either side of the cooling, fly-encrusted corpse. Coué squatted and studied Flynn's remains.

To save his aching knees, Jones remained standing and allowed the Frenchman space and time to complete his inspection. He tried to see things from the French officer's perspective.

The bloody gash between Flynn's shoulder blades, the blood on the floor, and the damage to the back of the kidnapper's head didn't exactly scream "accidental death". The handcuffs and the chain wrapped around Flynn's ankles added to the impact. It didn't look good at all.

Jones' warning mechanism tickled once again. The darned thing had been working overtime in the past few hours but its batteries showed no signs of running low.

After a few moments silence, the colonel craned his neck and studied Jones through dark brown eyes.

"Chief Inspector Jones," he said quietly, "I expect you are wondering why we are 'ere?"

Jones nodded.

"You could say that."

Coué's emotive face creased into a quizzical frown.

"But I just *did* say that."

"Sorry, it's an expression we use in England. I should have said yes. I am wondering why you're here."

Coué paused for a moment and tilted his head in concentration.

"Two-and-a-half hours ago my *gendarmerie* received a telephone call from a Detective Sergeant Pel-ham. He told us about your runaway girl and that you were in Brittany without official permission. He also gave us the name of Ellis Flynn and we found his address on our register of housing."

He stared at Jones and waited for a response.

Bloody Pelham! You'll pay for this.

Jones wondered whether he should ask for a lawyer. He cleared his throat and spoke with as much confidence as he could muster given the circumstances.

"Colonel Coué, I must point out that Hollie Jardine is fourteen and this animal"—he pointed to the corpse—"*abducted* her around four o'clock yesterday afternoon. She is most definitely *not* a runaway. Did my colleague, Detective Olganski tell you what I found in the cellar?"

"*Oui*, and that is why I used the satellite telephone. I called in our forensics unit from Rennes. They will be here in three to four hours."

"How long?"

Coué gave a Gallic shrug. For some unknown reason Jones found the action comforting rather than grating.

"We are a rural establishment, *monsieur*, and Rennes is nearly two hundred kilometres away. Our unit in Brest does not have the experience or equipment for a multiple homicide case with cross-border *implications*. Our regional resources are limited? You understand?"

"Yes, Colonel," said Jones. "I understand completely."

Coué stood tall and tugged out the wrinkles in his tunic.

"*Monsieur* Jones, we are professional police officers, *n'est-ce pas*? My name is Jean-Luc, the same as your Captain Picard in *Star Trek*."

His smile straightened his moustache and deepened the crow's feet at the corners of his eyes.

Jones breathed easier and returned the smile.

"Hi, I'm David. Pleased to meet you, Jean-Luc."

They shook hands. Jean-Luc's grip was firm, his hand dry.

"*Enchanté*, David."

Jones half expected a heel-click and a bow.

"Now that our introductions are completed," Jean-Luc continued, "I have to tell you that I am, of course, officially *mortifié* that you did not come to us directly and I will lodge a strongly worded complaint to your superior, when I have the time." His smile broadened. "*Mais, je suis toujours très occupé.* I am always very busy, yes? It might take me some little time to post the letter, you understand?"

"The policeman's lot." Jones smiled.

The Frenchman frowned again.

"I mean we policemen are always busy, Jean-Luc," Jones offered. "So much to do and so little time to do it."

"*Précisément.*" He nodded towards Hollie, who was receiving treatment for her cuts and bruises. "*J'ai une fille de douze ans* ... Um, excuse me. I have a twelve-year-old daughter and understand your sensibilities in missing children cases such as this. So I am inclined to act with lenience under such circumstances." He paused and stared at the body again. "However, this is a serious situation *et compliqué.*"

He placed his palms together as if in prayer and pointed at Flynn's body.

"Would you care to explain to me how *monsieur* Flynn came to be in this ... *condition?*"

Jones thought for a moment before answering. Everything he'd seen of Jean-Luc so far screamed "professional police officer". He had shown consideration and intelligence from the start. The man's eyes seemed to miss nothing and Jones was certain Jean-Luc had interpreted Flynn's injuries in the only way possible. Jones made the decision to trust the tall Frenchman. Even his warning mechanism reduced in volume.

He told Jean-Luc everything he could remember, including details of how Hollie struck the fatal blow. Jean-Luc interrupted only when the language barrier required a clearer explanation. Otherwise, he listened in deep concentration, nodding occasionally.

Jones concluded with, "But you must understand, Hollie was not responsible for her actions. I must insist that is made absolutely clear to your coroner."

When Jones finished he expected a barrage of questions and accusations, but received silence until Jean-Luc pursed his lips and said, "*Je comprends.*"

The Frenchman's deadpan expression gave nothing away, and Jones decided never to play poker with the man.

"And now I must visit the *cave*. I mean, the cellar."

Jones made a move towards the staircase but Jean-Luc raised his hand.

"No, David, I must do this alone. You understand."

Part 1

"I can assure you, Jean-Luc," Jones said, "I have not interfered in any way with the evidence."

He pulled the latex gloves and shoe covers from his pocket and showed them to Jean-Luc.

"I am sorry, *mais*, this is our procedure. I mean no disrespect." Jean-Luc fished a torch from a pocket in his utility belt, and an image of "Batman" flew, uninvited, into Jones' head.

Jean-Luc called from the doorway and a short, but powerfully built fair-haired man with metal sergeant's chevrons on his epaulettes arrived at the double. Jean-Luc spoke in low tones to the sergeant as he pulled on his own gloves and shoe covers. The sergeant turned cool eyes on Jones and rested a hand on his holster.

Jones swallowed hard.

As Jean-Luc made his way to the trapdoor, the sergeant stayed in the doorway, surveying the room. His hand remained on the gun, but the pistol stayed in the holster.

Small mercies.

After a sideways glance at Jones, the colonel reversed into the cellar as Jones had done less than half an hour earlier.

Rather you than me, my new friend.

With the colonel out of sight, Jones signalled to Alex. She left the girl with the medic and joined him near body.

"How is she?" he whispered.

Alex grimaced and waggled her open hand.

"You saw us all go into the bathroom, yes?"

"Rape kit?"

"Yes, and Hollie spoke the truth, she is, er … intact. You understand? Cuts and bruises only. We will now take a blood sample to test for drugs, and dress her wounds."

Jones closed his eyes for a moment and nodded.

"She's one lucky girl."

"You saved her."

"We both did, but I can't help wondering whether I could have done more." He hiked a thumb towards Flynn and shook his head. "Wish I knew what Coué's thinking. Seems reasonable enough, but I can't read him at all."

"You told him everything?"

"Had to, he's one sharp cookie. He'd have seen straight through any lies."

It didn't take long for Jean-Luc to re-emerge, ashen faced, from the cellar. He pulled in a deep breath, straightened his tunic and dusted off his trousers, and approached them. Alex backed towards the couch.

"Please stay, Detective Constable um ... Olan-ky?"

"Olganski," Alex corrected.

"*Pardonnez-moi s'il vous plaît*, Detective Constable Olgan-ski, but I need to talk to Chief Inspector Jones, and I may need you to translate. For this I want no confusion."

Jones bristled at the use of his rank and surname.

What's happened to 'David' and 'Jean-Luc'?

Coué continued.

"*Un moment s'il vous plaît.*" He ignored Jones and returned to his colleague at the doorway. Coué showed them his back and spoke quietly to his man.

Jones felt the colour drain from his face. Had he misjudged Coué? He studied the men in the doorway and hardly dared to breathe.

"What's happening, boss?" Alex whispered.

"Don't know. Can't say I like the look of it, though."

Coué slammed the front door behind the sergeant and returned to the middle of the room. He spoke slowly, pronouncing each word clearly.

"This is the worst case I have ever investigated. Ours is a small rural community. We have very few attempted murders, abductions, or violent crimes each year, and now this. *Merde!* I am lost."

He paused to scratch his chin.

Jones cast a sideways glance at Alex who stood to attention and stared straight ahead.

Coué brushed a cobweb from his sleeve and coughed. He stood over the corpse and shook his head.

"Detective Chief Inspector Jones, I have to say I was completely wrong in my initial appraisal of the situation. What you told me is definitely not what actually happened."

What?

The walls closed in around Jones. He found it difficult to breathe.

Chapter Nineteen

FRIDAY AFTERNOON - ARTHUR "JENNINGS"
Time since Ellis Flynn's stabbing: thirty-eight minutes

A SEETHING Jennings ripped the speaker-jack from his ear. He'd heard every word spoken in the cottage lounge, and French held no mysteries to him.

Poor Ellis. The poor simple-minded boy. It had taken fucking years to train the lad in his image, and now he was gone. His second-in-command, his hope for the future. Gone.

What was he going to do now?

Jennings forced himself to keep the car within the speed limit—ninety kph. Not that he'd seen any police patrols on the near-empty roads—one of the many joys of having a significant base of operations in Brittany. The Bretons hadn't installed the same number of speed cameras and CCTV stations that had mushroomed all over England in recent years. In fact, it would have been a joy to drive here if not for the piece-of-shit Citroën, and if a fucking teenage girl and a bastard of a copper hadn't screwed his plans.

He blamed them for everything.

Part 1

Everything.

Things had been going so well until the arrival of DCI David-fucking-Jones and his blonde bitch of an assistant, Detective Constable Alex-fucking-Olganski.

Jones' fault

David Jones.

A name he'd remember long after the bastard was dead. The son-of-a-bitch was going to pay. Him and that big blonde cow, *and* Hollie-fucking-Jardine. They'd die one-by-one. But Jones' death would be last, and by Jennings' own hand. Up close and very, very personal. He wouldn't contract out that particular deed. Oh no. Not a bloody chance.

"Nobody screws wi' me or mine," he screamed at the windscreen.

The cogs whirred inside his head.

"I'll show him 'Davey Jones' shittin' locker'."

Jennings imagined tying a concrete block to Jones' scrawny legs and dumping him over the rail of his seventy-foot cruiser in the middle of the English Channel. He'd watch the cold grey waters close over the fucker's head, but not before he'd chopped off the bastard's bollocks and force-fed them to him as sweetbreads. The thoughts placated Jennings and he unclenched his jaws. Revenge would come, but first he had to get back to England. Back to the safety and comfort of his like-minded friends.

As he drove, Jennings tried to make sense of what happened and worked hard to answer the questions charging through his head.

How much time did he have before the gendarmes identified the crappy Citroën and sent out the alert?

That one was easy. The car had been in the Flynn family since the late 1980s, but they'd bought it privately and never had it registered. The shitting gendarmes wouldn't be able to associate the Citroën with Ellis, and Jennings hadn't seen a single cop car so far. He was probably safe for an hour or two. Time enough to board the plane to England.

The car's speedometer crept above ninety-five, and he eased back on the accelerator.

How the fuck did the police find the cottage?

That one was more difficult. Jones must have linked Ellis with the girl somehow. Ellis, the poor malleable boy was still a relative novice in the enticement game. Jennings should have been more careful, should have schooled the lad better. Why did he let Ellis pick her up outside the school? It was bound to raise alarm bells. The campervan stood out like a groom in a fucking gimp suit. For fuck's sake!

Yep, that was it—the camper. But that led to the next uncertainty.

Could the cops connect him to the sap, Ellis?

Unlikely.

Jennings had never visited the house in Tile Hill, and Ellis had never been anywhere near Jennings' home. Heaven forefend. There was a distant link, but it would take a better man than DCI fucking Jones to find it, especially since he didn't, couldn't know what Jennings really looked like.

Jennings squinted into the wildly vibrating wing-mirror. Road behind empty. He increased the pressure on the accelerator pedal. The Citroën shuddered, coughed, and the speedometer needle trembled clockwise another five kph.

So who was this Jones arsehole?

He'd Google the fucker as soon as he reached home.

The French and English police were going to release the details soon enough. A crime like this would be all over the bloody news. Police Press Officers would milk the story for all its worth. Good news for the piggies was bloody gold dust these days.

Jennings pictured the headlines:

English and French Police Work Together to Save Abducted Teenager.

FUCK. The story was a PR man's wet dream.

Jennings needed information on Jones and he knew exactly

where to go. His 'friend and associate', PDC—Paedocop—was going to start earning his fucking corn, and Jennings' silence, and not before fucking time.

The road cut through a small village, little more than a hamlet. Young children kicking a football in a school playground prickled Jennings' interest, but he drove on—this time. He touched the brakes, but nothing much happened until he pumped the pedal a couple of times.

He prayed to God Almighty that he wouldn't have to stop in a hurry.

What about the film set?

Fuck!

Jones had already discovered the cellar. The film set wouldn't take them long to find. Damn it all to hell. All that expensive equipment wasted, but he'd bought it through seven different shell companies, so the cops wouldn't be able to link it back to him. No bloody way. He'd have to take the second site—the one back home in Scotland—out of mothballs.

"Bloody fucking bastard Jones!" he screamed again. "Such a fucking ball-ache."

Next question.

Would the girl be able to identify him?

Unlikely. Without his disguise, he could probably walk right past her in the street and she'd never recognise him.

Jennings' hands cramped from gripping the steering wheel too hard. He flexed his fingers and emptied his lungs before sucking in a huge gulp of the car's hot, exhaust-filled air. Even with both front windows open, the fumes from the Citroën's cracked exhaust made him gag. On top of everything else, he was now fighting a bloody awful migraine.

Any more questions?

Oh yes. Would the gendarmes be able to link any of the carcases back to him?

Although he had artistic and directorial control of the product, he didn't just stay behind the movie-camera lens. Oh, no. He liked to be hands-on for the kill, but he always wore gloves in the cottage and a smock when doing the actual butchery.

At sixty-odd kilometres from the cottage, Jennings slowed the car and drove close to the grassy edge of the road. With the tips of his thumb and forefinger, he removed each pea-green contact lens and flicked it through the open passenger window. He massaged his eyes and tried to blink away the strain.

Jennings hadn't seen another vehicle since the village, but checked the mirror before ripping off the shaggy blond wig and scratching at his close-cropped hair. What a relief to be free of the shitty hairpiece. He used the wig to wipe the make-up from his face and neck, and removed two prosthetic cheek inserts. He rubbed his face hard and stretched his mouth. It would take a while for the skin to return to its natural tension, but there was time enough before he reached the airport.

Wig, cheek implants, contacts, and makeup. That's all it took. Less is more, as his school drama teacher used to say.

A quick glance at his face in the rear-view mirror confirmed that the smudged, dark foundation made him look like a sun-baked son-of-the-sod in dire need of a bath. Not brilliant, but good enough until he could find a rest room. A cap taken from his carrier bag would hide the shiny white bald patch.

He wrapped the cheek-pads in the wig and dropped the bundle on the passenger's seat.

The blare of a horn nearly caused him to lose control of both the Citroën and his bladder.

"Jesus!"

The reflection of a dirty great big Volvo truck filled the rear-view mirror.

"Where the fuck did you come from?"

The truck-driver flashed headlights and waved an angry fist. Jennings checked the speedometer—forty-five kph.

Fuck's sake.

Driving too slow was as bad as speeding for attracting attention. He gave the impatient driver the finger and mashed the throttle pedal hard to the floor. The Citroën's engine coughed, spluttered, and died. Jennings tried the ignition again and pumped the useless accelerator pedal. Nothing worked and the dead car juddered to a faltering stop in the middle of nowhere. He rolled it to the verge.

The truck overtook with its horn blaring fiercely. Gravel from its rear wheels rattled the Citroën's grill.

"Damn it all to fuck!" He screamed and slammed both hands on the steering wheel with enough force to crack the feeble plastic rim.

He didn't have time to do much more before a Mercedes Benz pulled in close behind him. The driver, a sixty-something wrinkly, with a blue-rinse perm and glasses hanging around her scraggy neck on a string of pearls, waved at him through the windscreen.

A sign from God.

Jennings smiled, recognising a golden opportunity when one presented itself on a plate. He rounded his shoulders into a dowager's hump, and set his expression to "ever-so-grateful". He pushed at the Citroën's door, and it opened with an angry, extended moan —a sound mournful enough to do justice to the set of a horror flick.

"Excuse me, Madam," he called as he slid out of the useless Citroën. "Thank you so much for stopping. You might have saved my life."

With one hand gripped on the silver handle of his walking cane, and the other behind his back to hide the eight-inch gutting knife, Jennings hobbled towards the Good Samaritan.

Chapter Twenty

FRIDAY AFTERNOON - "THANK YOU, DAVID"
Time since Ellis Flynn's stabbing: forty minutes

JONES STIFFENED and opened his mouth to object, but Coué silenced him with a raised hand.

"No," he said, and pointed at Flynn's body. The swarm of blowflies and buzzing houseflies fought over the patches of matted blood. "I had it completely wrong. I now see it this way." Coué cleared his throat. "*Monsieur* Flynn attacked you, David, and *mademoiselle* Jardine stabbed him in your defence. You restrained him with the handcuffs and the chain, *afterwards*, while you, Constable Olganski, took care of the *mademoiselle*. Only then, did the vile creature perish."

He stopped talking and lifted his head to peer down his nose at Jones.

"Is that not the way it happened, David? Think carefully before you answer."

Jones couldn't believe he heard correctly. He turned to Alex.

"Can you leave us for a moment please, Alex?"

Part 1

He waited until she'd rejoined Hollie on the couch before answering Jean-Luc's question. He kept his voice low.

"Are you sure you want to go down this route, Jean-Luc?"

"*Excusez-moi?*"

"I mean, what are the consequences for Hollie?"

"Eventually, she will have to return to France and make a statement, but for now …"

"You mean you're letting her go home?"

"But of course. She needs to be with her parents, does she not?"

Jones ran a hand through his hair. He'd been so wrong about the French police, or at least one of them.

"Um, I don't know what to say, but thank you, Jean-Luc. Thank you very much. *Merci.*"

"There is however something you can do for me."

"Name it."

"As I said, in Brittany we have a small *gendarmerie*, er, police force. We do not employ many detectives. Would you be able to stay for a few days in France to help us with the case, as a liaison? I wonder, perhaps if we could obtain approval from the head of your department." He leaned close and lowered his voice. "Especially since, according to the passports you found in *le camping-car*, three of the potential victims are British citizens. Furthermore, I fear there may be more than simply the three bodies."

Jones paused for a moment and weighed his options.

"I'll have to contact my Chief Constable in the morning, but this is a high-profile case and I can't see a problem."

Assuming I still have a job after going off-reservation without a permit.

Jean-Luc gave a brief nod and the moustache twitched again.

"Excellent. I am certain your help will be extremely useful. You will make a statement, of course. And we have another *pédophile assassin* to detain, yes?"

Jones nodded and opened his hands in agreement.

Jean-Luc continued.

"There are fresh tyre tracks made by a small car leading from the barn. We are looking through our records for vehicles registered in France to *monsieur* Flynn. The accomplice might be using it to escape the area. It is worth a try, *n'est pas?*"

"It is indeed." Jones nodded. "And DC Olganski?"

Jean-Luc tilted his head again and frowned.

"She must accompany *mademoiselle* Hollie *en route* to England. I cannot send the poor child back without a chaperone."

"I agree, Jean-Luc." Jones grinned in relief. "She's far too young to travel all that way alone."

A great weight lifted from his shoulders.

———

THE FRENCH PARAMEDIC took a further fifteen minutes to treat Hollie's visible wounds, take the necessary evidentiary samples, and declare her fit to travel. By the time she'd completed her ministrations, Jean-Luc had booked Alex and Hollie on the next available flight to England. He'd also tasked the medic and a second gendarme to act as bodyguards for the return journey to the airport. To top it all, he gave Jones his satellite phone to arrange a reception committee for them at Birmingham Airport.

Hollie's safety and ultimate long-term recovery depended upon the care she received and the speed of its delivery. Jean-Luc's ability to see beyond the diplomatic and investigatory challenges ahead and focus on the human issues impressed the heck out of Jones.

Alex helped Hollie into the back of the second Renault. Jones waved them off, overcome with an immediate sense of relief and satisfaction. A risky decision had turned out pretty well so far, but there were other pressing matters to deal with. These included the former contents of the freezer, and the missing accomplice.

Jones stood in the sun, watching the driver execute a sedate three-point turn, but as the vehicle pulled through the opening in the wall where the three-bar gate used to stand, the SUV skidded to a halt, shooting up another cloud of dust. Hollie jumped out and ran to Jones, flinging her arms around his neck and hugging him tight. She smelled of Alex's perfume, and looked so much better than when she climbed out of the cellar.

Hollie cried into his lapel.

"Thank you, David. I'll never forget what you did."

Jones' mind floated back to another hug he'd received that morning. Hollie's huge blue eyes could have belonged to Jamie Cryer. The emotion was too much. Jones patted Hollie's shoulder and swallowed hard.

"My pleasure, lass," he mumbled.

Pathetic, Jones. Bloody pathetic.

Hollie sniffed and loosened her grip. Jones walked her back to the waiting Renault. Once in her seat, she smiled bravely and snapped her safety belt into place.

Jones cleared his throat and managed a, "Good lass. See you back in England," before the catch in his voice forced him to cough and fall into silence.

Hollie waved and kept her eyes on him until the big SUV rounded the first corner and disappeared behind a large bush. All the while, she kept mouthing the words, "Thank you".

Jones coughed again and turned to Jean-Luc.

"Right, *mon ami*, shall we start work?"

Chapter Twenty-One

FRIDAY AFTERNOON - ARTHUR "JENNINGS"
Time since Ellis Flynn's stabbing: One hour, forty minutes

JENNINGS PULLED off the dual carriageway at the final service station before Brest, and parked the shiny new Mercedes at the far end of the deserted car park. The battery on his mobile didn't have much life left and he needed to keep the call brief.

"Hello, is that the Hammer?" He made himself sound calm and controlled.

"Just Hammer."

Prick.

"Okay," Jennings sighed. "Is that Hammer?"

"Yes."

"You know who I am. You've received my introductory texts and checked my bona fides?"

"Yes."

"You've been highly recommended."

Part 1

"By whom?"

Jennings had to remember the next part carefully. A single wrong word here and he'd have to find someone else. He not only needed the exact words, but also the correct inflection.

"A man with a Military Cross, and a *silver* axe to grind." Fuck knows what it meant, but is was what PDC told him to say.

"What else?"

Shit. Had he forgotten something? He tried to remember the brief conversation he'd had with his pet police officer. Damn it, there was nothing else. He said the right phrase, emphasised the word "silver".

"What else?" The man's guttural voice bled brooding power through the speaker.

"Nothing. Nothing else."

Jennings held his breath and waited for Hammer to ring off.

"Okay, what do you need?"

A test?

Fucking stupid cloak and dagger, spy school bullshit. Jennings forced his voice to stay level.

"How long will it take you to reach Birmingham International Airport?"

"Dunno. Few hours. I'm in London, south of the river."

Oh, for fuck's sake!

"I'll be on the plane from Brest arriving at half-past seven tonight. Need you to help me do some spring cleaning."

"Neat and tidy? Or big and showy?"

"Haven't decided yet. Bring equipment for both, and a bugging kit. And there might be interference so you'll need a partner and some firepower."

"Right."

Without warning, Hammer broke the connection.

PDC had told Jennings his mechanic didn't waste much time or energy on words, and he hadn't been kidding. With backup on the way, Jennings' blood pressure eased a shade, and not before time. He'd been fretting so much since killing the old crone, the added stress did nothing to ease his back, or reduce the strength of the acid churning in his guts. He popped another pill.

He'd killed her easy enough: sliced the old biddy's throat when she got out of the car to help. Her warm blood hit the back of his hand like every other throat he'd ever sliced. Young, old, they died the same way with that questioning, disbelieving look spread all over their shocked faces. All those emotions expressed through dying eyes. The final ones, shock and defeat, always left Jennings with an unbeatable sense of power. Morality told him he should have felt guilt, but he didn't. He never felt any guilt. Did that make him a bad person? Probably, but what the fuck, he didn't give a shit. Kill or be killed. The laws of life and death.

After the deed, things had turned messy. He tried to stuff the body in the boot of the Benz, but the old bitch was a damn sight heavier than she looked. His useless fucking back couldn't take the strain and he had to roll the carcase into the drainage ditch after emptying the cow's pockets.

He searched the handbag the Good Samaritan left on the passenger's seat: purse, cosmetics, tissues, a notepad, driving licence. When the gendarmes found the body, at least they wouldn't have an identification or know the car she'd been driving. At least, not for a while. It would give him time.

It was a fucking mess, but he still had a chance.

He'd always been crap at the action stuff, even before the illness made him little more than a cripple.

As he did in the Citroën, Jennings thumped the steering wheel. This one, made of steel and covered in leather, absorbed his assault and didn't so much as creak.

He'd have to trust to luck and hope for the best.

Yeah. Right.

He'd had a hell of a lot of luck so far, and every bit of it bad.

The rest-stop pause lasted long enough for him to drop the disguise in a metal barbeque pod, pile on some papers he'd found in the back of the car, and set it ablaze with the car's cigarette lighter.

"Try getting DNA off that lot, little piggies," he shouted at the flames.

Part 1

Jennings pointed the big Benz to the exit. The clock on the dashboard showed thirty-five minutes before he had to check-in at the airport. After that, he'd have another two hours to plan the next move.

Whatever he came up with would have to be fucking good.

Chapter Twenty-Two

FRIDAY AFTERNOON – Annabelle Dupré
Time since Ellis Flynn's stabbing: two hours, thirty minutes

ANNABELLE DUPRÉ, Senior Customs Officer at Brest Airport, remembered the tall blonde woman from earlier that day. This time she accompanied a girl who had cuts and bruises to her face.

"Ah *mademoiselle* Olganski," she said, after reading the woman's passport. "You have had a short visit."

"I came to collect my niece. She had a car accident and is in a little pain."

"Should I call for a doctor?"

"I don't think that's necessary. What do you think, Hollie?"

The girl shook her head with great care and gave a weak smile.

"I'm okay, Aunty Alex. I just want to get home to Mum and Dad."

The child spoke quietly, but in a clear and steady voice.

Annabelle studied the passports. The child, Hollie Jardine, was fourteen but looked a great deal older. The woman, a police officer, appeared respectable and pleasant. Annabelle opened the barrier and watched them walk arm-in-arm across the runway to the awaiting plane.

Eight passengers later, Annabelle took a passport from a tall, thin-faced man. He wore a purple baseball cap with the word "Lakers" embroidered across the front of a yellow baseball emblem. He leaned on a fancy silver-handled cane.

"I am sorry, *monsieur*," she said, and pointed to his dark sunglasses. "Please remove the *lunettes de soleil*. The hat, also."

The man tilted his head downwards and removed the dark glasses to reveal a pair of washed-out grey eyes. He lifted the hat and held both items in the same hand.

"So sorry, Miss. Forgot I had them on."

"*Pas de problème, monsieur.*"

She compared his face with the picture on the passport. The man had lost a great deal of weight and had cropped his hair since having the photo taken, but the likeness was close enough. She pointed to the walking stick.

"Will you need assistance to climb the steps to the aircraft, *monsieur*?"

"I can manage perfectly well, thank you."

Annabelle smiled.

"And have you had a good time in Brittany?"

"Yes thanks. The weather's been wonderful."

"Ah, you English and your talk of the weather."

"Hey, mind who you're calling English. I'm from Scotland," he smiled, replacing the shades and the hat.

"*Désolée, monsieur* Jennings. Have a pleasant flight."

"*Merci, mademoiselle.* I will."

He tipped his hat, stepped through the exit door and limped across the runway.

Part 2

Jennings mashed his fists into his thighs. The bastards killed Ellis Flynn; murdered the boy in cold blood.
Now they were going to pay. He'd take care of the bitches first, and then he'd do for DCI-fucking-Jones.

Chapter One

FRIDAY AFTERNOON – *The Barn*
 Time since Ellis Flynn's stabbing: four hours, fifty minutes

FIVE MINUTES after the departure of Alex and Hollie, Jones collapsed in a heap in the middle of the courtyard. He had no warning—a slight greying of his peripheral vision and the sense of the ground rushing up to meet him. Nothing more.

Strong arms encircled his chest and stopped him hitting the concrete. Jean-Luc shouted in French, dragged Jones into the shade of the cottage, and propped him against a wall. Someone removed his jacket and wafted cool air in his face. It felt wonderful, refreshing.

Jones opened his eyes to find a concerned Jean-Luc squatting in front of him, blocking the worst of the sun.

"Are you feeling better, *mon ami*? You are pale."

Jones took a long breath and nodded.

"I'm okay now, thanks," he said. A second later, he leaned to the left and vomited into the base of the same rosebush that had scratched his face. Acid bile tore at the lining of his throat and stung his nostrils. He spat out the bitter phlegm and heaved again.

Rather than jump back as Jones might have done in his place, Jean-Luc stayed close and handed over a clean white handkerchief. He called to one of his officers who arrived at the double with a bottle of water.

Jones sucked at the liquid until he'd drained half the bottle. Revived, he thanked the gendarme but remained seated with his back against the wall and his knees bent up around his ears. Slowly, the dizziness melted away.

"Sorry about that, Jean-Luc. Don't know what happened." He breathed through his mouth and tried not to swallow. "Don't usually keel over like that."

"You have been exerting yourself too much. And you are no longer a young man, I think."

"Can't argue with that. I'm too old for all this." He splashed a few drops of the precious water on the hankie and wiped his face. It did as much to revive his spirits as the drink had done. Jones looked at his watch and sighed. "It could also have something to do with the fact that I haven't eaten much since yesterday lunchtime, and combined with this heat …"

Not to mention the contents of the cellar.

Jean-Luc's jaw dropped.

"But that is unforgivable of me, David. I should have realised, but with all that is happening … I will send one of my men to the village for provisions." He checked the time. "The *boulangerie* will be open now, as will the *Bar Tabac*. We will all need nourishment before the end of the day, I think. *Les sandwichs* will suffice until our mobile command centre arrives tomorrow morning with *une cantine*. Unfortunately, this is all I have for the moment." He handed Jones a tube of mints.

Jones took one and popped it into his mouth.

The sweet fire gave him an instant sugar-rush. He popped a second and revelled in the way they rolled around on his tongue.

"That helps." He offered to return the packet but Jean-Luc

raised his hands in a, "no you keep it", gesture. Jones slid the sweets into the breast pocket of his shirt and nodded his thanks.

"What's this about a mobile unit?"

"*Mais oui, mon ami.* We have a fully equipped field operations trailer. *En France*, the Gendarmerie is part of the French Military and is under the control of the *Ministère de l'Intérieur.* We share our equipment, including the forensic suite, with the army. It is essential for a rural police force such as ours. I think we will be spending a great deal of time at this crime scene. *Donc*, we will need a canteen, latrines, tents, cold storage for any perishable evidence we may find. Until it arrives we will have to make do with what we have, *oui?*"

"That all sounds most impressive."

Jean-Luc straightened his tie and puffed out his chest.

"We may be a small establishment, David, but we are properly funded and well supported." He glowed with pride as he added, "When the forensics team arrives they will bring with them a field laboratory. If necessary, they will be able to analyse tissue samples for DNA. In particular, I am thinking of the freezer in the cellar."

"Portable DNA analysers? I'm in the wrong police force. We have to wait weeks for test results." Jones shook his head. "Now, if you'll help me up"—he offered his hand—"we can get this investigation started."

Jean-Luc pulled Jones to his feet. He was forced to lean against the wall as a vicious head-rush threatened his balance.

"But," Jean-Luc said, "we can do nothing in the cottage until the forensics team arrives from Rennes. *Un moment s'il vous plaît.*"

Jean-Luc sauntered away to make a call while Jones brushed at the seat of his trousers. He'd been doing a great deal of brushing himself down recently. He also realised he'd been foolish enough to accept Jean-Luc's invitation to stay in France without as much as a toothbrush, let alone a change of underwear. Since arriving in France, he'd done little but ruin his one set of clothing.

One look at his reflection in the cottage window told him no amount of cleaning would rescue his trousers, or his shirt.

The chinos, torn at the left knee, filthy from his crawl through the pasture and his examination of the cellar, were fit for nothing but the rubbish bin. Then he remembered the stench released by the dead freezer and gagged. He turned away from his mess at the base of the rosebush and tried to clear his fuddled brain.

Jones' hands, stiff with grime and Flynn's dried blood, his captured evil, no longer felt part of him. They needed a good scrubbing with bleach, but he couldn't use the kitchen in the cottage.

After three deep breaths, he felt strong enough to walk to the SUV where one of Jean-Luc's men guarded the equipment. He pointed to the medical kit and mimed washing his hands. He also said the words "alcohol wipes" slowly.

The gendarme remained stony-faced but opened his hand in a "be my guest" gesture towards the rear doors. It didn't take Jones long to find the large medical kit and in it, a bag of foil sachets. He tore open the first of many and pocketed a handful. The clean, sharp smell of the evaporating cleaning fluid reminded him of a hospital ward. He breathed it in, and scrubbed his hands and face until they were raw. He dabbed at the graze on his cheek, the present from the rosebush. It didn't matter that the cuts and grazes stung as though he'd immersed them in battery acid, he was simply delighted to remove Ellis Flynn from his skin, if not his mind.

It took seven wipes before he considered his hands being even close to acceptable, but the black lines of dirt under his fingernails proved resolute, immovable.

While Jones scrubbed, Jean-Luc paced the courtyard and waved his arms with increasingly frantic gesticulations. This time, his phone call only lasted a few moments, but by the end, Jean-Luc's voice had risen to a shout. He ended the call and yelled "*Merde!*" into the dead mouthpiece.

Jones returned to the cool luxury of the shade and leaned against the rough wall. The dirt under his fingernails didn't matter anymore. Well, not as much.

Jean-Luc joined him. The frown on his lean Gallic face and the set of his angular jaw showed frustration.

"I am sorry, *mon ami*, but there has been a bombing on the Rennes tramline. Terrorists. Many casualties. This has taken priority over our little crime scene. Police headquarters has apolo-

Part 2

gised, but they are sending a helicopter unit from our sister force in Nantes. It will take time to organise, but it is the best they can do."

Jean-Luc smoothed his moustache and gave Jones the benefit of another of those Gallic shrugs. He pointed through the open cottage doorway at Flynn's body.

"You are the expert in murder investigation, David," he said with a grimace. "What do you suggest we do next?"

Good question.

"As we can't enter the house, it would be a good idea to search the farm again. There are a few outbuildings to sweep. And we could look for any disturbance to the grounds."

Jean-Luc's eyes narrowed. Deep vertical furrows creased his tanned forehead.

"You think there may be bodies here?"

"'Fraid so. Ellis Flynn's father was imprisoned for abduction and murder in the mid-1990s and the Flynn family has owned this property for decades. There's no telling what we might uncover when we start searching. But …" Jones scratched at the stubble on his chin.

"But?"

"Forgive me, Jean-Luc, but I didn't want to insult your men by reminding them not to disturb anything they find."

Jean-Luc tilted his head and graced Jones with a lop-sided grin.

"Your sensitivities do you credit, David, but I can assure you my officers are well trained. They know how to conduct a search with the fingertips?"

Once again, Jones felt the need to open his hands in shrugged apology.

"In the meantime," Jones said, "I suggest we secure the house and make sure the evidence remains undisturbed."

Jean-Luc nodded and issued quick-fire instructions to his sergeant who marched towards the remaining SUV and joined the rest of the men. Two gendarmes dived into the back of the vehicle and removed four heavy-looking canvas packs. A third fired up the engine, weaved in and out of the shattered remains of the gate, and headed up the lane, presumably off in search of food. The sergeant unloaded the bags while the remaining three gendarmes split up to search the grounds.

"I have summoned other support teams, but with darkness approaching, I am afraid we will not be able to commence the full exploration until morning. The forensics equipment, when it arrives, will include ground penetrating radar, and we will be able to explore the forest, but in the meantime we will do what we can with the few resources at our disposal."

Jones pointed to the sergeant and asked the obvious question.

Jean-Luc smiled with pride.

"We have a mobile communications system that will give us access to our internet facility in Brest via satellite, and through it, the national police database. Sergeant Brunö is my best communications officer, but it will take a few minutes to make the system operational. In the meantime we will assist my men with the search, if you are able?"

Jones took another sip of water, rinsed his mouth, and spat into the unfortunate rosebush. He'd recovered a little but couldn't ignore the rumbling in his stomach.

The sun dipped closer to the western hills and the resulting shadows provided a welcome respite from the cloying heat. Jones caught the ripe smell exuding from his armpits and considered dragging his jacket on again. What wouldn't he do for a long hot bath, or at the very least, a shower. He pumped his shirtfront but the resulting air movement acted only to push his body odour into his nostrils. He stopped.

To take his mind off the personal hygiene issues, Jones headed towards the campervan in the barn. Jean-Luc followed in close attendance.

"Would you mind answering a few questions for me?" Jones asked.

"*Bien sûr.* Please continue."

"What's the quickest way to get from here to England?"

The Frenchman pursed his lips.

"You want to return home, perhaps?"

"Not at all, I'm wondering about Flynn's accomplice, the elusive green-eyed man. Assuming he wants to return to the UK, what are his options?"

Jean-Luc paused for a moment before answering.

"From here, he could drive to Roscoff and take the ferry-boat to Plymouth, or he could travel further east along the coast road and take the St Malo, or Caen routes to Portsmouth. The alternative to a long drive through to the ports in Normandy would be to fly from Brest, Dinard, or Rennes Airports. Brest is the closest, of course. As you know, it is only a small airport. There are a number of direct flights to the United Kingdom, but only one per day to Birmingham. Also, flights from Dinard go to Stanstead, East Midlands, and Scotland."

The warning mechanism in Jones' brain, which had been mercifully silent for an hour, decided it was time to wake and jab him in the back of the eye.

"Are you able to check on the progress of your search for Flynn's second vehicle?"

Jean-Luc answered quickly.

"I have alerted all the gendarmeries along the most obvious escape routes. As soon as the communications system is operational, I will check on the progress of the vehicle licence authority."

"You'll be able to do that from here?"

Jean-Luc stood tall.

"David, when Sergeant Brunö initialises the satellite system we will be able to contact the whole world from this isolated little courtyard."

Jones smiled. The wonders of the Blessed IT.

Despite the lowering of the sun, the debilitating heat showed an aging, fatigued Jones no mercy. It boiled his weary brain and, with the cottage out of bounds, only the barn and a couple of outbuildings promised deeper shade. There were the woods of course, but Jean-Luc's men were handling that part of the search.

Jones had a need to see the camper. Although he'd followed it hundreds of miles, he'd yet to lay eyes on the pigging thing. Flynn used it to transport Hollie, and perhaps others, and for that reason, he suggested they search the area near the campervan first.

He and Jean-Luc turned the corner at the side of the house, passed the water butt and woodpile, and approached the big open-sided barn. It ran east-to-west at ninety degrees to the cottage and parallel with the stream.

The cool, fresh smell of the water proved too much of an enticement. Jones excused himself and made a quick detour. He strode right up to the flat banks and stared into the fast-running water. Shards of sunlight shot through the trees and diffracted on the surface to form starburst flashes that sparkled and danced in the shade of the trees. Jones had rarely seen running water so clear and never so inviting. So beautiful.

Must be the fatigue. Eyes playing tricks.

Jones licked his lips with a powder-dry tongue and dropped to his knees. He dipped Jean-Luc's handkerchief into the water, wrung it out, and pressed the cool, damp cloth to his face. He held it there and breathed in the moist air through the cotton. The freshness revived him better than a shot of adrenaline. He would never underestimate the recuperative power of cleanliness.

Jones lifted his face to the sky and took another breath—in through the nose, out through the mouth.

Wonderful.

He dipped the hankie again and dabbed the back of his neck. The cool air on his skin made him feel like, well, if not exactly a new man, then a very much improved one.

Jones struggled to his feet and turned to face the barn once more. "Sorry, Jean-Luc. Couldn't resist. Not used to such clear water where I come from."

"Brittany is beautiful. It is a pity we have to contend with this travesty." The French officer waved a hand towards the cottage.

The huge Dutch barn—little more than a slate-tiled A-frame roof on stilts—had a fifteen-by-ten metre footprint. At some stage in the recent past, someone had fitted a wooden tool-shed the size of a single garage into the far gable end. The big white campervan was the only other thing underneath the reasonably well-maintained roof.

Part 2

"It was a clever thing to use the parking alarm on the *camping-car* as a distraction. I applaud your ingenuity."

"Thanks." Jones gave him a tired smile. "It worked better than I'd hoped."

As they closed on the barn, the camper's strange orientation caught Jones' eye. It sat skew-whiff on the wrong side of the entrance. The fresh tyre marks showed that the driver had used a difficult entry route. He had chosen a line with little room for manoeuvre between the woods, the edge of the cottage, and the banks of the stream.

Why'd he done that?

It would have taken quite a bit of skill to reverse the camper into the hangar, yet the big vehicle had been edged to one side and didn't line up flush with the six-inch square oak roof supports, or the barn's opening. Jones raked his fingers through his matted, grubby hair. Why had Flynn parked the camper awry? Was Jones being his usual hyper-finicky self again? It probably didn't mean anything.

The camper stood on a slab of grey concrete, caked in mud and carpeted with piles of blown leaves, some of which were skeletal and had been ground into the dirt.

Fresh tyre tracks told him that a small car once occupied the space on the far side of the camper, but the tracks were far enough away not to have affected the camper's unusual parking position. He drained the last of his water. The liquid gurgled in his stomach, making almost as much noise as the babbling stream.

Jones studied the ground again and something else caught his attention. Numerous scuffed footprints trailed in front of the vehicle. They started at the driver's door, tracked to the passenger's door and back again, and then moved towards the cottage. He made out two sets of shoe-prints, one with ribbed soles, the other flat. The ribbed ones matched those of Flynn's expensive trainers. The others had to have come from Fat Face. A third set of prints, barefoot, belonged to Hollie. Scratches and ridges in the dirt showed she put up a fight when they dragged her from the cab. Only two tracks lead away, and the ridged ones were slightly deeper than before. Flynn must have carried Hollie to the cottage.

Bloody animals.

A fourth set of prints, fresher than the others, and slightly more distinct, appeared from the back of the van. The clear, crisp tread of Alex's walking boots, led to the driver's door and from there, headed to the courtyard. Her tracks stayed well clear of the others.

The trail showed a clear chronological order of events.

Jones almost missed them, but other impressions didn't make sense. Shallow holes, the diameter of a five-penny coin, dotted the tracks at irregular intervals. He had no idea what had made them, or whether they were important, but it annoyed him not to be able to complete the picture the tracks were painting.

What the heck were they? No matter how hard he tried, his fatigue-muddled brain wouldn't provide him with the answer.

Stop worrying away at it. Let it percolate. It'll come.

"Jean-Luc, could one of your men take photos of these tracks? There's no telling what sort of a mess the helicopter will make when it lands."

Assuming the damn thing ever arrives.

While Jean-Luc issued the instructions, Jones turned his attention to the structure of the barn. It didn't take long for something else to bother him.

"Tell me, Jean-Luc, do these open buildings always have concrete floors?" He pointed to the ground beneath the camper.

"*Oui*, David. Today all such buildings are built with cement floors."

"But the weathering of the oak struts and the jointing of the cross braces attaching the roof beams to the legs suggests the barn is old. A hundred years, maybe more. Would they have used concrete that long ago?"

"You understand construction?"

Jones hesitated. He was lost and vulnerable, tired and dirty, but relieved too. He didn't like to talk about his background, but after the support he'd received from Jean-Luc, the friendship, he felt the need to open up to someone. Perhaps a foreigner would be the ideal confidant—they'd hardly be bumping into each other very often.

"One of my foster fathers was a builder. Taught me a few things," he replied.

"Ah, interesting. I am afraid I know little about practical matters. My wife handles all the doing-it-yourself chores. I leave painting to artists like Monet and Matisse, you understand?"

The narrow moustache twitched again and stretched even thinner. It seemed to have the job of emoting, or punctuating, Jean-Luc's words. Jones appreciated the man's self-deprecation. The colonel appeared to be an individual who knew his limitations and didn't try to bluster.

"Hate DIY, eh? I bet you'll get on well with my sergeant," Jones said, but shook his head when Jean-Luc pursed his lips in confusion.

"But to answer your question, David, long ago it would have been unusual to put concrete floors in this part of the country. Cement is *très cher*, very expensive, and a place this old would normally have *boue*, mud floors? These are prepared with *calcaire*, powder of lime. Neighbours and friends come around to compact the ground. Some historians believe this is where the origin of our Breton dancing comes from. A great party is made of the day. But recently, concrete floors have become more affordable." He sighed. "The advancement of the modern age. I regret its arrival sometimes, but with the new times comes technology, no? A useful aid to police work as I'm sure you will agree."

Jones managed a grudging nod.

"In that case," he said, "this floor might be a recent addition. Why did Ellis Flynn or his father go the expense of laying concrete?"

Given that he'd recently used a whole bunch of alcohol swabs to clean his hands, Jones hated the idea, but dropped to all fours to look under the camper. What he saw confirmed his suspicions.

Bloody hell!

He scrambled to his feet and steadied himself against another dizzy spell.

"Jean-Luc, can you drive one of these big things without destroying any forensic evidence?"

The Frenchman waggled his head.

"But of course," he said. "I have a *camping-car por les vacances*. It is not as grand as this one, but it will not be a problem, and I will be most careful."

Jones took the keys Alex had used to release Hollie from the chains and lobbed them to Jean-Luc, who snatched them out of the air left handed.

"What did you see?"

"Something that has no right to be there. If you move the camper, I'll show you. But I don't think we're going to like it."

Jean-Luc shot him a questioning look but said nothing. He pulled on a fresh pair of disposable gloves and climbed into the cab. A few seconds later, the camper juddered as Jean-Luc struggled to find the biting point of the clutch, and then inched out of the barn.

As soon as the vehicle cleared the building, Jones scooted around the side. He stared at the freshly exposed space and sighed. The warning mechanism in his head fired off a two-claxon alarm.

"Jean-Luc," he called. "I've a horrible feeling things just become a whole lot worse."

Chapter Two

FRIDAY AFTERNOON – Observations
Time since Ellis Flynn's stabbing: five hours, thirty minutes

JEAN-LUC ROUNDED the side of the campervan and approached Jones. Like Alex before him, he stayed well clear of the footprints.

"What is it? What do you see?" he asked.

Jones scuffed at the concrete to clear the build-up of mud and dead leaves from the newly exposed floor. His boot hit a raised lip and stopped. "This shouldn't be here."

"What?"

"None of this is normal." He swept his arm at the floor of the open bay. "Flynn positioned the campervan to avoid driving over this area, but there's too much dirt to see the surface." He pointed to the tool-shed. "There might be a yard-broom in there."

"A yard-broom?"

Jones mimed brushing the floor and Jean-Luc raised a finger.

"Ah, *un balai*."

Jean-Luc strode to the wooden hut, and without breaking stride, turned sideways and snapped out a leg. The kick demolished the z-framed door.

"Impressive, Jean-Luc. Breton martial arts?"

The tall gendarme shrugged and ducked into the hut. He reappeared a moment later with a stiff-bristled broom and a crowbar. "This will be useful I think." He started to pass the broom to Jones, but hesitated. "But will you not disturb the evidence, David?"

"Probably, but what if there are girls down there, alive and suffering? Do you really want to wait for the forensics team?"

Jean-Luc gave Jones the broom and he set to work clearing a six-metre square patch. Two dozen hearty sweeps had Jones breathing hard and sweating heavily. Leaves and dirt billowed aside exposing two rectangular aluminium sheets lying flat, set into a thin flat-bar frame.

"This metal was covered for a long time, I think." Jean-Luc pointed at the piles of rubbish either side of the frame.

"Unless Flynn spread this stuff as camouflage."

Grey, and with a diamond embossed pattern, the metal plates looked fairly new. Three heavy steel hinges, rust-free and riveted in place, attached each panel to the frame. A large clasp and a padlock secured the two panels together.

"Not much pitting or tarnishing on the aluminium. And this padlock is new." Jones looked at Jean-Luc. "I don't like the look of this one little bit."

Heavy furrows etched into Jean-Luc's forehead and the moustache concertinaed into a crooked arch.

"*D'accord.* I think we need to be careful here, *mon ami*. There is no telling what we may find down there."

Bile returned to Jones' throat.

Jean-Luc spoke into his personal radio. A couple of moments later, one of his men arrived carrying a camcorder. Jean-Luc spoke a few terse words and pointed to the hatch.

The camera operator pressed a button on the device and a halogen light illuminated the area at his feet. The man signalled his readiness.

Jean-Luc placed the forked end of the crowbar into the clasp of the padlock and leaned on the handle. The sinews on his neck bulged and he grunted. For a moment, nothing happened. Jones took a pace forward, and was about to add his weight to the bar, when the lock snapped apart. A sonorous metal ding echoed in a hollow space below the aluminium sheets. Jean-Luc shifted his balance to avoid toppling, and allowed the crowbar to drop from his hands. It landed on the aluminium with another loud clang.

Jones reached for the shattered clasp and tried to raise one of the door flaps. It didn't budge. "Lend a hand here, mate. This thing's heavy."

While Jones tugged on the handle, Jean-Luc levered at the join with the crowbar. Again, it took more force than Jones expected, but after another metallic snap, the hatch rose silently on well-oiled hinges. Jones released his hold on the panel and it continued to rise.

"There must be a spring or a weight below, counterbalancing the door to make it rise."

When the metal flap reached vertical, it stopped and emitted a soft click. Jones gave the door a shake and nodded in satisfaction. "Something's holding it in place."

"A safety catch?" Jean-Luc offered.

Jones nodded. "What the hell do we have down there?"

Jean-Luc shook his head.

A metal bar, attached by two bolts to the underside of the aluminium plate hung down, bent and broken. It matched a corresponding piece of steel protruding from a metal housing below.

"Hell," said Jones, "will you look at that."

"*Qu'est-ce que c'est?* What is it?"

"I've seen these before. It's a trapdoor opening mechanism." He scanned the barn. "Somewhere around here, above ground, we should find a switch to open the doors automatically."

"There is an electrical panel inside the *cabanon*. But I would like some backup before we search the place, agreed? What if somebody is still down there?

"Doubt it. Somebody padlocked it from the outside. There could be another entrance, I suppose, but …."

Jones considered the possibility. What if Green-eyes didn't

escape in a car at all? Could he be hiding down there, having accessed it through another entrance? Could he be holed up inside with an armoury?

A young gendarme arrived at the jog and stood next to Jones, weapon drawn and index finger resting along the trigger-guard.

Jean-Luc entered the tool-shed, and snapped a loud switch. Two seconds later, a diesel generator somewhere in the background coughed twice, and fired up. Lights, suspended from the barn roof flickered, cut out, and then bloomed into brilliant life.

A moment later, the second aluminium door rose to the accompanying hum of an electric motor. Once it reached vertical, it too, locked into place. Both doors stood open but hardly inviting. Cool, stale air and the pungent smell of damp and rot rose from the depths. Jones sniffled. He caught another smell, too. Sharp. Caustic.

Bleach?

Concrete steps, one and a half metres wide, tumbled into the blackness.

The camera operator, silent until this point, whispered, "*Putain!*" The guard shuffled his feet, preparing for action.

Jones' heart rate leaped and the pulse boomed in his ears. The horrors of the cellar had been left more-or-less in plain view and little had been done to clean the congealed matter in the freezer. Yet Flynn and Green-eyes spent a hell of a lot of effort camouflaging this opening. What did they have hidden down there? Jones and Jean-Luc stood over the opening, looking down.

"What do you think, *mon ami?* Go down prepared for battle, or treat it as an abandoned potential crime scene?"

"Your call, Jean-Luc, but I'd hate to go down there with loads of men and destroy trace evidence. The dust on those steps hasn't been disturbed for a while. I doubt there's anyone down there, not anyone breathing at least. Shall we risk it?"

Jean-Luc held up a hand when his radio buzzed. After a brief conversation he said, "Sergeant Brunö informs me the communications system is now working."

"Any news of the accomplice?"

"*Je regrette*, but there is no record of a vehicle registered to Ellis or Edward Flynn *en France*. Nor is there a trace of the accomplice. I have informed all the ferry and airports, but we have the barest description and we cannot lock down the whole country."

Jean-Luc's mouth formed a thin line before he spoke again.

"Would you like to contact your colleagues in England?"

"Not yet. We need to look down there first. It might dictate our next move."

Jones stepped aside to allow the cameraman an unrestricted view of the entrance. The camcorder's spotlight threw the top four steps into sharp relief and illuminated a panel of five light switches on the left inner wall.

Jones and the gendarmes donned surgical gloves and overshoes before making the descent. "Shall we?" he asked.

Jean-Luc nodded and Jones took the initiative. He placed his foot on the top step, crouched, and threw all five switches on the wall panel. The familiar flicker of strip lighting dispelled the darkness below. With Jean-Luc at his side, weapon drawn, and the cameraman and guard following close behind, they descended.

Chapter Three

FRIDAY AFTERNOON – *Below*
 Time since Ellis Flynn's stabbing: five hours, thirty-five minutes

TWELVE STEPS LED DOWN to a rectangular room around eight metres long and five deep. It stood two metres high from the floor to the thick, reinforced ceiling. The bottom step finished at a small landing, surfaced in cream-coloured ceramic tiles. The same textured tiles covered the floor stretching out before them.

Jean-Luc signalled for the cameraman to stay on the steps and film from there while he, the guard, and Jones stepped into the chamber.

The underground room, decorated in the clean, harsh style of an operating theatre, stood out in sharp contrast to the dark grime of the cellar. Polar opposites. With walls painted a harsh clinical white, and spotless, the room reeked of bleach, pine air-freshener, and an underlying tang of mould.

Jones couldn't explain why the ambience of the place matched the vibe he received from the torture chamber in the cellar, but it definitely did.

"This is a bad place."

Jean-Luc swallowed, clearly picking up the same sense of foreboding. His tanned face had lost a few shades of colour. He removed his hat and combed long, artistic fingers through his cropped hair.

"Recent, judging by the door mechanics and the electrical equipment," Jones said, "but how could anyone build this here and keep it quiet from the locals? They'd need some major equipment to excavate a hole this large."

Jean-Luc frowned. "I may have a partial answer. During the last war, the resistance would dig hiding places for weapons and escaped prisoners." He whispered as though he wanted to avoid waking the ghosts that were crawling up Jones' spine.

The colonel stepped alongside Jones and continued.

"This farm is secluded and would have made an ideal location for a bolt-hole. However, the later modifications, I agree, would need considerable resources."

Jones and Jean-Luc stood against the wall at the foot of the staircase to allow the camera operator a chance to film the room in one slow, panning shot.

As he did when first entering Flynn's cottage, Jean-Luc stopped and swept the room with his eyes rather than go blundering ahead. Jones did likewise.

Only the background hum of an air conditioning unit broke the oppressive silence. This, together with the smell of disinfectant, reinforced the clinical atmosphere, but the under-note of rot punched through the superficial cleanliness.

A jumble of images assaulted Jones' vision. Stainless steel fittings reflected the ceiling lights in a dazzling flash of information overload. He closed his eyes and balled his hands into tight fists. When calm returned, he scanned slowly, from left to right, as the cameraman had done. To retain control of his emotions, Jones concentrated on one object at a time.

Treat it like an inventory, a stock-take.

Ahead of him to the left, a stainless-steel washbasin hung from the wall, and beyond that, a metal toilet without a seat. The setup offered no privacy to anyone using the facilities. Next to the basin, a wet-room area, complete with shower and bidet, filled the first corner. Again, no shower curtains obstructed the view.

The oppressively low ceiling made Jones want to stoop, but he counter-intuitively stretched to his full height. He would not be cowed. He'd be strong, even though he would have preferred to run from the ominous place.

He glanced at Jean-Luc. The tall gendarme's bunched jaw-muscles and flared nostrils showed him to be as uncomfortable as Jones. Like Jones, he too stood with fists clenched tight. The guard, eyes wide, skin pale, licked his lips and gripped his rifle firmly. Jean-Luc signalled him to stay on the plinth. The guard looked relieved and happy to obey.

Jones continued his sweep.

A floor-to-ceiling mirror, three metres wide occupied half of the far wall. He approached and pressed his finger to the surface. The absence of a gap between his fingertip and the reflected image confirmed his suspicions—one-way glass.

A flat-panelled door broke into the wall to the right of the mirror. The place had all the hallmarks of a laboratory observation suite.

In the middle of the floor stood a marble butcher's block on top of a solid tubular metal frame. Drip-grooves in the block's surface and a drain hole near the foot made its utility clear—a mortician's slab. Far more horrific to Jones were the straps attached to each corner of the gruesome tablet.

"*Merde!*"

The cameraman voiced Jones' thoughts precisely.

Shit!

Jean-Luc spoke in a hushed tone.

"This is not good."

His right hand reached up to smooth the moustache once again. Jean-Luc's nervous tick.

A side-table, like some macabre serving tray on wheels, stuck out

Part 2

at right angles at the head of the marble slab. Its top was free of the expected implements of torture. Perhaps the animals who'd set this place up, Flynn and Fat Face, used the same tools from the cottage dungeon? For continuity.

To the right of the slab, the final third of the room was set up as a bedroom, complete with four-poster bed, but minus the curtains. Empty bedside-tables stood either side of the headboard. An ominous stain darkened the centre of the bare mattress.

Apart from the stained mattress and the absence of a window with a view, the space could have passed for a bedroom in a medium-class hotel anywhere in the world.

Jones cut a sideways glance at Jean-Luc who studied the same mark on the mattress and made the sign-of-the-cross, eyes closed and head bowed. Jones lowered his eyes, too. He admired Jean-Luc's faith, and he used to wish he'd held onto the comfort of a religion, but … not anymore.

God hasn't reached this place, Jean-Luc.

Jones scratched his stubble.

"Shit!" he muttered.

"Did you notice the cameras, *mon ami*?" Jean-Luc's words broke into his thoughts.

Jones nodded and took in the half dozen closed-circuit units set high into walls in the centre and at each corner. Together, they would probably have covered every square centimetre of the room.

"It is like the Big Brother house, no?"

"I imagine so." Jones had never watched the so-called "reality" TV show, but knew what it involved. He pointed at the door beside the mirror. "I'm guessing that's the command and operations centre for this … place."

Jean-Luc signalled the camera operator to follow. The guard accompanied them.

The unlocked door opened into a room as wide as the chamber but only two metres deep. It was full of audio-visual equipment, communications devices, monitors, and computer servers. The screens were dead, the LEDs inactive.

"Someone spent a small fortune on this facility, this observation room," Jones announced, instinctively knowing how the owners recouped their investment.

"Jean-Luc," he said, and pointed to the DVD recorders. "You know what all this is for, don't you?"

"I think so." Further colour leached from his face.

"Are you familiar with the term 'snuff movies'?"

"*Oui*. People pay large sums of money to watch those things. *Incroyable*."

"I agree. Sick bastards."

"David, we must secure this, er … facility until the forensics team arrives, *n'est-ce pas*?"

"Absolutely."

Jean-Luc spoke rapidly to the video operator and guard who hustled from the observation room.

"The cameraman will have Sergeant Brunö upload the images to the main server and the guard will remain at the top of the steps." Jean-Luc paused and took a final look. "At least there are no cells down here. I feared we might find—"

"Me too."

Jones struggled up the steps and stumbled out of the barn's shadow. His hands shook and the acid taste of the foetid air remained on his tongue and cloyed at the back of his throat. He popped another mint into his mouth and passed the packet to Jean-Luc. This time the colonel accepted the offering and took a tablet. Anything to take the taste of the observation room from his mouth.

The courtyard offered relief of sorts, and Jones welcomed the much gentler warmth of the fading sun. The vivid greens and browns of the woods, and the pale blue sky overhead were welcoming contrasts to the white austerity of the underground chamber. He rested his back against his favourite wall and took appreciative note of the newly-erected tent that housed Sergeant Brunö's communications hub. It included a large-screened laptop, a complicated radio setup stacked on a heavy-duty camping table. The sergeant sat on a fold-away chair, working the equipment. Jean-Luc hovered over him and conducted operations via his satellite phone.

Part 2

Jones sucked in clean, clear air through his nose hoping to drive out the residue of stink from the room under the barn. Thoughts of Hollie Jardine jagged into his head—her bruised face and cut lip. Anger bubbled up and threatened to overwhelm him. He pressed the rough wall with his palms, gaining comfort from its solidity and pitted texture. He shuddered again as one question kept repeating itself. The question had no answer.

How long would Flynn and Green-eyes have kept Hollie alive before strapping her to that marble slab?

Chapter Four

FRIDAY AFTERNOON – *The locals*
Time since Ellis Flynn's stabbing: six hours

JONES HAD SEEN SO MUCH during his career, more than anyone should have to contend with. He knew what people were capable of doing. He'd seen deaths, both accidental and premeditated. Bodies torn apart and smashed by drunk drivers, corpses burnt, crushed, mutilated. Families left behind to grieve and wonder why.

But this?

This was something else entirely, something far more depraved and calculating. The cellar and the observation room were bad enough, but the beautiful setting, the light breeze fluttering the leafy canopy, the musical stream, the chittering birds and buzzing insects seemed to make it so much worse.

Jean-Luc left him to his thoughts. The considerate Frenchman seemed to know exactly what to do and when.

Jones closed his eyes and tried to bring his senses into balance, but the gentle head and shoulder rotations did nothing to ease the stabbing crick in his neck. Nor did they fix the ache in his heart.

Part 2

How could anybody treat other human beings the way Flynn and Fat Face had treated Hollie and the others? And who were those "others"?

He retrieved the three passports Alex had found in the camper from Jean-Luc. Three girls, young and pretty, two blondes, and a redhead, aged between fourteen and eighteen. Each had blue eyes, fresh, clear skin, and the sweet, wide-eyed innocence of youth. Were they dead, buried somewhere in this picturesque countryside? Were there others?

Torture, butchery, and barbarism. Christ, where the hell would this case lead?

Alex had written a list of the names and dates of birth from the passports, and would have someone search the MisPer database as soon as she arrived in England. Three families, maybe more, grieved, but if they found the remains buried here, the families might at least have some form of closure. Whatever good that did.

Jones felt sorrow for the lost lives, of course he did, but grieving would do no one any good. He needed to focus. Needed to find the people responsible and destroy the operation, or more families would grieve.

For the second time that day, flashing lights and a two-tone siren interrupted his thoughts and heralded the return of the SUV, which raced down the lane. This time the blue-flashers stood out clear in the reduced evening light.

At some stage during the underground exploration, the SUV which had taken Alex and Hollie to the airport had also returned, and the extra gendarmes swelled the numbers of the search teams. The second SUV pulled alongside the first. An officer jumped out, marched across the concrete to Jean-Luc, and delivered his report in a quiet aside.

While his subordinate spoke, Jean-Luc kept glancing at Jones, but Jones couldn't dredge up the energy to approach the Frenchmen. What little remained of his strength had leached away during his walk from the barn. He sank to his haunches and buried his face in his hands.

Jones kept playing the scenario in his head. He imagined Hollie down in the cellar, terrified, beaten, raped, and dragged to the false comfort of the observation room. She'd be confused, compliant, and maybe even grateful. How long would it have taken her to work out the significance of the marble slab? How would she have reacted? How many thousands of sick bastards would have watched her ongoing torment? Were they going to broadcast the pictures live or sell them as DVDs? Maybe both.

Not helping, Jones. Pack it in.

The remaining gendarmes took a break from searching the grounds and gathered around the rear of the newly arrived truck. Jones took little notice of their animated chatter until a hand touched his shoulder. He raised his head to see the stoic face of a twenty-something officer. His dark eyes showed concern and sympathy as he handed Jones a mug of steaming coffee, a bottle of water, and half a baguette stuffed to overflowing with cheese, tomatoes, and lettuce.

Jones didn't have the heart, or the vocabulary, to tell the gendarme he preferred tea, so he took the offerings and mumbled a faltering, "*Merci, monsieur.*"

The gendarme broke out a wide smile, exposing a set of uneven teeth. He gave Jones a thumbs-up, and returned to his comrades by the trucks. The other gendarmes raised their drinks to him and nodded their encouragement. To show willing, Jones sipped at the scalding black liquid and gagged at its sweetness. Then he took a bite of the sandwich to mask the powerful taste of the acrid brew.

Exhaustion had dampened his appetite, but the act of chewing made his mouth water and hunger returned with a vengeance. He vacuumed up the rest of the excellent baguette and washed it down with the whole bottle of water before Jean-Luc called him across to the comms tent. He left the unfinished coffee at the base of the rosebush.

The food revitalised him. Energy flooded through his system and he rose on much steadier legs.

Jean-Luc munched on an apple and offered Jones one from a bag on the camping table.

"We have some new information, David."

Part 2

With the apple halfway to his mouth, Jones said, "Please, go on," before he took a large bite. The sharply sweet juices ran down his chin and he mopped it with his sleeve.

What the hell. The shirt's already ruined.

"My officer interviewed the *maire* of the village, Carhoët Grande, when he collected our provisions. We now know the *marque* of the vehicle our green-eyed, fat-faced man used to make his escape. It is an ancient Citroën. I have transmitted the details to our traffic division. Unfortunately, there is no further description of the man. No one in the village admits to having seen him."

"That's strange."

"*Oui, d'accord.* In a small community, everybody knows the business of everybody else." Jean-Luc paused for a moment and, as he looked towards the barn, his smile faltered. "Or so we thought. But we have more information about the room beneath the barn."

"Yes?"

"The modification began three years ago, in the summer."

"How do we know this?"

"The office of the *maire* received a complaint from the owner of these woods." Jean-Luc shrugged and his moustache drooped. "It would seem that Mr Flynn did not obtain *un permis* before commencing building works, and the *maire* of the village decided to pay close attention. Flynn told them he planned to set up an orchard and the underground room would house a press and storeroom for cider and calvados. He said it would create jobs. The community levied fines for the failure to receive *le permis*, but granted permission to proceed. However, the *commune du Carhoët* monitored the work closely from that point onwards."

Jones stopped chewing the apple and swallowed quickly.

"That's interesting. The construction began only a few years after Flynn walked free from detention. I wonder where he found the capital, the money. The work would have cost a small fortune."

Jean-Luc spoke quietly. "He had a sponsor, I think."

"Fat Face? Have you learned anything else?"

"*Oui.* The *boulanger* said that *monsieur* Flynn usually bought bread when he visited, in amounts that suggested he had guests. The most recent visit before today was nearly two months ago."

Jones' emotions prickled. Flynn's last visit took place shortly before he'd first met Hollie.

"What do you think, Jean-Luc? Should we talk to the owner of the woods? He might have seen something."

"But the one who owns the woods and the *maire* is one and the same person, David. In the country, these things occur rather often."

"So, let me get this straight. The neighbour, who is also the mayor, made a complaint about the work. The Commune levied a fine, but ultimately allowed the work to continue. And this same mayor fails to tell your officer about a procession of visits and visitors to the farm. On top of that, he can't put a name to Flynn's accomplice, nor can he offer a decent description. Does this strike you as a little suspicious?"

Jean-Luc smoothed his moustache and nodded.

"It does indeed, David. I will have the man investigated. I will also find out whether any local teenager girls have gone missing."

"If the mayor … what's his name?"

"Plouay, Albert Plouay."

"Well, if *monsieur* Plouay is mixed up in this, he's highly unlikely to kidnap a local girl and draw all that attention. But you might want to check his background and maybe his bank accounts. He sounds like a man not averse to dipping his hands in the till."

"Excuse me? What is 'dipping in the till'?"

"I mean, *monsieur* Plouay might be happy to accept a bribe for his silence and maybe to guard the farm in Flynn's absence."

"Ah, *je comprends*. Do you think I should arrest Plouay in case he decides to disappear?"

"I would. If he knows what's been going on here, I imagine he's pretty worried about now."

Jean-Luc sent the same officer, and a backup, to arrest Plouay, and the Renault disappeared once more.

While they watched the Renault climb the hill, Jones said, "This is bad, Jean-Luc. As soon as word of what happened here leaks out, it'll be the centre of world attention. The media loves a multiple murder case, and when it involves young girls …."

"But we are not yet certain anyone has been killed. We have found no bodies."

"We will, Jean-Luc, we will. I've never been more certain of anything in my life."

He stared at the farm and the darkening woods and knew he was right.

"*D'accord*, David, *d'accord*. But this place is simple to isolate. We will have no trouble keeping the farm free of the media locusts, and I can impose a no-fly restriction if they send up helicopters to spy on us."

"You can?"

"*Bien sûr*. Of course. It is a simple matter."

"Blimey. Wish I had the same authority in England."

Jones tried to digest the new information. Flynn had evidently made numerous visits to the farm since his release from detention. Had the bastard brought a fresh victim each time? Jones shuddered at the thought.

The quiet little cottage in the middle of nowhere might have been turned into a bloody charnel house. The empty chest freezer in the cellar wouldn't have held more than one body at a time. But why use the freezer in the first place? It's not like there wasn't plenty of land around to bury the bodies. He couldn't see Flynn dragging corpses too far away.

"Jean-Luc? Does the local hunt go through these woods?"

"*Oui*. I imagine it would. We have many deer and wild boar in this region. Why?"

"People hunt with dogs here, right? Wouldn't the dogs have smelt decaying bodies?"

"I do not know. But the forensics unit will have equipment for analysing odours."

"Electronic noses."

"Ah *oui*, electronic noses." Jean-Luc checked his watch. "And do not forget the ground-penetrating radar. If there are bodies in the woods or fields, we will find them."

Oh, there will be bodies, Jean-Luc.

At any moment, Jones expected the caw of a big black crow to startle him.

If this were a movie, an old crone would burst out of the woods and scream a dread warning. He searched the groaning tree-line, but no one appeared, crone or otherwise.

He felt a great sense of loss. No one brought here would have survived.

No one before Hollie.

How many bodies would they eventually locate? Five? Ten?

Jones' fist wrapped around his cool bottle of water. Too full to take another drink, he touched the bottle to his forehead and rolled it from side to side. So cool, so good.

"Jean-Luc, might I ask you a favour?" Jones asked, as he tugged at his shirt and grimaced. "I don't suppose you carry spare coveralls in your vehicle?"

Jean-Luc removed his *képi* and waved it in front of his face. "You wish to change from your dirty clothes, yes? But of course, *mon ami*, I am so sorry I did not think to offer. My team and I always carry spare clothing. We never know how long we will be away from base. And we sometimes need to take away the *vêtements* ... the clothing of suspects for examination."

Once again, Jones found himself impressed by his newfound friend's empathy. They tracked to the remaining Renault and Jean-Luc handed him one of half a dozen packages stored in a plastic crate. It contained a dark-blue one-piece, one-size-fits-all uniform wrapped in cellophane, an individually wrapped bar of hospitality soap, and a small towel. A care package from the angels.

"David," Jean-Luc said with a sympathetic smile. "In the tool shed there is a sink with running water. You will not need to use the stream again, unless you prefer to."

Jones couldn't believe his luck. He scuttled with his treasure-trove to the barn where he found the ceramic sink with a tap that issued clear cold water. Jones stripped off his outer garments and bundled them into the empty carrier. He luxuriated in the crisp fragrance of the soap and had nearly worn the tiny cake down to the nub by the time he was ready to use the wonderful, scratchy towel. The crisply starched cotton one-piece fitted well enough—after he'd turned up the cuffs on the sleeves and the legs. He returned to the courtyard a grimly smiling new man. He only needed a shave to complete the transformation, but a razor would be too much to expect, or to ask for.

"You look much better, *mon ami.*"

"Thanks. Getting out of those filthy clothes is wonderful." He raised the package. "You'll need these for evidence."

Jean-Luc nodded to Sergeant Brunö who took the package and headed back to his equipment. Clean and revived, Jones took the time to look around. The gendarmes stood in a group, eating. Brunö busied himself with his communications equipment, and Jean-Luc jotted notes on a pad.

After a few minutes, the colonel paused his note-taking and barked orders at his men. They immediately broke away from the impromptu cafe and resumed their searches. Moments later, torch beams sliced through the woods, and sporadic radio traffic broke the silence.

The sun dipped behind the western hills and dusk settled in the valley. Jones cast his eyes to the sky. "If your forensics team doesn't get here soon it'll be too dark to land."

"They will arrive in five minutes. But before then perhaps we can discuss the case?"

"Good idea."

"One thing puzzles me," Jean-Luc continued.

"Only one?"

Jean-Luc tilted his head, and smiled. "Ah, I see you have a sense of humour, my friend. The question I have is this. Why would the *pédophiles* use the cellar in the house when they have the facility in the barn?"

"Been wondering that myself. It may have been a way of softening up the new victims."

"*Excusez-moi*? Softening up?"

"Perhaps they used the cellar as a shock tactic to make the new arrivals more compliant. Why else would they have stored body-parts in the freezer? It was asking for discovery. Alternatively, they might have killed those particular victims before the observation room became operational. Maybe Green-eyes used it as an alternate backdrop for their hideous movies. A change of film set, if you will. I don't know, but I'll be sure to ask the bastards when we catch them."

"Them?"

"Yes. This is has to be the work of a group. Ellis Flynn and Fat Face couldn't do something like this alone. This sort of operation is hugely expensive and will have an international perspective. There'll be a distribution network and a list of customers somewhere. Without customers, there's no profit, and no profit means no business. There'll be a money trail, alright."

"Ah yes, we follow the money."

"Exactly. And it won't all have been done via telecommunications. Some of it would have been face-to-face. And I want all of them, every sick bastard locked away for a very long time."

A dark shadow blotted out what remained of the light and the whooping, drumming sound of a twin-engine transport helicopter split the silence. The downwash from its rotor blades pushed dust, leaves, and loose rubbish into the air, forming helical dust devils at Jones' feet. He turned his head and clamped his eyes shut while the chopper banked and made its final approach to land in the field outside the wall.

"That'll be the forensics team then," he shouted.

Nice one, Jones. Sharp as a bloody knife, mate.

Chapter Five

EARLY FRIDAY EVENING – Alex Olganski
Time since Ellis Flynn's stabbing: five hours

HOLLIE SPENT the flight staring through the window as first the English Channel and then England itself passed below the wing. Alex spent much of the time wondering how to help her young charge cope with the after-effects of the abduction and the killing of Ellis Flynn. Cuts and bruises heal quickly, but emotional stress was a different matter entirely.

Alex cared nothing for the loss of Flynn, the creature deserved no better, but she should have stopped Hollie getting the knife.

Fan också. Shit!

Alex would never forgive herself if her momentary lack of concentration led to bad things for Hollie and the boss.

"Do you need some water, Hollie? Something to eat?"

Alex brushed the girl's forearm and she jumped, but her gaze remained fixed on the aerial world outside the fuselage.

"You'll be happy to reach home, yes?"

Hollie tucked her chin into her chest but did not take her eyes from the window. What did she see out there? The cellar? The blood pumping from the wound in Ellis Flynn's back?

And what of the boss, tackling the strongly-built Flynn with nothing more than pepper spray and a truncheon? She smiled at the memory of the quiet, unassuming policeman who looked frail enough that a light wind might knock him from his feet. But beneath that lightweight exterior lay a resilient police officer. A powerful, honest, and reliable man.

After taking down Ellis Flynn, the "old man", as Wash called the boss behind his back, looked so dishevelled. So what? Normal? Yes, that was it. His usual impeccable tidiness had been shattered. Phil Cryer once used the phrase "prim and proper" to describe the boss. At the time, Alex had looked it up in her English phrasebook and laughed. The description suited David Jones to perfection. But today, after tackling Flynn he looked, well, magnificent. Messy hair, scratched face, dirty hands, and stubbly chin—a true Hollywood action hero.

Bruce Willis with a full head of hair and an air of quiet heroism.

She and the boss had done a good thing that day. Ellis Flynn was now dead and could harm no other young women. Hollie was safe, headed for the love and support of her family, and for counselling. Hopefully, she would heal.

Others had not been so lucky.

Alex closed her eyes and considered the list in her pocket—the list of names. Three girls, three daughters, all probably dead. Attached to the list would be three inconsolable families. To lose a loved one is a terrible thing. What would she do without her beloved Julie?

Alex could not wait to reach home and hold her wife tight. The return to normality would help her cope with the memory of a deeply trying day.

THE *FASTEN SEATBELTS* sign lit up with a jaunty electronic *bing-bong*, and Hollie bounced into life as though the cheery noise had

Part 2

activated something in her head. She reached for the lap-strap with trembling hands and said something Alex did not catch.

"Excuse me, Hollie?"

"I need to get off this plane. I-It's stifling in here. Can't breathe."

Alex had the answer to her unspoken question. Staring out the window must have been Hollie's way of battling claustrophobia. A legacy from the cellar, perhaps.

"It won't be long now," Alex said, trying to keep the poor child calm.

She helped Hollie fasten the lap-strap, and Hollie rubbed her thighs, as though trying to dry wet palms.

After a few moments quiet, Hollie spoke again.

"Thank you for saving me. I … I'll never forget you and David as long as I live."

Her chin trembled and she breathed the words quietly.

Alex grinned.

"Why are you smiling?"

"You used DCI Jones' given name. I wondered what his reaction would be if we called him 'David' at the office?" She made an exaggerated shudder and Hollie's shoulders relaxed a little. "We would never put that particular sacrilege to the test. In public, our sergeant, Phil Cryer, still calls him 'boss', and David, as you call him, is akin to a godfather to his children."

Alex rested her hand on top of the girl's clenched fist. This time she did not flinch.

"You have an accent." Hollie lifted her head and their eyes met for the first time since boarding the plane. "Scandinavian?"

"Yes, you are exactly right. I come from a small place in Sweden, called Lysekil. It is on the coast, five-hundred kilometres west from Stockholm."

Hollie gave an apologetic smile and shook her head.

"I'm sorry. Don't know anything about Sweden, but I'd love to learn. I'm studying languages at school. What's Lysekil like?"

"Ah, it is so beautiful. You would love it. Not a single IKEA for miles," she said, smiling, "but we do have meatballs."

Hollie's return smile brightened her whole, bruised face.

Alex continued.

"There is caviar and fishing and tourists. We are too far south for the midnight sun but in the summer it is … magnificent. Long, long days. Often sunny and warm. However in the winter, it's … quiet."

Hollie's eyes shone.

"It sounds really beautiful. Why did you leave?"

"That is a story for another day." Alex cast her mind back ten years to when she first met Julie Harris, her one true love. After a fortnight's blissful exploration—a romance that shook her to her very soul—Alex would have followed Julie to the ends of the world, but that turned out to be Birmingham. The tenth anniversary of their first meeting was less than a week away, and Alex planned a big surprise, which included a visit to Lysekil.

"Please?"

Alex shook her head. "I found love."

"Would you take me to Lysekil?"

Alex leaned away, surprised by the request. After a moment of thought, she nodded.

"One day, perhaps."

When you're a little older.

"Can you teach me some Swedish?"

"Yes of course. Um … I know. Can you say - *Alla Danska folket är dumma?*"

Hollie frowned in concentration. "Er … *Allah Dansker falsket yeah doomaha?*"

Alex waggled her head. "Close, but no prizes."

"What does it mean?"

"It is not good, really. It says, 'All Danish people are fools." Hollie returned Alex's grin. "But I don't really mean it."

"The Swedish and the Danish are enemies?"

"Not at all. The friendly rivalry of neighbours. It's the same between England and Scotland, yes?"

"Oh, I see."

Part 2

"Now, we need to get ready to land and you must prepare yourself."

Hollie lowered her head and twisted her fingers in her lap. Her hands shook.

"What's wrong?"

"I've been so stupid. I was planning to run away. Broke into my father's office and stole some money and my passport. Don't know what I'll say to him."

"Hollie, listen to me." Alex spoke quietly. "We all make mistakes. Your *mamma och papa* will be waiting for you at the airport. I promise they're going to forgive you. Parents always do. It's their job, yes?"

Alex handed her a tissue. Hollie dabbed her eyes, taking care not to smudge the makeup covering the bruise. They could do nothing but clean the cut on her lower lip, but the girl looked a million times better than when she and the boss first found her.

The plane made a steep descent and a hard landing, bouncing twice and jagging left as they hit the runway. Some of the passengers screamed. Hollie squealed, grabbed Alex's hand, and held on tight until they taxied to a complete halt. As soon as the seatbelt sign deactivated, Hollie unsnapped her lap-strap, jumped out of her seat, and brushed past Alex.

"I need to get out."

She pulled Alex along the aisle and barged to the head of the disembarkation queue to the vocal annoyance of the other passengers. Alex flashed her police warrant card at the queue. The complaints subsided, but the angry glares continued.

Scowl if you wish, but Hollie takes priority.

Alex met the fierce glare of a particularly overweight middle-aged man wrestling his flight bag from the overhead locker. She stared him down until he lowered his gaze.

Alex continued to stare him down. The man thought he had been insulted. The idiot knew nothing. In her mind, Alex urged him to go home to his food and his wine and thank his God for his easy, safe life.

She threw a protective arm around Hollie's shoulders and faced the exit door.

A young steward peered out of the window. He held them back while the runway crew secured the mobile staircase before swinging open the door.

The Midlands air, fresh by comparison to the warmth of the plane and the heat of Brittany, re-energized Alex and she waited for permission to exit with growing impatience.

Chapter Six

EARLY FRIDAY EVENING - ARTHUR "JENNINGS"
Time since Ellis Flynn's stabbing: *five hours*

JENNINGS SAT in his seat and stewed. He hadn't believed his eyes when he first spotted the little bitch, Hollie-Hottie, and the buxom copper, Blondie, at the airport. Perhaps his luck had changed for the better—and not before time.

He had a damned near perfect view of them both. They sat on the opposite side of the centre aisle from him, three rows ahead. The girl spent the whole flight with her forehead pressed against the window. Blondie spoke to her occasionally, but the murdering little cow never responded.

He'd make the bitch suffer for what she did to Ellis. But how? What was he going to do when they landed?

The old bastard, Jones, would have arranged a reception committee at Birmingham. What half-decent copper wouldn't? If not, and if Hammer arrived in time, they'd take care of Blondie at the airport. Jennings wouldn't attempt it alone, not without a gun. The knife was okay for the decrepit Good Samaritan in France, but

Blondie looked like she could handle herself in a fair fight. To take Blondie down, he needed a surgical strike, clean and simple. What phrase did Hammer use? "Neat and tidy"?

Yes, that's right. Neat and tidy. Love it.

So what about Hammer the contract mechanic? Jennings had never met the killer or any of his business associates, but the guy came highly recommended and from an unimpeachable source. Dirty coppers had so many uses. Hammer's rep was good enough, faultless even, but who would he bring along as backup? A Nail perhaps?

Jennings smiled to himself.

Hammer and Nail.

Yes.

What a great title for an action flick.

Jennings thought about it for a moment.

Wouldn't it be fantastic to make a mainstream movie for a change? Go legit. On the other hand, the profit margins in his current enterprise were so much better, and he didn't have to worry about paying the actors. Their acting skills didn't matter either. In any event, he'd have to take care of this little piece of business first.

Blondie would definitely have to go, and go soon. But not Hottie, not yet. Jennings had other plans for the murderous little bitch. She'd killed Ellis. Stabbed him with his own bloody knife according to what Jennings heard through the bug. He'd make sure she suffered all the torments of perdition. Ellis, his main man, deserved retribution.

Divine retribution.

After getting rid of Blondie, taking the girl would be simple. Then he'd be able to carry on where he'd left off in France. Of course, he'd have to relocate, which presented continuity challenges for the product. But he'd deal with that in the editing suite with a bit of judicious cutting and artful lighting. Or maybe he should start again with fresh meat? Make things easier.

Decisions, decisions.

He'd have to think about that one. Perhaps things weren't a complete disaster after all. He'd still have his bit of profitable film-making fun. The new release would more than offset his losses from the cottage. But the girl was now damaged goods. Should he cut his losses and start again?

Replacing poor Ellis for future projects would be difficult, but not impossible. Jennings knew plenty of good-looking boys who could take Ellis' place and reel in the pretty little fishes, but they'd all need training.

They'd never fully replace Ellis, though. None of them.

In all the years they'd known each other, Ellis had never let him down. He'd always remained faithful and true. Obedient too.

For Jennings, obedience was an essential part of any relationship.

He'd learnt obedience through the gentle and ongoing chastisement of his father.

Jennings balled his fists and tried not to cry when thinking of the poor old man, planted in a pauper's grave, lamented only by a son and a pious mother. At aged eleven, he'd vowed over his father's grave that he would never die poor. With that vow in mind, he'd lied, cheated, stole, and killed to climb out of the gutter and buy a new respectability. Over the years, he'd thrived through ruthlessness, cunning, and brains. After all, God gave him brains and self-determination, and by default, must have sanctioned his activity. God even made sure he was nowhere near the cottage when Jones struck. How fortuitous was that?

Ergo, God Himself supported Jennings' actions.

Some people might call his a twisted kind of logic, but fuck them. Those people would forever be nonentities—the world's cannon fodder. Jennings was better than they were. He was successful. He was a veritable pillar of the British establishment. As a result, nobody could touch him.

Nobody would take away his good name or his money. Nobody. Not Jones, not Hollie Jardine, and not Her Majesty's Inspector of fucking Taxes.

Jennings relaxed into his seat but kept his eyes on the prize—the prey. He bought a bottle of water from the flight attendant but refused her offer of food. One glance at the plastic-wrapped sandwich triangles perched on top of the service trolley in the sweltering heat of the over-full cabin was enough to turn his delicate stomach.

He sipped the drink and turned his mind to the thorny issue of Jones. What to do with the old bastard?

What to do?

Jesus. Of course!

The idea hit him with such blinding clarity he couldn't contain a laugh. Ellis would have approved. He'd have loved the irony. Jones, the bloody Boy Scout, risked everything to rescue the Hottie, and he had a vested interest in the child's safety.

Brilliant!

Decision made. That left nothing but the logistics.

While he pondered the details, a smooth-toned pilot announced they were about to make their landing approach. He hoped they'd all had a pleasant flight and would fly with his airline again.

Not fucking likely, matey!

Jennings normally travelled business class or better, but as his sainted mother used to say, "needs must when the devil drives". Whatever the fuck that meant.

———

THE *FASTEN SEATBELTS* sign glowed bright and took Jennings by surprise—he'd lost himself in his plans to punish Jones. The plane descended through widely spaced, marshmallow clouds.

Hottie sat up straight and turned to face Blondie. Her eyes scanned the cabin and alighted on Jennings for a microsecond before moving away. He caught his breath, hooded his eyes, and pretended to wrestle with his seatbelt.

Did she recognise him?

Granny in the next seat lowered her handbag to the floor and showed him a denture-perfect smile.

"Would you like me to help you with that seatbelt, dear?"

"Er, no thanks," he answered. "I … I can manage."

He must have sounded nervous because the old bitch squeezed her bespectacled eyelids together in what he assumed to be her version of a comforting smile. Stupid cow. It made her look like a bulldog suffering with a stomach ulcer.

She continued.

"There's no need to be scared, dear. I fly to see my grandchildren all the time. Aeroplanes are as safe as cars these days."

Considering what Jennings had done to the old bat in the Benz, that didn't say much. He risked a glance up, but Hottie faced forward again, seemingly unaware of his presence.

"Do you have grandchildren?" Granny asked.

"Huh? Er, no. My good lady wife and I were never blessed with offspring."

Thank fuck.

The woman patted his forearm and nodded sympathetically.

Jennings' heart rate returned to normal or as near an approximation of normal as it was likely to get under the circumstances.

A couple of the passengers screamed when the undercarriage hit the runway with a heavy thump and the plane skittered sideways before straightening and taxiing to the terminal buildings. The pilot's urbane tones returned with an apology and an excuse about being surprised by a heavier-than-expected crosswind. Jennings shot a glance out of his window at the orange windsock hanging limp and motionless from the control tower.

"Fucking liar," he mumbled.

"Excuse me, dear?" Granny asked.

"Nothing."

As soon as the seatbelt sign extinguished, Hottie stood and pushed past Blondie. Carrying one small bag each, the two barged along the aisle to the front of the queue at the exit near the cockpit.

Jennings allowed a dozen passengers to filter between him and his quarry before turning towards the back of the plane. He waited for the queue to move and ducked to avoid hitting his head on the fuselage rim when he finally stepped through the rear doorway.

To his right, Blondie and the bitch skipped down the front staircase. Camera flashes accompanied their descent. Clearly, some asshole had notified the media.

Shit. Shit. Shit.

Noise from a jostling pack of reporters near the door of the arrivals building rose in volume as Hottie and Blondie disembarked the plane. More flashes exploded when the two females met a reception committee that included the girl's parents and four police officers.

Fuck. That's "Plan A" out the window.

Of course, DCI-fucking-Jones would make sure someone was waiting for the girl. Jennings had seen it coming, but it was still a royal pain in his arse.

He'd move on to Plan B—follow Hollie Jardine, and await a better opportunity. One would come. He was certain.

The early evening sun bounced off the concrete apron. Jennings shielded his eyes from the glare. A strong breeze chilled the sweat on his brow and the stark change in temperature from Brittany and the aircraft made him shiver. He lowered the peak of his baseball cap and pulled his jacket zip up to his throat.

While trying to minimise his limp and hide the stick, Jennings turned his head away as he passed within three metres of the celebrating family group, and merged with the crowd hustling towards the arrivals lounge. He hurried through the forecourt and waited at the empty carousel for the arrival of his bag.

Jennings boiled in frustration as the minutes ticked by and his annoyance grew. He gripped the handle of the stick and twisted, practising what he was going to do to the neck of the fucker, Jones.

Chapter Seven

EARLY FRIDAY EVENING - ALEX OLGANSKI"
Time since Ellis Flynn's stabbing: six hours, thirty minutes

AS THEY DESCENDED the steps from the aeroplane, Alex tried to shield Hollie from the camera lenses and the eyes of the reporters who were camped by the entrance.

"Hollie, keep your head lowered, and stay behind me."

The group with Mr and Mrs Jardine included Ryan Washington, Charlie Pelham, and two uniformed officers. Alex recognised the first constable but did not know his name. He stood tall and strong, and his broad shoulders and bulging arms stretched his shirt tight. The other constable was the Family Liaison Officer she'd last seen at the Jardine home. At least Hollie would have another female for company when she and Alex separated.

Dark lines had formed under Frank Jardine's eyes in the hours since Alex last saw him, and the dark grey stubble told a sad tale. When he saw Hollie, and her damaged face, his mouth formed an "oh", and his eyes glistened. He rushed towards the foot of the staircase. Tears glazed Mrs Jardine's eyes, but she ignored the handkerchief clutched in her fist in the excitement of her daughter's return. Each jostled to be the first to reach their child. Wash, Charlie, and the uniformed officers maintained a respectful distance, and their eyes kept scanning their surroundings.

Hollie stumbled in her haste to scramble down the steps, and threw herself into her father's open arms.

"Daddy, Daddy, I'm so sorry."

Frank Jardine's response was lost in the background noise from the hubbub of disembarking passengers. The Jardine family's arms meshed as they hugged in a tight little triangle. They simultaneously laughed and cried and embraced, and laughed some more. Mrs Jardine held on tight and repeated, "My baby. My poor baby," over and over again.

Alex stepped aside to allow them a moment's privacy. They needed as much alone time as they could find. Time to heal.

Wash tapped her arm. "Nice one, girl," he said.

Alex gave him a quick hug.

She glanced at Charlie Pelham who jerked up his chin in scant acknowledgement of her presence before looking away.

Charlie's mistimed call to the *gendarmes* had been calculated to cause the boss embarrassment, but it had actually turned out helpful in the end. Alex could not wait to see how the boss reacted on his return from Brittany.

"Where's the boss?" Charlie demanded.

He leaned to one side, trying see around Alex as though fearing David Jones was hiding behind her, ready to pounce.

"He stayed in France."

"Not in any trouble for going over there without permission, I hope?" The sharp glint behind the eyes of Charlie Pelham showed his concern for what it really was—a blatant lie.

"Not at all, Sergeant Pelham," Alex said, trying not to sneer. "In fact, they begged him to stay and help with their investigation. The evidence suggests there are at least three British girls buried out there. The case is very large and very important. If not for the boss, Hollie would have been added to the list of fatalities. The Ellis

Part 2

Flynn case will cause ripples around the world, and the name, David Jones, will be forever associated with it. He's a real hero."

Charlie Pelham snorted and turned to follow the Jardines and their escort towards the VIP entrance.

Ryan fell into step beside Alex.

"Damn it, girl, you kept everything so quiet. Why didn't you call me? I'd have jumped at the chance to help the old man. Don't know why he called you and not me. I have seniority, after all."

"Yes, Wash. By three whole days. But the boss didn't call me. In fact, he did his best to prevent me from going. He didn't want any of us involved in case he got into trouble. He was trying to protect us."

"I understand that, but why did he take you?"

Alex stood tall.

"I convinced him he needed a translator and someone to help with Hollie. A woman was essential, no? And, he couldn't have stopped me even if he wanted to. I'm bigger than he is."

Wash gave her one of his one-sided smiles, which made his hooked nose stand out even further from his gaunt face.

"Fair enough," he said. "So, changing the subject, this Colonel Coué, what's he like?"

"I would say Jean-Luc Coué is an excellent police officer. And a good man."

"Must be a decent sort. Could have kicked up a real stink." Wash smiled. "I'd love to have seen the old man take down Flynn, though. It must have been a hell of a sight. I mean, the boss doesn't look like he packs much of a punch."

"I didn't see the actual fight. I saw the result only. When I arrived Flynn was already down on the ground."

"And in a world of pain?"

"Exactly, so."

Alex prepared for the dreaded next logical question. How did Hollie get the opportunity to kill Flynn? But before Wash could ask, the clamour of voices and clatter of approaching footsteps interrupted their conversation. The media crowd, armed with cameras, microphones, and recording devices, burst through the barrier tapes in the arrivals paddock and dashed across the concrete towards them.

"*Knulla!* Who warned them of our arrival?" Alex yelled, and rushed to protect Hollie.

With Wash at her side acting as a defence shield, they hurried the family towards the sanctuary of the VIP lounge.

On reaching the double-doors, Pelham stepped across and raised both hands, taking the opportunity to have his brief moment in the spotlight.

"Ladies and gentlemen, as you can see, Hollie Jardine is safe and well, thanks to the efficient professionalism of my team. We'll be taking her to Queen Elizabeth's for a check-up. Please respect the family's privacy during this sensitive time. The West Midlands police will be issuing a statement later this evening, and we will arrange a press conference for tomorrow morning." He ducked through the opening and slammed the doors behind him. "Damned vultures," he said, smirking.

"Bloody hell, Charlie. What did you mean, 'your team'?" A red-faced Wash seethed. "You did fuck all and wanted to hand the whole thing over to the French. And why the fuck did you tell them where we were taking her? The poor girl won't be given a moment's peace."

"Don't talk to me like that, son," Charlie Pelham barked. "I know what I'm doing."

"Yeah? Like you knew what you were up to when you tried to drop the old man right in the shit?" Wash's pointed chin jutted out in challenge, his eyes aflame.

"Don't know what you mean." Charlie Pelham glanced across to Alex, who held his gaze until Pelham looked away.

Wash lowered his voice. "He told you not to talk to the French until he checked out Flynn's place. You could have screwed the whole operation."

"Operation?" Charlie Pelham made a throwaway gesture with his hand. "That weren't no bloody 'operation'. That were the old man playing the vigilante cop. I weren't going to stand by and have my reputation sullied if he screwed up."

Part 2

Charlie Pelham checked to make sure the Jardines were out of earshot and jabbed the index finger of his right hand repeatedly into the palm of his left. "I went by the book and that's exactly what the old man's always banging on about." He sniffed. "Nah. I don't have nothing to be ashamed of. Did the right thing. And more to the point, Superintendent Peyton agrees with me."

Wash shook his head in disdain and glared at his overweight partner.

"I dare say old Duggie Peyton agrees with everything you told him, and he might even remember it in the morning, *when he sobers up*."

"That's more than enough of that, *Constable* Washington."

Pelham straightened his tie and turned from Wash to be confronted by Alex who barred his way.

"Who told the press we were going to be here?" she asked, barely able to contain a growl.

Pelham glanced in the direction of the Jardines.

"I have absolutely no idea. Now stand aside, DC Olganski. Right now!"

Alex wanted to gouge the smug sergeant's eyes out with her thumbs, but not even the boss could save her if she lost that much control, although the satisfaction gained might make the sacrifice worthwhile. She hesitated a moment and flexed her fingers, but stepped back. Pelham strutted by her, chest pumped out as far as his belly, as though he had won a great victory.

Inside the haven of the first-class lounge, painted in pastel yellows and pale browns, the family stopped and searched the place in confusion. Frank Jardine released his daughter's hand for the first time since the apron, and turned to Alex. He looked lost.

"Where's passport control. We need to get Hollie out of here."

Wash shot Charlie Pelham a look of such contempt it needed no subtitles, and he stepped between him and the Jardines. He pointed to the uniformed constables.

"These officers will take you through the priority gates and escort you to Queen Elizabeth's Hospital. They'll stay with you until the doctors have examined Hollie. Alex and I will be along tomorrow to take statements, but for the moment, we want Hollie to have as much peace and quiet as she needs."

Hollie broke free of her mother's embrace and closed on Alex. "Aren't you coming with us?"

Alex hesitated, but could not ignore the desperation in the girl's voice, or the look of fear on her face.

"Yes, okay. I can stay with you until the hospital, but I need to go home once you are admitted. Okay?"

Frank Jardine beckoned Hollie, and she returned to the family fold.

Another commotion, this time at a security door, caused them to turn.

Wash cursed.

"What the hell? How did that mollusc bypass security?"

The local reporter, "Old" Lucas Wilson, together with a cameraman, forced their way towards the Jardines. Wilson's habit of wearing a dishevelled tweed jacket with leather patches at the elbows earned him the nickname "Old", but the creep had yet to reach his middle twenties.

Never the most subtle of journalists, Wilson waved a pencil and notebook and fired off a series of frivolous questions.

"How does it feel to be home, safe and sound?"

"What happened to Ellis Flynn?"

"What do you think of DCI Jones?"

"Can you give us a quote?"

"Can we have an exclusive interview for the Chronicle?"

As the questions flew, the cameraman took shot after blinding shot of the startled family who huddled together—a group of deer trapped in a hunter's telescopic night-sight. Hollie yelped and pressed her face into her father's chest. Her mother threw a protective arm around her daughter's shoulders and screamed at the press to go away.

"*Jävla skitstövel!* That is enough!"

Alex advanced three paces, grabbed Wilson by his left wrist, and twisted it outwards, away from his body. The reporter squealed, dropped the notepad, and snatched his arm away, elbowing the

Part 2

photographer in the process. The man's 35mm camera spilled from his hand and landed with an expensive-sounding crack on the border of ceramic flooring tiles surrounding the bar. Its telephoto lens snapped away from the camera's body, which broke with a loud crack. The lens rolled under a sofa.

The paparazzo's jaw dropped. He strangled a cry and dived to collect the broken pieces of his livelihood. Alex beat him to it and retrieved the camera. She snapped open the small retaining cover, removed the memory card, and dropped it into a discarded glass half full of red wine.

"Oops," said Alex, and frowned to Wash. "Is that what's called in England being a 'butter-fingers'?"

Wash smiled and wagged a finger at her.

"That's exactly what we say. You'd better apologise to the nice man. As I understand those things are rather pricey."

He took a step closer to Wilson.

"Now then sir, do you have any more ridiculous questions, or would you prefer me to charge you with obstructing a police inquiry?"

"Wanton destruction is what I call that … and assault. You wait 'til I have a word with my editor. You can't treat the press like this."

Before Charlie Pelham could intervene, Wash took an intimidating step towards Wilson, who backed into the bar and nudged a beer glass. It wobbled but didn't fall.

"I think you'd better leave before you cause any more damage, sir," Wash said, waving his hand dismissively. "As I understand it, those tumblers are nearly as expensive as this idiot's camera lens."

The reporter and his chastened colleague backed towards the exit accompanied by a round of applause from the smattering of first-class patrons.

"What the hell do you two think you're doing?" Charlie Pelham shouted, his ruddy, puffed-out face threatening to explode. "You can't go around attacking the press. We need to keep them on our side."

"Is that why you were sucking up to those bloodsuckers out there, Charlie?" Wash said, his finger pointing to the runway.

Alex turned her back on them and nodded to the constables who had formed a barrier in front of the Jardines. From the corner of her eye, she saw Charlie Pelham talking in a huddle with Lucas Wilson. They looked friendly—too friendly. Was the correct term, "thick as thieves"? She'd look up the phrase when she reached home.

They pushed their way through the concourse and shepherded the Jardines to a waiting border guard who did no more than glance at Hollie's passport and wave them along.

Alex followed in close attendance. Once outside the building, she telephoned Julie, said she loved her and was looking forwards to a hug, and asked her to put dinner on hold.

Chapter Eight

FRIDAY EVENING – Calls to home
Time since Ellis Flynn's stabbing: eight hours

THE BIG TRANSPORT helicopter banked and hovered above the farm, searching for a landing spot. One of Jean-Luc's men stood in the field on the other side of the wall waving a torch. A pair of powerful beams erupted from the chopper's underbelly, one from its nosecone and the other from its tail, shattering the dusk. The collar of Jones' boiler suit flapped at his neck. Choking dust coated his nostrils. He sneezed.

Before the helicopter touched down, Sergeant Brunö called and waved from his comms tent. His actions screamed "urgent".

Jones tried hard to follow the rapid, two-way radio conversation between Jean-Luc and someone, probably a colleague. His excitement rose when Jean-Luc mentioned Flynn's missing Citroën, but dipped again when the Colonel's shoulders sagged, his jaw clenched, and his voice took on a bitter edge.

Jean-Luc ended the radio conversation with what sounded like an expletive and slammed the microphone on the camping table.

He stormed from the tent and slumped against the cottage wall, ripping off the nitrile gloves and tucking them into his pocket. Jones couldn't help thinking how much support the old stone wall had offered them both that day.

The colonel stared at the ground between his feet and massaged his temples with his index and middle fingers.

"What's wrong?"

Jean-Luc stared up at Jones through heavy lids.

"My search teams found the empty Citroën of *monsieur* Flynn. Sixty-five kilometres west of here."

"Great," he said, "at last we've something to go on. The accomplice might have left some physical evidence behind."

The gendarme frowned and shook his head slowly.

"He left far more than that, *mon ami*." Jean-Luc glanced at Jones for a moment, unable to hide the pain and anger in his normally controlled expression. "The man abandoned the Citroën on a deserted road in the countryside. He tried to burn the vehicle, but there was no *essence*, er … petrol in the tank and the car did not ignite."

"Excellent, it means he couldn't destroy all the evidence and he can't have gone far."

Jean-Luc glanced at his open hands, they trembled.

"*Le salopard* stole another vehicle and murdered its driver in the process."

"Oh God."

"Yes. An old lady, *madame* Deauville. She had eighty-three years of age." Jean-Luc chewed on his lower lip and stared at the helicopter as it settled and cut its engines. "The murderer sliced her throat and dumped her body in a *fossé* … a ditch at the side of the road. *C'est catastrophique.*"

The anger on Jean-Luc's face told Jones plenty. Here was a man with genuine compassion. If Jean-Luc's benign and thoughtful treatment of Hollie hadn't told Jones enough about the man's character, his reaction to the news of yet another murder in his jurisdiction certainly did. Jones felt for the colonel, but an obvious question occurred and demanded an answer.

Part 2

Jones reached across to drop a hand on Jean-Luc's forearm but decided against it. Never one for the touchy-feely stuff, he allowed his arm to fall.

"I am so sorry, Jean-Luc, but how do you know the victim's name and age?"

"Excuse me? Oh, I see. The local gendarme recognised *la dame* from his village. He gave us a description of the missing car. A Mercedes Benz. My people are looking for her now. But it is strange, no?"

"What?"

"Why did *monsieur* Fat Face leave the victim's body at the side of the road where it would be found? Why not put her in the trunk of the stolen car?"

"Yes, I wondered that too. He's starting to make mistakes. How large was the victim?" Jones asked.

"One metre-fifty-five. Slim. No more than sixty kilos."

"Interesting. Even as dead weight, most men would be able to lift a body of that size into the car boot." Jones tried to think. "Is his physical condition, his limp, more debilitating than we thought? I wonder what's wrong with him."

A dull light switched on in Jones' head. Something scratched away at his mind, trying to dig to the surface. He'd missed something.

Come on man, think.

Jean-Luc jerked away from the wall and straightened his tunic, the professional demeanour restored.

Jones tried to clear his mind. The answer would come if he didn't try to force it. He looked down at their footprints in the dust.

Footprints.

"Bloody hell!"

"What is it, *mon ami*?"

"The prints by the camper. I'm a bloody fool."

Jones spun on his heels and sprinted across the concrete courtyard. Jean-Luc followed and his size twelve boots clomped in pursuit. As they darted around the corner of the house and approached the barn, Jones skidded to a halt and peered down. His shoulders sagged in much the same way Jean-Luc's had done a few moments earlier.

As he'd feared, the downwash from the helicopter had obliterated the scuffmarks in the dust. He turned to the slim Frenchman, whose breathing rate had barely increased while Jones sucked in air like an asthmatic in a dust storm. Sweat prickled his hairline and damp patches darkened the armpits of his fresh coverall.

"Jean-Luc, please tell me you had photos taken of the tracks."

"But of course. Sergeant Brunö has the images loaded onto the system. What do you have?"

"Not certain. I need to see the pictures."

The return march to the front of the house gave Jones time to clear his head and recover his breath. On the way, Jean-Luc spoke into his personal radio and, by the time they reached the courtyard, the quietly efficient Brunö had loaded a photo library onto his screen.

Jones leaned over the man's shoulder and peered at the main VDU screen.

"*Permettez-moi?*" he asked.

Wow, the schoolboy French is coming back.

Brunö raised his eyebrows, rose from his packing-crate seat, and indicated Jones should take his place. Jones sat still, trying to remember what to do to make the images scroll across the screen. He'd seen Phil, Alex, and Ryan do it hundreds of times. There was a button somewhere, but he'd never taken the time to learn how do to it himself.

Bloody idiot.

Jean-Luc came to his aide.

"Our photo gallery program must be different from yours, David. Click the enlarge button. It is the green icon with the big box. No, that is minimize. Up to the left. There. Now double click it with the left button. Now press that right arrow and you will advance the pictures one at a time. Hold it down to move quickly through the gallery."

Jones did as instructed and the image on the screen changed. In five taps, the picture he needed appeared, close-up and in brilliant colour.

"There. Do you see?" He pointed at the circular holes next to the scuffed shoe-prints. "What do they look like to you?"

"I do not know—a pole or a stick? A walking stick?"

"Yes. Don't know why I didn't think of it before."

The next thought hit Jones like a blow to the stomach and the temperature in the comms tent seemed to drop about ten degrees.

"Where exactly did Fat Face abandon the Citroën?"

"Huh?" Jean-Luc frowned. He was doing a lot of that recently. "What did you say?"

"Where did you find the Citroën?"

"It is due west of here, in the general direction of Brest."

He pointed to a place on the map Sergeant Brunö had uploaded onto his monitor.

Brest? Oh hell no.

"When was the old lady killed?"

"The local doctor puts time of death at between fifteen-hundred and sixteen-thirty hours. Why?"

"Don't you see? Fat Face was on his way to the airport. He's following the girl!" Jones checked the time on his watch: 20:38. The plane would have landed in Birmingham over an hour ago. "Hell, I need to call Alex. Right away."

With a growing sense of helplessness and desperation, Jones reached for his mobile and hit speed-dial #4 now he had a signal following Brunö's heroic efforts with the comms equipment.

While Jones paced the courtyard waiting for the call to connect, Jean-Luc took his place at the console and hit a series of keys before reaching for the microphone again. Jones pointed to the mike and raised his eyebrows in question.

A sparkle of excitement appeared in the Frenchman's eyes and he answered Jones' unasked question with a grim smile.

"I have an idea."

Jean-Luc raised an index finger for silence and turned his back to make the call.

Alex's mobile went straight to voicemail. Jones tried to convince himself she'd forgotten to turn her mobile back on after disembarking the plane. He left a message and dialled her landline.

"Hello? Alex?"

"Hi, you've reached the haven of peace that is the home of Julie and Alex. As you can gather, we're not here at the moment. Wait for the tone and, well … you know the rest."

"Alex?" Frustration combined with worry boiled Jones' blood. "If you're there, please pick up. This is DCI Jones … Alex? I tried your mobile but there's no answer. Listen carefully." He gave her the latest news and finished with, "Stay with Hollie at the hospital until I can organise a protection detail. The gendarmes have set up a satellite system so I can receive calls here now. Get back to me on my mobile as soon as you receive this message."

Jean-Luc had donned a headset and was now sitting in front of the TV monitor. He tapped at the keyboard and spoke in quick, authoritative bursts.

What's he up to?

Jones hit the #1 speed-dial and paced for an infuriating minute and a half before the desk-jockey answered.

"Holton Police Station Command and Control Unit. How may I direct your call?" The young woman's voice was hesitant. She sounded unsure of her lines.

"This is DCI David Jones, Serious Crime Unit. I don't recognise your voice. Who is this?"

"I'm sorry, sir, but I'm not at liberty to tell you my name at present. How may I direct your call?"

"Put me through to the senior duty officer on call, immediately."

"Sorry sir, but I have instructions not to put any calls through to the Superintendent until I have verified the caller's identification. May I have your warrant card number, please?"

Jones cursed under his breath and repeated his badge number by rote. "Now, please put me through to Superintendent Peyton. This is urgent."

"I am sorry, sir, but I am required to call you back to confirm you are who you say you are. Please hang up and I will call the mobile number we have on file."

Part 2

"Wait! I'm in France. You'll need to use the international dialling code—" The line fell silent. "Hello?"

The silence continued.

"Hello, are you still there? Damn it! What in the hell's going on?"

Jones snapped the phone closed and stared at its display clock. The seconds ticked by while he waited with growing anger for the idiot at the call desk to ring him back. After two minutes, he nearly threw the phone at the wall in frustration. He hit the redial button and, eventually, the same voice answered.

"Holton Police Station, Command and Control Unit, how may—"

"This is DCI Jones again. You rang off before I could tell you I am in France. Damn it woman, who are you?"

"I am the out-of-hours service receptionist, sir," she answered stiffly, "and there is no need for that tone."

"When did we outsource the reception desk?"

"My company took over this morning."

On a Friday? Why wasn't I told?

Jones paused a moment before saying, "I'm sorry, but this really is a matter of life and death. Please put me through to Superintendent Peyton. I promise you won't get into any trouble."

"One moment, sir."

After another endless pause, the line clicked and a loop of insufferable electronic music dripped water torture into his ear.

"That you, Chief Inspector?" Duggie asked after what seemed like an age.

"Superintendent Peyton. Sorry to be abrupt, sir, but you need to listen carefully. Hollie Jardine is still in danger."

"Hollie Jardine? You mean the runaway? DS Pelham briefed me this afternoon. I don't know what you thought you were doing running off to France on a whim. You'll have a disciplinary board to face when you return, you bloody fool. DC Olganski's in serious trouble too, but I guess we can protect her if she acted under orders."

"You heard what we found here?"

"Some sort of farm, right? Possible crime scene?"

"Yes, sir. And it's not just a farm, it's a house of horrors. Underground torture chambers, one-way mirrors, rusted knives, secret access points."

"Um ... oh dear. Serious eh? I suppose you ought to be congratulated for uncovering a major incident and apparently saving the girl, but you need to get back here, pronto. Leave the rest of the investigation to the French. The farm's on their turf and they can pick up the bill for the forensics. And by the way, who's paying for your little jaunt?"

Who's paying? What the bloody hell?

"If you're worried about the budget, sir, I'll cough for the damned tickets myself."

"Mind your tone with me, Chief Inspector. I'm your superior officer and don't you forget that."

Jones bit back the obvious knee-jerk response and spoke with as much calm as he could manage.

"Superintendent Peyton, I have reason to believe Hollie Jardine, the girl who was *abducted* yesterday afternoon, is still in great danger."

"Go on ... how?"

Jones told him about Fat Face, *madame* Deauville's murder, and the man's suspected destination.

"So what do you expect me to do at this time of night?"

"Call in an Armed Response Unit. I want a protection detail on the Jardines. Right now."

"Don't be so melodramatic, Chief Inspector. Miss Jardine and DC Olganski were met at the airport by her parents and four police officers, including DS Pelham and DC Washington."

"That's not enough. She needs an armed guard. We're talking about a multiple murderer here."

"Nonsense. The two constables will escort her to hospital and take turns on guard duty. I'm certainly not going to send in an ARU on the off chance a crippled man might be after her. Do you have any idea how much that would cost?"

"Damn the cost, sir. Hollie's life is in danger. Why the hell won't you listen?"

"Chief Inspector, don't you dare use that tone with me. I understand you're overwrought and wrapped up in this girl's story, but this is for your own good. We might be able to save your career now you've apparently rescued the girl from something distasteful, but if I send in an ARU on false alarm you'll be laughed off the force."

"What the hell's the matter with you … sir?" Jones couldn't prevent his voice rising to a shout. Jean-Luc and the stocky Sergeant Brunö turned to stare. He lowered his voice. "Let me ask you this. What happens if Hollie's killed on *your* watch, while I'm stuck here in France?"

Silence.

"Sir?"

"Listen. Tell you what I'll do. I'll run this past the Deputy Chief Constable and see if he'll okay the budget. I can't be fairer than that. In the meantime, you do what you can to smooth Anglo-French police relationships, and get back here on the next available plane. Let's see if we can't make this right. Okay?"

Damn your bloody eyes, sir.

Jones knew what the man was up to. Passing the buck upstairs, covering his useless arse. Superintendent Douglas Peyton was one of the worst kinds of police officers: useless, careless, and obstructive.

"Sir, you're breaking up. Hello? Did you say something? Can't hear you … battery's dying …"

Jones broke the connection and gripped the phone so hard his knuckles cracked. He wondered how much force it would take to break the casing. He also wondered what Jean-Luc was up to at the communications desk. But another question stood uppermost in his mind. This one wouldn't allow him to rest.

Why wasn't Alex answering her phone?

Chapter Nine

FRIDAY EVENING - ARTHUR "JENNINGS"
Time since Ellis Flynn's stabbing: eight hours, twenty minutes

JENNINGS SPENT A MONSTROUSLY frustrating twenty-five minutes stewing in the baggage area, waiting for his case to appear on the slow-moving beltway. He'd checked the bag into the hold at Brest to avoid it being searched, but the added delay was now causing him palpitations. A further quarter-hour spent in another apparently infinite queue at passport control had him spitting flames.

Despite the stomach-churning, fear-inducing attentions of a suspicious officer from the UK Border Agency, Jennings' second stolen passport—this one chosen to reflect his lack of hair and his natural eye colour, did its job, for the final time. He had plenty of other IDs ready to use. After today, John C Jennings would be no more. A name consigned to the dustbin of history. A past that never was.

He dropped his small bag onto a trolley and pushed it through

Part 2

to the concourse slowly to minimise his limp. He searched the forecourt. Where was Hammer and, more to the point, what the fuck did he look like?

Individuals, couples, family groups, uniformed officials, cleaners, and baggage-handlers driving carts towing trains of wire-encased luggage, all jostled for his attention and hampered his search. Old people pushed carts loaded with bags, and recent arrivals greeted loved-ones. The bastards all got in his way.

He climbed a staircase to a balcony for a better view and answered with relief the moment his phone vibrated.

"Yes?"

"Where are you and what are you wearing?" asked the deep-voiced Hammer.

Jennings told him.

"Scratch your ear. ... Okay, got you. Leave by Exit B. Head for the main car park. Walk slowly."

How else am I gonna fucking walk?

Hammer's voice hadn't lost any of its menace since the first call. In fact, knowing the man was so close made it even more threatening—if that were possible.

Jennings descended the stairs and crossed the hall as fast as his crumbling back would allow. He continued through the automatic exit doors, checked the signage, and turned left. He stopped every few metres to rest his back and give Hammer time to check for a tail.

A man materialised at his side, ghostlike, and said, "You're clear."

Jennings jumped.

Hammer?

Jesus Christ, where had he come from?

At least Jennings assumed it was Hammer. He hadn't heard the hired killer approach. One second he was alone, the next he had company. Simple as that.

The man didn't look particularly threatening, though. Average height and weight, bland face, no distinguishing features. He wore black trousers, dark trainers, and a dark blue polo shirt under a sober golf sweater, grey with a dark blue panther logo. He might have passed for a tourist in any airport in the world. The epitome of nondescript. Jennings grinned. Nobody would look at the guy twice. In fact, the perfect undercover killer.

"This way," Hammer said, and led him to an inconspicuous blue Nissan Micra.

Hammer keyed the lock, and Jennings dumped his bag on the back seat.

Once inside the car, Hammer removed a headphone bud from his ear. He pressed a button on the steering wheel and tuned the radio to the BBC news.

"You need to hear this."

Hammer's voice rumbled low in the car's confined cabin.

Jennings opened his mouth to ask a question, but Hammer raised a finger to his lips and pointed to the radio.

"Wait."

Who's the fucking boss here?

Jennings fumed, but he was not about to argue. Wouldn't want to antagonise a man with twenty-eight confirmed kills to his name, and that total was going to increase by at least two before the end of the week. Jennings bided his time, but he wouldn't be able to wait long before exploding.

While the late-evening news droned on, Hammer fired up the Micra and drove out of the car park at a sedate twenty-five mph. At least they were on their way. The movement went some way to calming Jennings' jangling nerves.

As instructed, Jennings listened to the radio and wondered what the fuck had happened to Hottie bloody Jardine.

A speech by the Chancellor of the Exchequer meant to calm the markets had led to a run on the pound. A hurricane in Guatemala had sucked the roof off a church and killed the congregation of one-hundred and twenty-odd pious souls.

"Here it comes. They broke the story before you landed," Hammer said, as their road merged with the A45, headed towards the M6, and Birmingham's City Centre.

"And finally, in a remarkable good-news story, we can tell you

Part 2

that the missing fourteen year-old, Hollie Jardine, has been found alive and well. She was rescued by Detective Chief Inspector David Jones of the West Midlands Police.

"The twice-decorated holder of the Police Bravery Award, and thirty-year veteran, DCI Jones and a colleague organised a joint operation with the Brittany police to rescue the kidnapped girl. It appears that the abductor, whose name has not been released, died whilst trying to avoid capture. But the details are …"

Jennings slammed his hand on the dashboard panel.

"The lying bastards. That's not what happened. Nowhere near!"

Hammer's mouth twitched. It was the first expression Jennings had seen on the hard man's immobile face.

"Hollie is now at the Queen Elizabeth Hospital, Edgbaston. When asked for details as to her condition, the hospital spokesperson refused—"

Jennings killed the radio and turned to face his hired assassin, careful not to hurt his aching back.

"You saw her get off the plane?"

Hammer nodded.

"Arrived just in time. The cops bypassed the standard arrivals gate and took her through the VIP lounge."

"What about the blonde copper, is she still with the little bitch?"

Hammer nodded his shaven head.

"Far as I know. Roy, my oppo, followed them in a taxi." He brought the Micra up to the maximum motorway speed—seventy mph. "Where to?"

Hammer kept his voice low, but it carried more than enough force to drown out the noise of the high-revving engine. Jennings wondered whether the man could shatter gravel with a voice that low.

"Call Roy-the-Nail. I want the bitch copper done right away."

Hammer's cheek twitched again.

"Roy-the-Nail? Hammer and Nail. Hmm. Hardly original."

Jennings shot a surreptitious glance at his driver whose dead, coal black eyes stared, unblinking, at the road ahead.

Despite the late hour, Friday night traffic on the M6 ground to an inevitable halt behind the usual gauntlet of road works and the sheer number of vehicles.

Hammer fished a mobile from his trouser pocket, pressed a button, and said, "Roy-the-Nail, speak to your new boss."

He handed the phone to Jennings.

"'Ello, Hammer. How's it hanging? What was that called me? The Nail? Ha. Love it."

"This is Mr Jennings. You've been following the copper, Blondie?"

"Oh, hello, sir. Er … yeah. That's right." The Nail's young voice, although normal, sounded almost feminine by comparison with his partner-in-killing. "She went straight home after dropping the girl at the hospital. Got here 'bout five minutes ago. Met a skinny brunette at the door and they kissed. Hey, what about that? The copper's a fuckin' dyke."

"Irrelevant. I want her and her partner dead by morning and I don't care how you do it. If there's a dog, a cat, or a fucking budgie kill them too. But watch out … Blondie looks like she can handle herself."

The Nail let out a high-pitched chuckle. The sound sent a minor tremor down the fine hairs on the back of Jennings' neck.

"I'd like to handle her, Guv, if you know what I mean. Tasty looking tarts, the both of them. Don't you worry 'bout nothing. I got it sorted. You want me to wait 'til you get here?"

Jennings pressed the mute button and turned to Hammer.

"The man sounds a bit … highly strung. You sure he knows what he's doing?"

"Huh?"

"The Nail, is he any good?"

Hammer glowered. "If not, I wouldn't have brought him along."

Jennings stared at Hammer. A cheek twitch and a glower, he wondered whether that was the killer's whole repertoire of visual emotions.

"What's his speciality?"

"Arson."

Part 2

"Perfect." Jennings released the mute. "Torch the place. Make sure neither of those bitches gets out alive."

Jennings cut the line on a second chuckle.

"Where to?" Hammer asked.

"I'm feeling a little unwell. Take me to the hospital."

―――

JENNINGS' personal killer-for-hire reversed the Micra into the nearest free space to the main hospital entrance. It wasn't that close.

"We're five bloody minutes' walk away from the admissions building. Bloody useless for a fast getaway with a reluctant passenger. And I don't like the idea of going in there under prepared." Jennings waved a hand in front of his face. "There'll be security cameras all over the place."

"No sweat." The man-of-few-words grunted as he retrieved a well-filled sports bag from the back seat. He peeled back the zip and handed Jennings a pair of tinted spectacles, and a flat-cap.

Jennings perched the glasses on his nose to find the blue lenses were non-prescription glass. He stuck the cap on his head and checked his "disguise" in the courtesy mirror. The change wasn't exceptional, but it would have to do. Perhaps he should have kept hold of the cheek implants.

"Have you got any cotton? Something to bulk out my cheeks?"

Hammer shook his head. "Keep your head down. Avoid the cameras."

Jennings sniffed.

"It'll have to do, I suppose. I want this done tonight."

Hammer dropped the sports bag into the foot-well and tugged the golf sweater and polo shirt over his head to reveal tanned skin, a rock-hard abdominal wall, and "Arnie" pecs. The man didn't carry a gram of spare fat. In the torso department, he looked like Ellis.

A curved tattoo above Hammer's left nipple read "Who Dares Wins", the motto of the British Army's Special Air Services. Jennings' admiration and awe for Hammer grew. His police mole, PDC, told him Hammer was ex-military, but the SAS?

Nice. Very nice.

Jennings' mouth dried as he considered Hammer as a possible replacement for the poor Ellis.

The hired gun tugged on a loose-fitting grey T-shirt and dropped a green baseball cap on his head, the peak facing backwards. What he did next astounded Jennings, and his respect for the assassin shot through the Micra's sunroof.

Hammer took a breath and closed his eyes. He rolled his head to loosen his neck, stretched his mouth into a thin grin, narrowed his eyelids into Oriental slits, and raised his eyebrows a couple of millimetres. At the same time, he hunched his shoulders and lost a couple of inches in height. Finally, he relaxed his stomach muscles and appeared to gain five kilos in weight.

The transformation was subtle, but astonishing. If he hadn't seen it happen for himself, Jennings wouldn't have believed it possible. The new-look Hammer appeared years younger and a continent away in terms of ethnic origin.

"Bloody hell. How'd you do that?"

"Practise," Hammer said, but kept in the new character. Even his voice had softened to a gentle whisper.

Jesus, the man's a freak.

"Did you bring the electronics?"

Hammer's hand dipped into the bag again and came out with a small, black case. He passed it to Jennings who worked the zip. A metal bug the size of five ten-pence coins stacked in a tower, rested snug in the centre recess. Two microphones with built-in transmitters, shaped like digital wristwatches, and two white plastic earbuds occupied another segment. He handed one to Hammer, and placed the other in his left ear.

"What's the range?"

"'Bout a mile, depending on the terrain."

Hammer had adopted an Asian accent. Hong Kong Chinese perhaps. Thai?

"Will they operate in a hospital?"

Hammer nodded.

"Dunno. Never tried it. Should do well enough."

Part 2

The one-way conversation had started to get on Jennings' nerves. Talking with this guy was like having root canal work done without anaesthetic, but there was no way he'd ever say so aloud. Hammer was nothing more than a hired gun. A skilled one, no doubt, but he'd turn on Jennings in a flash if someone else offered more money, or maybe just if he felt like it.

"What's your plan?" Hammer asked, staring out of the windscreen and focusing his attention on the hospital grounds. His eyes scanned left and right, up and down.

"I don't have the time to hack into the patient's database and there's no way they'll give me the girl's room number. I'll plant the bug near the reception desk and wait for someone official to ask for her."

"That's a bit hit-and-miss."

"Can't think of a better way."

Hammer sniffed again.

"I can."

"Really? What?"

"You want the girl alive?"

"Yes, I have plans for her."

"Complicates matters. I could go in and do a 'smash and grab'. Take a medic and force him to escort us to the girl."

"What about the police. Didn't she have a police escort?"

Hammer's upper lip curled.

"A brace of unarmed Woodentops? No worries there."

Jennings decided to up Hammer's fee and put him on retainer. Exclusivity of tenure might pay dividends in the long term. Since his illness, Jennings needed reliable muscle to compliment his superior mind, and he could definitely use a man with Hammer's particular skill set.

"I don't have a problem with you topping a couple of cops, but leave the parents alive if you can. Think of how they'll suffer when I take their cow of a daughter again. Exquisite punishment, I call that, but don't let things get too messy. While I eavesdrop at reception, you can take a scout around."

Hammer jerked his head up once in a curt nod.

"You're the boss."

Yeah, and don't you ever forget it.

Hammer took a watch from the little case and strapped it to his wrist. He tapped the surface. The sound transmitted through to the receiver in Jennings' ear.

"Hear that?" Hammer asked and opened the car door.

"Loud and clear."

"I'll be in touch."

The mechanic slung the strap of the small sports bag across his shoulder and sauntered towards the rear of the admissions block.

Jennings eased himself out of the passenger door and looked up at the hospital building. He shivered in anticipation. Hottie might well be behind one of the lighted windows facing him. He couldn't wait to meet her again and almost rubbed his hands together in glee.

It was so nice to be visiting an old friend in hospital.

Chapter Ten

FRIDAY EVENING – Forensics
Time since Ellis Flynn's stabbing: ten hours

AFTER ENDING the call to Duggie Peyton, the world closed in around Jones. He growled and kicked at a stone out of pure pent-up frustration. The stone bounced off a larger rock and ricocheted left to cut a small gouge into the side panel of the remaining SUV. Jones gasped and covered his mouth with his hand. The gendarmes had been nothing but helpful, and he had dented one of their trucks.

Bloody idiot.

Two of Jean-Luc's passing men shouted "Goal" and gave him a short round of applause. Jones shot them a relieved smile.

He tried to force his anger at Duggie Peyton's bloody-mindedness and stupidity to the back of his mind. The disciplinary situation would wait, but he needed to protect Hollie. If he couldn't go through Peyton, he'd have to go around. Hollie was his responsibility and he couldn't allow her to face more danger without proper protection. To make matters worse, Alex might find herself in the firing line, too.

Jones scrolled through his mobile phone's address book. The fourth name on his pitifully short contacts list, Giles Danforth, answered as soon as the number finished dialling.

"Hey, David, how are you? Still in Brittany?"

"Hi Giles. You've heard about my little … jaunt, then?"

"Are you kidding? You and Alex are the toast of the Division. Saving the girl was brilliant."

"Yeah, try telling that to Superintendent Peyton."

"That drunken old accountant giving you a hard time? Don't worry about him, mate. Nobody takes that fool seriously. I've heard rumours the Chief's trying to ease him out. Early retirement on health grounds."

Jones finally understood why Peyton was being even more of a pain than usual.

"Interesting. Sorry to be abrupt, Giles, but I need a favour."

"Name it."

"Are you sure? I'm overstepping my authority again. We're going to have to do this off-book."

"David, I said 'name it', and I meant it. What do you need?"

"Flynn had an accomplice. We suspect he might have travelled on the same plane as Hollie and Alex. Can you arrange a protection detail for the girl? They're on the way to Queen Elizabeth's."

"I know. It's all over the news."

"What? The press has the story already?"

"Yes. A whole press posse was waiting for them at the airport."

"Who the hell tipped them off?"

"No idea, but DS Pelham made a statement telling them where Hollie was headed. There's going to be a pack of journalists camped outside the hospital's front doors."

Jones pressed the mobile hard against his ear.

"Giles, you need to get there quickly. I tried warning them, but Alex isn't answering her mobile."

"Don't worry about it, mate. I'm on my way. Nothing better to do tonight but watch telly anyway."

"Giles, I'll owe you."

"Rubbish. I'll never forget what you did for me and Beth."

Part 2

"I've told you already, don't mention it. What else was I going to do? You were in Afghanistan and Beth needed help."

"Nevertheless, that stalker needed stopping, and I owe you big time. I'm on my way to the station to pick up my weapon first, but it's not far out of my way. When will you be back in England?"

"Next flight's not 'til tomorrow morning, so I'm stuck here overnight. Can you stay with Hollie 'til I get there?"

"Of course. I'll call a couple of my men. We'll mount a twenty-four hour guard until you say otherwise. You can make it official later. There's no problem in the short term, but we can't keep the Jardines under house arrest for the rest of their lives. We'll need to find this sicko. Whoever he is."

"I'm working on it. One more thing, can you make sure Alex goes home? If I know her, she'll want to stay and help. But she'll be exhausted."

"Will do. And get some shut-eye yourself. You sound knackered. Don't go overdoing it again. You aren't a kid anymore."

"No need to remind me. Learnt my lesson. But I'm not doing much here, offering advice only. Call me when you get to the hospital? My phone battery's dying so take this down just in case."

Jones dictated the number given him by Sergeant Brunö.

"Right. No probs."

"Thanks again, Giles," Jones said and ended the call.

Despite his relative youth, Giles Danforth was one of the most cool-headed, reliable police officers Jones had ever met. He felt a lot better knowing Giles was on board, but there were still plenty of things to worry about and questions to answer. Like where was Fat Face? And what the hell had happened to Alex?

———

DURING JONES' phone calls, the forensics team had disembarked the helicopter and started unloading their equipment. Within minutes, a petrol generator chugged in the background. Seconds after that, four halogen lamps on tripod stands illuminated a pathway from the chopper to the cottage. The French Scenes of

Crime Officers worked as a well-disciplined team and could have passed for a Formula One pit crew.

"David," Jean-Luc called, and pointed to the comms screen, his voice high-pitched and excited. "I have uploaded the closed-circuit film from the airport. Would you care to find out what our green-eyed and fat-faced murderer looks like?"

His eyes shone and the left side of his moustache rose as he broke into a lop-sided grin.

"How did you manage that?"

"I told you, David. We are a tight-knit law enforcement community here. All of our agencies work in close co-operation. My colleagues at the *gardes-frontières* sent us this video." He pointed to the screen with one hand and raised his microphone in the other. "As soon as we see the man with the limp I will have my friend on the other end of this telephone search the passenger records. Then, we shall have his name."

"Or at least the name he travelled under," Jones said. "I doubt he'll have used his real passport."

The black-and-white images reached them in such crystal clarity, Jones might have been sitting in front of his television at home. The time-stamp 17:33—twenty-seven minutes before departure—clicked at normal speed as the passengers paused at a barrier to show their passports.

Alex and Hollie appeared at the top left of the screen and advanced slowly. At 17:39, they reached the fair-haired border guard, exchanged a few words, and were waved through the gate.

The next few passengers aroused little interest. A family of three, a man, a woman, and a pre-teen child took an age to find their papers, but eventually exited, stage right. An elderly couple, both sprightly and neither with an uneven gait, followed without incident. A woman in light summer clothing, shoulders exposed, passed through next, but the next three in the queue, all men, drew Jones' close interest.

The first, squat and overweight, rolled forward, and presented his ID without fuss. He looked straight ahead and gave the camera a full-face shot. This was not a man in hiding, unless he was brazen in the extreme.

Man number two, slim, around six-feet tall, judging from his height in relation to the others in the queue, wore a baseball cap and sunglasses. The cap hid most of his clean-shaven, narrow-jawed face but he didn't seem to favour one leg over the other. When he reached the counter, the border guard spoke and the man removed the sunglasses, and the peaked cap, but turned his head away from the camera. The two spoke again and the security officer returned the passport. She waved him through with a nod and a smile. The slim man moved out of sight, keeping his head turned from the camera the whole way. Jones couldn't see much of the man's stride pattern, but something about his actions didn't look right.

"Can you roll the film back?"

Jean-Luc operated the keyboard and the movie stopped, rewound to the fat man's exit, and moved forward again, when the target reached the desk. The man removed his dark-glasses and ….

"There, did you see that?" said Jones. He wasn't able to stop his voice rising in pitch.

Jean-Luc frowned and shook his head. "No. What did he do?"

"He removed the sunglasses and hat with his right hand and lowered them to his left. He then took the passport from his pocket with the same hand."

"So?"

"Well, it's not efficient. His left hand should have come up to meet the right half way. Think about it for a second. It's the natural thing to do. His left hand stayed down at his hip the whole time … because it was holding a cane! Look. See how he keeps his face and his left side facing away from the camera? I know I'm right. That's our man."

He tapped the screen with a forefinger.

"But he does not limp."

"I bet that's because he's in a slow-moving queue. He's our target. I know it. The time-stamp reads 17:48. Can you use that?"

"Of course, *moment s'il vous plaît.*"

While Jean-Luc raised the phone and spoke to someone he called Annabelle, Jones studied the still image on the screen.

The man's baseball cap had a Lakers logo. It looked grey in the black-and-white picture. His ensemble included the glasses, a dark top, possibly a sweater or a hoodie, and dark trousers, not jeans. The shot cut off the man's lower legs so Jones couldn't make out his footwear. He tried to estimate the man's age from the way he carried himself and the little he could see of his face—mouth and jawline only. Jones' best guess put him at between forty and sixty. Not much to go on, but at least they were further ahead than they had been five minutes earlier.

Jean-Luc pointed to the screen.

"David, that man used the name, Jonathan C Jennings."

Jones repeated the name in his head and frowned.

Jonathan C Jennings.

The name seemed familiar, but he couldn't place it.

"Can you do an internet search from here?" he asked the colonel.

"But of course. We have access to the Interpol and Europol databases. Also Google and all the usual *moteurs de recherche*."

On Jean-Luc's instruction, Brunö retook his seat and ran the searches. Fifteen minutes of eyestrain netted them a grand total of three men in the Midlands region with the same name, but none looked even remotely promising. One, a convicted fraudster, resided at Her Majesty's Pleasure in Blakenhurst Prison, Redditch. A second played semi-professional football and had three unpaid parking tickets. The third turned out to be a retired Civil Servant renowned for his prize-winning vegetables.

Jones phoned Holton Police Headquarters again. This time the chastened receptionist put him straight through to the communications room. He issued search parameters: name, approximate height, age, IC1—White European—English-speaking according to border guard, Annabelle Dupré. He told them to get back with the results and asked Brunö to send them a still from the video. Jones knew the search would prove futile—there was no way their quarry would have used his real name, but he had to try everything.

Part 2

While waiting, Jones tried his go-to guy, but Phil Cryer failed him for once.

"Sorry, boss," Phil said after a couple of minutes racking his considerable memory database. "I've got nothing. Why do you ask?"

"We've a lead on Flynn's partner, but don't worry about it. You know me, never let anything lie."

Jones decided against telling Phil about the new threat to Hollie. Knowing his sergeant as well as he did, Jones wouldn't have been surprised for Phil to shuffle off to the hospital in Hollie's defence, and he daren't put temptation in his way. The thought of one limping man chasing another down endless hospital corridors might be of comic interest to a Hollywood film director, but Jones couldn't see the funny side.

Jones thanked Phil and ended the call but his internal warning mechanism screamed, jumped up and down in his head, and wouldn't let him rest.

Jonathan C Jennings. John Jennings. Jennings.

Why was the bloody name so damned familiar?

———

WHILE THE FRENCH SOCOs continued their unloading dance, Jones used the dying embers of his mobile battery to call England once more.

"Ryan? Where are you?"

"Hi, boss. Still at the airport, but I'm about to head back to the station. What's up?"

Jones gave him a brief sitrep.

"I've given your number to the techie guy here, Sergeant Brunö. He's sending you a still of the man we're looking for. When my mobile battery dies, you'll have to contact me through him. And, don't forget to forward the photo to DI Danforth."

"You want me to search the airport CCTV?"

"Yes please. Make sure you look for anyone Jennings might have met."

"Could be a struggle getting permission to scroll through the CCTV logs. You know what Airport Security's like these days."

"I know. Do your best. Raise a search warrant if you have to."

Jean-Luc didn't have any problems this end, damn it.

"What about Charlie Pelham?" Ryan asked. "Do you want me to call him in to help?"

"No," snapped Jones. "Keep that useless bugger well away from this. I've had more than enough of his … assistance."

Jones ended the call and turned his attention to the activity in and around the helicopter. While the setup operation continued it gave him more time to question a distracted Jean-Luc.

"What are you going to do about the other crime scene? I mean the Citroën?"

Jean-Luc thought for a moment before speaking.

"My officers have closed the road and a team of crash investigators is on its way from headquarters in Brest. Sadly, we have great experience of investigating road traffic incidents." He raised a fist to his nose and twisted. Jones recognised it the French sign for alcohol overindulgence. "You understand?"

Jones nodded.

"And the victim?"

"The body of *madame* Deauville will be taken to the morgue in Brest. I have asked our Medical Examiner to conduct a preliminary post mortem examination overnight. Perhaps the old lady put up a fight. Scratched the man, Jennings? Evidence under her fingernails might help identify the monster? One lives in hopes, yes?"

A gendarme appeared armed with two mugs of steaming coffee and two baguettes on a tray. Jones wondered how these guys managed to find fresh bread in the middle of nowhere in the middle of the night. He suspected the forensics team might have brought a baker along to add a touch of home comfort to a place that had already taken on the appearance of a holiday campsite—albeit a deeply sombre one.

Jones blew across the top of his coffee and took a careful sip. This time the expected sugar-and-caffeine-rush came as less of a shock. If he spent enough time in France he might be able to get used to the burnt, bitter flavour of coffee, but he longed for a nice big mug of comforting, unsweetened tea. He bit into the sandwich and his salivary juices flowed again. He couldn't identify the filling, but the salty meat and sliced pickles tasted as good as anything he could remember.

"And the Citroën itself?" he asked between chews.

Jean-Luc had accepted the coffee but rejected the baguette. He took a sip and kept his eyes on the progress of his men.

"We will take crime scene photographs and then the *voiture* will be sealed under a tarpaulin and transported to our garage in Brest. Once there, my men will examine it under the microscope. It is the only way to inspect the vehicle correctly. Is that the procedure you would adopt in England?"

"Pretty much. It should be fine so long as none of the evidence is lost in transit."

"Oh no, David. We will place the protected vehicle inside a covered truck. I can assure you, any evidence will remain secure. I am also going to have the crime scene examined for one kilometre either side of the vehicle, in accordance with our normal protocol." He looked up at the sky. "Unfortunately, my men cannot begin the search now, since there is not enough light. The fingertip search will commence at dawn."

"I don't suppose there are any CCTV cameras along the route near the incident."

"Alas no. It is the middle of the countryside. And what about you, David? Everything is well in England? You were having trouble, I think?"

"My superintendent isn't happy about my unsanctioned visit to Brittany, but I'm more worried about Jennings and his plans. I've taken steps to protect Hollie, but it can only be a temporary measure."

"You would prefer to be in England than here?"

Jones shot Jean-Luc a pained smile and nodded.

"I'm sorry."

"I understand, *mon ami*. I therefore release you from your promise to help with my investigation. Those alive deserve our priority. More so than the dead, I think. You are free to return to England on the first flight tomorrow."

"Jean-Luc, you are a gentleman. I'll help as much as I can until then, but to be honest, nothing I've seen here suggests you need me to hold your hand. I'd say you know exactly what you're doing. My time would be better spent finding the animal responsible for this setup." He nodded toward the barn. "And I think I can do that much better in England. Don't forget, I'll only be a phone call away."

"*D'accord*. But in the meantime, you may find this interesting." He pointed to a tall man who organised his forensics team like a conductor. The only thing missing was a white baton. "That is *capitaine* Gérard Assante, a highly capable man. I will afford you the introductions as soon as I have briefed him. You can see we have enough people to analyse the *camping-car*, the cellar, and the room under the barn simultaneously, yes?"

Jean-Luc touched the peak of his *képi* and marched towards Assante.

Jones watched in fascination as four of Jean-Luc's gendarmes manhandled a large canvas sack from the helicopter. They placed it on a flattish area of the pasture Jones had crawled through earlier that day, and untied the straps holding the bag together. Six side-flaps opened like the petals of a flower reaching for the sun. Jones recognised the contents as a furled tent, which he guessed would become the camp's centre of operations.

Wow, these boys are good.

Chapter Eleven

LATE FRIDAY EVENING – *Roy-the-Nail and Nobby*
Time since Ellis Flynn's stabbing: ten hours, fifteen minutes

IN A DARKENED ALLEYWAY, hidden between two privet hedges, Roy-the-Nail Harper watched for the lights to go out in the end-of-terrace house across the street—Blondie's house. Two fucking long hours he'd waited in the dark for the bloody women to turn in, and his patience was wearing precious thin. When the front room light finally went out to be replaced by one upstairs at the front, his long vigil approached its end. He smiled and licked his lips.

The Nail. Excellent.

When Hammer gave him his new moniker, he couldn't have been more pleased. Ecstatic even. The Nail. Absolutely fan-fucking-tastic. It still made him grin, but the long wait had dampened the buzz slightly.

Three years it had taken him to earn a cool street-handle. He'd have preferred 'Torch' or 'Pyro', but 'The Nail' would do well enough.

Hammer and Nail.

He repeated it in his head while he waited for the upstairs lights in the house across the street to go out.

Hammer and Nail.

It had a good vibe to it, powerful, and it locked him in with the right people. Gave him the handle he wanted. Hard as Nails. Roy-the-Nail.

Fuckin' ace.

Now he had to earn it. His first kill as Roy-the-Nail had to be a real "spectacular". Like 9-11 and the 7/7 London bombings, but on a smaller scale. More intimate.

Yeah, lovely word, "intimate".

Like the flames themselves, warm and engulfing, sensuous.

For as long as he could remember, flames had always made him feel special. He learned how to control them from an early age. Hammer actually called him a natural. A genius when it came to setting fires, but not when it came to controlling his needs, his desires. He'd worked on the self-control over the years, more recently under Hammer's tutelage, and now they'd finally accepted him into the fold.

As his wait continued, the neighbourhood grew more and more quiet, until most of the lights in the road had gone out. Every second streetlight was busted, including the one outside Blondie's house, which left the place in near total darkness. A real plus. Couldn't have been better for what he had in mind.

By ten-thirty, the traffic along the dead-end street had all but fizzled out. Nobody had passed his hiding spot for half an hour. Such a different place. Unlike this shitty hick town, London never slept. The Nail couldn't wait to get back home.

"Come on, come on," he muttered. "Turn the fuckin' lights off."

What was the point of being dykes if they weren't gonna hop into bed at the drop of a dildo and screw each other's brains out? Blondie had been away. They should have loads to get off their chests.

Finally, the light he'd been watching snapped off. The Nail pumped his fist and bared his teeth.

Part 2

"Yes," he hissed. "'Bout fucking time."

He waited another half hour and was ready to cross the road when a light broke the gloom somewhere behind the house. Its glow lightened the sky for a moment, and then vanished. He settled back into the shadows again.

What the fuck was that? What was out back? Had to be gardens. A neighbour pissing on his flowers or summat. Someone kicking the cat out for the night, maybe.

A white van pulled up and parked in the only available spot, blocking his view.

Bastard.

The van driver slammed the door closed behind him, and the Nail dragged his eyes to the lit match as the man paused to spark up a fag before moving away.

The Nail had to change position to reclaim his view of the house. All dark again. But there had been a light. No matter, he'd just have to wait a little longer, that was all.

He spat into the hedge and stayed put another fifteen minutes.

Nothing had stirred in Blondie's house for the best part of half an hour, so the little darlings were probably sleeping off the passion. The Nail wished he'd seen them going at it, naked and sweaty, but the fire would make them hot enough, as it would him. He grinned in advance of the delights to come.

Roy-the-Nail closed his eyes and saw the dream once more.

A man lying on the big messy bed. Passed out dead drunk after thumping his kid and wife—again. A lit fag falling from clumsy fingers and igniting the old bastard's spilled whiskey. The sheets catching and going up with a whoosh. Scorched flesh melting. The pork-like smell of roasting human meat and singed hair filling his young nostrils. The agonised screams of the dying man turned him on, big time. Always had, always would.

The Nail's excitement grew.

If he didn't set the fire soon, he'd explode. He couldn't wait to get on with it. This was going to be a good one. A couple of dykes, and one of them a cop. Things didn't get much sweeter than that.

After checking once more for pedestrians, he darted across the road, vaulted the low brick wall into the front garden, and made it to the side of the house in seconds. His breath came in short gasps as he melted into the comforting shadow cast by the fence.

He used to toss off when setting fires, but Hammer told him not to leave any trace.

"DNA doesn't survive flames," the Nail had told the killer, but the guy looked right through him and said, "You want to work with me, you learn my rules. Never take any unnecessary risks. Right?"

And that was that. He learned the rules of Hammer's little game and now he'd hit the big league. His first paid contract, although he'd gladly do the work for the pure pleasure—plus expenses.

The Nail crept along the paved path, skirted the side of the house, and pressed an ear against the glazed panel in the back door.

Silence.

His pulse quickened. Not long now.

The door wouldn't budge, but a child could have picked the three-lever mortise lock. Wouldn't cause him any trouble as long as they didn't have a chain or security bar on the other side. He'd studied the front of the house long enough to know they didn't have a burglar alarm.

Bloody morons.

A cop should know better.

Twenty-three seconds it took him to get in. He counted the time off in his head. The door opened into a small kitchen. He reached into his pocket for the special pipe-smoker's lighter and cupped his hand around the ignition nipple. With one light press of the starter button, a two-inch yellow flame with a deep blue core fired out of the blackened nozzle. The combination of the smell from the burning lighter fluid and the heat from the flame was intoxicating, and the accompanying hard-on was as familiar as it was welcome. He smiled when the flame showed him the gas hob on the cooker. The thing even had a gas-fired oven.

Mains gas.

Fuckin' aces.

Could this get any sweeter?

This was going to be no challenge at all. He'd use the bag of tricks slung over his shoulder for insurance, but he was almost disappointed. For a moment, he considered setting the electronic timer on the central-heating boiler and opening up all the burners on the cooker, but thought better of it. Instead, he followed Hammer's mantra: plan everything, don't take any risks, no showboating.

Hammer was a scary bugger, cut out a load of the Nail's fun, but the ex-soldier was right. The Nail would 'KISS' it: Keep It Simple, Stupid.

He estimated the volume of the room and worked out the time it would take the gas to fill the kitchen and combust. He did the calculations in his head. This was going to be a low-tech boom—but none the less effective for it.

A noise upstairs. A creaking floorboard, and then another followed by a third.

What the fuck?

The Nail froze. Held his breath, and pulled a switchblade from his jeans pocket. So what if one of them came downstairs? He'd have preferred a flame, but a knife would do the job well enough. Up close might be even better. With a flick, the stainless steel blade snapped open and flashed in the flame from the lighter. He scooted across the floor, hid in the space behind the internal door, and extinguished the flame.

He waited.

An upstairs door opened on squeaky hinges and closed with a soft click. A dribble of urine passing through a drain followed by a flushing toilet allowed him to relax. The footsteps retraced their path through the upstairs, presumably to the bedroom.

He stood in the corner of the kitchen behind the closed inner door and waited. If one of the dykes needed the loo, perhaps the other would follow. Time passed slowly. He waited a full ten minutes to ensure the women upstairs had gone back to sleep.

Scary how noisy an old house could be at night. The place creaked, groaned, and sighed like an old man stretching out the kinks in his back. But the upstairs doors stayed silent and the footsteps didn't return.

The Nail sheathed the blade, shrugged off his backpack, and

pulled out a glass bottle containing his favourite homemade combustive preparation. He opened the oven door and poured the colourless, odourless liquid into a crusty black roasting tray.

The Nail was unable to contain a smile of pure glee as he set the oven regulator to '1' but didn't press the ignition button. He left the drop-down door slightly ajar.

Back up to the hob, he lit the smallest gas burner and set it to the lowest flame. And that was that.

The smell of his best mate, North Sea Gas, or more precisely, the smell of the odoriferous safety additive, *ethyl mercaptan*, seeped into the small room.

Christ, what a rush.

It would take around fifteen minutes for the gas to reach enough density to ignite. When it did, the smallest of flames would set off the concoction in the roasting tray and … *kaboom!*

Oh Jesus, what a sound. What a sight. What a smell.

The Nail breathed in deeply and released the air slowly.

That's it, time to go.

He re-locked the back door behind him and jammed a match into the keyhole; he always carried backup matches in case the lighter failed. It paid to have a failsafe option. He was careful like that. If the smell of gas woke the dykes, they wouldn't be able to get out the back door. Climbing through windows would take time, as would making their way through the house to the front door.

All bases covered.

The Nail sauntered across the tiny front lawn, hopped over the wall, looked left, and then right before strolling along the pavement. A smile formed on his face so wide he knew it would show his immaculate front teeth.

Without a care in the world, Roy-the-Nail strolled onwards and didn't look back.

———

RETIRED STAFF-SERGEANT NORBERT GERALD WINTERTON, Royal Electrical and Mechanical Engineers, "Nobby" to his family and friends, stirred from his comfortable but worn armchair. He rubbed heavy lids with the heels of his hands and struggled, groaning, to his feet. Scruffy, his aging black-and-white border collie, raised his head, and stared at him through pleading, cloudy eyes. His tail beat fast against the threadbare carpet.

Nobby smiled down at his best friend.

"Yes, okay boy. We're going *walkies*."

The dog leapt to attention and, on command, scampered to collect his lead from the hall table. Paws scrabbled and scratched on the faded vinyl flooring. He returned with the leather strap clamped in eager jaws.

"That's my good boy."

Nobby rubbed the sensitive spot behind Scruffy's ears and the dog's eggbeater tail swished with delight. He barked once, and once only. A single bark was all Nobby allowed him. Scruffy's pink tongue tickled the inside of Nobby's wrist.

"We can't go far tonight, lad. Hip's playing up big time, and I'm afraid it's a little late. Your Daddy's a thoughtless old man, isn't he? Yes he is. Leaving it 'til now to take you out. And look at you, boy. You're getting as tubby as I am. We both need the exercise, eh?"

Scruffy panted as Nobby straightened from attaching the leather strap to his collar and groaned. He clutched at his hip and waited for the spasm to recede. Bloody useless thing got worse every single day. He'd been waiting sixteen months for an operation. Last time he checked, he was no further up the queue than when his consultant first put him on the cutting list. No chance of going private, neither. The pension barely stretched to food for him and Scruffy, let alone for the surgeon's knife.

"Still," he told the dog, "mustn't grumble. There's always someone worse off than you are. Ain't that right, boy?"

Nobby looked at his front room and shook his head. He hadn't decorated the place since Maire died back in '01.

Strewth, she'd been gone nearly twenty years? Poor Maire. God love her.

He should have stripped the wallpaper and spruced up the place years ago. Now he could barely walk to the park to let Scruffy do his business. Decorating was out of the question. He had no family left alive to help either. Pete died in Iran, and little Andy had given up the fight as a baby. Chemo didn't work so well back in the '60s. Nothing did.

Nobby sighed and patted Scruffy's flank gently. The dog stared up at him with the patience of a St Bernard in the summer, but the tail maintained its frantic rhythm.

Nobby sighed again and tugged on his best friend's lead.

"Come on, boy. Let's go. But remember, slowly, slowly. I can't walk so fast no more. Now, to heel, lad. To heel."

Scruffy circled around behind, and followed close to Nobby's right leg.

"Good boy," Nobby said, and limped towards the front door.

He grabbed his walking stick and his light summer jacket, and pushed through to the path, but not before locking the door firmly behind him. Couldn't be too careful these days. There had been a time when leaving the doors unlocked would be safe, but not today. Not anymore. Burglaries and muggings in the area worsened every bloomin' year. He'd even been warned about a local street-gang. Christ, the neighbourhood resembled a battleground some weekends.

How times changed.

Outside, the road was dark.

Intermittent streetlights offered patchy light, but Nobby tramped familiar streets with his companion half-a-pace behind. Straight on past the off-licence, he avoided the pothole near the pillar-box and turned left at the railings on School Lane. Twenty-five metres later, he turned right into Hobb's Lane—and crashed straight into a scrawny youth who barrelled towards him, head down.

Their shoulders collided and the youngster pushed him away with a straight-armed punch to Nobby's chest.

Nobby's hip clicked and a stabbing pain shot through the back of his leg. He grunted and tottered backwards. His breath caught in his throat and his lungs struggled to take in enough air.

"Fuckin' 'ell, Granddad," the ignorant delinquent yelled. "Open your eyes, you useless old bastard."

Part 2

The young man stepped back and raised a fist. Nobby flinched at the expected blow and raised an arm in defence. Scruffy, the brave little lad, darted forward and planted his forepaws out front and wide, standing at hound attention. He exposed his fangs and let out a series of increasingly angry, howling barks interspersed with deep-throated growls. Nobby struggled to hold him back. The ignorant bugger might have been carrying a knife. Scruffy stood brave and tall, and refused to quieten.

The thug danced back a pace or two and ducked his head. The baseball cap hid his face.

"Keep that fuckin' mutt of yours under control, Granddad or I'll 'ave the fucker put down."

"Up yours," Nobby shouted, hiding his fear with bravado. It wasn't Nobby's fault if the ignorant cretin was in too much of a hurry to look where he was going.

The young arsewipe stepped into the road and took a wide berth to avoid the near-hysterical dog. He shouted, "Cock-sucker," and hurried away without a backward glance. A few seconds later, he disappeared down a street the other side of the school buildings.

"Good boy, Scruffy."

Nobby ignored his hammering heart and the stabbing pain delivered by his worn-out hip, and bent at the waist to pat his best friend's head. "You're a big brave boy. Probably saved me from a thumping." He sucked in a breath and added, "Thirty years ago, I'd have taken that young sod apart, but that was then. That's a good boy. You can quieten down now, lad."

Scruffy soon calmed enough to lick Nobby's hand. He wagged his tail again and silence returned to the deserted street. With an extended grunt, Nobby straightened. He dug a fist into his buttock and tried to massage the pain away.

Bloody hip.

Nobby continued their interrupted walk.

"What a nasty little toerag, eh boy? It's the parents I blame. Gave him no respect for his elders."

Scruffy padded closer to heel. His tongue lolled to the side and his breathing subsided. Nobby tried hard to calm down, but he panted worse than his heroic little dog.

"C'mon, Nobby," he muttered to himself. "You faced worse than that in the Falklands."

Nobby took another five paces and …

Whoompf!

The end-of-terrace house on his right disappeared in an explosion of noise and light. The roar sent Nobby right back to June 14th 1982, the horror of war—the battle of Mount Tumbledown, Falkland Islands.

Screams, the insistent boom-crack-boom of cannon and light-artillery, flying shrapnel, choking black smoke, noise, and more screams. Always the screams. Tracer bullets flew through the air in fiery white-orange parabolas. His best mate, Graeme Wilkinson, died that night, torn apart by a grenade.

The well-remembered images flashed through Nobby's mind. He staggered, but kept his feet.

Bloody Argies. Where's my chuffing rifle?

"Wilko? Where are you, mate?" he screamed. "Wilko!"

The smell of gas snapped Nobby back to the present.

A second bright yellow flash followed by a blast of superheated air punched him to his left. Something hard and angular struck his right arm, between wrist and elbow, shattering the bones and sending an electric shock of agony through his forearm. A blow to the back of the head, and another to his knee dropped him to the pavement.

A fraction of a second after Nobby met the ground, another shockwave hit, bringing with it rubble, dust, and shards of flying glass.

Debris and building material peppered his back. Reflexively, his left arm flew up to protect his head from shrapnel. The broken arm wouldn't move.

Scruffy yelped once and fell silent.

Oh God, Scruffy?

Car alarms, activated by the blast-wave, burst into a cacophonous, tuneless chorus, but the ringing in Nobby's ears drowned most of it out.

Acrid black smoke stung his eyes and singed the little hairs inside his nose. He sneezed, violent and shuddering. The edges of his broken bones grated together and sent a new wave of pain through to his brain. He groaned and rolled onto his side to seek relief. Strangely enough, his hip didn't hurt as new agonies overpowered the long-term ache.

"Scruffy? Where are you, my boy?"

He could hardly hear himself above the roar of the bright orange flames, the car alarms, and the ringing in his ears. Great tongues of mustard-yellow fire consumed the front of the gutted house. Nobby pushed with his good arm and struggled to a seated position. He wished he hadn't.

A wave of nausea brought with it the remains of his evening meal as he caught sight of his beloved Scruffy.

"Oh Jesus, no."

His poor broken dog lay three feet away in a tangled, crumpled heap. A triangle of glass sprouted out of his ribcage. A growing pool of blood bloomed on the pavement under the hideous gaping wound.

"Scruffy? Oh God, Scruffy!"

At the sound of Nobby's voice, the old dog flicked his tail and tried to raise his head.

Scruffy whimpered.

Blinded by smoke and tears, Nobby dragged himself by his working arm and leg to the side of his dog and rubbed his friend's nuzzle.

Scruffy licked his hand once.

"Scruffy, Scruffy, boy. Stay with me. Please."

The dog stilled. The blood-pool on the pavement stopped growing.

In Nobby's devastated mind, Scruffy and Wilko lay side-by-side on the concrete paving slabs.

Nobby hugged his dog the same way he'd hugged Graeme Wilkinson all those years ago, and he wept.

A QUARTER MILE AWAY, the boom made Roy-the-Nail come in an exploding orgasm of pure, trembling joy.

He stopped, leaned against a nearby fence, and turned to soak in the glory of his work. The sky laughed with a gorgeous orange glow. No sunset or sunrise had ever been as beautiful.

The Nail thought about the geriatric and the vicious fucking hound. Would the old bastard be able to recognise him later? On the other hand, they had been headed in the right direction and the timing was pretty good.

With any luck, the old fucker and his mutt would have joined the dykes in the firepits of Hell.

Roy-the-Nail grinned, gave a little fist pump, performed a two-footed Ali shuffle, and began his search for an old car to steal. London beckoned as did a date with a nice piece of skirt—a very nice piece of skirt indeed.

He started whistling. Life was good. Things were on the up.

Like the house he'd just torched.

Chapter Twelve

LATE FRIDAY EVENING – ARTHUR "JENNINGS"
Time since Ellis Flynn's stabbing: ten hours

JENNINGS SQUIRMED IN HIS SEAT. The half-hour spent in the hospital waiting area, coupled with the delay at the airport had sent his blood pressure into the stratosphere. Although the last one had done little to help, he popped another pill.

The bug he'd placed behind a flowerpot on the reception desk had told him nothing. Nobody near the counter said word one about the girl. Jennings wondered how long he'd be able to keep still before exploding with frustration when the earwig clicked and Hammer's voice crackled in his ear.

"*The girl's … ward … oom 151. Over.*"

Jennings raised his hand and whispered into the wrist microphone. "You're breaking up. Say again."

"*…moved to the window. That any better? Over.*"

"Perfect. What did you say?"

"*I've found the girl. Private ward on the fifteenth floor. Take a lift to the fourteenth and climb up from there. I'll meet you on the landing. Over.*"

Jennings hesitated for a moment.

"Right. I'm on my way."

"*Can you climb stairs? If not, I can do this alone. Over.*"

Jennings bit back his immediate response. For fuck's sake, who did the arrogant prick he think he was talking to?

"Yes, I can climb stairs," Jennings hissed through clenched teeth. "Don't do anything 'til I get there. I want to see the look on her face when we take her."

Jennings struggled to his feet and located the bank of four lifts at the far end of the ground floor. He chose a route that took him past the reception desk to retrieve his bug. For once, he didn't try to minimise his shambling gait. If there was one place a limp wouldn't raise any interest, surely it would be a hospital.

He exited the brightly lit metal box at floor fourteen and followed a sign pointing to the staircase.

He lifted his wrist to his lips and whispered. "Where are you?"

"*Room 151. Top of the stairs. First door on the left. Over.*"

"What? I told you to wait for me. Damn it."

"*It's sorted. Get up here. Over.*"

What did the fucker mean by "sorted"? That was the trouble with having to hire others to do his dirty work. If his fucking back weren't so damned useless, he'd have done the heavy lifting without help. Degenerative spondylitis, a rare spinal condition that caused his vertebrae to crumble, and he had to have it.

God's fucking whacked out sense of humour.

Jennings climbed the stairs slowly, leading with his right leg, the left dragged behind like a reluctant schoolchild on its way to the headmaster's office. By the time he made the fifteenth floor landing, he was in a bath of sweat and a mood as black as the floor tiles.

The exit door pulled open on silent, recently-oiled hinges. On the private ward, Jennings would have expected nothing else.

He poked his head out into the spotless carpeted corridor stretching out to his right. Colourful landscape prints adorned the walls. Dark-wood shelves carrying cut flowers lined the spaces between the doors to the private rooms. The scent of flowers and the serenity reminded him of a funeral parlour.

Part 2

So fitting.

Jennings edged through the door. Voices from the far end of the corridor sent him diving back into the stairwell, breathing hard. He pressed his ear to the wooden panel and waited for a count of twenty before cracking open the door again, no more than a centimetre, to listen. The sounds died away.

Jennings ventured into the hall again, half expecting to see a couple of uniformed coppers on duty outside Hollie's room—or their dead bodies lying on the floor. He found nothing but the empty hallway.

Jennings followed Hammer's terse instructions and paused outside the door. What was he going to find behind it, a battlefield? An abattoir?

INSPECTOR GILES DANFORTH, team leader of the Midlands Constabulary's Armed Response Unit, dressed in civilian clothes, parked his unmarked police car in a space reserved for hospital consultants. In his experience, the chances of a consultant needing the space so late in the evening were as close to zero as anyone could imagine.

He jogged along the pavement and sidestepped his way through a scrum of reporters prowling the entrance. Without doubt, the news editors considered the story of Hollie's rescue and return to the UK as worthy of column inches, and hours of airtime. Big news. Happy news.

Representatives from both the national press and television news combined with the local hacks. Two white vans parked close to the ambulance bays, each adorned with satellite dishes, received the close attention of a gaggle of security guards. Giles smirked as he passed one uniformed jobsworth who demanded the vans be moved or he'd organise a tow-truck.

The automatic double-doors slid apart and Giles rushed to the main reception desk, ignoring the couple of dozen patients sitting in the waiting area. He flashed his warrant card discreetly at the receptionist and asked for Hollie Jardine's room number. The large-boned woman in a white lab coat, Pamela, according to the name-badge attached to the lapel, took his ID card and studied it closely through half-moon spectacles. The woman owned the tired eyes and waxy complexion of someone who spent too many hours indoors and too few hours on the exercise mat. She compared his face with the photo on the card, and jotted his name and serial number on a pad before handing it back.

"Come on, Miss," he said. "This is urgent. Hollie Jardine could be in danger." He opened his jacket and showed her his holstered handgun.

The woman's eyes bulged.

"D-do you mean the girl from France?" Giles nodded. "I … think they may have taken her to the private ward. Top floor. I'll look … one second."

She turned, tapped at her keyboard with trembling fingers, and strangled a curse when she made a mistake and had to retype.

While he waited, Giles scanned the people occupying the overcrowded lobby. The photo he had of Jennings passing through passport control at Brest Airport didn't help much. No doubt, the evil bastard would have changed clothes since then. No telling what he wore now.

Giles let his instincts take over.

The instructors had trained him to study crowds for anything out of place, unnatural—things that didn't fit. Search for eyes looking one way, while everyone else looked the other. Watch for people who didn't stare when they were supposed to. For people who smiled when others frowned, or vice versa.

What about the young guy standing in the corner by the water fountain? Why did he search the faces of the people in the waiting area? Why didn't he take a drink? Check his clothes. The youngster wore a thin T-shirt, tight trousers, and trainers. Giles doubted Mr T-shirt could be hiding anything bigger than a knife under those threads and dismissed him as an immediate threat.

Most of the people in the chairs, lost in their private worlds of pain and impatience, paid no attention to anyone else in the room. None were worthy of serious consideration.

A woman with a black eye and a cut lip cried silent tears. She was either a first-class actor, or an innocent patient awaiting care. The man in the next seat had an arm around her as though to console, but, judging by the woman's body language, she took no comfort from his touch. Mr Wife-beater gabbled into a mobile phone, ignoring the signs on the wall telling him to switch off the device. Mr Wife-beater didn't worry about rules. A bastard, thought Giles, but not the specific bastard he was searching for.

A thin-faced man with five-o'clock shadow, wearing a grey baseball cap caught his attention. Mr Shadow sat in the corner at the back, scanning the room as avidly as Giles.

Watch him, Giles. Something's off there.

The SIG Sauer P226 in the holster under his armpit gave him some comfort. Its twenty-shot magazine held 9 millimetre Parabellum rounds. The gun had enough stopping power to halt a charging rhinoceros. At least that's what the manufacturers claim. Giles was unlikely to ever test it on such a target.

The last time he'd drawn the lightweight firearm for anything other than target practice, he'd killed an armed robber. Two years ago.

"Excuse me, Inspector." Pamela leaned towards the speech portal cut into the Perspex security barrier and spoke quietly. "Hollie Jardine is on the fifteenth floor. Room 151, in the private recovery ward. You can take the express lift. The pass code is 1984."

She pointed to a bank of lifts behind and to his right.

"1984, eh?" he grinned. "Very Orwellian."

The woman looked confused.

"Sorry, sir?"

Clearly no fan of modern classic literature.

"Never mind. Thanks for your help."

Giles turned away and headed to the service area. A glance at the reflection in a plate-glass window showed Mr Baseball Cap rushing to embrace a young woman with her arm in a sling and a plaster cast on her wrist.

Nice one Giles. Read him totally wrong, didn't you?

Giles hit the final number in the sequence and the express lift doors opened with a verbal warning, "Mind the doors, please".

He took one look at the crumpled body on the floor in the far corner and yelled over his shoulder, "Nurse! There's a man down."

The man on the floor—green hospital scrubs, plastic clogs, mussed blond hair, pale skin, blue lips—didn't move.

Jesus.

David was right.

Giles rushed into the lift and placed an index and forefinger to the man's cold neck.

No pulse.

Crap!

Two faint bruises showed on either side of the fallen victim's throat. Giles recognised the marks as the result of a lock-down hold, the so-called "extended sleeper". Because of its inherent danger, only highly trained operatives used such a precision manoeuvre. Whoever used the hold on the poor chap either screwed up big time, or intended the kill. Giles guessed the latter. His defences switched to high alert.

He knew what he was up against now—a real, seasoned threat.

An alarm warbled through the halls.

Pamela's amplified voice cut through the din calling, "Code Blue, Code Blue … elevator one."

Seconds later, a team of three nurses with a "crash" cart arrived and shoved Giles aside as he reached for his phone and quick-dialled the ARU's on-call number. He dashed across the polished corridor and dived into another lift as its doors opened. He hurried the two sluggish passengers out and punched the button to floor fifteen. It took forever for the doors to slide across and the lift to begin its ascent.

Giles paced the car and cursed.

He passed the seventh floor before his phone clicked in response.

"Hello?"

"Giles here. That you, Dylan?"

"Yes, sir," answered Sergeant Roger Dylan, Giles' second-in-command.

Briefly, he explained the situation and summoned Dylan and the ARU's on-call team. Even at flank speed, it would take them the best part of thirty-five minutes to suit-up, draw firearms, and reach him from across the city. Until then, he was alone. The hospital's unarmed and undertrained security people would be more hindrance than help.

The lift ascended at a speed calculated to eviscerate a desperate man. An audible warning dinged each time it passed a floor. Giles watched each button on the service panel light and extinguish.

"Come on, come on."

Would it be quicker to run up the bloody stairs?

With a ding and another, "Mind the doors, please," the car jolted to a stop at floor eleven.

"What?" Giles jabbed at the red "Close Doors" button, but the metal panels slid open, revealing a pair of orderlies waiting at either end of an empty bed.

He flashed his warrant card and pressed the red button again. "Sorry. Police emergency."

The porters stared at each other in open-mouthed silence as the lift doors slid closed. Giles repeatedly hammered on button fifteen as though it would make the bloody lift move faster.

Floor Fifteen.

"Mind the doors, please."

Giles' hand flashed to his holster, unclipped its retaining strap, and drew the weapon in automatic response. He held the gun in a two-handed grip, muzzle pointing to the ceiling.

The lift doors slid open. His senses tingled. There should be noises, chatter, machines, nurses—something.

Silence.

Down on one knee, he edged to the doorway. Still no sound. Not even from medical equipment. Where were all the bloody *bleep-bleep* machines and the rattling medicine trolleys? Giles expected movement, activity.

This was a hospital ward. Should have been teeming, shouldn't it?

He risked poking his head around the door and his heart stopped.

Oh Jesus, where's the guard?

JENNINGS PUSHED into the private room and stood open-mouthed at the scene.

Hammer, dressed in a doctor's white coat, stood beside the white-sheeted, blue-blanketed bed. A stethoscope hung from his neck and the business end, the diaphragm, rested in the coat's breast pocket. All he needed was a patient's chart and he could have played the lead in any TV medical drama.

Hollie sat in a wheelchair with a blue hospital blanket tucked over her legs. Her head was slumped to one side and she looked even younger in the white hospital gown.

"What the fuck?" Jennings seethed. "Where is everyone?"

Hammer nodded to a door to Jennings' left.

It opened into a small but well-appointed toilet and shower-room, all shiny chrome fittings and blue-grey marble tiles. On the floor, crumpled, and in a bad condition judging by their unnatural positions, lay two police officers.

Neither breathed.

The first, a huge man with the arms and shoulders of a bodybuilder, had a misshapen jaw. His face resembled beef passed through a mincing machine, and his right elbow bent the wrong way. The second, a small brunette, suffered less external damage, but heavy bruising to her eyes and a deflection across the bridge of her nose indicated shattered facial bones at the very least. Jennings grinned at the sight of the downed piggies.

Fuck. He wished he'd been there to see Hammer in action.

Jennings closed the door and scowled. "I told you I wanted to be here. I'm not happy."

Hammer stared at him, cold malice in his grey-green eyes. "Live

Part 2

with it. You pay for my brawn *and* brains." He spoke quietly. "I saw an opportunity and took it."

Jennings dialled his anger back a notch. "What did you do to the parents?"

"Sent them to the canteen while I examined their little girl. They left me to it since she had a police chaperone."

Jennings' allowed himself a thin smile.

"Good. They'll suffer more when they see what I do to their little bitch. They'll be at the top of the CD mailing list."

"As for the cops, they weren't part of the original contract. You'll receive a bill for the added work, but with a fifty percent reduction for unplanned collateral damage. Anything else is open to negotiation. I don't do *pro bono*."

The bill had started to mount, but that was fair enough, Jennings already had more money than he could ever spend.

"What about her?" Jennings nodded towards the female meat in the wheelchair.

Hammer pointed to a syringe on the bedside locker.

"I came prepared. She'll be out for a few hours."

"I won't ask how you found her room number or where you got that coat." He peered at the nametag pinned to the lapel. "Dr Ericsson."

"Yeah, you owe me for him, too," Hammer said and tapped his wristwatch. "Let's go."

He opened the room door and every alarm in the building exploded into strident, caterwauling life.

Chapter Thirteen

LATE FRIDAY EVENING – First the bad news…
Time since Ellis Flynn's stabbing: ten hours, forty hours

IT TOOK LESS than half an hour from when they'd finished unloading the helicopter until Captain Assante declared the Field Annex of the Finistère Forensics Laboratory open for business. Jean-Luc glanced at Jones who gave the Frenchman an appreciative and heartfelt thumbs-up. Jones would not have believed they could install such a facility so quickly. Despite his worry over the fate of Alex and Hollie, he managed to find the reserves of spirit to appreciate a job well done.

While half Jones' mind fretted about the activities in England, the other half studied the French criminologist's methods and discovered little difference to those of their UK counterparts. No need for crime scene tape here, the farm was isolated enough, but in most other instances, the protocols matched.

The twelve-strong forensics team, each in hooded white coveralls, overshoes, and facemasks, set to the tasks allotted by Captain Assante with the proficiency of the true professional.

First priority was the carcass in the cottage.

After taking hundreds of *in situ* photos and trace samples, two men carried out Ellis Flynn's corpse, zipped into a black plastic body bag on a stretcher. They placed it in a coffin-sized chill box balanced on trestles next to the laboratory tent. Flynn's remains held no interest for Jones. The SOCOs would find nothing useful on the body. He knew where Flynn had been for the previous day and a half, and what he'd done. The animal had nothing on him to help with the case.

Inside the cottage, another two men grid-quartered the ground floor collecting evidence. Numbered markers, orange rather than the bright yellow ones the SOCOs used in England, indicated areas of specific interest. Purple fingerprint dust darkened huge swathes of the room, especially on door handles and other high-touch surfaces. Flynn's knives and torch were bagged, and blood and skin samples taken to the tent-laboratory.

A coolly efficient woman took Jones' fingerprints and a cheek swab DNA sample, for elimination purposes.

She examined the scratch on his face and tutted before soaking a piece of gauze with antiseptic and dabbing the wound clean. The antiseptic stung worse than the damned mosquito.

"You do not require stitches. It will heal well," she said, and walked away.

Jones thanked her and she waved without turning.

They all speak English here? Puts us Brits to shame.

Photoflashes and chatter from the direction of the barn told him the observation room-cum-film studio and the camper were receiving the same close attention as the cottage. He doubted the criminologists would find much of value underground. Jennings and Flynn's copious use of bleach showed an attention to detail not in evidence at the roadside crime scene. Which was a point worth noting.

Jennings seemed fine when acting to a pre-determined plan, but struggled to think and act clearly when placed under pressure. Did he panic in a crisis? If so, the information might prove useful. If Jones could keep Jennings off-centre, unbalanced, reactive, perhaps he might force the man into making more mistakes. But how could he do that? They had to find the bugger first.

Jones had better hopes for the camper and the Citroën. Flynn hadn't had time to clean the van after his arrival. He and Jennings may have left evidence in both vehicles.

So far, Jones couldn't fault the French procedures or the care they took in gathering evidence. Once again, he became a fifth wheel—an unwanted and unaccompanied guest at a wedding. Occasionally, Jean-Luc stopped and asked him a procedural question, but it seemed more for politeness, to include him in the process, rather than out of any real need. Most of the time, Jones stood and watched the activity unfold with a growing sense of helplessness. He couldn't stop his mind drifting to thoughts of England.

Where the bloody hell was everyone?

Jones hadn't heard from Giles for nearly two hours. Not a good sign. He tried to work out how long it would take the ARU man to travel from his home to his office, sign for his weapon, and reach the hospital. Factoring in the light evening traffic, forty minutes? Sixty at most. What had he been doing for the remaining hour? And where in God's name had Alex disappeared to? He tried calling her again, but still couldn't get through.

Why, damn it? Why?

An icy hand reached into Jones' chest, crushing hard. He couldn't breathe properly. His heart hammered and his lungs moved like old leather. He had to do something. Anything.

Jean-Luc's mobile buzzed as he approached Jones for another chat. He stopped and listened for a moment before closing his eyes in clear annoyance. He shook his head sadly before saying something to the caller and ringing off.

"Not more bad news." Jones didn't know how he'd cope if anything else went wrong.

Jean-Luc answered him with a sigh. "It seems that your suspicions about the *maire*, Albert Plouay, appear to be correct. He has disappeared. My men could not find him in the village, or at his

Part 2

home. I will launch a nationwide search and have a magistrate block his bank accounts. We will also explore the land registry for other properties he may own. We will find him David, and discover why he ran. That I promise."

Jean-Luc stormed away to join Sergeant Brunö, leaving Jones alone with his thoughts once again.

The news about Plouay's sudden departure lifted Jones' spirits. The first little crack had appeared in Jennings' protective shield, his network of monsters. Sometimes it only took a single breach in a wall to bring the whole damned structure collapsing around a criminal's ears. The fact that his instincts, which he had doubted over the previous few hours, proved to be bang on, gave Jones hope, and improved his mood.

Jones turned his mind back to matters in England. He checked the battery scale on his mobile—one bar. Should he call Giles?

As he stared at the display screen, it buzzed and he nearly dropped the mobile to the concrete. He checked the caller ID.

"Ryan?"

"Boss? Can you hear me?" Ryan's voice sounded strangled—tight and breathless. Traffic noise in the background should not have been there.

"Just about. Are you driving? You should have reached the airport ages ago."

"I … I was … but I'm on my way to Alex's house."

"Why?"

Ryan would never have left his post without good reason. Something was wrong. Except for the traffic noise droning through the phone speaker, all sound faded to silence.

With a sense of dark foreboding, he raised his voice.

"Ryan? Speak to me. What's wrong?"

"There's been an all-service emergency shout, boss. I got the call from control a few minutes ago."

"What emergency? Come on man. Spit it out." Jones couldn't avoid shouting.

"There's been an explosion … Alex's house. About twenty-five minutes ago. I'm on my way there now. I … Hang on, coming up to traffic lights." Ryan turned on his two-tone siren. The deafening noise made Jones snatch the mobile away from his ear.

Alex? Oh God. Please no.

"What about Alex? Are there any casualties?" Jones yelled.

The siren cut out.

"The Fire Services call log says, 'persons reported', and you know what that means …" Ryan's words caught in throat. "More than one casualty … Jesus, boss. Alex … and Julie?"

Jones' hands shook and he closed his eyes to concentrate.

"Ryan. Take it easy. We know nothing for certain … yet."

Oh God, what have I done?

"I'm … fine, sir." Ryan sniffed. "Be at the scene in ten minutes. I'll call you as soon as I know anything."

Jones closed the phone and stared at the mute black and grey casing with hatred, but the phone wasn't responsible for the news it delivered. Responsibility belonged elsewhere. Jones wasn't naïve enough to discount the possibility of coincidence. Flukes happened all the time in life, but an explosion, tonight of all nights, could not be chance.

Has to be that bastard, Jennings.

If Alex was dead, it was as much Jones' fault as it was Jennings'. And now Jones might have Julie Harris' death on his conscience too. Julie, the exact opposite to the athletically built Alex—a petite brunette with a ready laugh and an eye for a good photograph—had always been friendly, welcoming. Now she was gone, they were both gone.

Dear God.

Jones listened to the noises around him radiating through the intermittent patches of light and dark. What could he do stuck in the middle of nowhere?

The phone chirruped again. Dazed, he answered without checking the ID.

"Jones here." His voice only just made it past the sob he couldn't stifle.

"Boss? It's Alex. I am near the hospital."

Blood drained from his head. He slumped against the wall.

Part 2

"Alex?" he gasped, "is that really you?"

"Yes, boss. You sound strange, what's wrong?"

Jones couldn't stand still. He dragged a hand through his hair and returned to pacing the courtyard. He tried to sound calm when he wanted to scream with relief and joy.

"Have you been home?"

"Yes. Julie and I were ... occupied when you called. I couldn't reach the telephone in time. Every time I tried to call you, your phone was busy. You haven't activated your call waiting option."

"My what? ... Never mind. Where are you?"

"Turning into the hospital car park."

Jones ran a quick calculation. Alex's house was no more than half an hour from the hospital at this time of night. She must have left home a few minutes before the explosion.

Julie?

Jones made a desperate grab at a passing straw.

"Is Julie with you?"

"Of course not, I'm on duty. She's at home in bed. Why? What's wrong?" A discordant tone of worry coloured her words. Jones' heart lurched.

"Alex," he tried to sound calm, authoritative. "Stop the car as soon as it's safe."

"Boss? You're worrying me."

Jones waited.

"Are you parked up yet?"

"One moment ... Yes. Okay, what's wrong?"

"Pull the handbrake up and turn off the engine."

"Boss, what's happened?" Her words tumbled out, the voice raised in pitch, filled with fear. She sensed something and not being in the car with her to offer comfort tore Jones apart.

"Alex, I ... don't know how to say ... I have some bad ..."

The sound of Alex's cries of anguish after he delivered the news would live with him forever. Jones couldn't stop her racing home. He prayed she'd be safe to drive. The first responders, fire, police, and paramedics, would all be all over the scene by the time she reached home. They would take care of her.

With the dregs of his mobile battery, he called Ryan to prepare him for Alex's arrival. The young detective took the news with a mixture of elation and sympathy.

"I'll look after her, boss," Ryan said. "Jesus, she's alive. Thank fuck ..."

The rest of his words were lost as Jones closed the phone and sank to his knees.

For fifteen minutes, Jones prowled the courtyard with half a baguette and a mug of cold coffee in one hand, and his dying phone in the other. He couldn't think of anything to do but pace, and worry. Things were moving inexorably beyond his control. He hated being so helpless, but what could he do?

His phone bleeped again. This time he checked the display screen.

"Giles? Thank God. Tell me everything's okay?"

"No David. It's a complete bloody disaster."

David Jones stopped pacing. The plastic cup hit the concrete slab and bounced. Black coffee exploded from the spinning lip and might have passed for blood-spatter in the dim evening light.

JENNINGS RUBBED his hands together and turned to face Hammer, who drove the ambulance—sirens blaring and blue lights flashing—with the skill of a rally driver. "I have to hand it to you, Hammer. That was totally brilliant, but I nearly wet myself when the alarm went off."

He considered patting the man on the shoulder, or the knee, but remembered the ex-soldier's tattoo.

"In and out, like a pickpocket in a crowd. You've earned yourself a big bonus tonight, my friend."

For a brief moment, Hammer turned those cold, dark eyes on him. A shudder rippled down Jennings' disintegrating spine.

"Get this," Hammer said. "We aren't friends." He jerked a thumb to the back where Hollie lay strapped to a gurney. "Don't know what you want with her, and I don't care, but I'm taking you

Part 2

where you wanted as arranged and then I'm off." He turned eyes-front again and added. "I took on this job 'cause the money was right, and completed it 'cause I always fulfil a contract. Always. That's it. I'm done."

"Really? I was hoping you'd be inclined to join my operation in a more permanent role. There are fringe benefits." Jennings jerked his head towards Hollie who hadn't stirred since they'd transferred her from the wheelchair to the stretcher.

Hammer's mouth thinned into a gash. Once again, His eyes drilled right through Jennings.

"Not interested," he growled.

"Are you sure? I can offer big money to a man with your particular skillset."

Hammer snapped off the blues-and-twos, and eased his foot off the accelerator pedal.

"How much money?"

Chapter Fourteen

LATE FRIDAY EVENING – *Graves*
Time since Ellis Flynn's stabbing: eleven hours, twenty hours

WHEN GILES DESCRIBED the scene in Hollie's hospital room, the murdered constables, and the doctor in the lift, Jones' world collapsed for the second time that night. How much more bad news would he have to endure? If he'd been alone he might have screamed and ranted, but he would never allow himself to show such emotion with strangers close by.

The doubts and self-recriminations returned and grew in force and volume.

He'd been so damned clever. Ridden to the bloody rescue on a white horse and saved the day like the US sodding Cavalry. But his efforts had only given Hollie a few hours reprieve. Now here he was, stuck in rural, isolated Brittany until morning with Julie Harris probably dead, Hollie Jardine missing, and no opportunity to help.

Siân, help get me through this.

He checked the time—eleven-twenty. Which meant twelve-twenty French time, since he hadn't reset his watch. The next flight didn't leave Brest for another seven hours.

All that time wasted. What the hell could he do?

Giles' concise, commanding voice cut through his thoughts. "I've locked down the hospital."

"Sorry, Giles. Repeat that."

"When I reached the room, Hollie's bed was cold, so they'd been gone a good few minutes. And get this. As it's a private ward, there aren't any bloody surveillance cameras up here, so no identification. Christ, David, security here's a bloody joke. Jennings and his accomplice might have strolled right out the front doors." Giles grunted. "The place is on lockdown now and I'm organising a floor-by-floor search. If she's still here, I'll find her, but it'll take time—"

"Do you have anyone looking at the hospital surveillance tapes?"

"Not yet. I was going to call Ryan Washington."

"Hell, you mean you haven't heard?" Jones scratched his head. "No, no, of course you haven't."

Jones could not believe how matter-of-fact he sounded when he relayed the news, callous even, but his training had taken over. He'd make time to mourn later.

"Jesus Christ," Giles whispered. "Arson?"

"I'd bet my pension on it."

If I still have one after this bloody fiasco.

"I don't know what to say. Is there anything I can do?"

"Keep searching for Jennings and whoever's working with him."

"Jennings can't be his real name, can it?"

"Doubt it." Jones clutched at another straw. "You've never come across anyone called, John Jennings, or Jonathan C Jennings on your travels, I suppose? The name's been bugging me ever since I heard it."

Giles paused for a moment before answering.

"Sorry, David. No."

"No reason why you should. As for the surveillance tapes, call in someone from the night shift. Even Duggie Peyton won't sit on his hands after this." He paused for thought before things could get away from him again. "Call on Phil Cryer for help, but nothing hands on. I don't want him anywhere near the action. He can access the PNC from his home—assuming the bloody thing's up and running again—and anything else online. He's great with the IT stuff, but make sure you do it on the QT. I don't want Peyton or the brass finding out. Phil's not insured for active police work. And draft in all the warm bodies you can find. I want the whole bloody force involved in the search."

At least those who aren't investigating the explosion.

Jones' thoughts raced. He'd forgotten something.

"What about Hollie's parents?"

"The Jardines are unharmed, but the mother collapsed. The doctor's admitted her for shock. Frank Jardine's bearing up. Doesn't look it, but he's a strong one. As for the PC's Johansson and Brown … Christ, never seen anything like it. Whoever killed them knew their stuff. Took them both out like a fucking ninja. Neither stood a chance. Especially the lass. David, it was bloody horrible. Wait 'til I catch the bastard."

"Couldn't have been Jennings," Jones said, thinking aloud. "He's damn near disabled. Wasn't able to pick up and carry a little old lady. I'm guessing he drafted in some muscle."

"That's what I thought. Whoever he is, the guy's a pro. The way he took down Johansson and the doctor in the lift suggests ex-military, possibly special forces." Giles paused again. Alarms wailed in the background. Giles must have opened a door and entered a different part of the hospital.

"Who going to notify the officers' next of kin? Not bloody Peyton, surely?"

"Nah, the Force Welfare Officer is doing that now old Duggie's ducked his head under the parapet. The bugger knows he should have listened to you." Giles paused for a moment before continuing. "One good thing. There's no blood on the bed, so Hollie might still be alive."

"Of course she's alive. Jennings has something horrible planned for her, and it'll be a lot worse than what he did to the others—slower. Why else would he risk kidnapping Hollie a second time?" asked Jones, thinking aloud again.

Part 2

"David, unless there's something else …" Giles sounded distracted. "I need to supervise the search."

Jones ended the call and stood in the centre of a bustling crime scene, but felt very much alone.

Multiple generators fed power to electrical equipment. A dozen halogen lamps on tripod stands illuminated large areas in various parts of the farm. Jean-Luc and Captain Assante marshalled their men like twin conductors at the head of the same orchestra, but without entering a competition. Gendarmes in dark one-piece uniforms, and SOCOs in white coveralls, scurried about their duties. Some carried boxes of electronic equipment, others digging tools.

In the meadow between the perimeter wall and the cottage, a woman wearing a set of oversized headphones pushed a wheeled trolley containing ground-penetrating radar. She worked slowly. Jones calculated it would take most of the night to cover the whole field.

A powerful looking man in a white one-piece operated a second, lighter radar unit in the woods. He surveyed the open spaces between the trees.

Jones had never felt so helpless in his life. If he thought that praying would do any good, he'd have dropped to his knees in the middle of the courtyard, but he'd given up believing in God decades ago, at the end of a long, hot summer in Wales.

As the minutes ticked by, Jones' desperation increased. He'd hit a total dead end.

He paced the patches of dark, made gloomier by his mood and by the counterpoints of brilliant glare thrown by the powerful lights, and rolled through the information he had. There was precious little.

Ellis Flynn and his father Edward were both dead.

They'd found no close relatives of the Flynns left alive, and Ellis had no known associates. The other suspects on the Sex Offenders list had all been traced, interviewed, and eliminated as suspects, at least in this particular crime. On that front, the cupboard stood empty.

They had a miserable, useless photo of Jennings, and a sketchy description. What about that damned limp? Jones had only assumed the man's fragility because of the way he'd dealt with *madame* Deauville's body. Perhaps Jennings had simply killed the woman and left the scene in a panic. Was the walking stick a prop? The prop of an actor?

Christ, what a mess.

And the biggest question of all?

Why?

Why had Jennings taken the enormous risk of recapturing Hollie? With little to link him with the killings, Jennings might have faded away and set up his repulsive operation somewhere else. In fact, he still might. What was so special about Hollie Jardine? Why risk so much to take her again?

Rage? Bloody-mindedness? The psychological need to finish what he'd started? What drove an animal like Jennings to risk everything and plot against Hollie?

Jones scratched and picked and worried away at the information, but came up with nothing. A psychiatrist or a psychologist might suggest a motivation. Maybe Jennings had a deep-seated need to demonstrate his power over young women because of his physical infirmity. Maybe he'd been mistreated by an older sister or by his mother. Maybe he'd been bottle-fed and missed out on the breast. Maybe the bastard had been bullied by a large-breasted teacher. On the other hand, maybe there was no real reason. Perhaps Jennings was nothing more than an evil shit with no motivation other than simple bloodlust.

Bollocks to the psychologists. What do they know?

Jones treated the dark arts of the unconscious mind with the same scepticism and suspicion as he treated mediums, gypsy fortune-tellers, and astrologists. Their words were little more than guesswork and bullshit designed to skim money out of the pockets of the gullible.

John C Jennings, or whatever his real name was, orchestrated the torture and death of young girls for the entertainment of others, and for profit. During his desperate flight, he'd sliced open the

Part 2

throat of an elderly woman and tossed her in a ditch like a piece of litter.

Hollie Jardine was back in the hands of the amoral, vindictive sociopath to whom life meant nothing, and Jones couldn't do a thing about it.

He wanted, no, needed to scream.

It didn't take Jones long to pass the news to Jean-Luc, who took it better than he had.

"I am so sorry, David. I do not know what to say, or do."

"That makes two of us."

Jean-Luc smoothed his moustache with both hands and stared into the distance. Jones could almost hear the cogs in the colonel's mind spinning. In Jean-Luc's place he'd be wondering what sort of useless moron would allow a recently rescued girl to be abducted for a second time. The Frenchman would have had a point, too. Jones should have seen it coming. He'd been so cock-sure he'd saved the day, that he'd let his guard down, and Hollie was the one paying the price. Hollie, the two uniformed officers, and the doctor.

Siân, what have I done?

A yell from the woods behind the barn made them both turn, and took part of Jones' attention away from his self-recriminating fug. He followed Jean-Luc along the well-worn path to the barn. Someone had placed a pair of planks across the stream to form a bridge.

On the other side of the water, a few metres inside the treeline, a bright light shone from a yellow tripod stand. Dark tree trunks and the outline of bushes interrupted the beam and gave the scene an otherworldly, backlit glow.

Two SOCOs knelt and scraped at the ground with what looked like bricklayer's trowels. Two others replicated the activity six metres to their left. A female gendarme stood to one side, filming their work.

"What is it?" Jones followed Jean-Luc across the makeshift bridge, which groaned and sagged under their combined weight. Jones' mind turned back a few months to a flat roof, which bounced underfoot, collapsed, and put Phil Cryer in a hospital bed for six weeks. He blanched at the memory. So much hurt, he could barely stand the pain.

"The radar indicates a shallow grave and human remains," Jean-Luc answered after speaking to his man. "It shows at least four bodies buried in this clearing."

Jones and Jean-Luc stood over the grave and watched the progress in silence until Sergeant Brunö interrupted their vigil when he rushed towards them with a phone in his outstretched hand. His face was as pale as his swarthy complexion would allow. Jones was surprised. Who would have thought the coolly efficient, monosyllabic sergeant capable of registering discomfort?

Instead of handing the phone to Jean-Luc, Brunö passed it to Jones. "It's for you, Chief Inspector."

"You speak English?"

And with an American accent.

"Of course, sir, but you have to take this. It's the *putain*. It's Jennings!"

Chapter Fifteen

LATE FRIDAY EVENING – Ultimatum
 Time since Ellis Flynn's stabbing: eleven hours, forty hours

"WHAT?" Jones shot a glance at Jean-Luc whose quizzical expression told it all. "How?"

Brunö passed him the mobile. "He called the *gendarmerie* in Brest and demanded to speak with you. The animal says he has *mademoiselle* Jardine."

Jones' world condensed into a black object the size of a packet of cigarettes. Everything else faded to silence as he reached for the mobile. The tremor in his hand returned.

Sergeant Brunö tapped his ear and handed Jean-Luc a white plastic earpiece. "We'll both be able to hear you, Chief Inspector, and I'm recording the call. Depress the mute button when you're ready to speak."

Jones pressed the cold phone to his ear. "Any chance of tracing the call?"

Brunö opened his hands and shrugged. "The *gendarmerie* in Brest is trying, but …"

Jones closed his eyes before releasing the mute.

"Hello?" he said, with a mouth dry as talc.

"Ah, at last. Have I the honour and privilege of speakin' tae DCI David Aaron Jones, head of the Serious Crime Unit, Holton Police Headquarters, and the man responsible for the death of the poor defenceless Ellis Flynn?"

Poor and defenceless Flynn? Damn your eyes.

"Yes," Jones answered. This time his voice sounded stronger, even though he felt as sturdy as wet tissue paper.

Jennings' gentle Scottish accent, lowlands, possibly east coast, seeped through the speaker like molten tar. He sounded calm and considered, almost conversational. He made perfect glottal stops and each consonant stood out clear and precise. Here was a well-educated man, or at least a man with faultless diction, but how had he learned Jones' middle name? He hated the name Aaron, and never used it. The only places it appeared were his new birth certificate, and his Police Personnel file.

Jesus, he has access to my records. Someone working on the inside? Another hacker as skilful as Corky?

Jennings barked out a cruel laugh. "I know everything there is tae know about you, ye wee bastard. You're an orphan, aren't you? Spent time in foster homes. I know all about those places. Poor little Jonesy-boy."

Jones gritted his teeth and bit off an angry response.

"As I understand it, you're looking for me. Is that so?" Jennings' smooth taunt drove home Jones' helplessness.

"Yes." Jones replied. "Fancy meeting up sometime?"

Lame, but he couldn't think of anything better.

"Oh aye. Most definitely. Looking forward tae it, in fact. How soon can ye make it here?"

Not the response Jones expected. Had he heard the animal correctly? A meeting?

"If you like. Where?"

"Oh no, *Detective Chief Inspector,*" Jennings spat the rank with venom and derision. "I'm no' making it that easy for ye. You found Hollie once. Now find her again. You have until midday tomorrow. Hear that? High Noon. Like the classic movie." His laughter sounded like the hacking cough of a man dying from lung cancer. "Think of yourself as Gary Cooper, at least for the next few hours. But if you're one second late, Hollie dies. If you don't come alone, Hollie dies. If you're armed, Hollie dies. Get it? And it won't be quick. I'll make the wee bitch suffer. And you know what kind of suffering I'm capable of producing. You know the mess I can make. Don't ye!"

Jones checked the time. He had a little less than thirteen hours. Images of the freezer in the cellar and the marble slab in the viewing room bled, unbidden, into his head. He ground his teeth.

"So, you have another movie studio?"

"Ye'll find out. If you miss the meeting, I'll send you a preview copy of my next special feature." Jones could hear the smile in the animal's voice. "Hollie Jardine's first, and last, starring role."

Blood pounded in Jones' ears. He wanted to throw up again.

"I'll never make it in time. It's not possible."

"Okay then, tell me. Should I start the cutting at the face, or the feet? Actually, I normally like tae keep them pretty to begin with. Aye, The feet it is then. After that, I'll work up tae the sensitive bits. I'm going tae love that. What do you say? Does that suit your viewing tastes?"

Bastard.

"I have no idea where you are. I don't stand a chance." Jones made his voice sound even more helpless and pathetic than he felt. Not an easy task, but he let the nuance bleed into his tone. Maybe playing to the sociopath's ego would net him something.

He'd take any advantage he could find, no matter how small.

"Aw, so inept. Clueless. Little Ellis was like that when we first met, but he turned out all right in the end. He had promise. I saw it in him early on, but you snuffed out his life, his talent, and the fucking bitch is going to pay for your mistake unless you find her. Tick-tock, tick-tock. *Tempus fugit,* Jonesy-boy."

"What happens if I *do* turn up in time, alone, and unarmed?"

"Why then, I'll release Hollie and you and I can have our little chat."

Yeah. Right.

"Why should I trust you?"

"Och, I'm mortified," Jennings gushed. "I give you my word that Hollie won't be harmed before you get here. She's here right next to me, in a nice little sanctuary. A home-away-from-home. A refuge, if you like. She's goin' nowhere for the moment. And you don't have a choice, do you? Don't come, Hollie dies. But if you do … and if I'm telling the truth … well, Hollie has a chance. That's the gamble you're running. Imagine your life if you don't at least try. Remember, I know all about you, Jonesy-boy. I know about your first beat in Wales. I read all about how you rescued that black bitch and her harelipped future husband. Most laudable. Most people would have let the bitch drown in that cave."

Jennings paused again, giving Jones more time to stew.

"And then of course, think of the mess I'll make of poor little Hollie afterwards. Don't like mess, do you, Jones. Must have been horrible for you to go down into that filthy cellar after you'd scrambled on your hands and knees in the dirt to get to ma poor wee Ellis."

Jones tried to block out the thumping in his head. The paedophile killer seemed to know every intimate detail of his life. And what did Jones know about Jennings? Nothing. He couldn't allow the feelings of impotence to engulf him. That was what Jennings wanted.

"But I don't have a clue where you are."

Jennings sighed, long and loud.

"And here I was thinking you were a dangerous adversary. You pathetic old man. Sneaking up on wee Ellis like that. You wouldn't ha' stood a chance face-to-face. He'd have torn ye apart."

A train's horn sounded in the background. Was Jennings near a station, or a railway track? How did that help? There were thousands of miles of track and hundreds of railway stations in the UK.

"Shall I give you a wee clue?"

Part 2

The line fell quiet for a moment, and Jones thought Jennings had broken the connection.

"Hello?"

"Had you worried there, didn't I? Well, let me see. What hint should I give you? Tum-ti-tum. Ah yes. Meet me at the place *my* boy, Ellis, was born."

"What?"

"You heard. I'm no' repeating myself."

Jones didn't want to push it. The man could cut the call any time he wanted. He had Jones at his mercy for the moment.

"How do I know Hollie's still alive?"

"Delaying tactics? Trying to trace this call? Don't waste your time. I've routed the signal through a dozen different satellites and carriers. You'll never find me that way. But I'll let you speak to Hollie if you ask nicely." Jennings paused again. "Go on, ask nicely."

The smile in his voice told Jones how much the creature enjoyed the situation. Taunting was fun.

Jones dragged civility from a dark place and spoke calmly, fighting for control.

"Mr Jennings, please may I speak to Hollie?"

The words tore from his throat as though wrapped in razor wire.

"Well, since you said please, I'll put her on. Just a sec' …."

The silence down the line stretched for an eternity. Jones, Jean-Luc, and Sergeant Brunö exchanged worried glances until Hollie's fragile "David?" broke the quiet and tore at his heart.

Jones would have done anything to trade places with her. Gouged eyes, smashed through walls, beaten Jennings to a bloody pulp. His fingers mashed into the phone's hard case. He took a breath.

"Hollie? How are you?"

"I … I'm okay. Mum and Dad, are they …?"

Her voice pulled at him from the distance.

"They're fine, Hollie. A friend of mine spoke to them a few minutes ago. Worried about you though. Where are you?"

"He won't let me tell you. He has a knife—"

273

"Hollie, are you still there?"

Silence.

Jones shouted, "Hollie?" but the next words chilled him to his bones.

"That's the last time anyone will hear from the little bitch unless you obey my instructions to the letter. Understand?"

Jones tried to think of something to say to make Jennings put Hollie back on the line, but he had nothing.

"I asked you a question, Jonesy-boy. *Answer me!*"

"I have the message, Mister Jennings. But I can't reach England in time to meet your deadline. The next plane won't land in Birmingham until ten-thirty tomorrow morning. And I don't have a clue where you are."

"Don't be obtuse, wee man. You have all the information you need. Think man! You're a detective, so fucking detect. As for gettin' here in time ... work something out."

The line clicked into silence.

Chapter Sixteen

LATE FRIDAY EVENING – Old school letters
Time since Ellis Flynn's stabbing: eleven hours, fifty minutes

SERGEANT BRUNÖ RETRIEVED HIS PHONE, his expression glum, but eyes sympathetic. The three men returned to the courtyard in silence.

While Jones tried to come to grips with the enormity of Jennings' ultimatum, Jean-Luc stared towards the forensics tent and studied the progress of the white-garbed scientists, his expression deeply pensive. Slim fingers worried at his moustache. After a few seconds, he nodded. He seemed to have arrived at a decision.

"Forgive me, David," he said. "I have to attend to something, but before I go, consider this. Why does Jennings think you can identify where he is keeping Hollie?"

Jean-Luc touched Jones on the forearm as if to empathise with his predicament, gave Brunö a curt nod, and marched towards Captain Assante. The captain stood beside the large tent with a clipboard making notes as each new piece of evidence entered his field laboratory.

Jones couldn't blame Jean-Luc for deserting him. The colonel had more than enough on his plate. With a potential mass grave, the senseless slaying of *madame* Deauville, and the fleeing mayor, he didn't need the added responsibility of searching for Hollie Jardine, too. That task rested on Jones' shoulders alone, but he didn't have a clue where to begin.

Brunö slumped on his makeshift chair, leaning forward with powerful forearms resting on thighs. Head bowed, he stared at the ground beneath his feet.

A desperate idea formed in Jones' overstressed brain.

"Sergeant Brunö, have you had a chance to inspect the electronics in the room below the barn?"

The sergeant looked up and shook his head.

"No, sir. I've been too busy here." He pointed to his radio equipment. "The Colonel told me you found recording and broadcasting equipment. There must be a satellite here also."

Jones nodded.

"There's a dish on top of the barn. Pointing north. You can't see it from here."

He studied Brunö for a moment. The sergeant's right knee bounced and he clenched and unclenched his hands. The man's every gesture suggested agitation. Even though Brunö hadn't spoken to Hollie directly, he clearly cared for her plight.

"Can one of your men take over here while you search the facility room?"

"This is my post. I will have to ask the Colonel. Why?"

"If you took a look at the observation room, would you be able to trace a signal from here to its destination?"

Brunö smiled sadly and shook his head.

"I think you've seen too many cop shows on the TV, Chief Inspector. Given enough time, doing what you ask might be possible with a normal open system, but the one under the barn will be part of a sophisticated criminal operation. Jennings would have installed a shedload of defences. Passwords, firewalls, failsafe devices, booby traps. Without the correct start up sequence and codes, we might end up reformatting the main hard drive—destroying any information stored on the system. It'll be much better to wait for our forensic technologists, I think. And there is another thing. As *le putain* Jennings said in his phone call, he would bounce the transmission off a string of satellites. The receiving station for the broadcasts could be anywhere on the planet. China, Malaysia. Even Paris."

Brunö shrugged and shook his head.

Jones saw the futility of this line of investigation. He knew nothing about computers and his ignorance became more obvious with each passing year. Perhaps it *was* time for him to retire and make room for techno-savvy young coppers like Phil, Alex, and Ryan. But he wasn't finished yet. He returned to the tried and trusted.

"Okay, Sergeant. Scratch that idea as a bad one. Let's try the old-school method." He pointed to the large screen on Brunö's desk. "Can you pull up a map of England on that monitor and centre it on Birmingham?"

Brunö shuffled forward. A few keyboard clicks were all he needed to produce the map Jones asked for.

Jones checked his watch.

"I received Jennings call at twenty-three-forty-two. According to my officer, Giles Danforth, that's a little less than an hour and ten minutes after Jennings abducted Hollie. We need to work out how far he could have travelled within that timescale." He drew across a camping chair and sat next to the sergeant. "Jennings and his accomplice took Hollie away in a stolen ambulance. Too conspicuous for a getaway car so I'm guessing they would have dumped it as soon as possible. I don't know. Let's allow ten minutes to change vehicles? A bit of a guess, I know but they wouldn't have wanted to do it in the open and it might have taken some time. How long did it take Jennings to reach me on the phone?"

Brunö creased his face in thought. "Perhaps fifteen minutes, including the time it took me to bring you the portable? No more. Our comms people knew of your presence here. They didn't take long to realise the importance of the call."

Jones continued. "Jennings would have needed a few minutes to find the *gendarmerie's* telephone number and place the call. Let's call it ten minutes total?"

Brunö nodded his agreement. "A reasonable estimation."

"That gives Jennings around forty-five minutes to reach his destination. Less the time it took to carry Hollie from the new vehicle and secure her."

"And that assumes *monsieur* Jennings isn't moving her to a different location at the moment," Bruno offered.

"Understood. But Jennings asked how soon I could 'make it here'. Right? I had the distinct impression he was already at the meeting place. That's the assumption I'm working on. Any other variables are too difficult to account for. Agreed?"

"In the absence of other information, what else can we do but guess?"

"Not so much of a guess. As Colonel Coué suggested, Jennings actually *wants* me to find him. He wouldn't make it too difficult. Would he?"

"Perhaps not. So, at this time of night in England, how far could you travel in forty-five minutes?"

"Good question. Traffic would be light, but he wouldn't want to break any speed limits. Seventy miles per hour maximum in forty-five minutes would get you a little over fifty miles." Brunö gave him a quizzical look and Jones added, "That's about eighty kilometres."

"Ah, I see."

The sergeant worked the computer mapping system and superimposed a circle on the chart, centred on the Queen Elizabeth Hospital in Edgbaston, Birmingham.

"So, if we're right," he said, focused on the map, "Hollie should be somewhere within this circle. There's a lot of surface area to cover, *n'est-ce pas?*"

"Certainly is, but at least it's a place to begin."

Starting due north of Birmingham and moving clockwise, Jones read off the major towns within the target area: every large conurbation in the Midlands, plus Derby, Nottingham, Leicester, Coventry, Northampton, Gloucester, Hereford, and Stoke-on-Trent. All major towns with large populations. Of course, there was nothing to stop Jennings hiding out on a farm in the middle of the country. The Cotswolds, for example fell within the search perimeter. Jones noted that Edward Flynn's former property near Great Malvern, the cottage confiscated by the courts, also lay within the circle. Would Jennings keep Hollie there as some sort of tribute to his dead accomplice, Ellis Flynn?

Jones considered calling the West Mercia Police, the force local to the area, and having them check the cottage again, but that would be too dangerous. Jones had to attend the rendezvous alone. He turned to Brunö again.

"We need to narrow the search grid."

The light-footed Jean-Luc appeared at his side. Jones didn't hear him approach and used his hands as levers against his knees to stand to greet him. The tall Frenchmen stood with his right hand folded loosely in the crook of his left elbow. The left hand scratched at his gunmetal-blue stubble.

"I think you are forgetting something, David," said Jean-Luc, pointing at the circle on the map.

"I don't doubt it, but what in particular?" Jones wanted to collapse back into the chair. The weight of his body suddenly felt too much for his legs. The circle on the map seemed to taunt him.

"Jennings clearly expects you to find the location. He must have told you where he would be, no?"

"Really? Did I miss something?"

Jones' neck ached from the build-up of tension and his lack of sleep. His forehead pulsed. Even his damned fingers itched. Control was flying away from him. The initial fleeting hope provided by the search grid had changed to despair. He was in danger of losing control altogether, and from the look on Jean-Luc's face, the Frenchman could see it too. He signalled for Jones to follow him to a quiet spot by their favourite wall, now illuminated by the backwash from the temporary lights in the comms tent.

Once alone, Jean-Luc kept his voice low.

"Think, David. *Monsieur* Jennings wants you and is using Hollie as bait. Agreed?"

Jones nodded and smiled. Jean-Luc hadn't given up on Hollie at all. His spirits lifted with the realisation he wasn't in this alone, and he chided himself for not crediting Jean-Luc with more loyalty and concern.

The Frenchman sequestered a pair of camping chairs and took a small device from his utility belt.

"Sergeant Brunö gave me the recording of the telephone conversation. Let us go through what Jennings said and discover whether we can work out his message, yes?"

He pressed play.

They spent twenty-five minutes dissecting Jones' telephone call with Jennings and boiled it down to a small list of potential clues.

"Here's what we have."

Jones scanned through the jottings he made in the police notebook he never went anywhere without. He even took a fresh one with him on his rare holidays.

"Point one. Jennings has access to my personnel records. He might have inside help, a police mole or a hacker who broke into the police system. I don't know where that gets us, but I'll need to bear that in mind for future reference. We'll file that one away."

He flipped a page.

"Points two and three. Jennings is not his real name and he has a Scottish accent. Doubt that's important, but, again, it might be of use later—if we ever catch the bugger. Voice analysis and comparison."

Jean-Luc shook his head.

"The call was made via computer. Jennings may have altered his voice enough to fool the analysis. He may also have put on the accent."

The Frenchman paused for a moment's thought before adding, "However, none of these points helps us find a location for Hollie. Our next point, David. *Numéro quatre?*"

Jean-Luc made a rolling-forward gesture with both hands.

"Point four, right. I need to be able to reach him by midday. But how is that possible? Assuming the plane is on time, I won't reach Birmingham until ten-thirty tomorrow morning. That only

Part 2

leaves ninety minutes. Barely time to reach the city at that time of the morning. Even if we do work out where Hollie is, I won't be able to reach her. Not unless she's right next to the bloody airport."

"Is that possible?"

"Possible, but unlikely. There's nothing much around there but fields and housing estates. Urban sprawl. If he's in one of the housing estates, I'll never find him without an address."

"You are forgetting about the helicopter, David." He pointed to the transport aircraft.

"What about it? That thing won't make it all the way to Birmingham. Will it?"

"No, but I have talked with the pilot. He is arranging for a colleague to fly you to England. A lighter and faster helicopter will arrive within the hour. I am sorry, my friend, I do not know why I did not think of it sooner." Jean-Luc tapped his forehead.

"What? I ..." Jones didn't know what to say other than, "Thank you, Jean-Luc." It seemed woefully inadequate. With the promised transportation, the colonel had given him the hint of a chance, but it wouldn't do a blind bit of good if they couldn't work out the exact meeting place. He gave an embarrassed cough. "I'll make sure your department is compensated for all our expenses. Aviation fuel, the pilot's fee, and so forth."

Jean-Luc smiled. "But of course, we are now running a joint operation, *n'est pas*? My accounts department will send an invoice to yours. Now, shall we continue? There is something you are missing. I am certain."

Jones referred to his notes again.

"Point Five. Play that part about Jennings meeting Ellis Flynn again. It's at counter point number ... 436."

Jean-Luc dialled the number into the digital recorder and Jennings' voice sprang from the speaker:

"...was like that when we first met, but he turned out alright in the end. He had promise. I saw it early on ..."

"That's it, hold it there." Jones held up his hand. "So we know Jennings met Ellis Flynn when he was much younger."

Jones saw it, plain and simple. He jumped to his feet. The camping chair tilted and fell behind him.

"It's obvious. I'm a complete idiot."

"What do you have?"

"It's in the timeline. The bloody timeline. I should have seen it straight away. Hell, Phil Cryer pointed it out before we'd even heard of Jennings. His wonderful bloody memory …"

Jones paced in front of Jean-Luc who remained seated. He frowned in confusion but clearly knew better than to interrupt a man in full flow.

Jones shot quick-fire questions and answered them himself. Jean-Luc responded as fast as he could to direct questions, or when Jones stopped to search through his notes.

"When did Flynn renovate the room under the barn? Couple of years ago, right? Not that long after they released him from detention."

Jones paused and rubbed his palms together.

"How did he pay for the work? Couldn't have come up with the money himself, he'd been locked up five years and the courts confiscated most of his father's money. Ellis Flynn was broke. All he had was the house in Tile Hill and the family campervan. Someone sponsored him and that someone must have been Jennings. Makes sense, right?" Jones flashed the question at Jean-Luc who nodded but said nothing.

Jones continued his pacing.

"Now, this brings us to point six. Jennings said he'd be at the place where Flynn was born."

"Do you know where?"

"Yes, Phil Cryer told me. I wrote it down." He flipped back a few pages in the notebook. "It was a woman's hospital. Damn it, where did I … ah, here we are, Birmingham Hospital for Women, Edgbaston. But he can't be keeping Hollie there."

"Why not?"

"They tore the place down back in the 1990s. It's a multi-storey car park now in constant use. Hell. There must be something else."

Part 2

"What about the birthplace of the father? Might Jennings have known Ellis through his father?"

Jones thought for a moment, but shook his head.

"No. That won't work either. Edward Flynn was born at home in Tile Hill. A home birth. I've had officers posted at the house ever since we searched the place last night. I ordered them to report in to the station every fifteen minutes. I'd have heard if there'd been a break in protocol."

Jones punched his open left palm three times. The slapping noise was lost in the background hubbub.

"Play that part again. Counter point number 458."

Jean-Luc pressed the buttons on the device and Jennings' hateful, taunting voice scratched its way under Jones skin. They were getting closer. The electric prickle of excitement pulsed from Jones' toes to his hair roots.

" …worried there, didn't I? Well, let me see, what hint should I give you? Tum-ti-tum. Ah yes, I have it. Meet me at the place my boy, Ellis, was born."

"That's it," Jones said, "'The place where my boy, Ellis, was born.'" He stopped at the upturned chair, righted it, and sat. He leaned toward Jean-Luc and smiled. "Notice he said 'my boy'?" Jean-Luc nodded. "Why would he say that if he isn't his father? What if Jennings meant the place where Ellis Flynn was *re*-born?"

"What do you mean?"

"The Young Offenders Institute. Ellis Flynn entered as a naive thirteen-year-old boy, and left five years later, the fully formed underling of a sadistic killer. Don't you see? Jennings must have met Flynn while he was in prison. Jennings is either an inmate, a guard, or a social worker. Ellis was already partial to underage girls. We know that. It's what he was sent down for. Maybe Jennings has been tutoring him since he arrived … where was it?" Jones turned the notebook pages once more. "Ah, here we are, the Derbyshire Youth Detention Centre." Jones paused again. "Hang on a minute. Didn't Jennings say something about a home?" He flipped back a few pages in the notebook. "Number 398."

"…won't be harmed until you get here. She's in a nice sanctuary, a home-away-from-home, a sort of refuge, if you like, and she's going nowhere, for the moment ..."

Jones raised a fist to Jean-Luc.

"Don't you see? He's talking about the detention centre! We used to call them Boy's Homes, back in the day. And we already know the place was closed shortly after Flynn's release. It's abandoned. It's where Jennings is holding Hollie. I'm sure of it. And look"—he pointed at Brunö's screen—"Derby's inside the search grid."

"How close to Birmingham is this place?"

Jones rose and, followed by Jean-Luc, crossed to the comms tent. He handed his notebook to the sergeant. "Can you find the address for this place?"

The sergeant took all of two minutes to discover the detention centre's address: Sunnyhill, south-west of Derby.

They located Sunnyhill on the target map.

"Look," Jones said, tapping the screen. "It's less than forty-five minutes from Birmingham, up the A38, if they avoid the motorway network. The timings are right. Jennings could easily have driven Hollie to Sunnyhill in the time between taking her from the hospital and making the call. I'm betting the location suits Jennings' warped sense of justice, too."

They'd made a whole load of assumptions and wild-arsed guesses to reach the conclusion, but Jones somehow knew he was right. With Jean-Luc's help and calm encouragement, and Sergeant Brunö's support, he'd discovered the meeting place—perhaps. Furthermore, the imminent arrival of a helicopter gave Jones the opportunity to reach Derby well before the deadline.

For the first time since he received the hideous phone call from Giles, Jones felt the tiniest flicker of hope.

Chapter Seventeen

FRIDAY NIGHT, Saturday morning – Flight towards fight
Time since Ellis Flynn's stabbing: thirteen hours

JONES HAD NEVER BEEN in a helicopter before, and doing so would never have featured on his bucket list. He didn't want to visit any more amusement parks either, not after his first and only Big Dipper ride as a twelve-year-old. Never again. He detested the lack of control and the way his stomach flipped and lurched at each unexpected jag and twist. That one time, he'd thrown up over his new school shoes and spent the rest of the day splodging around with wet feet after plunging them into the nearest puddle. Vile. Why anyone would want to pay good money and stand in line for the privilege of being scared witless, was beyond him.

Being strapped into the helicopter's passenger seat, whipping over the Brittany countryside at a frighteningly low altitude, and at ridiculous speeds, was not the way he'd choose to spend the night. At one stage they flew so low, he could have reached out and grabbed an apple from a bloody orchard.

Every time the pilot toggled the cyclic steering control, or rotated the collective lever, the aircraft lurched violently. Jones wasn't able to predict the movement, up or down, left or right, and spent the early part of the flight breathing through his mouth, trying to keep down his baguettes and coffee.

Corkscrewing was the worst. Up, down, and around in one slewing, nauseating manoeuvre. His over-sensitive stomach heaved, and he continually fought the gag reflex. And worse, the pilot insisted on giving him the full tourist spiel as they flew over dimly-lit points of the utmost disinterest.

Thankfully, things improved when they reached the coast and started crossing the Channel, where the helicopter flew straight and true and reached its cruising speed of two-hundred-and-sixty kph. As his stomach settled, Jones closed his eyes and ran through the conversation he'd had with Jean-Luc while they waited for the helicopter's arrival.

"You cannot go alone, David." Jean-Luc had said, gripping his shoulders and staring into his eyes. "It is a trap. Jennings will surely try to kill you."

"If I don't go, he'll definitely kill Hollie. You heard what he said. She'll suffer and I can't have that on my conscience. At least this way, I'm going to arrive early. I'll have time to think of something. And besides … what would you do in this situation?"

The colonel sighed.

"Exactly the same, *mon ami*, but going unarmed is suicide."

"What else can I do?"

"You must take precautions, David. I would love to go with you, but I am needed here. Can you arrange protection?"

"Not much. Remember, there might be a police mole operating somewhere. I can't involve anyone I don't trust implicitly. Jennings might find out and cut his losses. I need to go in light and fast."

Jean-Luc released his grip on Jones' shoulders and looked towards the sound of the approaching helicopter.

"Who will you turn to?"

"Apart from Sergeant Cryer, who's out of commission, and Alex, who has other things on her mind, there are two people on the UK police force I can really trust."

Part 2

Jones passed the rest of the two-and-a-half hour flight organising his thoughts and trying to relax. He couldn't plan anything in detail until he clocked the layout of the centre, but at least the helicopter flight won him some preparation time.

Going in underprepared and alone was a huge and suicidal gamble, but what alternative did he have? Jennings had planned it that way.

Something touched Jones' arm. He woke with what felt like a mouth full of dry leaves. The pilot smiled and pointed through the glass dome of the cockpit. "Birmingham," his voice crackled through the helmet speakers. "We land in a few minutes."

He'd slept through so much noise?

Jones stretched as much as he could in the restrictive harness, while the young pilot touched the helicopter to the tarmac as gently as a feather landing on a pillow. He cut the engine and the chopper settled its weight on the skids. Jones closed his eyes and gave silent thanks to whatever had delivered him from the evils of whirligig flight, and waited for his stomach to land.

"Can I get out of this thing now, *monsieur*?" he asked, pointing to his restraints.

The pilot nodded.

Jones punched the central release mechanism, and the five-point harness fell away. It felt so good to move freely again. Even the creaking complaints made by his stiffened back and cramped neck muscles were a relief, of sorts. Jones gave the pilot his grateful thanks and, before the rotors stopped spinning, ducked low, slid from the cockpit, and scuttled towards the waiting Giles Danforth and Ryan Washington.

"How's Alex?" he asked Ryan, as they headed to the customs building dedicated to private-flights.

"She wanted to come with us today, but I had a support officer take her in hand. The counsellor's under instructions not to let Alex out of her sight."

"Is identification of Julie's body possible?"

"Not a chance. The fire … Jesus, what a mess. According to the ME, she wouldn't have felt a thing. Smoke inhalation would have killed her before the flames reached the bedroom."

"Do they know how it started?"

"Fire-fighters are still damping down, so the investigators won't get access for a while. But the guys I talked to reckon it might have been deliberate. A rigged gas explosion."

"Arson," Jones said through gritted teeth. "Anyone else hurt?"

"Yeah." Wash lowered his head. "A pedestrian walking his dog was hit by flying debris. Street's a real mess. Explosion destroyed the house next-door and caused loads of collateral damage. Looks like the aftermath of a battle. Smashed windows, ruined cars. Could have been a hell of a lot worse though."

"How's the dog-walker? Has he been interviewed? He might have seen something."

"Not yet. He's unconscious. I have a uniform with him set to call us the moment he wakes and the doctors give us the all clear. Major Crime Scene Unit is running the house-to-house interviews. Not sure we'll get all that much. Quiet street. The nearest CCTV camera's over a mile away."

Jones tried to relax his jaw muscles but his whole body remained tense. He turned to Giles.

"So it's the three of us now?"

"Not quite. I've pulled in my best officer." Giles raised a hand to halt Jones' impending interruption. "I trust Dylan with my life every time I go on a call, and I've known him since initial training. He's a damned good officer. Honest too. He's not your mole. Guaranteed."

Jones had to trust that Giles knew what he was doing, but he didn't like the idea of another variable he couldn't account for.

A lightning-fast transit through Border Control, followed by a rapid shower in the visitor's suite helped calm Jones' taut nerves. He changed into his own clothes, courtesy of Ryan, who'd grabbed the overnight bag from Jones' office, and felt a million times better.

Part 2

The crisp white shirt against his freshly scrubbed skin was a pure delight.

Within twenty-five minutes of the helicopter's touchdown, the four of them, Jones, Ryan, Giles, and Sergeant Roger 'Bob' Dylan, screamed along the A42 towards Derby in an unmarked police Range Rover. Dylan, a short, broad-shouldered man with close-cropped brown hair and a Geordie accent, drove. Ryan sat beside him. Jones and Giles took the rear seat.

Giles removed a folder from the parcel shelf.

"I had Phil Cryer run an online search of the detention centre and its surroundings and printed this off at the office from his email. We have an aerial view of the site. Phil found an architect's plans of the building and a few photos of the place from when it was still open."

Jones took the papers and studied each carefully. The map showed a group of buildings standing in the middle of large grounds. A railway track passed within one hundred metres of its rear fence. Further confirmation of his guess.

Hollie's there, she must be. Please let her be alive.

———

JONES and his hastily organised mini-team left the A38, joined Warwick Avenue, and arrived at Sunnyhill, a sprawling suburb some five miles south of Derby. Eventually, they found Park Drive, a three-mile long road that curved in a gentle anti-clockwise arc and continued towards the city centre.

To their left, undulating open farmland, with fields, hedges, and woods stretched into the distance. To the right lay the commuter-belt. Side roads gave access to estates of semi-detached and detached houses—featureless boxes for aspiring lives. Sunnyhill turned out to be little more than a dormitory town for people working in Derby and the much larger Birmingham.

According to Phil's internet research and downloaded aerial survey maps, the *Derbyshire Youth Detention Centre* occupied a three-acre site and backed onto the countryside on the western side of Park Drive.

Jones instructed Sergeant Dylan to enter an industrial estate of two, three, and four storey factory buildings some three hundred yards from the detention centre. Dylan found a quiet cul-de-sac and parked. The place was pretty much deserted, the factory outlets mostly closed for the weekend.

Jones and Ryan left the ARU men at the car checking their equipment and scouted the environs. They strolled back to the T-junction with Park Drive, playing two friends out for a Saturday morning stroll in the sun, ostensibly talking football.

Two hundred yards to the north, on the other side of Park Drive, an overgrown conifer hedge grew tall and spindly. Behind the hedge, Jones could just about make out a six-foot tall, red-bricked wall, which he knew would be topped with rusty razor wire. The wall defended the grounds to the former detention centre.

On the way back to the Range Rover, Jones nodded to a nearby warehouse, a Swedish furniture designer.

"Don't rush, somebody might be watching, but why don't you pop over there and see whether you can convince a security guard to let you and Dylan onto the roof? Looks like you'll have a pretty good view of the school from up there."

"See what I can do, boss."

Half an hour later, after Ryan's summons, Dylan, armed with a high-powered rifle and a radio comms unit, left the car to join him. It didn't take long for the ARU sergeant to announce that the rooftop site offered a three-sixty view of the area and a perfect observation point for the eastern side of the former grammar school.

"Excellent," Jones responded, "Ryan can act as spotter, but you're in command. Keep your heads down and your eyes open. Jones out."

Jones and Giles stayed with the car.

Giles spent most of the remaining time trying to convince Jones to call off the meet and drag in more backup. He counselled Jones to let the deadline pass, saying that Hollie Jardine was, in all probability, already dead, but Jones dug in his heels.

After half a dozen, "I don't like this one little bit, you'll be too exposed," and similar statements of gloom, Giles gave Jones a refresher course in hostage negotiations and urban military fieldcraft. Jones listened, humouring his friend who was trying to teach him to suck eggs.

"Never disagree with the hostage-taker … always say yes, and try to make him agree with you … make sure you keep your exits clear and scout for alternative routes in and out. Keep to one side of a room. Try to keep him between you and a window, I'll do the rest," and finally, "If he lets Hollie go, don't make your move until she's out of danger. I'll use the comms unit to let you know when she's safe."

Jones nodded his patient agreement the whole time, until Giles finally ran out of advice. Then they studied the architect's blueprints together.

A boarding school in a former life, the building was a maze of corridors, small classrooms, and dormitories. The most obvious venue for an open meeting—the Assembly Hall—occupied the front and centre of the ground floor. Accessible via a door in each wall and visible from the east side and front of the building, the hall became the focus of Giles' hasty plan. He used the American sporting term, "a Hail Mary", to describe the operation and Jones understood why.

The plan was pitiful in its simplicity.

Jones would head straight for the hall and try to make Jennings bring Hollie to him. The logic being that Jennings wanted Jones more than he wanted Hollie. If Jones dug his heels in, maybe Jennings would agree to his request. As soon as Hollie came under Giles' protection, things would be different. They could act, if Jennings didn't act first.

Giles marched to the back of the Rover and beckoned Jones to follow him. A large green medical kit took pride of place in the centre of the storage space. Giles grunted as he hefted the box to one side. "Hope we don't need this, but just in case …."

Moving the med kit exposed a metal weapons locker bolted to the floor pan. Giles dialled a number into the hefty digital lock and snapped open a pair of clasps. He pulled out a small, silver automatic handgun and offered it to Jones who backed away, raising his hands.

"No chance. Jennings said no weapons."

"Are you sure? He isn't likely to get close enough to frisk you, and I doubt he'll have had the time to set up a metal detector or an x-ray machine."

"I'm certain." Jones dug his hands into his pockets. "Wouldn't be able to fire it anyway."

"Even if Hollie's life depended on it?"

Jones shook his head.

"Never could pull the trigger. It's one of the reasons I had to leave the army and join the police." He gave Giles a half-hearted smile. "Not much use for a soldier who can't shoot, eh?"

"Gun-shy? You?"

Jones shrugged. "It's the way I'm built."

The stink of gun smoke and the gunpowder residue all over his hands hadn't helped, but there had been other reasons for his detestation of firearms.

After a final, "You sure you want to do this?" from Giles, and a, "Not one little bit," from Jones, Giles completed the final comms checks.

"Fifteen minutes to the deadline."

Giles dropped a hand on Jones' shoulder. It felt like a lead weight.

"Dylan and Wash are in a good position," Giles said. "They can cover most of the ground floor, east side. I'll be in front with you. There are a couple of blind spots, but we can't do anything about that. I'll be listening"—he tapped the earpiece—"but once you're inside we'll go to radio silence. Jennings has shown he knows his way around electronics so he'll probably be scanning you for a signal." He raised the tiny electronic device in his hand. "This is the absolutely latest bit of kit from the US army. Uses narrow-band microwave technology. They claim it can't be hacked or traced, but

Part 2

Jennings will probably have ears on you, so don't speak to us unless you absolutely have to, right?"

Jones nodded. He didn't trust himself to speak.

"Okay David, eleven-forty-eight. Off you go."

Jones closed his eyes and stood still for a moment. Birds chirruped, bees droned, and a sudden gust of wind drove the branches of the nearby conifer hedge into a gyrating frenzy. He wiped sweaty hands with a paper towel taken from a roll in the boot of the car and strode along the pavement towards Park Drive.

"Good luck, David. See you soon."

Hope so, Giles, but don't hold your breath.

Chapter Eighteen

SATURDAY MIDDAY – Hammer
Time since Ellis Flynn's stabbing: twenty-two hours

HAMMER LAY under a grey tarpaulin that matched the colour and texture of the third storey flat roof. He stared through the 30x50, high-magnification telescopic sight. At so short a range, less than four hundred yards, he'd make a kill shot ninety-nine times out of a hundred. The sound suppressor screwed into the end of the muzzle might reduce the accuracy by a couple of points, but it wouldn't affect the result.

The pane of glass between him and the girl had caused him some initial concern. When leaving her in the room he considered opening the window to remove the obstruction, but that presented a whole mess of potential trouble. If she woke from the second sedative, she might take it in her head to scream, and the sound would travel further with the window open. Jennings refused to allow him to gag her, because the limping man didn't want to risk her suffocating before Jones' arrival, which was a reasonable point.

Another problem with opening the window was visual. An open

window in a building supposedly locked and abandoned might arouse interest.

Decision made.

As usual, Hammer opted for fine crosshair reticles on the scope for better accuracy.

Although more difficult, he chose a head shot for an instant, painless kill. He didn't want the poor kid to suffer any more than she already had. After all, Hammer was a professional, not a fucking sadist like the limping arsehole, Jennings.

Hammer didn't like making war on children, but the money was good and that was all that mattered in the end.

He adjusted the parallax compensation nut and brought Hollie Jardine's forehead into even sharper focus. He'd bound the girl to a radiator and gaffer-taped her head into position. A fixed target. He really couldn't miss.

As for Jones, Hammer had offered a package deal for both hits, but Jennings declined. He wanted to do the middle-aged cop personally, but that was okay by Hammer. He'd made sure the payment arrangements were in place in case the cripple fucked up and was taken. Everything was cool. His job ended the moment he killed the girl, and that was fine by him. There were plenty more contracts in the pipeline to keep him occupied and increase his bank balance.

He inched the rifle five degrees north to check the wind strength. The strip of light plastic tape he'd tied to the guttering four storeys above the girl didn't so much as flicker. The big mother of a building acted as an excellent windbreak and took one important confounding variable right out of the equation.

Two hours earlier, Hammer managed to suppress a chuckle when an unmarked police Range Rover arrived and parked on the street fifty metres below his vantage point. The wily old bugger, Jones, had welched on the deal and arrived mob-handed. No matter, Jennings had predicted as much. The nut job wasn't so stupidly arrogant after all.

Everybody knew the deal was bogus. The girl's death had been preordained from the moment they took her from the hospital bed.

In the end, the Range Rover's proximity turned into a real advantage and allowed him to hear every word the cops said once outside the vehicle.

The big one, Giles Somebody, wasn't happy and tried his best, but Jones was going to risk his life for the girl, and Giles couldn't persuade him otherwise.

Hammer smiled. The old guy earned top marks for bravery, but none for street smarts.

What about the other two?

The scrawny-looking one with the sloped shoulders, Wash Something, and the squat one, Dylan, were five hundred yards away on top of a factory roof looking in the wrong direction. Neither would cause a problem. No, he was sitting, or to be more exact, lying pretty.

The situation became even better when Giles followed Jones towards the former school, leaving Hammer's rear exit open and unguarded. Couldn't have been more excellent.

Not long now.

Lungs full, he held his breath for the count of five, and exhaled slowly. He repeated the mantra his instructor drummed into him week after week in sniper school.

"Relax. Slow your heart rate. Fire at the bottom of the exhale. Squeeze the trigger, don't pull it."

He rolled his shoulders to ease a stiffening neck, and rested his index finger along the trigger guard. The scope's cross hairs lined up with the centre of Hollie Jardine's forehead.

This was going to be the easiest seventy-five grand Hammer had ever earned.

Chapter Nineteen

SATURDAY MIDDAY – Sunshine and hot glass
Time since Ellis Flynn's stabbing: twenty-two hours

THE HOT SUN beat down hard on the top of Jones' head. The clean, fresh feel the airport shower had given him disappeared as sweat bled through every pore on his body. He thought about removing the light summer jacket, but if he was about to die, he'd go as he lived—neat, tidy, professional.

His tongue stuck to the roof of his mouth and he found it difficult to swallow. Dark thoughts raced through his mind, tumbling over themselves in a jumble of broken images and half-finished questions. Foremost amongst them were for Hollie Jardine.

Had he worked out the clues correctly and guessed the right location? Was she here and still alive?

Nothing in the training manual or regulations allowed him to risk his life like this, to take such a ridiculous gamble, but he had no choice. It was his life for Hollie's.

Is it worth it?

As he headed towards his fate, Jones ran through a scant checklist. He'd reached his fifties, and what did he have to show for his life?

No family left alive, few friends outside work, and a dilapidated ruin in the country he would never finish, not now.

That was it.

"Lived alone, died alone."

Not much of an epitaph for a life spent trying to make a difference.

What about professionally? What did he leave as a legacy? A desk piled high—although neatly—with unclosed case files. A half-decent career as a thief-taker, but that was all.

The SCU wouldn't continue without him, not with Phil out of commission however temporarily. Neither Ryan nor Alex would stay in a unit led by a promoted Charlie Pelham, or by someone else drafted in from outside.

He had a few years until retirement and then what? A couple of decades spent trying to eke out a living on a Civil Servant's pension. The occasional reunion bash where he and a cabal of other has-beens would get together to remember the good old days, the days when they were still valued? In a few years, he'd have nothing to look forward to but a long slow decline into a loneliness and oblivion.

Oh, Jesus. Remember you're doing this for a young girl who said, 'Thank you, David'. And for the memory of a girl you loved and the boy who never had a chance to grow up.

Jones gritted his teeth and marched on, resigned to the fact that this was likely to be his last hoorah.

He had one slim chance.

Giles Danforth.

Ordinarily, Jones would have had every faith in Giles, but he'd given his friend a near-impossible task. Protect Hollie first, and Jones second. In that order. Protect them from an unknown threat, in an unknown environment, and without the necessary resources.

He chewed his lower lip and bunched his hands into fists. He'd done it again, hadn't he? Called in old favours and endangered the lives and careers of his few remaining friends. Julie Harris' face popped into his head. Poor Alex. She'd jumped in to help and look what happened to her life partner, her wife.

Jones wiped his mouth with the back of his hand. Sharp whiskers scraped the sun-tender skin of his wrist. He'd have awful sunburn in the morning, but that wasn't likely to be an issue.

C'mon, Jones. Concentrate. Check your surroundings. At least pretend to go through the routine.

A prickling in the middle of his back told him someone other than Giles watched him.

He made the right turn onto Park Lane and strode onwards, his footsteps muffled by the accumulated dirt and the dead leaves littering the pavement.

Jones tried to take a deep breath, but it caught in his throat.

The time on his Seiko read: 11:54.

Get a move on, man.

Three hundred metres.

He marched on, stretching his legs to increase his stride.

TWO HUNDRED METRES.

Close up, the conifer hedge was more ragged than he'd imagined. Three of the trees, brown and dead, teetered dangerously close to collapse. It didn't take long for places to corrupt and die. Jones' cottage would do the same thing after his death.

Ashes to ashes, dust to … For pity's sakes, man. Stop it!

One hundred and fifty ….

There it was. The entrance.

Chapter Twenty

SATURDAY MIDDAY – *Face-to-face*
Time since Ellis Flynn's stabbing: twenty-two hours, forty minutes

JONES STOPPED.

Two large brick columns, three-metres tall, supported a huge pair of rusting wrought iron gates. He stared up at the overarching and badly formed sign, *The Darbishire Detention Centre for Juvenile Offenders.*

He re-read the words and frowned.

Darbishire?

The spelling was wrong. Pitiful. He filed the information away for later—not that he *had* a later—and peered through the gate's vertical bars.

Although the entrance gates were closed, someone had unclasped the padlock holding the rusted chains together. He freed the chain and pushed at one of the gates. It opened with a rusty, careworn screech.

His shoes crunched on a sparsely gravelled drive that curved

Part 2

uphill to the former school-the former Boy's Home. He had to tread with care to avoid the dips and potholes. It wouldn't do to twist an ankle at this late stage in the game. Former lawns, now weed-covered pastures, spread out on either side of the pathway. The run-down appearance reminded Jones of his approach to Ellis Flynn's cottage. At least this time, he didn't have to crawl on his belly.

As he drew closer, Jones studied the crumbling edifice.

Built in the middle of Queen Victoria's reign, the building's age-dirtied orange bricks and grey stone window surrounds could have been the setting of many a Dickensian novel. A pair of doors—black paint peeling to reveal bare oak panels—stood closed, forbidding. Two dozen small windows dotted the facade, some boarded, some broken, others intact but filthy. He wondered what sort of a hellish life the inmates of this establishment had endured, back in the day.

This was the place of Ellis Flynn's rebirth. The place he had morphed from nascent child molester into a serial-killing monster.

How many more inmates had been turned into an Ellis Flynn?

The Seiko on his wrist showed, 11:58.

Atop the three steps to the grand porch and the imposing doors, Jones hesitated. A single static click in his earpiece told him Giles still had line-of-sight. As planned, the ARU man had scaled the crumbling wall using the cover of the hedge.

Jones took another breath and approached the stepped-back doors. A sheet of paper pinned to the one of the panels held a computer printed note:

"Hello, Jonesy-boy.
Bang on time, as I knew you'd be.
First door on the left.
JJ."

RELIEF AND FURY flooded through Jones. Relief that he'd guessed the correct location, and fury at Jennings' taunting welcome.

Unable to overcome a lifetime spent gathering evidence, Jones ripped the note from the door, slid it into an evidence bag, and placed it in the breast pocket of his jacket.

Jones twisted the tarnished brass handle. As the lock drew back it gave out a loud metallic clunk. He pushed and the hinges creaked in protest.

Somewhere off to his right, water dripped onto a floor. A cobweb brushed against his face. The smell of decay attacked his nostrils. The authorities had boarded up the old school and left it to rot. One day, when the recession finally ended, the place would no doubt fall under the control of a property speculator. But for the time being, it slowly rotted away.

Jones left the door wide open to help Giles and crossed the threshold.

The earpiece clicked twice.

Damn.

Giles was blind.

He took a half pace to the left, to keep clear of the open doorway.

Single click.

Better.

The entrance hall must have been twenty degrees colder than the air outside. The floor's black and white tiles—set in a chessboard pattern, many cracked—radiated waves of frigid air. Thick, plastered walls, damp with disuse, hosted spores of black mildew and showed the faded marks where oak half panels had once been. Fancy cornices, broken and yellowed with age, showed evidence of a once-magnificent building now corrupting and decaying. The walls opened into corridors and dark wooden doors were dotted everywhere. Was Hollie behind one of them?

"Well done, *Jonesy-boy!*"

Jones jumped. His heart skipped into a double beat.

Jennings' disembodied, electronic voice boomed and echoed through the deserted entrance hall.

Part 2

An old-fashioned grey funnel speaker above one of the doors, hastily erected with cables trailing haphazardly, magnified the sound and made it difficult to understand. A feedback squeal stabbed at Jones' ears. He clamped both hands to the side of his head.

"I knew you wouldn't let the little bitch down. You understood my message, then?" The volume diminished and with it, the screech.

"Where's Hollie?" Jones shouted.

"Turn right. Come into my parlour said the spider …"

"Where is she?" Jones yelled again, but Jennings continued uninterrupted.

"…to the fly. Come on. Come on. Hurry up."

A dark, four-panelled door blocked his way. He pushed it open. From his reading of the floor plan, he already knew it led to headmaster's study, or rather, the warden's office.

Jones' spirits lifted. The room would be in full view of the front gates. Giles would be able to see him clearly. They still had a chance.

Jones entered a bare room. Wooden floorboards, blackened with age and dotted with woodworm, creaked underfoot. He made sure to keep away from the windows.

Something whimpered to his left. He snapped his head around.

"Hollie!"

She sat scrunched sideways on the floor in the corner of the room. Two thick cable ties bound her hands and feet to a cast-iron radiator. Blood trickled from wounds caused by the bindings. She still wore the hospital gown, filthy now and stained with her body waste. The instant he saw her head taped to a downpipe feeding the radiator, he knew Jennings' plan.

Stupid idiot, Jones. All for nothing.

He made a move forward.

"Stop! Raise your hands!"

Jones complied.

Jennings' voice had a different sound, natural, not enhanced by electronics. It came from the doorway Jones had recently stepped through, which stood directly behind him.

The bastard was in the room with them.

Every cell in his body wanted him to rush towards Hollie, release her, and scoot her from the room. His earpiece remained silent.

Where are you, Giles?

"Make one move before I tell you and the girl dies."

"What happens now?" Jones risked the question.

"I get to watch you suffer."

"What?" Jones tensed, preparing for the inevitable.

Hollie groaned and tried to lift her head and pull her hands free of the radiator.

"Hollie," Jones whispered. "Don't move."

Her eyes opened and swivelled in her restrained head. Bare feet scraped at the floorboards trying to push away from the radiator. She caught sight of Jones and blinked.

"David?" A brief flicker of hope reached her blue eyes before they stared past Jones and opened wide in fear.

Jennings' voice screamed the single word that ended Jones' hope.

"Fire."

"No!"

Jones dived towards the girl trying to shield her, but he had no chance. Behind him, glass shattered. A high-pitched sizzle flew by his right ear. Heat scorched his hair as it passed.

The top of Hollie's head exploded in a bright red splatter of blood and hair. She slumped.

It happened in the half-second Jones flew through the air. He landed hard on the floor a metre short of Hollie and let out an animal roar.

"Hollie!"

Her hand trembled as the final vestiges of her short life ended.

No. Oh God. No.

The iron-rich smell of hot blood invaded his senses. The rage of lost hope boiled. His own blood pounded in his ears.

Behind him, Jennings chuckled.

"Oh dear. Terrible waste of a good cast member."

Part 2

Jones twisted and stared through tear-blurred eyes filled with rage.

A man stood in the doorway.

Jennings.

He leaned on a whitewood cane, its silver handle gripped tight in his left hand. The right hand clutched a dull black revolver, the barrel levelled at Jones' chest. The monster wore a baseball cap, dark glasses, and a broad grin. He shook his head in mock sadness.

Jones screamed and scrambled to his feet. Nothing mattered. He needed to rip, to maim, to kill.

Before he reached half way, the pistol exploded in a ball of yellow fire and a billow of blue-grey smoke.

The bullet hit Jones full square in the chest. It spun him around and lifted him off his feet. Another gunshot followed.

Jones' heart jolted. He stared up at the plaster ceiling. The ornate cornices, the reminders of a time gone by, faded to a smoky blur.

His vision misted, turned first to grey, then to black.

Part 3

PART THREE

"What the hell's happening to the world when an innocent child can be treated like this?"

Chapter One

SATURDAY AFTERNOON – *Giles Danforth*
   Time since the shooting: seven minutes

"DAVID?" Giles placed two fingers against his friend's carotid artery. His mind turned back to the last time he did the same thing, in the hospital lift. Miraculously, this time he found a pulse, and one that was strong and firm.

"Thank Christ. Rest there, mate. Young Wash called for an ambulance. It'll be here in a couple of minutes."

David's head moved, lips twitched.

"Can't breathe," he whispered. "Get this bloody thing off me, will you?"

Giles pulled at David's jacket and ripped open the shirt. Three of the buttons popped from the cloth and rolled across the floor. He released the Velcro straps from the micro-light ceramic body-armour. Jennings' bullet had struck dead centre, a black dimple marked the spot on the white surface. Without the protective vest, a certain kill shot. There would be damage though. Bruised ribs at least, maybe a fracture or two, but his mate was still alive.

David groaned and struggled to raise his head.

"Hollie?"

Giles glanced up at the girl he couldn't save. Her body lay crumpled in the corner, hands and feet still tethered to the radiator, the top of her head a real mess. Hair, blood, and scalp tissue plastered the wall behind her. The spatter, a graffiti tag painted by a butcher. Something Damien Hirst might have dreamed up but rejected as going a step too far.

So damned young. What the fuck did she do to deserve that?

David's eyes fluttered. He winced as he tried to sit.

"Hollie?" he asked again through gritted teeth.

The pain in his eyes didn't only originate from the bullet to the chest, Giles was certain of that.

"She's gone, David. I'm so sorry. I let you down."

David lowered his head.

"Why am I still alive? Jennings fired twice after Hollie was hit. How'd he miss with the second one?"

"No, David. I made the third shot through the window after the sniper killed Hollie. I had a clean shot. Don't know how the hell I missed the bastard. But there's no blood and he was gone by the time I arrived." Giles punched the floor with the side of his fist.

He continued. "The animal locked the front doors behind you and the comms went down after the first PA announcement. He must have jammed the bloody signal somehow."

"State-of-the-art, you said." David, lying prone, rubbed his eyes with the heels of his hands. "State of the bloody art!"

Giles shook his head. "Don't know how he did it without the signal frequency. But I'll find out." He'd screwed up. Hollie died because he didn't search the surroundings properly. Their early arrival should have given them the edge, but the sniper had arrived even earlier. He'd beaten them to it.

Hollie was the second hostage to die on Giles' watch. It got no easier.

Jones winced again. "How'd Jennings get away? He can't move fast with that limp."

Part 3

"Dunno. Dozens of rooms and corridors … We'll need sniffer dogs and the locals to form search teams. But it'll be too fucking late by the time they get here."

With another groan, David rolled onto his left side and struggled to all fours. Giles helped him stand. They avoided the corner of the room as too painful.

David stood, head bowed, shoulders slumped. Giles had never seen him look so damned … old.

Giles half-carried him to the window. Splinters of broken glass peppered the sill. He brushed them away with a gloved hand. They hit the floorboards like a shower of salt crystals, scarcely making a sound. He rested a hand on David's shoulder, forcing him to sit as the siren of an ambulance broke the oppressive silence.

"What about the sniper?"

"Away on his toes. He fired from a rooftop near where we parked the car. Wash spotted him after he heard my comms shout. He and Dylan are there now, searching.

"You sure he's gone? Are they safe?"

"Yes, he drove off in an old Ford. Dylan didn't have a shot and the bugger got away. Wash sent out a description of the car."

To Giles, it sounded so bloody lame. Such a total fucking balls up.

David rested his hands on shaking knees but kept his back locked straight, grimacing against the pain.

Giles paced the room but, in deference, stayed well away from Hollie's body. The place was now a crime scene, and he knew better than to get too close. He turned his back on the pieces of scalp and strands of hair stuck in the blood—the silken threads of a hideous cobweb. "So sorry, David. What a God-awful mess."

The siren stopped. Ambulance doors opened, slammed shut, and footsteps crunched on gravel. Giles rushed to open the main doors and escorted two green-clad paramedics into the Warden's office.

The leader, Pik Jessop, according to the name embroidered on the front of his tunic, paused in the doorway, took one look at

David's pallid face and pained expression, and headed straight for him.

"You've been shot, sir?"

"I'm okay." David raised his head and pointed at Hollie. "Go to her."

Jessop turned his head to the left. A shock of long brown hair flopped over his eyes. "Oh ... right, sorry."

The ambulance men crossed to the body and squatted. Jessop placed the medical bag on the floor and removed a stethoscope. He handed a scalpel to his mate and fixed the stethoscope's buds into his ears.

"Cut those ties. I need to—" His whole body tensed. "Jesus, there's a pulse! This girl's alive."

David jumped to his feet, arms wrapped tight around his chest, and took two paces towards the corner. A look of disbelief twisted his ashen face.

"Don't play silly buggers. How can she be alive?"

He clenched a fist and his face contorted in pain. He teetered. Giles rushed across and grabbed his arm.

The paramedics released Hollie's hands, feet, and head, and gently laid her on her back. Her chest moved.

Christ, she is *still breathing!*

The second paramedic race out the door and returned moments later with a collapsible stretcher.

"How's that possible?" Giles asked, his voice little more than a whisper.

Colour returned to David's face and he tore his arm free of Giles' grip. He knelt beside Hollie, took her hand, and closed his eyes.

"Head wounds bleed profusely, sir," said Jessop. "Her scalp's a mess, and I suspect there might be a depressed skull fracture. She'll need a scan ... heart rate's slow but regular ... breathing shallow."

He removed a penlight from his breast pocket, gently raised Hollie's lids one at a time, and waved the light in front of her eyes.

"Pupils evenly dilated and responsive." He broke off from the examination and stole a glance at each of them. A thin smile played

Part 3

on his lips. "She's still in danger, but there's a chance. A lucky young woman."

David moved back to allow the medics room. After fixing a neck brace, they took great care moving Hollie onto the stretcher. They draped a loose bandage over her wound and attached a clip monitor to her left index finger.

With Jessop at the head, and his mate at the feet, they hefted the stretcher carefully, and carried Hollie towards the door.

As Jessop passed, he spoke to Giles. "There's a bullet hole in the wall back there you'll want to take a look at."

"Where are you taking her?" David's voice strengthened as he spoke.

"Saint Mary's cranial suite. We've got to go right now."

David raised an open hand. His fingers trembled.

"Wait."

"But, sir—"

"No, wait. Please," he repeated, insistent and urgent.

"David," Giles said quietly. "She needs to go to the hospital. She's still in danger."

David straightened and fixed him with an impatient glare.

"I know that, Giles, but Jennings and the sniper are still out there somewhere. If Jennings hasn't bugged this room, he'll still think Hollie's dead. We need to keep her condition quiet. At least until we've set up a secure room at the hospital. Okay?"

Giles wondered why he hadn't thought of it himself.

The light returned to David's pale eyes, and he recovered some of his old composure. He looked calm, centred, controlled. Sharp as the scalpel the paramedics used to free Hollie. Giles smiled and thanked fuck he had his old friend back.

"Mr Jessop," David said with the tone of quiet authority Giles recognised and admired so much. "Would it harm Hollie's chances to cover her face with that sheet and disconnect the monitor?"

Jessop hesitated and studied Hollie for a second. He pursed his lips.

"Only until you get her into the ambulance?" David added. "Someone's tried to kill her twice in the past twenty-four hours."

"Um … yes. But we'll have to hurry."

Giles followed them to the foyer as Ryan burst through the entrance door. His jaw dropped when he spotted Hollie on the stretcher, still breathing. He broke into a smile wide enough to span the Thames at London Bridge.

"How the fuck—"

David cut him off with a raised hand.

"Go with them to the hospital. Tell no one. Not even her parents. I'll contact them later. No one's to know Hollie's still alive but us. Got it?" Ryan nodded. "And stop grinning, man. Droop your shoulders. You're desperately sad, right?"

Ryan changed his expression to deadpan and augmented it with an additional stoop.

"Got it, boss. What about Dylan? Should we get him to mount guard while we're there?"

David looked to Giles for permission—Bob Dylan was under Giles' command, not David's.

"Good idea," said Giles. "But make sure he changes into plain clothes. Wouldn't want people wondering why an armed officer is protecting a corpse."

"Yes, sir."

Jessop cleared his throat. "We're ready."

Hollie lay on her back, the sheet pulled over her head. David leaned close to her and whispered, "Stay with us, Hollie. Be strong," and squeezed her hand.

Giles stood aside, head lowered, while the paramedics loaded the stretcher into the ambulance. Jessop and Ryan hopped in the back and the other man drove away slowly, without the sirens and flashing lights. To begin with, they weren't in a hurry. No need to race to the mortuary.

By the time Giles retraced his steps to the office, David had returned to the windowsill. He sat, face in hands, shoulders shaking.

Giles coughed as he entered the room. The old man wouldn't appreciate anyone seeing him cry. David straightened slowly and took a stuttering breath.

Part 3

"Are you okay, David? You took a hell of a blow to the chest. Should have gone with them to the hospital."

DCI David Jones stood, pulled his shirtfront together, straightened his tie, and tugged the creases out of his jacket. The eyes, though still shiny, had their old fire back.

"Time enough for the hospital when I'm dead, Giles." He turned to face the window and squinted. He studied the glass closely for a moment.

"What's that?" he asked.

He pointed at the bullet holes. One cut through the top left quadrant of the window. The other, smaller than the first, was ten inches lower and to the right.

"Top one's from the sniper. The lower one's mine."

David frowned and leaned to one side to study the damage from an oblique angle.

"Something's wrong with them. You're the expert. What do you think?"

Giles stepped closer to the window and fingered the two cone-shaped bullet holes. They were smaller than he expected, and the edges crenulated when they should have been smooth. The spider web pattern of cracks radiating out from the centres didn't look right either. They were tighter, more concentrated than they should have been.

"You're right, well spotted. What the bloody hell does it mean?"

"Take a look from the side. The glass is much thicker than you'd expect. It could be why you missed your shot, and why Hollie's still alive. I want a ballistics report—"

He pressed a hand to his breastbone and sucked air through his teeth.

"You sure I shouldn't take you to the hospital?"

"No, a twinge is all. Be alright in a minute. Let's go find Jennings, or whatever the fuck he's really called."

"Wow, never heard you swear."

"Sorry." He winked. "Don't tell the team, or they'll think I'm human."

"Never seen anyone more human than you, mate," Giles said

and clapped David on the back before remembering his friend's ribs.

"Easy, Giles. I'm a broken old man, remember."

"No you aren't. Not broken at least."

Giles couldn't stop himself from smiling.

Chapter Two

SATURDAY AFTERNOON – *Fruitless searches*
Time since the shooting: six hours

JONES' frustration had built to breaking point. He'd never felt so bloody helpless.

Six hours spent searching for Jennings proved fruitless. Sniffer dogs lost his trail within minutes of entering the dank building. The lame killer had disappeared faster than an early morning mist under a hot sun. The hired gun, the sniper had vanished, too.

The Officer-in-Charge and Jones' local counterpart, DCI Mike Fuller, had been apoplectic when he arrived to find Hollie's body gone, but dialled it back after receiving a full—and private—briefing. He shot question after question, obviously concerned for Jones' sanity, before agreeing to keep Hollie's condition quiet for as long as he could.

AT HALF-PAST SEVEN THAT EVENING, and with a great deal of reluctance, Jones left the local murder team and crime scene investigators to their painstaking business. He'd been forced to admit that Jennings had escaped him yet again.

The estimable DCI Fuller organised transport to the hospital where Jones spent the rest of the evening pacing the corridor outside the operating suite. Mr and Mrs Jardine sat patiently in the dedicated waiting area. God only knew how they had managed to cope with the events of the previous two days. A pale-skinned and sunken-eyed Emma Jardine sat in silence. Frank's shoulders sagged, but his tired eyes glistened with hope and he kept smiling and thanking Jones for bringing his daughter back to them again.

Jones had to admire the man's inner strength.

A few minutes before midnight, a balding surgeon, Mr Albright, breezed through the operating suite doors. He wore washed-out green hospital scrubs and a tired smile.

An exhausted Jones only caught snippets of Albright's explanation after he told the Jardines that Hollie had survived the operation really well. Jones eased into a hard-backed chair and forced his shoulders to relax, wondering when someone had taken the meat tenderiser to his neck without him noticing. His back and ribs radiated pain each time he took a breath, but emotionally, he couldn't remember being as ecstatic. Hollie was alive, and he somehow knew she would recover well from her ordeal.

Albright explained Hollie's injuries in such detail that another doctor might be able to understand him, but Jones didn't.

As Jessop, the paramedic diagnosed, Hollie had suffered a compressed cranial fracture. During the extended operation, Albright and his team drained a build-up of fluid on the brain, and rebuilt her damaged skull. As for the prognosis, Albright made no promises.

"Brain injuries are notoriously difficult to diagnose," he said, but he was, "optimistic." The scan had shown a "slight swelling …" and "they wouldn't know Hollie's condition until she woke …" Albright predicted "severe concussion", and said they would "keep Hollie

Part 3

under close observation for a few days to guard against further inflammation of the brain tissue."

In the end, Albright gave the Jardines a leaflet explaining the signs and symptoms of brain compression injuries, and concluded by saying Hollie's physical outlook was "promising". At one stage, he actually used the word "miraculous", but by then Jones was too exhausted to take in anything new.

After Albright's detailed and convoluted explanation, Frank Jardine insisted he examine Jones. The surgeon diagnosed three heavily bruised ribs and a possible cracked sternum.

Thank you, Doctor. I could have told you that without the finger-prodding torture.

"What's the treatment, Doctor?" he asked while tugging on his jacket.

"We don't strap ribcage injuries anymore," he said. "There's no point. So all I can offer is a prescription for heavy-duty painkillers and bed-rest. Visit your GP in a week if the pain doesn't ease."

Bed-rest, yeah, right. With a murdering paedophile and his gang on the loose? Thanks for that.

Jones rejected the offer of a confirmatory x-ray, but thanked Albright for his time and the prescription, which he folded and slipped into his pocket. He'd run it through the shredder later. Apart from the occasional glass of beer or wine, Jones didn't take drugs—ever. In his experience, the side effects could often be worse than the benefits.

"I hate to ask, but when do you think Hollie will be fit to make a statement?"

The doctor's eyes widened and his nostrils flared.

"Are you serious? After what that girl's been through over the past few days, you want to interrogate her?"

Jones clamped his jaws together and counted to five before responding.

"Hollie might be able to lead us to the monsters who did this to her. I promise to be extremely gentle."

"Be that as it may, Chief Inspector. My prime concern is for Hollie's wellbeing."

"Mine too."

Albright tried to stare him down, but Jones refused to be intimidated. He'd been confronted by more frightening gerbils.

"She is heavily sedated at the moment, and I doubt she'll be conscious until morning at the absolute earliest. You will not be allowed to talk to her until I'm satisfied she's out of danger."

"Fair enough," Jones conceded. "Sorry, doctor, but this case is bigger and uglier than you can possibly imagine."

Albright softened his stance a little.

"I do understand, Chief Inspector, but I'm not going to rush her."

They shook hands and the surgeon retreated through the operating suite doors—returning to his personal fiefdom.

After receiving more of the Jardines' undying and somewhat embarrassing gratitude, and avoiding their hugs, Jones secured an armed guard for Hollie consisting of Giles, the strong and largely silent Dylan, and a couple of locals armed officers assigned by DCI Fuller. The protective detail would suffice until they could move Hollie to a safe house in Birmingham, or until they found Jennings.

Jones didn't feel safe to drive, and with a generosity that took Jones by surprise, DCI Fuller provided a patrol car to take him home. An hour and twenty minutes later—at five past two in the morning—he closed the front door behind him.

Home. Thank God.

The place may have been a half-finished old ruin in the middle of nowhere, but it was *his* half-finished old ruin in the middle of nowhere.

The instant he slid into the scalding hot bath and soaked away the grime of Brittany, the detention centre, and the hospital, his mood lightened. He towelled off, refreshed.

A frozen pizza with his favourite topping, Bolognese with extra cheese, had cooked in the oven while he soaked. The smell from the kitchen was amazing and made his mouth water. Drizzled in piquant olive oil, and sprinkled with grated parmesan for added bite, the pizza hit the spot dead centre. Accompanied by a small glass of Burgundy, it set him up for a wonderful night's rest.

Part 3

Thirty minutes after finishing his meal, Jones relaxed into the paradise of clean, crisp sheets, and his head hit the pillow.

Chapter Three

SUNDAY MORNING – *The value of literature*
Time since the shooting: twenty-one hours

FIVE-AND-A-HALF HOURS OF RESTORATIVE SLEEP, the longest unbroken rest he'd had in months, found Jones awake and refreshed. He rolled onto his back carefully, stared at the ceiling, and took time to assess his physical state. Apart from the damaged ribs stabbing him with red-hot pokers each time he breathed or moved, everything was hunky-bloody-dory—if he excluded all the other mess.

Before moving from his bed, he reached for the phone and dialled the hospital in Derby. It took him a while for the operator to put him through to Frank Jardine.

"Chief Inspector," he said, with the joy of a man with wonderful news to impart. "I would have called you, but Hollie said you looked tired and needed your sleep."

"What? Hollie's awake?"

"Yes, Chief Inspector. Didn't I say?" Frank laughed. "Sorry, but we're a little overwhelmed, as you can imagine. She woke about an

Part 3

hour ago and asked how you were. She remembered you coming to save her."

Not for the first time that week, Jones was lost for words. He promised to call again and speak to Hollie after Albright had finished his assessment, and then dressed, all the time unable to wipe the stupid relieved smile from his aching face. Although he didn't look in the mirror, Jones knew the smile was stupid—he rarely had cause to use it.

He finished a breakfast of cereal and tea before making perhaps the most difficult phone call of his life. Commiseration calls were never easy, but one to a close colleague was impossible. The mobile had been on charge overnight and Jones stared at the screen for a full five minutes before dredging up the strength to hit speed-dial #4. Alex answered the call within two rings.

"Hi, boss." Her voice was subdued, but he'd expected nothing else.

"Alex. How are you?"

Stupid question. How do you think she is, idiot?

"Fine, boss. You know. Still getting used to … the situation."

What could he say to make things easier?

Absolutely nothing.

"Wanted to call last night, but I didn't get in until … Oh, hell. I'm so sorry, Alex. I …"

"Not your fault, boss." She made her voice stronger, more defiant. "Jennings is responsible, not you."

Perhaps, but I dragged you into this mess.

"What happened?" he asked. "How did you escape the … fire?"

"Julie parked the car in the garage after dropping me at the airport yesterday. I must have driven out the back way moments before the arsonist broke in. It would appear that the house exploded ten minutes after I left." She paused and gulped in a huge sigh. "Oh, boss. Julie …."

She broke down.

Jones held on in silence. He hated the sound of her distress, but he was useless with emotion. He'd let himself go once, lost control when his family died. Spent weeks wallowing in a moraine of despair. He couldn't go through that again, not with so much work still to do. Jones owed Alex answers, and a disjointed, depressed boss would do no one any good.

He let her cry.

"I heard about Hollie," she said through the sobs. "I'm so sorry we couldn't save her."

"You mean nobody's told you?"

Bloody fool, Jones. Who'd have told her?

"Alex, Hollie's alive. The doctors say she's going to be fine."

Okay, perhaps he was being a little premature with the prognosis, but good news was good news.

Alex burst into tears again, but these were different.

"Thank you so much for telling me, boss. It's going to help when I … make arrangements. Julie's parents arrive this morning …." Her voice cracked again.

"Are you staying at the Grand?"

The inappropriately named and past-its-sell-by-date Grand Hotel, in the old city centre, offered a discount to police officers and their guests.

"Yes. It's quite comfortable."

"I'll call on you tonight and offer my … well, you know."

Jones didn't look forward to the meeting with any relish. Not while the men responsible for so much destruction and death roamed the country, free as skylarks.

"Boss? Promise me one thing?"

Oh hell, here it comes.

He hesitated.

"If I can."

Don't ask. Please don't ask.

"Let me be there when you arrest Jennings?"

Bloody knew it.

"Oh, Alex. You know that's not possib—"

"Please, boss. I need to see his face when you put on the handcuffs. I promise I won't touch or speak to him. You have my word." She sobbed again.

What can you say to that, Jones?

Part 3

"I have no idea who or where the bastard is yet."

"But you'll find him, this I know. Please, boss? I need to be there."

At least she didn't say you owe it to her.

"We'll talk about it tonight."

"*Tack så mycket*, boss. Thank you so much."

Jones ended the call and stared into the dregs of his morning cuppa. He knew he'd been in the wrong, but he simply hadn't been able to refuse her request. Now all he had to do was find Jennings even though he didn't have a clue who or where the bastard was.

John Jennings.

He repeated the name, this time saying it aloud.

"John C Jennings."

Where had he heard the bloody name before?

"Jonathan Jennings?"

He cast his eyes around the room. The packing crates stored in the far corner of his kitchen-diner caught his eye. He'd put them there when he cleared the lounge to add a new radiator. They were a bloody eyesore, but he wouldn't be able to move the heavy wooden boxes until his ribs healed.

The fifteen boxes housed the few precious mementos of a long life spent mainly alone. They contained his memories: wedding photos of unknown and long-deceased parents; pictures of his dead sister aged twenty-three; school certificates; graduation photos of him as a fresh-faced constable; Siân and the baby who would never grow up; and baby toys he'd bought as presents but never had the chance to give. Eight of the boxes contained books.

He'd planned to start on the library over the winter, but police work always took priority. Bookshelves, another project he needed to put on hold. The books would remain packed for another summer. He hoped damp hadn't reached them.

The books!

"Bloody hell. The books!"

The answer hit him with the stunning force of a brick to the back of the head. A decent night's sleep had freed his mind, unblocked the logjam.

Could it be that simple? He had associated the name Jennings with work, a criminal from an unremembered case, or maybe a victim. But no, Jennings wasn't an enemy, but a long-forgotten *friend*. A character he'd spent many hours with as a lonely, sensitive child.

Jennings. Of course!

"Jones, you bloody idiot!"

He'd been too tired to make the connection in France, and too busy since. With a bark of laughter, Jones pulled the handwritten inventory from a filing cabinet in his makeshift office, a corner of the spare bedroom. Drawn up nearly a decade earlier, and written in longhand, the catalogue listed each item in each box in alphabetical order.

Crate Six: Books, childhood, A-to-M.

He didn't even have to search the boxes. The comprehensive list had it all. Crate Six contained half the books he'd pored over as a child. One series in particular grabbed his interest, thirty-two novels in all. Stories that had kept him company from the orphanage and through each foster home. The books that had wrapped up his early life. The author, Anthony Buckeridge, had been his all-time boyhood hero.

Jones read each title on the list. The fourth stood out as large as a beacon and reaffirmed his working theory—*Jennings and Darbishire*. He yelped in delight and punched the air. The damaged ribs screamed in complaint, but he didn't care.

Rare times such as these made police work worthwhile.

Got you, you bastard.

His next phone call woke Phil Cryer, yet again.

"Jesus, boss. How many more times are you going to wake me up in the middle of the night?"

"It's nearly eight o'clock, man, but I promise, you're gonna thank me. Listen …"

After setting Phil the confirmatory task—desk research only—he made three more calls. With the first, he dispatched Ryan to help the team investigate the arson at Alex's home. With the second, he tasked Section 14, the West Midlands Police's covert observation unit, to liaise with Phil and put a twenty-four hour watch on the man who'd passed himself off as John C Jennings.

Now that Jones had an actual ID, he wasn't going to let the murderous arsehole out of his sight until ready to make his move. Police mole or not, "Jennings" wasn't going to escape this time. The third and final call was to Giles and asked for an unbiased sitrep on Hollie.

"She's really weak, but wants to see you."

"What does Albright say?"

"He says she shouldn't be questioned, but Hollie's insistent. Won't take no for an answer."

"That's great. What about her parents?"

"They think you're a superstar, and they deffo wouldn't dream of saying no to her. Not for a while, at least."

"Tell Hollie I'll be there as soon as I can."

"Will do mate. Any sign of Jennings overnight?"

"You could say." Jones looked at the crate across the room and grinned down the phone as though he was making a video call.

"David, you sound pumped. You found him, didn't you?"

He told Giles what he knew.

"That's fantastic, can I tell Hollie?"

"No, not yet. If you don't mind, I'd rather like to do that myself. I need to see how strong she is before breaking the news. Don't want to do anything to set her back. She needs to recover."

"David, she's a remarkable young woman. Sharp as a tack. Brave too. Demanded to see a sketch artist the moment Albright left her room. Says she can identify the bastard, Jennings. We actually have an eyewitness to go along with your theory."

Since he was alone and no one else could see, Jones allowed himself a little fist pump. Things were definitely popping into place.

"Give her anything she needs but don't push. I'll have Phil email you an electronic identity parade, subject to Mr Albright's approval. Wouldn't want to upset the good doctor now, would we?"

As per Jones' instructions, Phil would run a full background check on the suspected killer, but although he now knew Jennings' real identity, or thought he did, Jones had to play things carefully.

He needed more than half-baked theories, childhood memories, and coincidences. In court, any decent defence barrister would cast doubts on the memory of a traumatised teenager with a head injury, and Jones had only caught a fleeting glimpse of Jennings at the detention centre. He needed hard evidence and was willing to bet the crime scenes would provide it.

When they finally arrested the creature, Jones wanted the case airtight and with no wriggle room. He still had too many unanswered questions. The correct pressure might even force Jennings to give up his accomplices. Jones wanted the lot: the money trail, the customers, the identities of the other victims, everything. Most of all, apart from Jennings, he wanted the sniper, and the bent copper.

He drained his third mug of tea for the morning and gazed through the kitchen window before heading to the bathroom. The sun shone bright through the trees bordering his back garden, bringing with it the promise of a beautiful day.

Jones smiled.

Chapter Four

MONDAY MORNING – Devil's Island
Time since the shooting: forty-six hours

JONES WAITED in the Birmingham International Airport's arrivals lounge for Jean-Luc's plane, which had been delayed. He spent the time reviewing the investigation since Hollie's miraculous recovery and his own revelation.

Sunday had been one of those rare days where everything slotted into place like the pieces of a child's wooden jigsaw puzzle. It didn't happen often, but when it did, it was best to go with the flow. He'd spent the day flitting between the arson site, Holton Police Station, and Saint Mary's Hospital, Derby.

The visit to Eldon Road had been hard to take. The extensive damage wasn't simply limited to Alex's house. The fire had gutted the adjacent building and the immediate vicinity reminded him of the bad old days and the IRA bombing campaigns of the 70s and 80s. A time that had scarred his life to the core. A time he never wanted to revisit.

As for the arson investigation, credit had to go to Ryan. He made the breakthrough Sunday afternoon when the doctors finally allowed him to interview the passer-by who had lost his dog and had suffered serious, but not life-threatening, injuries.

Young Ryan put everything together with minimal help from Jones, who allowed him to run with the evidence. The Detective Constable raised an arrest warrant for a known pyromaniac, one Roy Harper. He also arranged for the Metropolitan Police to arrest and detain the arsonist in a cell at his local nick, ready for Ryan's arrival.

Jones smiled at the young man's excitement.

"Didn't even need the computer, boss," he said, pulling on his jacket in preparation for the trip to London to collect the prisoner. "Did it the old-school way. Only took a couple of phone calls. Can't thank you enough for letting me run with this."

"Who are you taking to London with you?"

"One of DI Danforth's men. Don't worry, boss, Harper won't be giving me the slip."

"Good man. When you get back, book him in the cells overnight and go home. I'll let you handle the early stage interview tomorrow."

"Really? Fantastic. Thanks."

"You deserve it." Jones pointed to Pelham's empty desk. "Where is he?"

Ryan's smile fell away. "Took the weekend off sick. Made himself scarce, I reckon."

"So he should." Jones massaged his aching ribcage. "Ever heard the term *persona non grata*?"

"Yep."

"Keep this between us, but I'll be having a quiet word with DS Pelham tomorrow, assuming he recovers from his 'illness' by then. There are going to be some changes around here."

"Great. You'll never guess, but Superintendent Peyton's gone missing as well. Funny that, eh?"

"It's a real hoot."

After visiting Alex and meeting Julie's parents in the late afternoon, Jones returned home early, in preparation for the big day to

Part 3

come. He then phoned Jean-Luc to invite him to witness Jennings' arrest.

And, as a result, there Jones stood, Monday morning, Birmingham International Airport, awaiting the delayed arrival of the morning plane from Brest.

He was relaxed. In no rush. The investigation had reached the endgame and things were under control. Section 14's latest report showed Jennings at home, unaware of the surveillance team, doing nothing more exciting than watching breakfast news with his wife of thirty-six years. The couple had no kids, no pets, and apparently, few joint interests.

Jones' meeting with Jean-Luc was subdued. The Frenchman knew about Jones' damaged ribcage, and when they met at the customs barrier, he curtailed the expected backslap and cheek-kissing frenzy, and made do with a restrained and polite handshake.

"David, it is good to see you again. And you look refreshed." The pencil moustache stretched wide as he broke out a teeth-baring smile. "You have been busy since we last met, I understand."

"Certainly have. I'll explain everything in the car on the way to the station."

"As it happens, I have brought something with me to help with the, er … festivities." He raised an aluminium attaché case attached to his wrist by a chain. "Evidence I think you will find somewhat useful. But first let me tell you about the *maire* and the crime scene."

Jones grabbed him by the arm. The man's corded bicep was rock under his hand. "You found the mayor?"

"*Oui*. He owns a holiday property in the Pyrenees."

"Did he explain why he ran?"

"Alas no. We found him hanging from one of the roof beams."

"Suicide?"

"Initial indications suggest so, but the investigation has only just begun."

"Did he leave a note?"

"Again, no. But we found a bank account with funds far in excess of the amount one would expect for the *maire* of a small village in Brittany."

"You're following the money?"

"But of course," the tall Frenchman said, grinning hard. "As you know, we must always follow the money."

"And the bodies you found at Flynn's farm. Any closer to identification?"

"Not as yet, but the days they are early, *n'est-ce pas?*"

SENIOR SCENES OF CRIME OFFICER, Patrick Elliott, welcomed them into the forensics lab with a grin as wide as Jean-Luc's had been at the airport.

"Ah now there you are, Chief Inspector. You must be psychic. I was about to give you a bell, so. I've matched the prisoner's blood and tissue samples to the arson scene, and to the fingerprints on the button. There's little doubt. DNA analysis will follow, but not for a few weeks. You're good to go ahead with the interrogation whenever you like."

"Thanks, Patrick. You worked through the night on this?"

He shrugged.

"Sure and it's the least I could do. Julie Harris was a wonderful girl. You go get the bastard who killed her, eh?" He took a second look at the Frenchman and scratched his dark beard.

Jones took the point and made the introductions, and after a detailed explanation regarding its contents, Jean-Luc handed over the evidence sachet taken from his briefcase.

Patrick signed the official receipt from the French *Ministère de la Justice*, and broke the seal.

"I see things are moving on this case, both sides of the Channel," Patrick said. "Leave this with me sir, and I'll see what I can come up with. It won't take me long to search the DNA and AFIS databases."

"*Excusez-moi*," Jean-Luc said. "Ayfees?"

"Automated Fingerprint Identification System," Jones answered, ignoring Patrick's bemused grin. "How long, Patrick?"

Part 3

"Give me 'til mid-afternoon. I need to verify the analyses of the fingerprint first." He glanced at Jean-Luc. "If you'll forgive me, sir."

Jean-Luc gave him a quick nod. "I would expect nothing less, *monsieur*."

On the way back through the station, most of Jones' colleagues avoided eye contact, probably for fear of upsetting a respected senior officer. After all, as far as they were concerned, Hollie Jardine had died and her killer still roamed free—not a great result for the West Midlands Police's most respected and celebrated detective. The news of Hollie's death had made the local paper, and the national breakfast news. No one knew how the media had unearthed the information so quickly.

Jones had told no one he'd leaked the Derby story to "Old" Lucas Wilson—anonymously. Jones sincerely hoped the fairy-tale wouldn't hamper the miserable hack's journalistic career. He really did.

To the world at large, Hollie was dead, and Jones hoped the man who'd been calling himself Jonathan C Jennings thought the same thing.

He showed Jean-Luc to the changing rooms so the Frenchman could make a quick change of clothes, and said he'd be back after completing a little "housekeeping".

Two minutes later, he burst through the SCU office door, slammed his fist on the desk, and pointed at his cowering future-former-acting-second-in-command.

"A word in your ear please, DS Pelham. My office, right now."

———

AT TEN O'CLOCK, Jones, Jean-Luc, and Ryan Washington stood in the corridor outside the interview suite. Ryan almost bounced with excitement at the prospect of leading his first major interview.

"Easy, Ryan," Jones said. "Take it the way we discussed. And, Jean-Luc, play it by ear."

"*Désolé*, David. Playing an ear?"

"Sorry, I mean, don't worry about what we say … play along

with it. I'm not going to introduce you. Please stand in the background and look menacing. If you want to say anything, take your cue from Ryan or me, okay?"

"Ah, I see," Jean-Luc winked. "You are going to … pull a fast one?" Jones gave him a thin smile and nodded. "Is this why you asked me to wear my uniform?"

Jones studied his friend and had to admit, the man looked damned impressive in his quasi-military rig. Dark blue top with a multi-coloured medal ribbon band across the left breast, light blue trousers, and black shoes buffed to a high-gloss military shine. He carried his *képi* clamped under his right arm and stood tall, imposing. The only thing missing was the pistol inside his holster. Despite his diplomatic status and his initial objections, Jean-Luc didn't have permission to carry a weapon in the UK.

"Interview Room 3," Ryan said.

"Ready?" Jones asked.

"Can't wait, boss."

———

ROY HARPER SAT on a hard metal chair, behind a metal table. Both were bolted into the concrete floor. As per Jones' instructions, the custody officers had manacled his hands and the linking chain passed through a ring attached to the table. They had looped the chain twice through the ring to restrict the arsonist's movement. It had to be said, the weasel looked decidedly the worse for wear. Under normal circumstances, Jones would have removed the handcuffs to put the suspect at his ease, but in this case, he changed tactics and let the killer suffer. He didn't need coddling. This one needed to feel the weight of police hatred, and no one had to put on an act to facilitate the effect.

"Where's my lawyer?"

Ryan met Harper's first words with a harsh glare.

"All in good time. We haven't charged you with anything yet. You are simply helping the police with our enquiries. All we're going to do at this stage is have a little chat." Ryan waved a hand around the small room. "Look, there's no recording equipment, no briefs, no one to get in the way. We wanted to take a close look at the bastard who firebombed our friend's house, and killed her partner the other night … before you go far, far away. Now, are you going to tell us who put you up to it?"

"I want my Miranda rights."

Ryan snorted and leaned forward, forearms resting on the table. "That might work if you commit a crime in America, but this is England. You can stay silent if you want. It's all the same to us."

"I didn't do fuckin' nothin'. I keep tellin' ya," Harper answered with an irritating nasal whine. "I ain't never been to this motha-fuckin' shithole afore. I's from London, ya know? The smoke? Bright lights, big city? What would I be doin' in this fuckin' Midlands toilet?" He smiled when he said it. "Why d'you have ta' drag my ass outta bed at midnight and fetch me 'ere?"

"And why do you have to sound like an East Coast rapper when you were born in Essex?" Ryan asked, adding a mocking sneer. He turned to Jones. "American rapper? More like a sweet wrapper, eh boss?"

Jones smiled and let Ryan continue. He handled the opening part of the interrogation well, setting the scene and laying out some of the evidence against the fire-starter. After half an hour, Jones took over. Time to draw out the big guns.

"Here in the West Midlands, we take a dim view of arson, and a dimmer view of murder," he began.

Sitting across from a man who'd killed a friend of a friend, and who'd attempted to murder Alex wasn't easy. Jones forced himself to remain calm. Letting loose the anger wouldn't get the job done. He knew how to work an interview. He'd been doing them long enough.

Harper kept looking up at Jean-Luc and frowning. As intended, Jones didn't make the introduction.

"So," Jones continued. "Let's recap a moment, shall we? You've never been to Birmingham before, and you didn't set fire to a police officer's house two nights ago in Eldon Road, Smethwick. Am I correct?"

"Ain't sayin' nothin'. Not without my lawyer."

Jones opened the concertina case-file he'd placed on the desk at the start of the interview and removed a photo from one of the segments. It showed the burned-out remains of Alex and Julie's modest home. The embers still smouldered.

Roy Harper stared longingly at the images. He shuddered, and his eyes glazed over. The little shit was getting off on the picture. Jones had read the man's psych profile before the interview—a pyromaniac who drew sexual gratification from setting fires.

In other words, one sick little puppy.

Jones turned the photo face down. Harper's eyes followed the movement closely. He frowned and licked his bottom lip, but said nothing.

Jones interlaced his fingers and cracked his knuckles. He leaned back and folded his arms across his chest taking care to show no pain even though the damaged ribs hurt like the devil.

"I'm going to tell you a little story, and you're going to listen. When I'm finished, I'll ask you one question. Only one. You don't have to answer, but if you don't I'm going to hand you over to my friend here." He jagged a thumb over his shoulder at Jean-Luc. "And after that, we will never meet again. Not ever. Do you understand?"

Harper gave Jones the finger, which was amusing given his contorted position.

"Dream on, CSI!" the moron added.

"What?" Jones sighed. "Will you please drop the ridiculous Americanisms? You're the twenty-three year-old son of a Baptist preacher and a midwife mother. You've lived most of your life in the leafy suburbs of Basildon, and moved to London to study chemical engineering."

According to the man's medical report, everything else in Harper's life stemmed from an overactive imagination and a psychotic dissociative disorder.

Harper frowned.

"My father died in a fire nineteen year' ago."

"No, Roy. You're making things up again. Both your parents are still alive and wondering what they're going to do with you."

Part 3

The prisoner blinked and frowned. "Huh?"

Harper shook his head in confusion and took in his surroundings as if for the first time. He fixed his gaze on Jones, his expression returned to one of defiance.

"I ain't telling you nothin' without my attorney." He made a ridiculous sucking sound with his teeth. Searching for "gangsta" but finding Bugs Bunny.

Jesus. This man should be in a psych ward.

"Okay, have it your way, Mr Harper. My story starts last Thursday evening when your boss and Ellis Flynn kidnapped Hollie Jardine from outside her school. That was their first mistake."

"Don't know nothin' 'bout that," Harper said.

This time Jones believed him.

"The pair's second error came when they took Hollie to Brittany. That's in France."

Harper's nervous eyes flashed up to Jean-Luc, and then locked on Jones. A light began to dawn behind his eyes.

"I know where Brittany is. And I told you, I've never heard of the girl. Hollie Jardine, wasn't it?"

"Ah. You've changed the accent back to Estuary English. Now we're getting somewhere."

Harper tried to sit up straight.

Jones returned the arson photo, still face down, to the case-file and took out another picture. This one had an aerial shot of Ellis Flynn's cottage. He rotated it so Harper could take a good look. Harper studied the picture and his frown deepened. He clearly didn't have a clue where it was.

"I don't care whether you've seen the place or not. Under French law you became an accomplice to the crimes these two committed the moment you took on a contract to kill my officer. It's all part of the same case."

Harper tried to settle back into the chair, but the restraints didn't allow him enough movement.

"Well now, Mr Harper, I see I have your attention at last."

"The Nail."

"Excuse me?"

"Not Harper, call me the Nail. Roy-the-Nail."

"Roy-the-Nail?" Jones snorted. He looked over his shoulder, first at Ryan, and then at Jean-Luc. The Frenchman gave Roy-the-Nail the benefit of a malignant glare. Actors called it staying in character, and Jean-Luc was clearly a natural.

"Yeah, Hammer and Nail, get it?" Harper's eyes wavered and fell to the floor. Roy-the-Nail knew he'd made a big mistake.

Oh you silly boy. That's the first 'nail' in your coffin, old son.

Jones smiled and mentally underlined one of the names on his suspect list. The PNC, in all its recently updated, hacker-defended, super-fast glory, had thrown out a list of all the known hit men operating in the UK with the skills to make the shot described by Giles Danforth. It wasn't a long list—only four names. One of them, Hammer, had never been caught or identified.

Hammer and Nail had to be someone's idea of a sick joke.

It wouldn't take much more to push this fool over the edge.

Next up, Jones slid the new photo across the table.

"This cottage is where Jennings and Flynn took Hollie Jardine. So far, we've found the remains of eight girls in and around that farm. That's enough to rate it as a mass grave. And that's really serious."

Roy-the-Nail swallowed, and some of the colour drained from his face.

"We now come to the interesting part of the story. Ellis Flynn is dead, but Jennings got away. During his escape, he killed a woman, and that makes nine deaths. You still counting? No? Well we are." The prisoner lowered his eyes. "If you include the murder-by-arson of Julie Harris, which is down to you alone, Roy-the-Nail, it takes the grand total to ten."

Jones swivelled in his chair, his action stiff due to the burning ribs, and looked up at Jean-Luc.

"I'm right, aren't I, Colonel Coué. The total is ten, the magic number?"

"*Oui, dix,*" Jean-Luc growled, but didn't take his eyes from Harper. The moustache barely moved as he spoke. "*Le nombre magique.*"

Part 3

Jones had to hand it to Jean-Luc. The Frenchman played the brooding menace with panache. If Jones had been in Harper's position, he might have wet himself by now.

Ryan, like Jean-Luc, played his part to perfection. He scratched his chin and blew out a silent whistle. He sucked air through his teeth, shook his head with exaggerated sadness, and made another note. The SCU's resident petrol head was coming across like a used car salesman appraising a second-hand wreck for part-exchange.

"What the fuck are you on about? What magic number?" Roy-the-Nail Harper squeaked and tried to ease his wrists as the handcuffs bit into the flesh.

"Ten murders, that's double figures. Takes us into terrorism territory. You heard about Guantanamo Bay?"

"What?"

Fear, deep and primal, shadowed the pyromaniac's light brown eyes. His lower lip trembled and dimples formed in his weak chin.

"Gitmo's a holiday camp compared with what the French have in place on Devil's Island. Terrorism is punishable by death in France. They still use the Guillotine, you know? And they ship all their murderers to Devil's Island for a couple of year's hard labour first. Isn't that right, Colonel Coué?"

Jean-Luc dipped his head in a nod, but remained silent.

Harper lowered his head to his hands and let out a quiet whimper.

One more push ought to do it.

Jones removed two more photos from the file and placed them next to the one of the cottage. He turned them face up and rotated them for Harper to see clearly. Jones pointed to one. It showed an old man with short, grey hair sitting up in a hospital bed. He had a three-inch gouge on his chin, a badly bruised cheek, and his head was swathed in a bloodied bandage. The bandage covered one eye, but the other stared directly and angrily into the camera lens.

"This man's name is Norbert Winterton. His friends call him Nobby."

Harper studied the picture carefully. Jones couldn't tell whether the eyes registered any recognition, but the kid trembled in his chair.

Sweat sprouted from his hairline and ran in little rivulets down the side of his pockmarked face.

"Never seen him before," Harper whispered, but raised his eyes to the right, a classic give-away for a liar.

"Really?"

Jones moved his finger across to the other photo. It showed a grey jacket. Scuffed and grazed at the elbows, covered in brick dust and spattered with blood. The lab techs had superimposed an arrow onto the image. It pointed to a button, third down from the top.

"See that? We found a fingerprint on the button. You'll never guess who it belongs to."

Jones scratched his earlobe and leaned back in his chair. Harper's heavy breathing and the rattling of the chain on the handcuffs as he tried to ease the pain broke the silence in the interview room. His hands had darkened with the restriction to his circulation.

If Jones didn't get what he wanted soon, he'd be forced to loosen the restraints—but not yet.

"Yep," Jones continued at last. "Surprise, surprise, the dab is yours." To reinforce the information, Jones took a document from the folder, a pro-forma AFIS printout. It contained two adjacent fingerprints, one from the button and identified as such, and the other from the database. The same lab tech, Patrick Elliott, had stamped the word, "MATCH" diagonally across the page, in blood red.

Jones paused to let the information sink in before continuing. He approached the important part and needed Harper's full attention.

"You bumped into our friend, Nobby, on Saturday night after setting the fire. You left your fingerprint on the button. Remember?"

Harper didn't acknowledge the question.

"So that catches you in a direct lie. You *have* been to Birmingham before, haven't you? And our witness places you within two-hundred metres of the arson. And there's one more little piece of evidence you might be interested in."

Jones leafed through the concertina file once more and removed a clear plastic evidence bag five centimetres square, zip-locked along

Part 3

its top edge. He pinched the top of the bag between finger and thumb and waved it under Harper's nose.

"This, Mr Harper, is what we found inside the lock of the kitchen door. Can you tell what it is?"

The Nail's eyes narrowed as he focused on the baggie's contents —the scorched remains of a matchstick further protected inside a hard plastic box.

"You screwed up again. The metal lock protected the match, and the DNA trace you left on it!"

Harper's chin trembled. His eyes glazed.

"That's it. With your record we won't have much difficulty convincing a jury you murdered Julie Harris and *attempted to murder my officer!*" Jones shouted the last five words. Until that point, he'd been quiet. The effect was as dramatic as it was unexpected.

Roy-the-Nail Harper burst into tears.

"I'm sorry," he wailed. "I … I can't help myself, see? I … I have this illness, right? A compulsion."

Jones allowed him to keep it up for a couple of minutes. Harper wailed on about how his doctors said he needed treatment, how his father beat him as a child and stubbed out cigarettes on his feet. In the end, he broke down, burying his face in his manacled hands. He finished his pathetic explanation with, "Help me, please."

It was pitiful.

Jones waited for the initial outpouring to quieten. He didn't believe anything the little creep said, and as for remorse? Jones had seen Julie's body in the morgue and the charred remains of the houses he'd destroyed. He held no sympathy for the cowering arsonist.

Time to go for the jugular, or in Jean-Luc's terms, the *coup de grâce*.

"Shut up and listen!"

Harper's head snapped back and he stiffened.

"Remember at the start of my little story I said I was going to ask you a question? Well it's coming, so you need concentrate."

Harper sniffed and dipped his head to wipe a runny nose on the shoulder of his baggy T-shirt. Jones tried not to look at the glimmering smear on the blue cotton.

"We've got you for one murder, but I'm not having you pleading diminished responsibility and spending a few years in some cushy hospital discussing your bedwetting problems with a do-gooder counsellor. Oh no." He paused for dramatic effect. "Shall I tell you what I propose?"

Harper looked up through cowed eyes. Jones caught the smell of fresh urine.

"I'm sending you to France with Colonel Coué. You're going to die." Jones stood and made a show of searching his jacket pockets. "Jean-Luc? He's all yours. Take him. Now, where are the keys to those damned handcuffs?"

Jean-Luc sneered and made a move forward.

Harper's jaw dropped. He shook his head and tried to speak, but the words came out as a strangled cry.

"Unless …" added Jones.

"What?" Harper managed between sobs. "Unless what?"

"Here's that question. Ready?"

Jones chose his next words carefully. If he chose badly, the whole act might be for nothing. But Roy-the-Nail had given him the opening and Jones took the gamble.

"Answer me this and I'll let you face trial here in Britain." Jones slapped his hand on the table. The sharp crack resounded through the room and Jones' ribs shot out an electric bolt of pain.

"Where's Hammer?"

"I don't know!" Harper squealed.

Damn it!

"But I know how to get hold of him. I promise."

As soon as Harper broke down, Jones released his bonds and offered him a drink of water. Harper was so pathetically grateful to have the threat of Devil's Island and the Guillotine lifted, he cried like a teething baby. He not only agreed to tell them how to contact Hammer, but also agreed to helped lure the hitman back to Birmingham on the pretext of another contract from Jennings.

Part 3

Giles Danforth would be in on the takedown—Jones would insist on that.

#

Jones closed the door to IR3 behind them and led Jean-Luc towards the canteen.

"You played that well, Jean-Luc, *merci*."

The Frenchman stared at Jones and tilted his head in question. "You do know that Devil's Island is now a holiday resort, and we have not had the death penalty in France since 1981? Its abolition is enshrined in our constitution."

Jones grinned.

"Yes, I do, but Roy-the-Idiot doesn't."

"Aha. Nicely done, David."

Jones' grin broadened into a smile and he slapped Jean-Luc on the shoulder. He had to reach up high to do it. "I researched French jurisprudence on the internet last night. Sergeant Cryer would have been so proud. I hope you have time to meet him before you return to France."

"And the matchstick. Surely, there can be no viable DNA evidence left after it was cooked in the fire."

Jones winked.

"Correct. Sometimes, stupid criminals make it too easy for us. Fancy a snack before our next appointment? We have plenty of time."

"What about Jennings?" Jean-Luc asked. "We should be searching for him, no? Your forensics man may have identified him by now if his fingerprints and DNA are on your database."

"No need to rush, Jean-Luc. I've had a covert observation unit following John C Jennings since yesterday morning. Right now, the man's sitting in his office, blissfully unaware he's being watched. We'll be going there after lunch. We need to leave time for our sniper, Hammer, to make his way to Derby." Jean-Luc followed him along the corridor. "I can't promise *cordon bleu*, but the tea and coffee is hot and the bacon rolls are excellent."

Jones spent the following couple of hours eating two wickedly unhealthy, but wonderful BLT rolls, drinking two mugs of tea, and fielding dozens of questions from an enthusiastic and inquisitive Jean-Luc Coué.

At two o'clock, Jones' mobile buzzed.

"Excuse me, Jean-Luc. I need to take this." He clamped the phone to his ear; the background noise in the canteen made the speakerphone redundant. "Hello Ryan, is everything ready?"

"Yes, boss. No problems raising the warrant."

"Excellent. What about the voice recordings and the video link to Saint Mary's?"

"The equipment's all prepped and we're ready to go when you are."

"Meet us out front in five minutes."

Jean-Luc stood. "As they say in the movies, 'we are ready to roll', yes?"

"Yes indeed." Jones smiled. "Shall we go arrest ourselves a serial killer?"

Chapter Five

MONDAY MIDDAY – *Arthur M Buckeridge*
 Time since the shooting: two days

ARTHUR MICHAEL BUCKERIDGE eased himself into his plush leather chair and emitted a grateful sigh. He hooked the ivory-handled cane over the arm of the chair and opened the broadsheet newspaper to the centre double-page spread. It followed on from the front-page story. The bold headline screamed, *"Hollie Jardine Murdered Following Second Abduction."*

Not pithy, but accurate.

Buckeridge allowed himself a satisfied smile. One problem dealt with, but the article's only comment on Jones was to say the detective had returned to England and remained unavailable for interview.

The bastard had to be dead or dying, didn't he? He'd taken a bullet square to the chest. He didn't have body-armour—at least none that showed through under that god-awful grey jacket, which the cheap bastard probably bought off the peg from bloody Tesco.

Buckeridge would have pumped a couple of rounds into the

miserable fucker's head but the big ugly copper, Giles Something-or-other, shot him from behind.

He touched the wound where the bullet entered his shoulder. His backpack absorbed some of the bullet's force, but the wound went deep and the resulting nerve damage might turn out to be permanent. His well-paid private doctor, another member of the exclusive "Club" advised bed-rest and a sling but that was out of the question. Antibiotics and over-the-counter painkillers would have to do. If he were to arrive at the office wearing a sling, he'd have to field too many awkward questions. Luckily, he held the walking stick in his left hand, and was still able to walk.

Fucking Jones. Pain in the arse. Why had he worn the ugly jacket on such a warm day? Was the bugger still alive?

Buckeridge had one sure-fire way to find out. He picked up his burner phone, a pay-as-you-go mobile, and dialled. The man Buckeridge called PDC behind his back, answered without preamble.

"That business in the hospital in Birmingham and at the school in Derby, down to you, right?"

"Sure was," Buckeridge answered with pride.

"You fucking moron! The girl was one thing, but killing three police officers and that doctor. Stupid. What do you think you were doing? Why draw so much attention to yourself?" PDC spoke in a stage whisper, but the underlying anger was clear.

Buckeridge took a breath. "Had to be done. The constables stood in the way of your man, Hammer. And as for Jones. He killed Ellis, and Ellis was one of mine. I had to make him pay for that."

"Such a stupid, stupid thing to do. You should have left the girl well alone."

"Perhaps, but I've sorted the mess now and it's fucking over."

"Oh dear, Arthur. There's no need for the foul language," the bent cop chided. "Swearing is the last resort of the feeble mind."

Cheeky fucker.

Who did he think he was?

"Okay, *assho*—" Buckeridge aimed at disdain, but a shoulder twinge made him cut the word short, lessening the impact. "Perhaps you'd like to start earning my silence."

PDC followed his sharp intake of breath with, "I wouldn't continue that thought if I were you, *Arthur*. I know who you are and where you live. Remember that."

A pause, followed by a muffled scraping on the speaker at Buckeridge's ear, told him PDC had covered his mouthpiece. After a few moments, the sound cleared and he spoke again. "Be quick, I'm busy." A conference of voices in the background grew louder, as the bent cop probably moved closer to the crowd.

"DCI David Jones, West Midlands Police. Tell me about him."

"I've already sent you his file, what more do you want?"

"Do you know him?"

"I've never been to the Midlands, but I do know him by reputation. Good, solid officer. Honest. From memory, he's only a few years from retirement."

"Is he still alive?"

"No idea. Why?"

"I shot him in the chest, but there's nothing in the news about it. Can you find out for certain?"

Hesitation.

"I'll make a few calls when I get out of this meeting, but it won't be for a couple of hours. Anything else?"

"The girl's definitely dead then?"

Despite the newspaper story, Buckeridge had to make sure. He'd already missed her once.

"Yes. Spoke to a mate in the Derbyshire force this morning after I saw the breakfast news. Head shot."

"Yeah. Hammer's a good man. Knows his stuff. Thanks for the intro."

"You're welcome. Never misses. I use him for all my wet work."

Buckeridge wondered how many assassinations a dirty cop would need to commission. He decided to tone down his aggression in future. He didn't want to end up the subject of one of those contracts.

"I'm thinking of putting him on the payroll."

"Right." PDC sneezed three times in quick succession. "Bloody hay-fever. Hate this time of year. Anything else?"

"I'm going to reopen the Glasgow studio. Need to find more film stars now. The buyers want the next film, and soon. You know anyone who can reel in another kiddie, or shall we take one off the street?"

"There's always some little scrubber in the pipeline. Shame about young Ellis though. He was pretty useful in that respect. I'll get back to you this evening after I've made a few calls."

"Okay, and I'll do the same. We can compare notes. Another fourteen-year-old busty blonde would be nice. I'll be able to use the footage we already have in the can."

Buckeridge ended the call and dropped the phone into his breast pocket. Paedocop, PDC, was an arrogant bastard, but he did have his uses. The bugger's attitude towards Buckeridge needed polishing, though. He might get Hammer on the case if it degenerated even more.

The intercom on his desk buzzed. Careful to avoid jarring his shoulder, he leaned forward and clicked the requisite button.

"Yes, Valerie?"

His personal assistant of twenty-three years replied. She was efficient, loyal, and owned the inconsequential body of a stick insect, which made her perfectly safe in terms of starring in any of his feature films.

"Sir Ellery Danvers, on line three, Dr Buckeridge. He's calling as arranged. On line two."

"Excellent. Thank you, Valerie. Please put him through." He took a breath to compose himself before connecting the call.

"Sir Ellery," Buckeridge said through an enforced smile, "how may I be of service to the Minister for Prisons?"

"Hello Arthur, I'll be brief. Just left a Cabinet meeting. The PM read your excellent report and approved the proposal."

"That's wonderful news, Sir Ellery." With fifteen years work nearing fruition, Buckeridge could barely contain his excitement. "Which parts of the plan is he going to sign off?"

"All of it, Arthur. The whole programme. You will have full funding for a National Youth Detention Centre that will be commissioned within the next two years. The PM is putting you in charge

Part 3

of the new Department for Youth Justice. Congratulations, Arthur. I wouldn't be surprised to see your name appear in the New Year's Honours list for your services to childre—"

The line fell silent.

"Hello?" Buckeridge pressed the intercom button again. "Valerie? My call's been cut off."

More silence.

"Valerie?"

The office door burst open. Four men and a woman stormed in. Buckeridge's heart lurched and pounded hard against his ribcage.

No! It can't be.

The first man, middle-aged, slim, with wavy grey hair, wore a light summer jacket, collar and tie, and a thin smile. The woman, blonde hair tied tight back from her face, white bud in her left ear, stood two paces behind the men and glowered. It looked like she wanted to eat him alive.

Jones and Blondie!

How the fucking hell?

The man beside Jones stood over six feet tall. He wore a smart grey suit and blue shirt, no tie. A trimmed moustache hovered above thin lips, his jaw clean-shaven. The other two men wore police uniforms.

Buckeridge turned his concentration to Jones.

"Good afternoon, Dr Buckeridge," Jones said. The senior cop's smile widened to show a straight row of gleaming white teeth. "Or do you still prefer, Jonathan C Jennings?"

Buckeridge tried to respond but the words stuck in his throat.

Chapter Six

MONDAY MIDDAY – *High office*
Time since the shooting: two days

JONES STARED at the man in the fancy chair, behind the fancy leather-topped mahogany desk, and inhaled the rich aroma of beeswax and expensive aftershave.

Here he was at last, Dr Arthur Buckeridge, PhD. High flying academic and bottom feeding paedophile.

In his early fifties, with short-cropped, dark brown hair, he looked like the average civil servant. No one would ever guess the man's dark secret, not by looks alone. But wasn't that always the way? The real monsters didn't look like Frankenstein's creation. That would make his job too easy. They always looked normal on the surface … but scratch a little deeper.

Buckeridge had been in charge of the Derbyshire Detention Centre for the best part of twenty years before its closure. Hell, he must have felt like a glutton in a bakery with unfettered access to its flawed population. He'd groomed Ellis Flynn for five years, moulding and shaping him into the image of his father, Edward.

God knew how many other young men Buckeridge had perverted over the years, and how many deaths he'd caused. And there he sat as the Chairman of a government prison reform committee.

What a sick irony.

On the wall behind Buckeridge's head, framed under non-reflective glass, hung his life's story told in paper and photographs. Academic honours, including a doctorate from the University of Abertay, citations, and commemorative photographs clung in even rows.

In each photo, Buckeridge stood beside a member of the great and the good—a rogue's gallery of the country's rich and powerful. Prime Ministers, Home Secretaries, TV celebrities, and film stars all happy to shake his hand. Finally, in pride of place at the centre, was a diptych, a matched pair. The first photo, in monochrome, showed a younger Buckeridge standing, without the aid of a stick, under a wrought iron sign in front of a large Victorian building. The sign read, *Derbyshire Detention Centre*. The second picture, this one in colour, showed the same tableau, but in this, Buckeridge was older, leaning on a stick, and the spelling on the sign had changed. Few people would have noticed the difference.

Some of the pictures hung off square, offending his eye. All of Jones' being wanted to straighten them, put things right, but he didn't trust himself to pass close to the monster. He thought of Hollie, lying in a hospital bed in Derby. He also thought of the mutilated corpses buried in a Brittany wood, Julie Harris, his two fallen colleagues, and the unfortunate Doctor Ericsson.

There the man sat, feigning offence.

Buckeridge recognised him. Of that, there was no doubt. Jones wanted to yank the bastard out of his chair and frogmarch him through the outer office in handcuffs, in front of all his subordinates. He wanted to humiliate him for the torment he caused his victims. In fact, Jones wanted to do a damned sight more to the animal, but he dared not. He needed to do things correctly, by the book, follow procedures. Nothing could get in the way of Buckeridge's arrest and conviction.

"Who are you people?" Buckeridge asked. He kept his voice low, and without any of the histrionics Jones usually faced during an arrest.

"And what do you mean by bursting into my office like this." He leaned towards the intercom and pressed a button. "Valerie? Call security."

Jones ignored him. He let Buckeridge stew a little longer and turned to the two constables.

"Search the place. There might be a gun in here somewhere."

Buckeridge grabbed hold of his walking stick and struggled to his feet.

"This is a Government building. You have absolutely no right to be—"

"We've served a search warrant to the building manager, and there's a team tearing up your house and grounds as I speak, *so sit down and shut up!*"

Buckeridge dropped back into his chair and placed the cane across its arms. He glowered at Jones and started rolling the stick along the leather padding. The ivory handle spun clockwise and anticlockwise, glowing in the sunlight flooding through the floor-to-ceiling window behind him.

The constables didn't take long to search the sparsely furnished office. Apart from the main desk, a low coffee table and two comfortable-looking leather chairs huddled next to the window. A small glass vase of cut flowers in the middle of the table might have been of use as a weapon of sorts. Jones instructed one of the constables to remove it. The second officer searched the desk and removed a silver letter opener and a pair of scissors.

"Search him too, and the cane. Wouldn't surprise me if it turns into a sword," Jones said, never taking his eyes from his target.

"Don't be ridiculous, man."

Buckeridge hugged the cane tight to his chest and the constable had to wrestle it from him.

"What's the matter?" said Jones, quick to seize the opportunity. "You need the cane so much?"

"It's easier with the stick, but I can manage perfectly well without, thank you very much."

That's number one.

This was going to be easier than he imagined.

Part 3

Jones turned to Alex who pressed a finger against her earpiece and nodded.

The uniformed constable raised his hand. "The walking stick's solid, sir. No hidden blade. Should I take it with me?"

"It is just as well," Jean-Luc said. "You English could never fight with swords."

As Jean-Luc spoke, a flicker of recognition crossed Buckeridge's face.

"Hey, mind who you're calling English. I'm a Scot and don't you forget it!"

That's number two.

It should be more than enough to bury him.

"Colonel Coué is quite correct. Why fight close up when a longbow will do?"

Buckeridge flinched at the name. He stole a look at Jean-Luc and closed his eyes.

"*Oui, mon ami. C'est vrai,* it is true," Jean-Luc replied, without tearing his stony gaze from the killer.

The constables left the room without the stick, but with orders to stand guard outside. Alex backed away and leaned against the closed door. She nodded to Jones and opened her hand twice before fixing Buckeridge with the death scowl. Jones smiled—Patrick Elliott had told Alex through her comms unit, he needed ten minutes to do his magic with the voice analyser.

Jones leaned on the back of a visitor's chair. He glared at the multiple-murderer and spoke quietly. "So, we meet at last, Mr Jennings."

Buckeridge leaned back and folded his arms across his chest. Jones couldn't be sure, but he might have seen Buckeridge grimace when moving his right arm.

"What the devil are you talking about? I demand to know who you are."

"Oh stop it, man. You're finished. Let's get it over with, shall we?" Jones stood tall and coughed. He brandished his ID card and recited the words printed on the back. He'd read the warning out many times before, but never with so much relish. He drew out the sounds, savouring the way they felt on his tongue.

"Arthur Michael Buckeridge, also-known-as John Christopher Jennings, I am arresting you for the murders of …"

LYING prone on a flat rooftop overlooking Saint Mary's Hospital turned out to be *déjà vu* for Hammer as he raised the rifle and took aim.

He'd been pissed to learn his first shot hadn't actually finished off Hollie Jardine, but less pissed than Jennings, whose scathing text demanded a refund or an instant contract completion. The text included the correct passwords and the girl's room number—sixth floor, front of the building, in full view of the tower block where he lay. It couldn't have been better. A shot of less than one-hundred-and-fifty metres. The double-glazed unit separating him from his target wouldn't matter, not with armour-piercing bullets, which he should have used the first time.

He'd never make the same mistake again.

Hammer adjusted focus on the 'scope. The girl lay on the bed with a tube in her nose, her head swathed in thick bandages, face obscured.

"Bye-bye, darling," he said, and took a deep breath. He waited for the next cloud to cover the sun and give him the perfect view.

"Armed police officers! Armed police officers! Lower your weapon and place your arms out, palms up to the sky."

GILES DANFORTH, on temporary secondment to the ARU of the Derbyshire Constabulary had the perfect shot, and the perfect backup. He and four highly trained marksmen stood in a semi-circle, each less than ten metres from their target. Red dots from five laser-scopes lit the spot between the hitman's shoulder blades. The lights barely moved.

Part 3

He repeated his instructions.

"Armed police officers! Lower your weapon and place your arms out, palms up to the sky."

Hammer twitched.

"Don't do it, there are five automatic weapons pointed at your back." Giles added. "You don't stand a chance. Lower the weapon."

The muzzle of the sniper's rifle remained steady. "I recognise that voice. Giles, right?" The assassin sounded calm and his hands remained steady. "Don't do a thing. I have the girl in my sights. This time, I won't miss."

"Haven't you got it yet?" Giles's asked his voice steady and as calm as Hammer's.

"Got what?"

"You're targeting a CPR mannequin."

The sniper rifle's muzzle dipped half a centimetre. "So the girl's dead? I knew I couldn't have missed that shot on Saturday." His shoulders relaxed.

"But you did. Hollie Jardine's alive with nothing more than a horrible scar and a nasty headache."

"What? How?" The muzzle moved again.

Giles felt, more than heard the men around him stiffen. The red dots wobbled but didn't leave their target.

"The window you shot through held thick leaded Victorian glass. Deflected your bullet a couple of degrees north. You should have left the window open. Now lower your weapon and spread your arms. This won't end well if you don't."

"Fuck. Harper sent the text, right?"

"Got it in one. He's singing like Michael Bublé."

"I should of known not to trust the lunatic fuckin' pyro." His spoke quietly and with resignation.

"Lower the weapon, Hammer," Giles repeated. "I won't ask again!"

For a moment, Giles thought Hammer might even comply, but the killer howled, twisted, and swung his rifle in an impossibly slow arc. He fired a single shot into the asphalt roof.

With an explosion of sound, light, and acrid gun smoke,

Hammer's left side, between hip and armpit, exploded under the force of two volleys. A ragged hole the size of a man's clenched fist appeared in his ribcage. The rest of his chest exploded out in a flume of blood, bone, and tissue. Gore oozed onto the roof's gritty surface and puddled under Hammer's torso.

Ten shots. Centre mass.

Shooting justified.

A rich metallic tang of blood fused with gunpowder assaulted Giles Danforth's nostrils as he stepped forward and stood over the wilting body. He ripped the rifle out of the assassin's warm, dead hands.

Giles understood why Hammer attempted the impossible. He faced life without the possibility of parole or suicide by cop. In the end, not a difficult decision.

He wasted no tears for the loss of this particular life form—a multiple murderer, assistant to a butcher, and a double cop killer. He handed the assassin's weapon to one of the marksmen, and pressed a button on his mobile. It didn't take long for David Jones to answer his call.

"Hello, David …? It's me, Giles. It's just gone down. As you expected, he didn't come peacefully."

Chapter Seven

MONDAY AFTERNOON – *Arrest*
Time since the shooting: fifty-two hours

JONES PAUSED to answer his phone. He'd been in the middle of arresting Buckeridge for multiple murders, the attempted murder of a police officer, incitement to arson, abduction, solicitation, jaywalking, littering, and anything else he could think of. He listened for a moment, stone faced.

"Thanks, Giles. Yes, I'm with Buckeridge now … No, he's going nowhere but the cells."

Buckeridge feigned disinterest, but furtive glances, eyes flitting from face to face, showed a nervous energy at odds with his otherwise relaxed exterior.

Jones ended the call and rubbed his closely shaved chin.

"Sorry about that. Interesting news. Now, where was I? Oh yes, I remember now. Ahem. I am arresting you—"

"Have you gone stark raving mad, Jones? I have no idea—"

Jones slammed the flat of his hand on the desk. The crack silenced Buckeridge, who jerked backwards and raised his hands in reflexive defence. Jones took note of another grimace. The animal was in pain, he had no doubt, but Buckeridge wasn't the only one. The act of slapping the desk aggravated Jones' injury and a shaft of pain raced through his damaged ribs, but he'd be damned if he showed weakness to a serial murderer.

Sweat popped on Buckeridge's forehead, but the air-conditioned office maintained a constant twenty-two degrees Celsius, according to the thermostat on the wall.

The two men glared at each other. Jones waited for Buckeridge to blink first. It didn't take long.

Buckeridge settled back and his leather chair squeaked under the load.

"I've done nothing wrong. What do you think you have on me?"

Jones finished reading Buckeridge his rights and continued.

"I'd normally do the rest at the station, but this is as good a place as any, and I'm in a upbeat mood all of a sudden."

He pulled up the visitor's chair, placed his briefcase on the floor and sat in front of the lauded public figure whose honourable name was about to be ground into the dust. For the second time that day, Jones told a story to a killer. This time, he had no need for lies or subterfuge.

"It took me a while to work it out," he began. "In my defence, I've been under a great deal of stress lately. An abducted girl to find, twice, a mass killer to arrest, and two hired assassins to catch. Lack of decent sleep is damaging to the little grey cells." Jones tapped his temple.

Damn it, Jones. Stop hamming it up. You're not Hercule Poirot.

"The first thing to give you away was your pseudonym, John C Jennings."

Buckeridge lowered his eyes and stared at his fingernails. His lips formed a tight circle and he blew a silent whistle. He aimed for nonchalance and did a reasonable job.

Jones continued. "It reminded me of something but, for the life of me, I couldn't remember where I heard the name. Racked my brains. Damn near drove me nuts. Even searched online using that Google thing, but came up empty. I filed the information away.

Allowed it to percolate. I'm good at that. An important part of my work is piecing little clues together and making them fit the bigger picture. As a child, I used to love doing jigsaw puzzles. And reading, of course. I read so many books as a kid. Great way to pass the time on long winter nights, don't you think?"

Jean-Luc circled around from behind Jones and took a pace closer to the desk. He stood at ease, feet apart, arms crossed over his chest, shoulders square, head facing forwards, his eyes locked on Buckeridge. Imposing his will on the man without saying a word. For his part, Buckeridge kept aiming sideways glances at Jean-Luc and Alex, a spectator at a tennis match. He was in danger of giving himself a migraine or neckache.

"Your second mistake was setting up shop in France. After that, you made error after error. Letting Flynn's Citroën run out of petrol was a doozie. There was a fifty-litre drum of petrol in Flynn's barn. Did you know that? No, I guess you didn't bother checking the tank as you only went for groceries. You tried to torch the car, but it didn't catch. That was perhaps your greatest blunder, but I'll come back to that in a moment."

Jones took a shallow breath before continuing.

"Killing the old woman was stupid, wanton, and it brought about an even closer cooperation between the French and English Police."

Jones hiked a thumb in the direction of Jean-Luc. "It shouldn't surprise you to know that the French don't take kindly to foreigners killing little old ladies and teenage girls. Nor do they like people setting up torture chambers and shooting snuff movies in their Republic. And who can blame them?"

Apparently, Buckeridge found some dirt under his fingernails. He started picking at it with a thumbnail.

"What are you talking about? Is this something to do with that poor girl who was killed in Derby the other day?" He shook his head and tutted. "Such a crying shame. I really feel for her poor parents."

Jones ground his teeth, but let the barb pass for the moment. He spread his fingers wide and placed the flat of his hands on the desk. The leather top was cool to the touch, its surface creases tactile, and the rich leather smell evocative of past times spent in libraries.

Buckeridge had a slight squint in his left eye, and his smile showed a crooked front tooth.

Won't be smiling in a minute.

"Now we come to the interesting part. Are you ready?"

Buckeridge ignored him, seemingly finding his fingernails more interesting.

"The link between you and Jennings didn't come to me even when I saw the misspelt sign above the entrance to your jail, 'Darbishire'."

Buckeridge flinched. A giveaway so subtle, Jones nearly missed it. He continued. "At first, I thought the sign maker must have screwed up, but you had the sign made specially didn't you?"

He pointed to the diptych, partially obscured behind Buckeridge's head, but the film director and butcher didn't turn to look.

"Seeing that misspelled sign sent all sorts of questions spiralling through my head. Why did you do that? Were you thumbing your nose at authority? Was it your little joke?" Jones shook his head. "I didn't put it together until I had a good night's sleep."

Jones shot Buckeridge a smile that contained no mirth.

"As I said, it's amazing, the recuperative powers of rest."

After knocking on the door, Ryan Washington strode in brandishing a white envelope, size A4. He handed it to Jones with a flourish.

"They match, boss. Both samples."

Two more pieces of the puzzle. Well done Patrick Elliott.

Now, Jones only needed the voiceprint analysis to complete the puzzle.

"Excellent," Jones said, rubbing his hands together. He stared at Buckeridge, who met his gaze full on.

Jones placed the envelope on the desk, unopened. Buckeridge pretended to ignore the buff-coloured rectangle, but his gaze kept sliding towards it. Jones braced himself against the pain from his ribs and hefted the briefcase to his lap. He removed a sheaf of photos and dealt them face down on the table, six in all, two rows of

Part 3

three. He lined each up with the edge of the desk, keeping things tidy.

Jones scooted to the edge of his chair, rested his elbows on the desktop and steepled his hands.

"Now where was I? Oh yes, *Jennings and Darbishire!*"

Buckeridge's jaw muscles bunched and his left eyelid twitched. Not much movement, a mere flicker, but to Jones it stood out as obvious as the tell of a dreadful poker player.

"Yes, *Jennings and Darbishire*, the fourth book in a series of children's novels written by your namesake, Arthur Buckeridge."

The killer sighed and swivelled his chair to face the window. Jones followed the man's gaze—the view from the eighth floor was nothing short of magnificent. Birmingham's City Centre shimmered in the bright afternoon sun.

"I didn't recognise the link at first, because the documentation we had on Ellis Flynn spelt the detention centre as 'Derbyshire', with an 'e' and a 'y'. And when I travelled to our little rendezvous on Friday you'd had it spelled with an 'a' and an 'i' as in 'Darbishire'. So 'Derbyshire' became 'Darbishire'. Why was that? A sort of homage? Was your namesake a relative? An uncle, perhaps?"

"No relation. Like you, I was a fan of the books as a kid, nothing more."

Buckeridge swung the chair around to return Jones' stare. He affected a look of boredom. Jones wouldn't have been surprised to see the sick bastard yawn.

Jones went on. "Like the predictions of Nostradamus—it's easy to find the answer to a puzzle *after* the event. When I finally put it together, I had a colleague dig into the detention centre's background and we confirmed your name. The association between you and Ellis Flynn became clear, too. You turned a damaged boy into a murdering psychopath. How many others did you train in the same way?"

Buckeridge pulled on the armrests and sat upright. "That sounds awfully melodramatic, but I still have no idea what you're talking about, Constable Jones."

Jones ignored the intentional jibe.

"All you have," Buckeridge continued, "is a fanciful association between me and this dead man. What did you say his name was, Elroy Flint?"

"You were Ellis Flynn's mentor and his boss. And you are going down for the crimes you committed as a team."

"Rubbish. Is that all you have?" Buckeridge grabbed his walking stick and used it to help lever himself from the chair. He limped across to the window and faced out. Sunlight bathed his face, accentuating the crinkling around his eyes and his pallid complexion. "A ridiculous, coincidental link between me, a children's novelist, and an unfortunately misspelled name? A little tenuous do you not think. Why on God's good earth would I choose to draw attention to myself like that? It's complete and utter nonsense."

"I'll let the psychiatrists answer that one. I agree, the connection is purely circumstantial, but it led me to you and, I'm afraid it's not the only thing we have." Jones flipped over the first five photos one at a time, leaving the final one face down. Buckeridge craned his neck and stepped closer to the desk. The limp made his approach more laboured than it should have been.

Jones pointed to each of the five photos in turn. "We took these shots in Brittany. They show footprints and scuffmarks on the ground inside the barn. One of the men who made these marks favoured his left leg. See the scrape marks? That shows a limp, and do you see these little divots, these holes? They look like the marks made by a walking stick to me. What do you think?"

Jones studied Buckeridge's reaction. He didn't show much, but his left eyelid twitched again. He started to raise his right hand to the eye, but winced and lowered it again. It confirmed Jones' suspicions. There was definitely a restriction in Buckeridge's arm movements. He had shown no such limitation on Friday when he levelled the gun at Jones and fired. Jones let it pass for now, but he would bet big money on the police doctor finding a bullet wound during the physical examination at the station.

Jones pointed to Buckeridge's stick.

"I wonder if there's any trace evidence on the tip of that cane to place you at the scene."

Part 3

Buckeridge sneered. "This cane's brand new. Bought it yesterday. Wish I still had the old one to prove you wrong, but I threw it away. Sorry. As I keep saying, you have nothing."

"Really?" Jones flipped over the final photo—the best still image they could capture from the passport control queue in Brest airport.

Buckeridge huffed.

"Is that supposed to be me, Constable? Lord above. Whoever that man is, his own mother wouldn't recognise him from that photo. And all your so-called evidence is nothing but conjecture. None of it will hold up in a court of law. And what's more, I have alibis for each murder."

"How do you know that? We haven't produced a time of death for any but the old lady in Brittany."

"Doesn't matter. I am a well-respected man, always in the public spotlight. I didn't kill anyone, so I couldn't have been at any of the murders. If needed, I could probably be able to find an alibi for any day over the past ten years. For heaven's sake, I'm the chairman of a Government think-tank on prison reform. I can't go gallivanting off to France whenever I choose. This is all completely ludicrous." Buckeridge backed towards the window again. "And by the way, I've never been tae Brittany in my life. Your case is pure speculation and will never reach court."

Buckeridge raised the cane and pointed the tip directly at the centre of Jones' chest. Today he held the walking stick in his left hand. On Friday, he'd held the pistol in his right. The images were identical in Jones' mind, but reversed.

The memory of the gun in Jennings' hand and the flash of the muzzle before the bullet struck caused Jones to tense up. His damaged ribs sent out another sharp stab of pain. He still owed Buckeridge for the shock of that bullet, and for everything else.

"Now, I am tired of your ridiculous accusations. Leave my office or I'll call my great friend, the Chief Constable, and then call my other great friend, the Home Secretary."

Jones had enough of the man's bluster. He was within a heartbeat of slapping the supercilious bastard across his smug face, but he couldn't hit a man with a disability. Or could he? He hadn't completely dismissed the idea when another memory flashed to his head. Hollie, bound to the radiator, the top of her head a bloody mess and the wall behind her spattered in red.

"Shut up," Jones hissed, and took three paces forward. He stopped an inch from the cane's tip. "The French forensics teams are examining the crime scene and the campervan as we speak. Hollie told us you were in the passenger seat for hours. You will have left evidence somewhere—flecks of skin, sweat, saliva, fingerprints. And there's the Warden's Office in the detention centre, you'll have left trace evidence there too."

Buckeridge's lips thinned into a slit.

"I used to run the damned Centre. My prints and DNA will be all over place." He smiled. "As I keep saying, you have nothing."

Jones took another pace, pushed the stick aside and grabbed Buckeridge by the upper arm, and made sure to squeeze the sensitive skin on the inside of the bicep. Buckeridge squealed and tried to pull the arm away, but Jones pushed him to his desk and dumped him in the chair.

Jones placed a hand on each armrest of the chair and leaned close to the now sweating murderer. He stopped when their faces were no more than a foot apart. Buckeridge's blue-grey eyes flicked left and right as he tried to find focus. His breath reeked of acid decay.

Jones said nothing. Buckeridge pulled his head away until it pressed against the back of the leather chair. After a five second count, Jones straightened and ripped his hands from the armrests. Buckeridge flinched in anticipation of a blow that never came.

Time for the endgame.

Jones returned to the other side of the desk and took his seat once more.

Buckeridge produced a white cotton handkerchief and wiped his forehead. Heavy breaths hissed through the slightly misshapen teeth. A bloodstain appeared on the shoulder of his white shirt. Jones studied the tiny spot as it grew.

The bugger's just popped a couple of stitches in a shoulder wound.

"And now we come to the contact lenses," Jones said.

Part 3

Buckeridge lowered the cloth and shifted his gaze to Jean-Luc before fixing Jones with a dead-eye stare.

"What contact lenses?"

"The green ones you used as part of your disguise. You flicked them out the Citroën's window on your way to Brest airport, didn't you?"

Jones' abrupt change in tack clearly rattled the man. His left eyelid started twitching again, and the squint became more pronounced. He would not be winning many games of prison poker—not that many inmates would deal a hand to a paedophile. They were more likely to remove one of his hands, along with other parts of his anatomy.

"My friend, Colonel Coué here, delivered the conclusive evidence this morning. You see, he wanted to meet the man responsible for all that carnage you created in his beautiful Finistère." Jones looked up at Jean-Luc and nodded. "Within hours of your abandoning the Citroën, Brittany's forensics team towed it to a police compound. They've taken it apart. And what do you think they found embedded inside the window groove of the passenger's doorframe?"

Jones grasped the envelope Ryan had delivered.

With obvious difficulty, Buckeridge managed to pull himself to the edge of his chair. He grimaced and flicked a glance at the blood on his shoulder. He should have said something, but Jones knew he wouldn't want to draw attention to the injury.

Jones tore open the seal and read the title of the first sheet: *Holton Forensics Laboratory - Fingerprint Analysis. Positive match: Arthur Michael Buckeridge.* He turned the page around and showed it to the killer.

The second sheet held the copy of a photograph. It showed a close-up of a wrinkled, dried ball of plastic-like material, tinted green. The third sheet showed the same item but, according to the printed note below the image, after a five-hour soak in a solution of distilled water.

"Did you know," Jones said, "that contact lenses are a wonderful surface for retaining fingerprints?"

Buckeridge's protruding Adam's apple bobbed.

"We have two partials. Thumb and forefinger. Both are a positive, six-point match to the ones we have on file for you. Remember your fingerprints were taken as part of your government security clearance?"

Jones paused to let the information sink in. Buckeridge must have known he was done. He slumped into his chair and took on the demeanour of a defeated man. His head dropped and his left hand crossed to cradle his right arm. The bloodstain had stopped growing.

Only popped one stitch then.

Jones broke the silence. "Still claim never to have been in Brittany?"

No reply.

"Now we come to the DNA evidence. You know how we police love our DNA evidence. Juries love it too, thanks to all those slick forensics shows on television. The French lab analysed the lacrimal fluid they found on the lens. That's teardrops to you and me. We tested the DNA against your Home Office records. And what do you know—they're absolutely identical."

Jones dropped the final page in the sheaf on top of the others.

"Alex?"

"Yes, boss?" she answered without drawing her eyes away from the killer.

"Are the results in yet?"

"Yes, sir. Another perfect match."

Buckeridge frowned in question. "What's this, more tricks?"

Jones tapped the photo of Jennings wearing the baseball cap. "Recognise where that shot was taken?"

No response.

"It happens to be a still from the passport control queue at Brest International Airport. Not many people know this, but they record all conversations with passengers as part of the new anti-terrorist security protocols. We now have an unmodified digital recording of you speaking as Jennings. There is no computer interface messing with your voice here, unlike when you phoned me in France. Our

Part 3

lab confirmed the match with something you said a few minutes ago about being Scottish. Your nationalism is going to be another nail in your coffin. And by the way, we have a hammer and plenty of nails."

Buckeridge's jaw slackened.

Jones continued. "Yes, you heard right. We know all about your contract killers. We know everything—Hammer, Nail, the mayor of Carhoët Grande, Albert Plouay. You're going down for life, Arthur Buckeridge. And do you know what? I'm going to make the case for you to be housed with the general population. You know what inmates think of sex offenders, don't you?"

Buckeridge shook his head.

"Rubbish. All that technical gibberish is nothing but smoke and mirrors. None of it will hold up in court without an eyewitness."

Jones had to give the monster points for bravado, but he'd held the best part back until last.

"Alex, would you mind coming closer for a moment please?"

She closed to the side of the desk, and stopped within arm's reach of Buckeridge who shifted sideways in his chair. A film of sweat sprouted like a pale moustache on his upper lip. Alex reached into her pocket and pulled out a mobile phone. She used it to tap a button on her lapel and spoke to the cowering murderer.

"This, *Doctor* Buckeridge, is a pinhole camera. We've been recording this whole interview and have transmitted the image and sound to our server hub in Holton police station. From there it was sent to a computer screen in Saint Mary's hospital, Derby." Alex pressed the speaker button on the mobile and raised it to her lips. "Please repeat what you told me a moment ago."

Hollie Jardine's steady voice sprang from the phone. "It's him, the man who kidnapped me. I know him as Jennings."

"Thank you, Hollie," Alex said, not taking her eyes from the killer. "You did a good thing today. I'll come to visit you this evening."

Buckeridge, white faced and shaking, collapsed in on himself.

"The fucking bitch is still alive!"

Alex jerked her hand back in preparation to strike.

"Alex! No."

Jones half-stood, but Alex lowered her hand and backed away. Her eyes filled with tears, and her lower lip trembled. Ryan darted forward and draped an arm around her shoulders. Alex straightened, but it looked as though the effort took all the strength she had left.

"Up you get, Buckeridge," Jones said. "We're going to the station. Ryan, cuff him."

Buckeridge screamed, and with a burst of speed surprising in a man who walked with a stick, he leaped from his chair. He ran to the window, arms pumping, and dived, head-and-shoulder-first into the glass panel.

He hit the window, bounced, and ended up sprawled on the floor at Alex's feet. Jones admired her restraint. In her position, he might have swung a foot at the bastard's head.

The murderer lay on the carpet in a crumpled, groaning pile.

Jones chuckled. If the murdering bastard wanted to save the country the cost of a trial by throwing himself out of an eighth floor window, he would be out of luck. Triple-glazed panels didn't break that easily.

Ryan burst into a loud, braying laugh.

"Jesus," he said, "I'd have paid good money to see that in a movie."

"Enough, Ryan," said Jones, keeping a straight face. "That must have hurt. Please check the poor man's alright."

"Right you are, boss."

At that moment, the two officers on guard duty outside burst into the room. They stopped, looked at the crumpled mess on the floor, and stood mouths agape, awaiting instructions.

Jones turned to the men.

"Help DC Washington take this man to the station. Put him on suicide watch until we can get a medic to give him the once over. And Ryan, make sure he doesn't trip over his walking stick on the way to the station."

Ryan nodded, and helped the dazed Buckeridge to his feet. The

Part 3

other two officers stood back to let him pass. As Buckeridge pulled alongside, Jones spoke into his ear.

"You don't get away that easily, Buckeridge. I'm going to watch you go away forever. Life without parole. How does that sound?"

Buckeridge blinked and stared at Jones in confusion. He said nothing as they took him, in handcuffs, from the room.

When they left, Jones collected his papers and Jean-Luc leaned in to help.

"Well, David, that was interesting."

Jones dropped the papers to the floor and slumped into the visitor's chair. The pain flared in his ribs and he studied his shaking hands.

"Hell, Jean-Luc, I've never been so close to killing a man with my bare hands."

Jean-Luc shook his head. "Never worry, David, I have done much worse."

"Really?"

Jean-Luc nodded sadly. The moustache twisted as he grimaced. "*Oui, c'est vrai*. Before joining the Finistère Gendarmerie, I was a member of the *Compagnies Républicaines de Sécurité*."

"The CRS? You?"

"*Bien sûr*, but of course. I am still a member of the CRS reservists. Did I not tell you?"

"No, Jean-Luc. You didn't." Jones didn't know what else to say other than, "Let's go for a drink. I'd love for you to sample our world famous warm beer and round off the evening with a fish-and-chip supper."

"And *monsieur* Buckeridge?"

"He'll wait. It'll be hours before a doctor passes him fit to be charged and interviewed. And I'm thirsty."

JONES ESCORTED Alex to her hotel and helped her break the news of Roy Harper's arrest to Julie Harris' parents. Afterwards, he left the three to grieve and joined Ryan and Jean-Luc at the *Bold Dragoon*.

So early on a Monday evening, the pub was quiet. Most of the after working stiffs had yet to arrive and the celebrating team had the Snug Bar all to themselves.

As the closest pub to Holton Station, the *Dragoon* earned its place as the favourite after-work watering hole for the West Midlands Police Service.

Ryan took a long pull on his beer and smacked his lips.

"That hit the spot," he said. "So, boss. What next?" He wiped his mouth with the back of his hand.

Jones looked away and sipped at his pint of Bombardier. The real ale, nutty and flavoured with rich Kentish hops, slipped down his parched throat better than a vintage claret.

"First thing in the morning, you can tear Buckeridge's life apart. Full background check. I want to know everything about the sick bugger from the second he entered the world: family connections, education, finances, inside leg measurement, the works. Drag in all the office resources you need. I'm sure Phil will be happy to help on the quiet. He's crawling the walls at home."

As is Manda.

"And you, sir?" Ryan emptied his beer in two swallows.

In times past, Jones could match heavy drinkers glass for glass, but he took things more steadily these days. He removed three sheets of paper from his briefcase. Each contained a copy of the photograph page from the passports Alex recovered from Ellis Flynn's campervan. He studied the pictures.

"We know three families with missing daughters. I need to tell them what we found." He took another sip, but the Bombardier didn't taste quite as nice this time.

"Don't envy you that job, boss." Ryan stood. "Anyone want another?"

Jean-Luc sipped his example of England's finest ale again and put the glass down. "No thank you, Constable. This is quite enough for me."

Ryan disappeared to refill his glass. Jones and Jean-Luc sat side-

Part 3

by-side in companionable silence. Jones nursed his beer. Jean-Luc left his glass on the table.

Jones cleared his throat.

"I, um … I never really had the chance to thank you properly for what you did." He turned his head towards the Frenchman. "After Jennings gave me that ultimatum, I was … well, lost. Without your help I'd never have worked out the meeting's location."

"Nonsense, David. I did very little. You put the ones and twos together." He reached for his glass and took a second sip. His lips thinned and he stuck out his tongue.

"Arranging the helicopter made all the difference."

"Ah, that reminds me. *Dans mon porte-documents* … in my briefcase, I have the bill for your accounts department. It totals thousands of Euros, I am afraid."

Jones smiled. "I'll make sure it's paid quickly and in full. I have a sense my bean-counters will play nice for a while."

Ryan returned carrying a tray with two beers, a bottle of wine and an empty wine glass.

"I saw what you thought of the beer, sir. Thought you'd prefer some grape juice."

"Ryan Washington," Jones said, "I always said you'd make a great detective one day."

Ryan beamed.

Jean-Luc pushed his beer to the other side of the table. He poured the wine, swirled it in the glass, and sniffed the bouquet. "A good nose." He nibbled the liquid and nodded in approval. "An acceptable claret. *Merci*, Ryan."

"I asked for the most expensive bottle in the house," Ryan winked. "Put it on Charlie Pelham's account. Didn't think he'd mind. Cheers." They touched glasses. "What are your immediate plans, Colonel Coué? If you like, I could show you Birmingham's nightlife. We could hit the city and party."

"Alas, Ryan, I need an early night. I must return home tomorrow and oversee the investigation. There is much yet to do. A team of forensic accountants is researching the financial dealings of *monsieur* Plouay. Hopefully, we will find a link between him and *monsieur* Buckeridge and from there …" He shrugged. "Who knows? Maybe we will break the vice ring?"

Jones nodded. "I agree, we aren't even close to wrapping this case up. In fact, we've barely scratched the surface. Think about it."

He rattled off a list that included locating the moneymen and following the distribution network from source to destination. After a pause for another sip of beer and some thought, he added, victim identification, finding the snuff-film clients, and researching the post-release records of inmates from the detention centre.

"And I'm not forgetting there's at least one corrupt policeman out there somewhere." Jones made a fist. "He's on my list, and I won't bloody rest."

"I'm with you there, boss."

"And don't you worry, Ryan," Jones concluded. "I'll make sure both yours and Alex's roles in the case are fully recognised. I imagine the Home Office and its French equivalent will be setting up an international task force. We have more than enough here to keep the Serious Crime Unit busy for a while. What do you think, Jean-Luc?"

The gendarme nodded.

"David, Ryan … I think I will never get used to that warm beer of yours. I will keep to the, er … grape juice."

Jones raised his glass, "Absent friends."

Epilogue

LYSEKIL, Coast of Sweden
Time since the shooting: three months

A TALL BLONDE woman in jeans and a thin woollen cardigan pushes a wheelchair along a smooth pavement.

The sun is low in the western sky. The light is crisp and clear. In the chair sits another blonde, this one in her teens. The girl is dressed in a warm coat. A blanket covers her legs. A cool wind whips off the sea.

Following behind the two is a middle-aged couple. The woman holds tight to the man's arm. They stride forward with confidence. The man smiles as he watches his daughter being pushed by one of her guardian angels.

The girl shields her eyes from the low sun and stares across the bay to the far shore. She points to a large stone church standing proud on a low hill. It gazes with benign benevolence upon a town of multi-coloured wooden houses.

"It's beautiful, Alex. How could you ever leave such a gorgeous place?"

A dark cloud casts a shadow over Alex's face. She smiles. It is a sad smile.

"I followed my heart."

The girl pushes the brake lever on her chair and struggles to her feet. She uses the arms of the wheelchair for support and turns to face her friend.

Her father rushes towards her, right arm outstretched.

"Hollie, it's too early, don't overexert yourself."

"I'm okay, Dad. I'll take care. Promise."

Frank Jardine returns to his wife's side and they hug and watch their brave daughter stand and face Alex. That Hollie can stand at all is spectacular, but her recovery is nothing short of miraculous. Frank pulls up the collar on his jacket as the sun kisses the horizon and the temperature dips. Emma leans against him for warmth and support.

Hollie takes two steps towards Alex and reaches out a hand.

"*Jag är så ledsen*, Alex. I'm so sorry," Hollie says. "I shouldn't have asked that."

Alex smiles, but sadness dims her eyes as she stares at the church where she and Julie were married so many years earlier.

The End

Next in the DCI Jones series

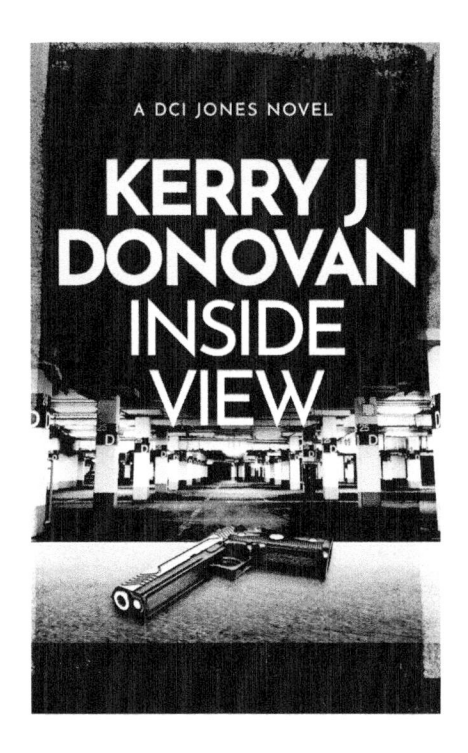

fusebooks.com/insideview

The DCI Jones series

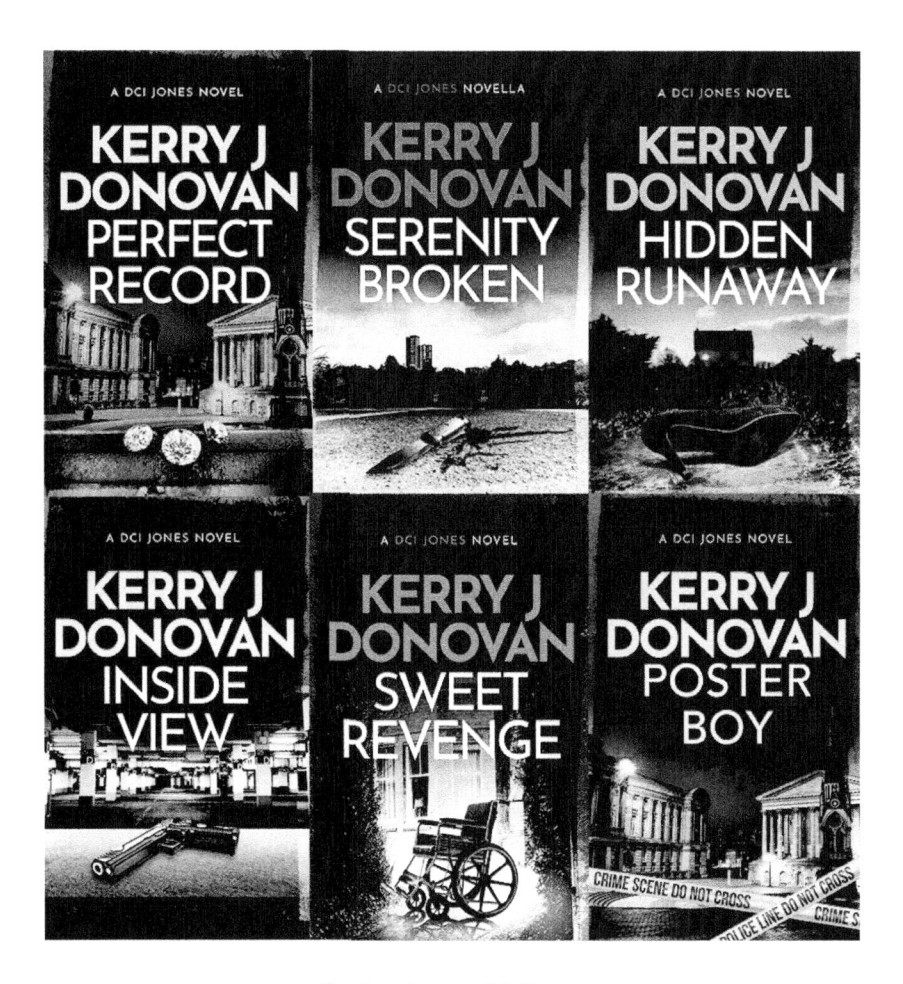

fusebooks.com/dcijones

ABOUT THE AUTHOR

#1 International Best-seller with *Ryan Kaine: On the Run*, Kerry was born in Dublin. He currently lives in a cottage in the heart of rural Brittany. He has three children and four grandchildren, all of whom live in England. As an absentee granddad, Kerry is hugely thankful for the advent of video calling.

Kerry earned a first class honours degree in Human Biology, and has a PhD in Sport and Exercise Sciences. A former scientific advisor to The Office of the Deputy Prime Minister, he helped UK emergency first-responders prepare for chemical attacks in the wake of 9/11. He is also a former furniture designer/maker.

kerryjdonovan.com

Printed in Great Britain
by Amazon